To Bonnie
Happy Reading
Michael J Smedley

Late Cut

Michael John Smedley

FastPrint Publishing

2

ISBN : 978-184426-899-3

Late Cut

In the long hot summer of 1984 life in the little Pennine village of Briseley T'ill centres around the cricket club.

A chance encounter with the spoilt daughter of the local MP leads to a tempestuous affair for nineteen years old Barnett Hall, rising star of the village cricket team.

By contrast, an unlikely candidate for romance is Edward Decker, the forty-six years old village constable, who has led a lonely celibate life for over twenty years. The accidental discovery of a body, buried in the Sinkhole close to the cricket ground, throws the even tenor of rural life into turmoil.

Suspicion falls on Barnett and Edward Decker is torn between loyalty to his friends and fellow players on one hand and his duty as a policeman on the other.

To further complicate the issue, police resources are stretched to the limit by the politically motivated miner's strike. Decker alone has to investigate what appears to be a motiveless crime and track down the ruthless killer.

His patience and local knowledge is finally rewarded by success... but at what price, as he discovers that even his closest friends have secrets he had never suspected. His loyalty is stretched to breaking point.

At the final count Decker stands alone, without support, unarmed, facing a ruthless proficient killer.

4

Contents

The Cut

The Cut. A devastating stroke when played by an expert.

The Killer was tall and powerful. He stood in the shadows. Waiting. Watching. His features were emotionless, very calm and very still. Death was his profession, the taking of life. He had trained himself to look at it from a distance, to remain uninvolved. On the rare occasions when thoughts of what he did entered his mind he persuaded himself that death is inevitable. That it comes to every living creature. That it is the ending of awareness. The ending of all sorrow. The ending of all pain.

That *he* was providing a necessary service, a remote and distant service that was far removed from his own personal life.

Except for this time…

Now his victim was at the sink. He watched the meticulous washing of hands, the ritualistic scrubbing of the fingernails, the thorough careful drying of each individual finger and the web-like spaces between them.

Then the black rage surged within him. The volcano of fury mounted, a rising tide of anger rose like lava seeking to escape the pressures of his internal conflict.

He moved quickly to strike.

His left arm crooked around his victim's head, pulling it violently back and to one side to expose the neck. His right hand held the slim-bladed knife with its razor-sharp edge, struck swift and true with deadly accuracy to the carotid artery. In one fluid continuous movement his victim was thrust forward over the white butler's sink. As the blood spurted in a crimson jet he already held the body perfectly positioned. The knife clattered into the white stone basin. Ice-cold water hissed from the tap. The Killer knew with professional certainty that his single strike would be sufficient. Death for his victim was as sudden as it had been unexpected.

There was no struggle. No time to struggle. It would have been ineffective against the power and strength of the Killer. His victim's lifeblood flowed into the old white butler's sink it mingled with the cold water into eddying patterns and with a swirl was sucked away to vanish down the plughole. For long, still moments there was no movement from the Killer. Outwardly calm, his brain raced ahead planning his movements.

There was no panic. He was a man on his own ground, completely and utterly sure of himself.

*

Briseley T'ill. 02.00. A cloudless night. There was frost in the air and upon the ground. A full moon rode across a clear sky. It was Good Friday. One of those years when Easter fell in the early part of April and the frost still lingered.

The ground was hard and the two men carrying their awkward burden stumbled over frozen lumps of earth as they crossed the open field. They were both big men, well over six feet in height, but here the similarity ended. One of them was fit and wiry, his muscles were hard and his voice silent. The second man was sadly out of condition. He breathed heavily and complained incessantly. Fear gnawed at the edges of his mind, weakening his resolve, loosening his tongue.

'Oh my God!' he blasphemed bitterly, 'That bloody moon... makes it light as bloody day. W-we'll be seen... b-bound to be...'

They came to an abrupt halt.

'Rest.' ordered the lean wiry one. He lowered his end of their burden to the ground and straightened his back, taking in a long slow breath. His eyes slowly and steadily scanned the familiar landscape. They had reached the boundary fence of the village cricket ground.

The village of Briseley T'ill is situated on the fringes of the Peak district and had grown over the centuries in a haphazard fashion. It was a stretched out meandering place that loosely followed a minor road that wandered in the shape of the letter 'S' from the railway bridge at its lower end, past the cricket ground and church, over a small stream, past the Cock Inn then steadily wound upwards until it ended at the railway station. The cricket field lay at the lower end of the village. It was south of the main road and the land sloped gently down from the north. A high railway embankment ran in a loop along the eastern boundary of the ground. Its thirty-foot high mound of earth screened the playing area from view and also served as an effective windbreak. A line of willow trees grew along the edge of a small stream forming the western boundary of the little ground. The stream flowed sluggishly down the gentle gradient and ended in a marshy depression.

The locals called this spot 'The Sinkhole'.

Here the sluggish stream disappeared underground, leaving an area of evil smelling viscous black mud. The villagers used the site as a dumping ground for garden rubbish and the cricketers found it a convenient place to dispose of their grass cuttings.

The nocturnal visitors came to a halt in the shadow of the pavilion.

'Wait.' the lean one commanded. There was the scrape of a rusty lock, the creak of warped hinges, the sound of objects being moved about, the noise of careful searching in the semi-darkness, then the tall silhouette re-emerged bearing a straight bladed edging spade. He knotted a piece of rope to form a sling and draped the tool across his back, then bent once more to lift their gruesome burden.

The second man was reluctant to move. He stared hypnotically at the shapeless mass upon the ground. The body had been wrapped in black plastic bin liners and secured with a length of yellow plastic-coated washing line. Common items both, and virtually untraceable. Frozen by his fear and trembling from more than the biting cold the man's breathing was harsh and gasping: frosty white jets in the thin night air.

The lean one seethed with barely suppressed fury. His anger was seldom vented in words. In the whole of his life few had heard a violent word fall from his lips. His anger was always contained within him. People sensed the writhing beast that dwelt inside. In company, without even speaking, he created an alien hostile atmosphere. The world had its reservations about him. He was unloved by many.

Sensing the resentment simmering in his companion the frightened one battled to master his fear. The awe in which he held his tormentor was greater than the sickness in his heart of what they were about to do.

Good fortune was with the Killer. The frost had made the ground around the Sinkhole firm. Normally it would have been impossible to walk on the earth without sinking knee-deep into its black slimy ooze. The keen blade of the edging spade bit through the frozen crust easily. Working with tireless strength the Killer shaped a shallow grave. Three to four inches down the cold had lost its grip. There was a sluggish seeping back of the liquid earth, but the man, working swiftly, stayed ahead in his race against the mud.

He cut through the plastic-coated line with his knife. Rolled the naked corpse into the shallow trench. Still supple, the corpse flopped over, face up, arms limply askew. Callously he kicked the limbs into place across the still white torso then rapidly shovelled back the earth. Finally he tossed a generous scattering of decaying grass cuttings to cover the freshly turned soil.

He stood back to study the ground, finally, satisfied, he turned to go. His unwilling accomplice still squatted, head down, shoulders hunched in misery against the biting cold. The Killer touched him upon the shoulder.

'Come.' he said. For the first and only time there was a hint of compassion in his voice and gesture. As the two silent figures picked their way back towards the cricket pavilion some two hundred yards away, the first traces of cloud scudded across the face of the moon. Later snowflakes drifted in on the north, westerly wind. Well before morning a two-inch sprinkling of snow had erased all trace of intrusion.

Luck was still on the Killer's side.

Maiden Over

Maiden Over: When the batsman fails to score.

Young Barnett Hall chuffed around the Briseley T'ill cricket ground like a clapped out steam engine. He was out of condition and he knew it. With the coming season only two weeks away he was determined to work off the flabby beer belly that lapped over his waistband and wobbled with every pounding step. A broken leg during the football season had drastically altered Barnett's normal winter sports schedule.

Instead, an indoor sport, a preoccupation as old as time itself, had lead to the young man's undoing. That, and a growing taste for the amber nectar on tap at the Cock Inn, a public house considered by many as the most popular pub in Briseley T'ill, was the cause of his present unhealthy state.

Beer and sex, it was a fatal combination, but then, for a young man of nineteen, life still has a lot of unfolding to do. Barnet, just like his father and his grandfather before him, believed in living life to the full. It seemed that there had always been a Barnett Hall living in the small Peak village of Briseley T'ill and currently there were three of them for it was a family tradition that the eldest son was given the Christian name of Barnett. Also inherited, through a dominant gene, was a head of flame red hair and a short fuse. Once lit the fuse, rather like a November fire cracker, flared briefly… and then expired. Whatever the cause of their anger, it was forgotten as quickly and as easily as it had arrived. Baring grudges had never been a family trait.

They were all natural cricketers. In his own time each and every one of them became the star batsman of the Briseley T'ill cricket club. They were tall athletic men talented sportsmen who moved with an easy grace and never ever understood why less gifted beings failed to perform with the same fluent ease.

Today Young Barnett Hall felt angry and frustrated. The even, settled tenor of his love life had been disturbed. A comfortable routine that had developed over the dark winter months had been brought to an abrupt halt. Twice a week, every Tuesday and Friday evening, Barnett had called upon Daisy Kutter. He had slipped around to her isolated cottage next to the church under cover of winter's darkness.

It had all started innocently enough. When the plaster was removed from Barnett's broken leg it revealed that his wasting muscles were in need of urgent treatment.

In the absence of a resident doctor, the medical care in the isolated Peak village of Briseley T'ill. was routinely provided by the Nurse, Daisy Kutter. The letters after her name were extensive and impressive. She was qualified as a nurse, a midwife and a member of the Chartered Society of Physiotherapists. She was welcomed as a visitor of the sick, as a comforter and a friend to everyone in need.

Barnett's first treatment session had been unremarkable. Daisy Kutter pummelled the muscles of his leg with clinical efficiency. She rotated his ankle joint, flexed his knee to a point Barnett had never believed possible and levered and stretched the sinews of his body with all the detachment of an experienced member of the Spanish Inquisition. At least that was how it felt and how Barnett explained it to his fellow club members in the snug comfort of the Cock Inn.

Later the situation changed far more rapidly than either one of them expected.

Entertainment in an isolated Peak village in the winter months is thin upon the ground. Especially if one is unable to drive, restricted by a lack of mobility and bored out of one's tiny flame-haired skull. Barnett was a virile, healthy and attractive young man and Daisy Kutter a warm-hearted voluptuous woman of thirty-three. She was single with no lasting attachments... and not lacking in experience.

His treatment became more... well... shall we say experimental?

For Barnett, an eager nineteen year-old and anxious to learn, life began to unfold...

Now, Daisy Kutter had gone away. It was quite a normal occurrence and it happened every year at Easter. She drove north into Yorkshire to visit her mother over the Easter break. Only this particular year her departure had been sudden. She had left late at night without a word of explanation and without even saying goodbye.

Illogically, Barnett felt aggrieved. He had now missed two therapy sessions. His leg was well on the way to recovery but his ego was bruised.

Taxing his body to the limit was Barnett's way of assuaging his battered pride. He drove his tired legs over one more circuit of the field, down the gradient by the stream, turning left short of the Sinkhole, a quick sprint towards the railway embankment, then short straining steps up the slope towards the road, round the sight screen and finally a sharp lung-bursting effort to collapse, exhausted and dripping perspiration on the pavilion steps.

Cynthia Ashley-Jayle nudged her horse, Dapple, through the five-barred gate at the entrance and onto the field. It was not part of her normal route and she knew how fiercely the cricket club objected to horses hooves ripping into their precious turf.

Over one hundred years of careful cultivation had gone into the cricket ground. It was the pride of the village of Briseley T'ill. An even, green expanse of velvet-like carpet, rolled, mowed and cosseted with an almost religious fervour by generations of loyal clubmen for decade after decade after decade. The land was now the property of the club having been presented to them by an ancestor of the intruding equestrian. Its donor, Giles Ashley-Jayle, long deceased, had been a true socialist at heart even though born a capitalist by inheritance and tradition. By contrast his grandson, Simon Ashley-Jayle, the father of the trespassing rider, was a socialist MP in name only.

He believed in the nation sharing its wealth… always provided it was not *his* money.

Cynthia viewed the track-suited figure sitting head down on the pavilion steps with interest. A lonely Easter break had left her bored and ripe for mischief. Barnett's flame-red hair was instantly recognisable. Although still a mere boy in Cynthia's book… he *was* a Barnett Hall.

In the village of Briseley T'ill and in the surrounding countryside the flame-haired family had a well-established reputation for masculine virility. And reputedly, Cynthia recalled, their sporting instincts went further than the game of cricket…

Perhaps a little encouragement would help, she mused as she unzipped her anorak. She drew back the garment from around her body to reveal a fine white silky blouse. Underneath, her lacy brassiere revealed just enough to excite the imagination. With her slim wiry body, shoulder-length blonde hair, violet blue eyes and clear outdoor skin, fine and softly textured as a peach, Cynthia's physical attributes quickly captured the admiration and attention of the young men in her circle. Sadly there was a strong wilful streak in her. The only daughter of wealthy parents, spoiled and over-indulged all her life she was used to her own way. Her body tensed as she slapped the reins against the horse's neck and drove down hard into the saddle.

'C'mon Dapple,' she urged, 'Go girl. Go!' The animal sprang forward, responding to her kicking heels. Little crescents of dislodged turf arced into the air behind the accelerating beast. A surge of excitement raced through Cynthia's veins. 'Go! Go! – Go!' she cried out. Horse and rider bore down upon the pavilion, hooves skidding in a curving run.

Barnett was jolted out of his reverie by the thudding sounds. His head shot up, took in the scene. The quick fiery temper that matched his flame-red hair exploded. He shouted angrily, starting towards the horse and its rider with the wild notion of stopping them. Then, thinking better of the impulse, ended by leaping frantically to the safety of the pavilion steps.

'You bitch!' he cried out, 'You crazy stupid bitch.'

How could anyone treat the sacred turf so... so... Words failed him.

Barnet dashed out onto the field and feverishly attempted to press the pieces of damaged turf back into place. Furiously he trod down with his heel in a vain attempt to repair the scarred earth. Tears of bitter frustration pricked at the corners of his eyes.

All those hours of patient work, he raged inwardly, *...all the raking and the rolling and mowing, the dedication, the untold years of careful attention...ruined by a single thoughtless act.*

'You bitch... you rotten bitch!' he called out aloud. His words went unheard and unheeded. His anger mounted. He felt violent, an unstoppable urge to punish her, to spank the thoughtless, stupid vandal's jodhpur-clad bottom until her skin was red raw.

Cynthia, an excellent horsewoman, reined in her mount a few yards short of the Sinkhole. She turned Dapple briskly, her hands and heels in full control and cantered back towards the agitated youth. Pulling to a halt before Barnett she hooked her right leg across the saddle and gave a slow contemptuous look around the field. Her eyes came to rest upon the young man. She feigned surprise.

'Why, it's Bar-r-nett. Hello Bar-r-nett.' Cynthia drawled out the first syllable of his name. It was insulting, deliberately insulting. The agonised Barnett could not contain his rage.

'You idiot.' he screamed at her, 'you great steaming nitwit. Look at the damage you've done... you... stupid female twit!'

'I something the matter Bar-r-nett?' Her treacly voice tormented him

'Of course there's something the bloody matter,' he stormed, 'Look at the turf... look at the damage you've done.'

' But Bar-r-nett ... it's only grass Bar-r-nett. You can't hurt grass, can you?' Her eyes were as round as an owl's, innocent dark blue orbs.

It was infuriating.

He made towards the horse with every intention of dragging her off. Cynthia reined back and balancing skilfully, pulled the mare onto her rear legs until she pawed at the air. Barnett hesitated. There was a wild gleam in Dapple's eye. He had always been nervous of horses. Especially big ones, and Dapple was an impressive beast.

Cynthia was enjoying herself. It gave her a tremendous kick to torment the powerfully built young man. His apprehension of the horse was quickly apparent to her. She twisted the screw another turn.

'D'you like to ride Bar-r-nett?' she drawled, 'Fancy a gallop? A quick jog-a-jog... Eh!' Her knees urged the animal towards the young man. Unaware of the double entendre in her voice, Barnett eyed the beast with growing terror. He edged back.

'Don't ride.' he muttered, 'Can't... never had a horse... never learnt.' Deflated at his admission his rage began to subside. His eyes began to take in more details of the girl. Of her slim lithe body beneath the silk shirt. Of her firm sensuous breasts, almost... almost, but not quite visible. He noticed her hair, her soft shoulder-length blonde tresses gently blowing in the mild spring air.

God! But she was beautiful in a sullen sulky way.

Barnett felt his senses quicken. There was trouble with his breathing... uneven... catching in his throat, its rhythm quickening as the air whistled past his vocal chords. He felt like a hypnotised rabbit transfixed by the sight of a stoat... two stoats under a layer of white silk... swaying... moving...with little pink noses... just... out... of... sight. Barnett became flustered. He began to back away. Cynthia urged the horse still nearer.

'C'mon Barnett, not frightened are you? I could teach you about riding?' She flicked her riding crop. Whether by accident or design the leather loop caught the corner of his eye a smarting glance. The young man reacted rapidly. As his head jerked to one side his right hand grabbed at the crop and gave a violent tug. His action was so quick that Cynthia was caught off balance. She toppled forward and fell into Barnett's fending arms. He staggered backwards, two short steps, before they both crashed to the ground. The weight of Cynthia's body knocked the wind out of his lungs. Stunned and gasping for air he slowly became aware of the situation. Her body continued to press down upon him. It squirmed and wriggled sensuously...not pulling away but pressing into him. Her firm round breast pushed into his open hand. He felt its yielding pressure, a sensation like no other in the whole wide universe.

A tight constricting band about his chest affected his breathing.

'Oh you Devil!' he gasped, vainly trying to push his body into an upright position, 'Oh God! You Devil... you little Devil. I ought to... to... to t-tan your bloody arse!'

Cynthia, still pressing down with her body, knew exactly what she was doing. She knew from experience the passions she was arousing. Her eyes

searched around. She spotted the door to the pavilion standing ajar. Saw
the darkened and private interior and seized her opportunity.

'You!' Her tone was contemptuous, tormenting. 'You wouldn't dare.
You haven't got the nerve. Poor Bar-r-nett!' She half raised her body, then
let it drop, hard, bouncing more air from Barnett's tortured lungs. Then
rolling quickly over she leapt to her feet springing up the steps and into the
dark interior of the building.

The cricket pavilion was typical of its kind, an overgrown timber shed
that had been extended over the years, higgledy-piggledy, metamorphosing
into its present form. At opposite ends were the changing rooms marked
respectively; "Home Team" and "Visitors". A large central lounge with a
bar also served as the tearoom. A kitchen and toilets had been added at the
rear. The whole structure was fronted by a veranda, its wooden floors
pitted by the tread of a thousand metal cricket studs. The pavilion's
windows were still sealed by shutters, padlocked into position, protection
against the winter storms and perennial attention of vandals. Overall
pervaded the lingering musty smells of stale sweat, damp cricket pads,
fusty leather and the clinging odour of raw linseed oil. Trestle tables stood
in the centre of the main room, stacked high with cricket pads, each pair in
a varying state of wear, some new, some worn but still serviceable and
others positively decaying; sprouting horsehair stuffing and splintered cane.

Into this room plunged Barnett racing after the girl. He grabbed at her in
the semi-darkness and locked together they crashed into the trestles which,
never very stable, promptly collapsed spilling the pads onto the floor. They
wrestled about the floor on a bed of cricket pads, wriggling and squirming
frantically, Barnett gasping for air in anger and frustration, Cynthia
thoroughly enjoying the skirmish, giggling and tormenting, aroused by the
close proximity of Barnett's young masculine body.

It was an uneven contest. Barnett, for all his quick temper and red
flaming hair, was totally incapable of genuine violence towards any
woman, young or old, even one as madly infuriating and tantalisingly
beautiful as Cynthia. He used his superior strength with restraint, trying
only to twist her buttocks into an exposed position to administer a richly
deserved judicial spanking.

Cynthia had no such inhibitions. Barnett's tracksuit offered poor
protection against her probing claw-like fingers. They quickly found and
fastened onto the waistband of his baggy bottoms and rapidly dragged them
down below his knees. In seconds Barnett's winter-white legs were
exposed from his ankles to his Y fronts.

Shocked by an assault outside his experience he twisted over in a vain attempt to prevent further intrusion into his underwear by the exploring, searching hands of the aroused young woman. He felt her lips and then her teeth nibbling and biting into the flesh of his arm, his shoulder, his neck. Quick and passionate movements... seeking... wildly seeking...

A thought flashed into his alarmed mind. It had never been like this with Daisy... with gentle, caring Daisy Kutter. Here was no tender exploration... no gradual subtle arousing of his emotions. Daisy Kutter's lips sent icy tingles down his spine. The feel of *her* fingers, a sweet ecstatic torture, set his skin afire and his muscles all atremble. There was warm genuine love in *her* touch, in *her* eyes and searching lips. Daisy's concern was all for *his* welfare, *his* pleasure, a shared and enjoyable gratification of mutual love.

It wasn't like this... this... this *rape*. Rape? The shock of it hit him with hammer-like force. The situation was crazy. It was back to front. Wasn't it always men who were accused of rape? Thoughtless, uncaring, selfish, evil men who used women... not like this, not the other way round.

Many times Barnett had fantasised, he'd conjured up passionate love affairs with nubile young women in his racing fertile imagination. But it had never been like this. Rabid teeth biting chunks out of his body and razor-like finger nails gouging at his most personal private parts. A wave of revulsion hit him. He felt suddenly sick. His ardour vanished instantly; went limp.

A tiny whimper of dismay escaped Cynthia's lips, a barely suppressed groan. 'God no!' she exclaimed.

What had started out as fun, as mischievous devilment to relieve her crushing boredom had run away with her, become a raging beast totally out of control. She crouched on all fours like an animal, a panting bitch on heat. Her long blonde hair hung down in tangled damp tresses. Her silk blouse had lost two of its buttons and gaped revealingly. Wild eyed she stared at him. Aghast at her actions! Then finally, as her composure returned she rocked back into a sitting position. Her head went back in a haughty gesture, eyelids drooping indolently. Her treacly upper-class voice returned laced with mockery. 'Oh dear! Barnett. How very disappointing. It isn't just your belly that's gone flabby is it?' Her head shook derisively. 'You were quite, quite right after all. You're not much of a rider... are you?'

With an outwardly calm demeanour Cynthia stood upright, coolly refastened the buttons of her blouse, tucked the bottom into her jodhpurs, zipped up her anorak and walked to the pavilion door. She paused, half turning back towards him. Her lips began to frame a word, then paused. She gave a quick shake of her head, turned and disappeared from Barnett's view.

Momentarily there had been an impulse to return, to place a gentle kiss on the young man's lips, to say that she was sorry. It was an unheard of happening in the Ashley-Jayle family.

One never, ever apologised to the lower classes.

Barnett lay recovering. His emotions shattered and in disarray. As thoughts trickled back into his brain the full realisation of what had happened began to dawn on him. How could he ever explain it? Suppose Cynthia Ashley-Jayle told everyone what had happened. In his horrified mind he imagined her upper-class circle screaming with laughter at his dismal failure to perform. Suppose Daisy Kutter was to hear? Oh no! It would be the end of their wonderful relationship. Suppose fellow members of the cricket club heard the details, distorted, grossly exaggerated, with added gloss. He knew full well what would happen then. Word would flash around the village of Briseley T'ill in no time at all. The reputation of the Barnett Hall's would lie in shreds. The gossips would have a field day. He groaned audibly.

Oh God! Barnett thought morbidly, *men have killed for less…*

Another thing, the sharp vicious spike of a cricket pad buckle had punctured the naked flesh of his pale white bottom.

*

Cynthia Ashley-Jayle rode away from the cricket ground with her vision blurred by a mist of tears. Why oh why? she asked herself, did she always destroy the very love and affection that she so desperately craved? Why did it always turn out like this? Why did she destroy men before she had even got to know them?

The answer was simple and lay in her upbringing. For her mother, Cynthia's conception had been an unfortunate accident. From the day of her birth she had resented the child for interrupting the social whirl of her butterfly existence.

Her father, Simon Ashley-Jayle was little better. He lived in and was absorbed by the political world, a power seeker, not for the benefit of his fellow beings but because of the authority it gave to him and the wealth such a position created. Both of Cynthia's parents were creatures inordinately interested only in themselves and in their own selfish welfare.

Their daughter never lacked for material belongings, only for love and affection.

Once through the gate horse and rider turned right, past the two small cottages that backed onto the cricket ground, proceeding east along the country road. Dapple, an intelligent mare, maintained a steady trot. With that uncanny intuition animals possess she sensed her owner's unhappy frame of mind and took charge.

Where the railway line crossed the road an arched stone bridge caused it to narrow considerably. It was a danger black spot. The scene of frequent violent braking, a fact indicated by the presence of multiple black rubber tyre marks on the tarmac surface. There was barely sufficient room for two vehicles to pass one another safely as they travelled under the bridge. On the eastern side of the bridge the approach road curved, severely limiting visibility.

John Emmett, driving his builder's truck, was suddenly confronted with a horse and rider heading straight towards him. Slap-bang in the middle of the highway and half way under the bridge. There was nowhere for him to go. He reacted rapidly, his foot slamming down on the brake pedal. John managed to avoid a direct collision but the sudden loud screech of brakes frightened the horse. It shied violently, turned and bolted throwing its rider to the ground.

The thwacking sound made by Cynthia Ashley-Jayle's body hitting the hard, unyielding tarmac stayed in John Emmett's mind for a long, long time. It sickened him. He sat for heart-stopping moments, paralysed, his brain refusing to function and face what he fully expected to find: a *dead* body.

People appear from nowhere when an accident occurs. One moment the road was deserted and then, seconds later, it is as though they have popped up out of the ground, appearing as rapidly as mushrooms that grow overnight. Silently they gathered around the victim and gaped at the limp motionless form. With the cold dread of uncertainty squeezing at his heart John Emmett joined the little group. He felt an uncontrollable trembling in his legs and an overwhelming sense of shock caused his teeth rattle and chatter like castanets. It was very sudden.

'She's still alive.' a woman's voice said.

Emmett looked towards the voice and saw a motherly figure, bustling and competent, already tucking a folded cardigan under the girl's head.

'Let's be 'aving yer coat.' said the woman to Emmett.

'Coat?'

'T'keep 'er warm. Treatment for shock.'

'Of course! Sorry.' Still in a daze, Emmett stripped off his thick warm donkey jacket and spread it over the motionless form of the injured girl. Understanding began to return... slowly. Trickles of conversation reached his ears.

'Dreadful place... a real danger spot...'

'Time they did summat about it.'

'Concussed I should think. Poor kid! Anyone rung for an ambulance?'

'Aye, me, I 'ave. Ain't it that Ashley-Jayle's daughter?'

A young mother from one of the nearby cottages arrived, accompanied by a little boy, her son. She produced a flask of hot sweet tea. The liquid scalded Emmett's throat but the burning discomfort helped him to recover a sense of stability.

'Is she dead Mummy?' asked the small boy with the uninhibited and avid curiosity possessed by the very young, 'Is she weally, weally dead? Will they dig a big hole and put her in the gwound? Will they Mummy, will they?'

What a horrid kid, thought Emmett, *How gruesome can you get?* Then, with the thought still in his head, he realised the paralysing sense of shock was losing its grip.

A two-tone cacophony of sound signalled the arrival of the ambulance. To the paramedics the accident was yet one more statistic, adding to the Easter carnage. They moved with calm and economical efficiency, easing the girl's body gently onto a stretcher and hooking on an oxygen mask. Cynthia Ashley-Jayle slid on silken wheels into the cool antiseptic interior of the ambulance. Inside twenty minutes she was in the intensive care unit of the nearest hospital. Thirty-seven hours later in the early hours of Thursday morning she regained consciousness. The previous three days of her life were a complete blank.

From the waist down Cynthia was unable to move...

Dead Bat

Dead Bat – A negative approach to stave off a disaster.

The funeral of Rowena Mole took place on the Wednesday after Easter. The dry weather continued with early morning frosts followed by warm spring sunshine. The daffodils in Briseley T'ill churchyard danced amid the sombre gravestones. Although the grass had begun to grow, it was, as yet, still short and reasonably tidy. Later, in the growing season a sparse but gallant band of aging helpers battled valiantly to contain the luxuriant growth that threatened to overwhelm the gravestones.

The Reverend Price hummed a hymn happily to himself.

'Lead kindly light, amid the encircling gloom…' It was a favourite hymn of the deceased and soon to be sung by request. They were familiar words which sounded so melodious when performed in the Reverend's mind but so discordant when the good man opened his mouth to sing in unison. An uncontrollable nervous disposition was his problem. A shy and timid man by nature, when called upon to perform in public the Reverend Price became a trembling wreck. Just when it was vital that his voice boomed out a vibrant message: the vital word of God, out came the sound, a tremulous squeak, reedy and high-pitched. Poor man, he genuinely believed in his calling… and passed through agonies of mind as a result.

Easter was a busy time for the timorous man of God. It was a traditional time for marriages. There were extra services, communions, evensong, matins, and now on top of everything, an unexpected funeral.

Yet the Reverend Price was happy, not an exuberant outgoing kind of joy but more from a sense of inward contentment. A peace of the heart and soul that came from the knowledge that he was needed as a necessary member of the community.

His community - Briseley T'ill.

In his imagination, prior to the service, the Reverend Price practised words of sympathy, it being very important to him to appear genuinely concerned for he had always been a fervent admirer of the deceased, the late lamented Rowena Mole. She had been a remarkably courageous woman and her death at the early age of thirty-nine had been both cruel and kind. Cruel because a vibrant life had been cut tragically short when she should have been in the full bloom of womanhood, yet kind because she was finally, mercifully, released from an agonising and crippling disease.

Six years of rheumatoid arthritis has seen the physical degeneration of Rowena Mole from a healthy young mother of thirty-three to a wheelchair bound cripple in constant pain.

Yet her spirit had never succumbed.

Rowena Mole raised two sons, twins, Leonard, older by an hour, and Norman. She washed, ironed, cooked and cleaned the house all from the confines of a wheelchair. Unbelievably she even tried to decorate. She stripped paper halfway up the walls for as far as she could reach, painted the skirting boards and the lower half of all the ground floor doors. She was incredibly determined... and brave. The entire village admired her and the entire village would attend her funeral as a final mark of respect. Every man, Jack and Jill who could, who was not previously committed, was certain to be there.

Knowing this the Reverend Price placed a collecting plate in a prominent position by the East door. The East door was always the one used for funerals. It exited onto the graveyard where Rowena Mole would be laid to rest.

The West door was the popular one the door used for weddings and christenings with its elegant stone archway had framed a thousand photographs of glowing brides and their smiling grooms. Wryly, the Reverend Price thought, there were many who had only ever used the West door... that was until their one last journey to eternity. He always felt a tiny morsel of guilt about taking collections at a funeral service. As though it gave him an unfair pecuniary advantage, then he thought of the many times when the congregation was sparse and the scattering of coins barely covered the surface of the collection plate. The church badly needed the money, as did the Reverend Price. A more unselfish man it would be difficult to find. He never spared himself. He gave his parishioners his time, his devotion, his experience, his regard, the bread from his table and the cloth from his back. Although it was unlikely that even the most needy down and out would have wished for the threadbare black cassock with its ragged hemline that hung from his back.

Any Oxfam shop stocked better clothing.

*

The mourners began to arrive in dribs and drabs, quietly tiptoeing into the ancient church dressed in respectful black and wearing suitably sad expressions. To those who had known Rowena Mole well it was inappropriate. She would have wanted them to be happy, to enjoy the spring sunshine, to revel in the fresh clean country air and to appreciate the glorious beauty of the dancing daffodils.

One of the earliest to arrive was Constable Edward Decker, known to his many friends as Ted. Decker was approaching the age of forty-six. A stocky substantial man although not excessively tall for a policeman. Unusually for him Decker was accompanied by a woman. Beatrice Leyland, his sister, had recently been widowed. She had arrived, uninvited, on his doorstep a week ago. Ostensibly, she claimed, to take care of her brother. He considered it to be a fatuous excuse for he had lived alone for over twenty years and cared for himself with fastidious efficiency.

Secretly he resented the intrusion into his organised bachelor existence but, too soft-hearted for his own good, he recognised the loneliness that crowded his sister's eyes and made her welcome. It was like making a stranger welcome, for although they had been siblings for a lifetime in reality their relationship for the last twenty-five years had barely existed. A bi-annual contact, at Christmas and on his, or her, birthday usually by a hand written and dispassionate card was the pinnacle of their affection for one another.

They had never been close even as children.

*

The hearse arrived, a sleek black Rolls Royce, neatly piloted by George Webb, the senior partner of G. Webb and Sons. 'Funerals, Weddings and Taxi Services'. The sound of tyres crisply crunching on the gravel drive heralded the arrival of the cortege. Heads turned surreptitiously towards the East door. Curious eyes peered discreetly from beneath the brims of sombre black hats. Four pallbearers carried in the coffin. Two of them were the twin sons, Leonard and Norman, of the deceased woman, Rowena Mole. The third man was the builder, John Emmett, and the fourth a tall Negro. They were all big, sturdily built men, immaculately attired in black woollen pinstriped suits and gleaming white shirts. On their shoulders the highly polished casket looked pathetically small. It was just five feet long.

John Benedict Mole, head bowed, walked two paces behind the coffin. Father of the twins, a sidesman of the church and the chairman of Briseley T'ill Cricket Club, Jack Mole was regarded as a prominent figure in the little community. Formerly seen as an active and vibrant personality he seemed to have aged unnaturally over the last six days. An enormous weight of despair settling squarely on his bowed shoulders.

Beatrice Leyland's head snapped towards her brother. Her voice hissed at him, low and venomous, 'That man's black!'

'Black?' startled, Ted Decker's mind failed to register understanding, 'So...?'

'That man, one of the men carrying the coffin. He... is... black.'

Comprehension dawned slowly to Constable Decker. He'd known Everett Jackson for so many years that he had long ceased to notice his colour. His only thoughts were of the man, not his race nor the fact that his skin was black. He found it hard to believe such racialism still existed in any person, in *his* sister, the stranger. Was it possible there were still parts of the British Isles where black faces weren't commonplace?

'Oh! Y'mean Snowball.' replied Decker, 'Well, that's what we call him at the cricket club. It's a daft nickname but he doesn't seem to mind... and it's stuck. His real name is Everett Jackson.' Beatrice's cold stony eyes gazed long and hard at the black man.

'He's got a mean and vicious look.'

'What?' the policeman replied in astonishment, 'Y'can't mean Snowball.' He thought of the easy-going friendly man he knew so well. Of the wide beaming smile that revealed his pearl-white teeth, of his bright intelligent eyes and his ever present readiness to help anyone and everyone. Thoughtfully he looked again at the man's black sombre face. In repose, mused Decker, perhaps he does look different, to a stranger, to someone unused to Jackson's familiar features perhaps the man did appear ugly. It was the contrast, the smile breaking through the sombre clouds that gave Everett Jackson his own particular charm.

Beatrice's comments, as unwelcome as they were, gave him cause to look around with fresh eyes. To look anew at people he had known for many years and others he had met only recently, to look clearly at his long time friend, Everett Jackson... and, with renewed interest, at Helen Argosy.

Helen Argosy was the latest newcomer to Briseley T'ill. She was certainly worth a second look. Hers was a new face in the village and she appeared to be unattached. Decker had interviewed her shortly after the accident on Easter Tuesday. Her account of the incident, the policeman recalled, had been detailed, clear and concise. He'd been very impressed by the calm un-dramatic manner in which the young mother had given her evidence. Ms Argosy, as she referred to herself, was not only an attractive young woman she was also imminently sensible and intelligent. But why, Decker wondered, did she have to use the prefix, 'Ms'. He thought it was an ugly word, 'Ms' He was never quite certain how to pronounce it or exactly what it was supposed to mean and if it was an abbreviation... of what?

Ted turned his head furtively to steal a second glance at the said Ms Helen Argosy whom he'd observed slipping quietly into the back row of the congregation. She was dressed in a soft grey suit, respectful without being too sombre. Her boy was with her looking a little overawed by the solemnity of the occasion and the cold echoing grandeur of the little church. She caught sight of his glance and flashed him a quick shy smile in return.

'Who's that?' hissed the low voice of Beatrice, her hawk-like eyes missing nothing. Decker started like a guilty schoolboy caught peeping into the girls changing room at the school gymnasium.

'It's... er... hmmm. Mrs... erm... Miss... Mizz... Argosy.' he replied awkwardly.

'*Mizz* Argosy?' Beatrice's haughty tone was sceptical. The strident sound of her hissing stage whispers was causing heads to turn in disapproval. Decker, acutely embarrassed, stared hard at the worn and lumpy hassock between his sturdy feet.

'Let us kneel and pray.' entreated the reedy voice of the Reverend Price.

Grateful for the distraction Decker, along with the rest of the congregation, thudded down onto the ancient hassock, compacting further its lumpy stuffing and causing a sudden cloud of dust to be expelled from the kneeling pad. But it was religious dust ... strictly Church of England. So no one dared to complain.

The common belief in the village of Briseley T'ill was that Constable Edward Decker was a confirmed bachelor; a man who was always friendly and pleasant towards the female of the species. But whose interest ended there. Common belief was wrong. As a young policeman Decker had once been married. Twenty-four years ago he and his pretty young wife had been headline news. Their faces had stared out from the front page of every tabloid newspaper in the land. For a few brief days their story had screamed at the nation in the large black print of banner headlines. Then just as quickly, with that transient fame bestowed by the media, they were forgotten. The rape and murder of the young policeman's wife soon lost its front-page news value. World events overshadowed Constable Edward Decker's private tragedy. Other terrible crimes were committed. Other blank dead faces stared out but they too only cast a brief impression on the insatiable but fleeting attention of the public mind.

The effect on Edward Decker was of a permanent nature. The wound ran deep, raw and lasting. His judgement was seriously affected by the emotional shock and when it became clear that his recovery could take years rather than months it was considered prudent to relocate the young policeman somewhere safe, to a place the escalating crime rate appeared to have overlooked, to the little Peak village of Briseley T'ill.

Now, after twenty-four years, during which time a serious crime had never been known to happen in Briseley T'ill, the policeman was a mature accepted member, well woven into the life-thread of the community.

The service inside the church drew to a close. The pallbearers moved towards the coffin. Speaking softly Decker whispered in his sister's ear.

'The two young men at the front of the coffin are the twins, Rowena Mole's sons, Lenny and Norman. The one walking behind, the chief mourner, that's Jack Mole.' His voice dropped a tone in sympathy, 'Poor Jack, he does look ill. I've never seen a man go downhill so quickly. It's terrible.'

'Mmm!' mused Beatrice, 'I take it *he* is the husband?'

What is passing through Beatrice's mind? Decker wondered. He answered her question warily, 'Ye-e-es.'

'When the vicar was speaking, offering his sympathy to the family, you know, consoling the relatives,' Beatrice probed in her subtle musing vein, 'He mentioned her sons and other relatives, but, I don't recall him ever actually referring to *her* husband. He sort of... fenced around it didn't he...?' Her voice tailed away leaving a half suggested question hanging in the air.

Damn Beatrice!

Damn her sharp perceptive mind.

Damn her uncanny ability to sense the very faintest trace of a scandal. He sighed heavily. There was no escaping from the inevitable where his sister was concerned.

'The fact is...umm! They were never married.'

His reluctant admission brought a positive gleam of malicious delight to Beatrice's eyes.

'A-ha! Never married eh? And why not?'

The policeman grew more uncomfortable by the second. He stayed silent.

The cortege began to move out through the East door which faced directly onto the cemetery. Silent mourners fell into an orderly line, following the coffin. Decker slid along the ancient oak pew, eased himself into the aisle and stretched cramped muscles. The Norman builders of the little church had failed miserably to anticipate the solid size of a twentieth century police constable. Beatrice scuttled after him, anxious to prevent his avoidance of her question.

'Why weren't they mar… ?'

'Collection.' barked Decker, with a brisk nod in the direction of the collection plate. He dropped a pound coin into the pile of notes and silver mounting up on the wooden plate. The little church and the Reverend Price were faring well today.

Exasperated, Beatrice searched fussily in her purse, found a coin and almost hurled a ten-penny piece onto the pile. The policeman gave his sister a glassy stare.

'How generous!' was his sardonic comment.

*

Outside the church the sun still shone, the daffodils continued to dance in the breeze, the birds sang noisily and the distant hum of traffic was faintly heard as a droning background hymn. The clutch of mourners gathered around the empty grave with an air of suspended belief. They all recognised that they too were mortal beings but no one was willing to admit it.

The Reverend Price, in his reedy tremulous voice, reached the final burial words. Despite his familiarity with the last rites tears glistened in his eyes as genuine sadness and emotion added sincerity to his shaky elegy.

'…Earth to earth, ashes to ashes, dust to dust…'

Soil thudded onto the coffin lid. Feet shuffled restlessly, anxious fearful feet.

'In the name of the Father, and of the Son, and of the Holy Ghost.' As the Reverend's reedy voice, like the soft and gentle breeze fell away to a lingering silence, a young piping voice was heard repeating his words.

'…Name of the Father, and of the Son, and in the 'ole 'e goes.'

A burst of sniggering laughter, instantly stifled and converted into a convenient outbreak of coughing by the disconcerted mourners, rippled around the group. A few of them, those who'd been closest to Rowena, smiled wanly to themselves. It was the kind of humour their late lost friend would have appreciated.

Helen Argosy, blushing furiously, tugged at her son's hand.

'Shush!'

'But Mummy.'

'Shush Jason.' She folded her son's face into her body. The muffled sound of Jason's piping treble voice could still be faintly heard.

'But Mummy, I told you they put bodies into the gwound. I told you. I did. I saw the two men do it!'

*

The mourners stood in little groups waiting to depart. Waiting to shake hands with the vicar. Waiting, awkwardly, to offer their condolences to the grieving family.

Decker found himself standing next to Young Barnett Hall.

'It's not long to the cricket season,' said the policeman conversationally, '... you'll be looking forward to it I expect?'

'Can't wait.' replied Barnett eagerly rubbing his hands in anticipation.

'And your leg... recovered has it?'

'Fine. It's coming on really well. Almost back to normal.'

'So you're still having treatment then?' Ted raised an enquiring eyebrow.

'Erm... yeah. Physio... y'know... twice a week... at Nurse Kutters.' Young Barnett, in trying for a light and nonchalant reply achieved only a vocal squeak.

'I'm very surprised she isn't here,' commented Decker, 'I felt certain she would be.'

'Gone up t'Yorkshire,' Barnett replied as he moved away, 'T'see her Mum. I'll be finishing off my treatment when she returns.' He turned to shake hands with the Reverend Price and to offer his condolences to Jack Mole and his sons.

Decker turned at the sound of a deep throaty chuckle. He faced a wiry little man with tanned weathered features who was busily packing the bowl of a disgustingly old pipe with fresh tobacco.

'It bain't just 'is leg she be treatin' be it?' said George Burke grinning broadly.

'It bain't! I mean, it isn't?' Decker corrected himself. It was so easy to forget and slip into the local dialect. 'Just what do you mean... exactly?' he asked.

George Burke took his time. He packed the bowl of his briar like a craftsman. Struck a succession of matches as he sucked noisily at the stem of his inseparable comforter. The pungent smell of tobacco filled the air as the fire caught hold and a cloud of insect-dispelling smoke drifted around his weathered head. The throaty chuckle was repeated.

'You'm sayin' you don't know what I mean?' His eyes twinkled wickedly at the policeman as he grinned impishly, 'Spry young fellow like Barnett. Seen 'im on more'n one occasion I 'ave... slippin' round ter that

Daisy's cottage of an evenin'. Hu-hur! Reckon I knows wot 'es up to… and it ain't jus phizzy-therapy wot puts a smile on 'is face.'

'George! I'm surprised at you,' chided the policeman, 'You, spying on young lovers?'

''Er bain't so young!' retorted Burke, 'And I wasn't a spyin' on purpose. No. I just 'appened along at the right time like. 'Sides, there ain't no 'arm in a young feller completin' 'is eddycation is there?'

'No-o! I guess not.' Decker smiled, a worldly, tolerant, remembering smile. 'That would be some education if all I've heard about Daisy Kutter is true.' He looked closely at the little man, continued, 'It's remarkable how many times you happen along at the right moment George… truly remarkable.'

'I 'ave ter take the dog a walk of an evenin'.' Burke replied easily. Then he smoothly switched the topic of conversation, 'Will you be at the meeting tonight? Six o'clock at the ground. Fust match is a week on Sat'day. There's a might o' work t'be done. Mowin', rollin' and the like. Us need yer help.'

Decker, with a mischievous twinkle in his eye, considered for a moment. 'We-ell, you know Briseley T'ill, George. It all depends upon the crime rate.'

'Ah! If that be the case… see y' there. Six-ish. Don't forget.' He drifted away in a poisonous haze of tobacco fumes. A fretting Beatrice bustled towards him.

'You never answered my question.' she snapped.

. 'Question?' he eyed her warily, 'What question would that be Beatrice?'

'You know what damn question,' she hissed at him, 'Why didn't they marry?' It was useless trying to evade answering. Ted Decker knew he would have little rest until his sister's curiosity was satisfied.

'They couldn't marry because they are first cousins.' he explained.

'But! – But! That's incestuous.' exclaimed Beatrice, 'What's more it's interbreeding. Their children can turn out peculiar… loopy… you know… subnormal.' Her eyes searched around and settled on the tall figures of Lenny and Norman Mole. 'I knew there was something odd about them.' she muttered, self-satisfaction oozing from her voice.

'Keep your voice down.' urged Decker, dismayed by his sister's attitude. She was like an evil affliction, casting gloom and despondency around. 'There's nothing wrong with either Lenny or Norman. They're just a little on the slow side… that's all. It happens all over the place.'

'Not where I come from it doesn't.' retorted Beatrice haughtily and she strode briskly away.

Taking Guard

To insure one is correctly positioned.

The Killer was worried. The little stream that flowed along the outskirts of the cricket ground was reduced to a mere trickle. Normally in the middle of April the water would be two or three feet deep and flowing strongly towards the Sinkhole. In the village of Briseley T'ill no one alive could ever remember the stream drying up.

The area fell into a natural depression. Water from the surrounding hills always coursed towards the Sinkhole. Hidden springs, underground streams and manmade land drains from the cultivated fields all flowed towards the black slimy ooze. But this year was unique. There had been dry summers before. Usually they were followed by a wet winter. What was so different this time was that the previous summer had been very dry and sunny during its latter half. A mild winter followed in which the rainfall had been exceptionally low. A succession of anticyclones drifting across the Atlantic was responsible. The pattern was maintained throughout the winter months and had continued well into spring.

He was one of nine members at the cricket ground. Part of a working party which had arrived around six o'clock. They hooked up the tractor to the gang mowers, started its diesel engine and set about mowing the outfield in an ever-widening circle, sweeping out from the playing square. Other volunteers dragged two motorised mowers from the equipment shed. They were ancient machines and had seen better days but both still functioned efficiently. The larger mower, which had a twenty-inch cutting swathe, had been designed with a seat mounted over a small concrete roller. It provided a hard and uncomfortable ride for the operator. It was used to mow the six hundred square yards of the playing square.

A smaller mower, with a fourteen-inch cutting blade, shaved the playing strip. Set to its lowest position it left the barest minimum of grass covering the turf.

The Killer put in his fair share of effort. He worked quietly. Conversation over the sound of the single cylinder engines being impractical. When the grass bins were full he emptied them into a capacious square wooden barrow. Mounted on twelve-inch wheels with solid rubber tyres the barrow had been designed and built by Everett

Jackson, one of his many contributions towards the efficient running of the club.

The Killer kept his eyes on the level of the grass in the wooden box, not wanting to risk anyone, other than himself, disposing of the contents at the Sinkhole. The fresh smelling green clippings began to spill over the barrow's wooden rim.

Now, he thought, and moved to take the wooden handles.

'I can take that.' said a familiar voice.

It was the voice of Ted Decker.

Decker, the quiet, observant policeman.

Dangerous…!

'S'alright.' he mumbled, tugging at the handles.

'I'll walk with you.' Decker offered.

Panic! Beads of perspiration broke upon his brow. Had it actually happened? Was there really a body in the black viscous mud of the Sinkhole? Or was it all a dream?

Sometimes life became a dream. Hazy. Vague. Unreal. A nightmare.

'Phew! It's warm work.' observed Decker, trying to break through the man's reserve. It was common knowledge how introspective the man was and only a very few succeeded.

'Yea. It keeps me fit.'

'You're always fit.' agreed the policeman. An answering smile of appreciation surprised him. Normally the man's reaction was akin to a black hole in space – it absorbed all light and gave out nothing. No response. No warmth. No emotion. No sense of pleasure. Nothing.

They reached the edge of the Sinkhole. A broken dry crust had formed on the surface, like cracks upon the moon. Or a newsreel shot of a drought-ridden lake in a remote African country. Ted Decker looked at his highly polished black policeman's shoes and hung back. He wrinkled his nose at the sickly sweet smell of rotting vegetation.

'God! It stinks worse than usual,' he complained, 'Must be the dry weather. Can you manage alright?'

The other man gave a single curt nod of his head. He gripped and tugged sharply at the front panel of the barrow. Ingeniously, Jackson had designed it to slide out from between wooden grooves. He heaved up on the handles tipping the barrow onto its end. The pile of grass clippings tumbled out and spilled over the evil smelling mud.

They covered the very spot where the body lay.

In time the cuttings would rot down and be absorbed by the mud. Silt would be washed down from the surrounding hills, feed into the Sinkhole and cover everything. That was what usually happened. Everything disappeared down the Sinkhole. Everything. But only when the rains came...

*

George Burke eased himself off the motor mower and turned off the petrol. A simple but effective metal plate shorted out the spark plug and cut off the power to the engine. He swung over a stiffening leg and using the sole of his boot pressed the plate against the top of the plug. The motor gave a few final jerks and died.

Thankfully George stretched his cramped muscles. He jiggled his underwear back into a comfortable position and proceeded to dig out his eternal comforter. When the briar was burning evenly he surveyed the even green stripes of the cricket square with satisfaction. He grumbled incessantly about the ancient mower. George would never admit it but were anyone else to usurp his twice-weekly chore he would be most upset. Ted Decker came towards him, striding easily up the slope.

'Looks good George. ' He said, nodding in the direction of the square.

'So it bluddy ort to. T'is sheer 'ell on that ode banger. Rattles yer knackers like tupenny marbles it do. Could ruin a young man's love life y'know.'

'A young man like you, eh George? Has your Mildred been complaining?' Decker sucked in his cheeks expecting a pungent reply. He was not disappointed.

'Hers got nowt to complain about on that score.' retorted George with a hint of wounded pride in his voice, 'I mebbe fifty but I'm not past it yet.' Then, turning away, muttered wistfully under his breath, '*Not as that does me much good.*'

The two men manhandled the cumbersome old mower into the storage shed. Decker, who was by nature and training a neat and tidy person, noticed the edging spade. Its blade was caked with dried black mud.

'Hello! Whose been putting the tools away in a mucky condition?'
His own tools were always immaculate, their blades spotless and gleaming, their cutting edges, razor sharp. Each one meticulously kept in its place in the racks of his garden shed. He sorted out a wedge of wood and used it to scrape clean the blade. Although the mud had dried hard on the outside, next to the metal it was still moist and sticky. It could not have been all that long ago since the edging spade was used.

'Have we been laying any turf George?' he asked. George Burke shook his head emphatically. 'Done all that last back end. October time it were afore the winter set in.' He thought for a moment and then added, 'P'raps sum'on borrowed it… Mucky devils…ort t'cleaned it up afore they puts it away.'

It was not an uncommon occurrence for a member of the Briseley T'ill cricket club to borrow a piece of equipment. The key to the padlock hung on a hook under the eves of the storage shed, a fact known to every member. Any one in the club could have borrowed it.

The heavy roller used to flatten the playing square into submission was a weighty cast iron object. Roughly a metre in diameter the roller was set in a cast iron frame which projected fore and aft ending in round metal handles. They had been worn smooth by countless hands and frequent seasonal use. Once the roller had been filled with water to add to its already considerable weight. Then at the end of one season the matter of draining the roller had been overlooked. A severe frost had caused a crack to open in the cast iron and the leak had never been repaired. It still required four men to move it in dry weather. When the ground was soft and wet, then it needed six.

Rolling the playing square usually began three weeks before the commencement of the season on the third Saturday in April. It was a pleasurable enough occupation and not over strenuous if eight or nine took the handles. It was a time for pulling together, both literally and in the metaphorical sense, a time to renew acquaintances and catch up on the local gossip after the long dark days of winter. A way of building up team spirit and a healthy thirst, which of necessity then needed to be quenched in the players second home – The Cock Inn.

There were eight men on the roller. Pushing were John Emmett the builder, Snowball Jackson, Young Barnett Hall and one of the Mole twins, Lenny. On the pulling side were Ted Decker, John Shackleton, Tim Taverstock and the remaining twin, Norman Mole. As they came to the edge of the square their roles became reversed. The pushers, pulled and the pullers turned into pushers.

George Burke, excused the exertion by virtue of his years, sucked comfortingly on his evil smelling briar and supervised. The *Old Captain,* as he was sometimes called, was looked upon as the self-appointed foreman and expert on all matters appertaining to the upkeep of the ground. Because George was employed by a market gardener he was able to *borrow* useful items like grass seed and fertiliser. A wealth of agricultural knowledge was attributed to him, some of it relevant…and some of it not. Whether it was George's knowledge or the *borrowed* fertiliser was impossible to decide but either way the little village team of Briseley T'ill reputedly possessed the finest ground in the district. Visiting teams found it a joy to play there and the club never lacked for fixtures.

Unusually the conversation amongst the players was desultory. Generally it ebbed and flowed naturally as they tugged away at the handles of the weighty old roller, sometimes witty, frequently reminiscent as the men recalled their former triumphs and successes, occasionally scathing at a player's failure but mostly it was the easy ribald humour of athletic young men gathered together for a common purpose. But today their interchanges were awkward and stilted.

Norman and Lenny Mole scarcely uttered a word.

That's to be expected, thought Decker who was surprised at their presence until Norman Mole quietly explained.

'Dad insisted that we come. He said it would do us good to get out of the house, said we haven't to brood... that life has to go on.' The tall young man turned his head away, his eyes unseeing, misty, looking into eternity. His voice dropped very low, scarcely audible. 'We're all going to miss her... our Mum... especially Dad.'

The silence that followed became uncomfortable.

Tim Taverstock, in an attempt to lighten the atmosphere, spoke to John Shackleton.

'So when's your sister's wedding then?'

'Wedding? What wedding?' Shackleton looked puzzled, 'Who's getting married?'

'Your sister of course,' replied Taverstock who ran a travel bureau, 'She's made two reservations for a ten day trip to Paris. Told me it was a honeymoon trip. Four star hotel, private suite, no expense spared. Nothing but the best, she said.'

'Nah!' Shackleton, looking puzzled, shook his head, 'Married – never. You must be mistaken.'

'Tch! Tch!' Everett Simpson's tongue clicked against his pearl-white teeth, 'Yo white fella's is all da same,' boomed his rich West Indian accent, 'Doan know a darn ting what is goin' on your own fam'ly'

'Huh!' snorted John Shackleton becoming agitated, 'I can ruddy-well guess. She's planned a dirty weekend... the mucky little tyke. I'll bet that's what it is... and her so prudish on the face of it. Pretends she saving herself for Mr Right, so she says.'

'Actually, it's for ten days.' corrected Taverstock.

'Right! Right!' John Shackleton's voice rose in protest, 'Two nights or ten nights, that doesn't make it any better... does it?'

'Mmm! But she could be going with a girlfriend.' Decker suggested reasonably.

'Don't be stupid,' Shackleton retorted scornfully, 'To Paris... with another *woman*? You wouldn't do that. No one would... well, not unless he was a man.'

'Oh Lord!' groaned Taverstock, 'that's true. It looks like I've let the cat out of the bag. Trust me. I should keep my big mouth shut.'

'I don't know what the world's a comin' to, young folk gaddin' off on 'oliday together,' George Burke muttered, ruminating on the decline in morality, 'It never 'appened when I were a lad. Jus' my luck... born too soon I were.'

'There's one poor lass who won't be gadding off anywhere,' murmured Decker softly, 'At least, not in the foreseeable future.'

John Emmett raised anxious eyes and spoke for the first time, 'Do you mean the Ashley-Jayle girl? How is she?'

'Still unconscious the last time I heard. Ted replied, his voice grave and serious.

'I feel sick inside every time I think about her,' John Emmett stared morosely at the slow moving surface of the roller, 'Just can't forget the sound her body made as it smacked onto the tarmac. It's here,' Emmett took one hand off the roller to tap the side of his head, '...in my head. T'was a truly dreadful sound.'

'It wasn't your fault John,' Decker consoled the builder, 'It seems a funny business altogether. She's a good rider. Knows how to handle a horse well. A bit frisky like, but always acted sensibly on the road. I can't understand it.'

'Nor can I.' Emmett's head shook slowly from side to side, thinking deeply, 'She seemed... preoccupied. Mind not on her riding. She nearly rode slap-bang into my truck. Quite unlike her usual cheeky self, waving at me, saucy-like.'

Young Barnett listened quietly, absorbing the conversation: the news of the accident came as a surprise to him.

How could it be, he wondered, *When? How? What time? How seriously was Cynthia hurt?* A host of question flooded into his mind, but did he dare ask them out loud? Trying to sound casual he asked.

'Accident? What accident? I've not heard of it. When did it happen... and where?'

George Burke, the old captain, hastened to inform him. 'Bluddy 'ell Barnett don't y'know nothin'? It 'appened Tuesday, yesterday afternoon. Under bridge... up 'ere near t'cricket ground.'

'But I was here then.' admitted Barnett.

'Then you must have seen her.' Ted Decker suggested shrewdly. His eyes watched the young man closely. Barnett felt his colour rising.

'Uh! Yea, well, I did... sort of.' he confessed reluctantly.

'Sort of?' Decker queried mildly, 'What does '*sort of*' mean Barnett?'

The blood ran hot under Barnett's skin.

'She was here, riding, on that horse of hers. I was training, doing laps around the outfield. She came onto the ground with that ruddy great dappled horse... tearing across the turf... cutting it to shreds. It made me so mad to think of the damage she was doing. I shouted at her. Gave her a piece of my mind. We had words... a bit of a row. Then she left.'

'Yet you didn't hear the accident?' pressed Decker.

'No. It must have been when I was inside the pavilion, changing out of my tracksuit.' Barnett's eyes shifted uneasily. He dare not admit the truth. No way!

John Emmett seized upon the excuse eagerly.

'That would explain why she wasn't paying full attention to her riding. If she'd had a barney, she'd be upset. That's it, she'd have been distracted.'

'Maybe so.' acknowledged the policeman. He felt sorry for John Emmett who had a wife and two small children. It was obvious he was deeply anxious about the tragic accident. It happened to people. If only they thought it through.

Decker sensed that Barnett was holding back. Whatever it was, may, or may not, have some bearing on the accident. But at least there was now a logical explanation for what had taken place. Thinking, perhaps, that the young man felt partially guilty, Decker put a suggestion to him he thought might ease his conscience.

'Cynthia, Miss Ashley-Jayle, was taken to the Royal Infirmary. She's still unconscious as far as I know, but when she recovers why don't you call in to see her Barnett. Ask how she is... perhaps make it up with her?'

'Make it up!' Barnett retorted hotly, 'What for? It was her flaming fault. Not mine.'

'Wow!' exclaimed Snowball Jackson, 'Take it easy man. Poor child is in a bad way. She gunna need friends. And she ain't got many... dat gel.'

'Well, is that surprising?' broke in Tim Taverstock, 'She's a stuck up bitch. Acts like she owns the place just because Daddy is a Member of bloody Parliament.'

Jackson rolled his eyes in horror, accentuating his West Indian accent, his deep bass tones rolling out. 'Now dat ain't Christian man. It looks like we po' black folks gunna have to send mission'rys to dis 'eathen place.'

A sudden burst of laughter helped to ease the atmosphere.

*

The working session came to an end, the roller gang having worked their way across the cricket square firming down the ground with slow steady traverses. Now it was time to manhandle the cast iron beast back over the boundary and away from the playing area. If left to stand on the field the sheer weight of the roller would create an unwanted depression. When all the equipment was safely stored away George Burke clicked the padlock secure and handed the key to Lenny Mole. The tall lean young man easily reached up to the hook hidden under the eaves of the storage shed. George Burke at only five feet five was dwarfed by a good eleven inches.

'Thanks Lenny.' George said, nodding. He wanted to start up a friendly conversation with the bereaved young man but wasn't sure how to begin.

Although twins, Lenny and Norman were not identical, they were *fraternal* twins. Both men were big and both bore a superficial family resemblance to their father. But whereas Norman had curly, mouse coloured hair and a round chubby face, Lenny was possessed of high cheekbones and lank black hair. There was almost an oriental look about the set of his eyes and features. Again, they were totally opposed in temperament. Lenny being reserved and quiet, an introspective man, Norman, by contrast, was outgoing and instantly likeable. He made friends everywhere he went.

'Going for a pint?' enquired Burke. Lenny looked thoughtful, he chewed on his lower lip and slowly shook his head. 'No, I suppose not.' George Burke replied to his own question. 'T'ain't surprisin' in the circumstances. I'm sorry about your Mam, she were a grand lass. Goin' t'be awkward for your Dad. You too... and for Norman. Still, bet Daisy'll 'elp out when she gets back. P'raps she'll find you an 'ousekeeper, one o' them 'ome 'elp people...' His words tailed away helplessly as he caught the bleak look on Lenny Mole's face. Only then did it come home to Burke just how close the twins had been to their mother.

Very close...

*

The members made their way across the ground towards the gate. George Burke to collect his antique Raleigh bicycle. Decker possessed an old but reliable Morris Minor. The Mole twins shared a mini-van; both the driver and the passenger seats raked fully back to accommodate their long legs. John Emmett used his builder's truck. Only Tim Taverstock owned a vehicle of any distinction. His sleek, metallic blue BMW boasted a personalised number plate. Barnett and John Shackleton had walked to the ground. Tim, keen to show off his car, offered the two pedestrians a lift to the Cock Inn.

'See you all Monday night,' called out Burke, 'Let everyone know, we've a team to select. Mebbe get some practice in if the light's good. Cheerio.'

The cars doors slammed shut, Taverstock's BMW with a satisfyingly solid clunk, the doors of the Mole's minivan with a tinny rattle. Their engines roared away into the gathering dusk. The last to leave was Ted Decker. He closed the gate and drove steadily along the bumpy drive leading to the road. A pleasant thought entered his head. Why not stop at the cottages backing onto the cricket ground. There was no real need for him to interview Helen Argosy again, on the other hand, why waste a good excuse?

She was a long time answering his knock, coming to the door looking flushed and more than a little flustered. Helen apologised for the delay, explaining that she was busy trying to persuade her son, Jason to go to bed.

Decker found the little lad hammering hell out of his bedroom carpet with a homemade cricket bat firmly clutched in his chubby hands.

'Hello!' he greeted the boy, 'What are you up to young man?'

'I'm making a block hole,' stated Jason proudly, 'Like the cricket men do when they go out to bat.' Helen Argosy gave a despairing shake of her head.

'He's mad keen to be a batsman.' she informed Decker, 'Heaven help my carpets.'

'Here, let me show you the right way.' offered the policeman. He stood over the boy, put his arms around him to guide the bat. 'Like this see. Just a gentle pat or two will do. We don't want to damage the wicket do we?'

'No-o-o. Not likely.' chirped the rising young star.

'It's called "Taking guard". Do you know why? So the batsman knows where he stands.'

A faint smile crossed Helen Argosy's face, a wry questioning look.

'Tell me Constable Decker...should *I* be taking guard?' she asked, 'So that I know where I stand...?'

Short Run

When a batsman fails to make his ground properly and forfeits one run.

Barnett telephoned the Royal Infirmary at ten o'clock on Friday morning. It was difficult making a private call from his place of work. The offices of his employer, an internationally known insurance company, were open plan. It was hardly the place from which to make a confidential enquiry. In the absence of walls all that separated him from his fellow employees were some strategically placed rubber plants and a series of low Hessian-covered screens. Behind the screens, he imagined, hid a dozen pairs of curious ears all waiting to listen in to his conversation. Perhaps if he had behaved naturally no one would have noticed. Barnett hunched protectively over the telephone, cupped the mouthpiece covertly in his hands and lowered his voice to an inaudible whisper. It invited curiosity.

'Can you speak up?' asked a voice on the telephone.

'I want to make an enquiry.' repeated Barnett hoarsely.

'You want to make a… a diary?'

'No! No! An enquiry. En-quiry.'

'Sorry. I still can't hear you very well. Do you have a sore throat?'

'No! No!' raged Barnett, 'An enquiry… about a patient.'

'Have you a name please?'

'Ashley-Jayle. Cynthia Ashley-Jayle.' he repeated, 'An accident case. Brought in on Tuesday evening. Can you tell me how she is?'

'As well as can be expected.' came the brisk and automatic response.

'What the Hell does that mean?' he replied loudly, annoyed. A dozen heads bobbed up and surveyed him over the Hessian screens.

'There's no need to be abusive.' A haughty voice replied, 'Are you a relative? We can only give out information to relatives.'

'Yes.' lied Barnett, 'Well, erm… no. Sort of… a friend.'

'Friend? Boyfriend… or perhaps her fiancé?' The voice on the telephone was trying hard to be helpful.

'Yea, her fiancé, that's it. Look can you tell me please… has she recovered consciousness yet?'

'One moment please.' There was a dull thump as the telephone was abruptly laid down followed by the echoing sound of footsteps walking away down the bare floor of a clinical corridor. Barnett hung expectantly on the end of the telephone. A dozen pairs of eyes watched him. A lot of pertinent questions were going to be asked. The waiting seemed endless.

Eventually the telephone clattered and the same voice informed him that, yes, Miss Ashley-Jayle had recovered consciousness and that visiting hours were from 6:30 until 8pm. But only two persons were allowed at any one time.

'Thank you very much.' sighed Barnett and replaced the receiver on its cradle. A circle of curious faces crept from behind the rubber plants and the low Hessian screens to surround his desk.

'What's all this about a fiancé?'

Eyes closed, Barnett searched his imagination for an answer. Life had suddenly become very complicated.

*

Simon Ashley-Jayle was angry, furious because he abhorred personal complications. More than anything else personal complications upset him, they interfered with the smooth running of his life... and worse, with his parliamentary career. In particular he abhorred family problems. He found it easy to stand up in Parliament and harangue the impersonal faces of members of the government. It was so detached, so impersonal. Quite unlike family problems that required personal family decisions, private decisions from which there was no easy escape.

The slightly built Asian doctor faced the MP calmly. He was unafraid. Many times in the past he had faced angry men, brutal vicious men with angry faces and murder in their hearts. They had been far worse than this man. By comparison he was a pussycat.

Born a Ugandan Asian, the doctor had been forced to flee from the brutal regime of Idi Amin. He had come to England to find sanctuary. Working for long, hard and conscientious hours the doctor had built a fine reputation for himself in the eyes of the only critics who mattered; his medical contemporaries.

Also, this was England. People did not disappear without trace in England, overnight, ending up in a remote grave, unheard of and never to be seen again.

'I'm very sorry Mr Ashley-Jayle,' he told the MP, 'but we are unable to tell you exactly what is wrong with your daughter. All we can say at this stage is that she is unable to move from the waist down. There is very severe bruising to her back and spine. She also has concussion from the impact to her head but X rays don't reveal any fractures. There is some loss of memory, which is understandable, but other than that we can find nothing wrong.'

'Nothing wrong!' thundered Ashley-Jayle, 'Nothing wrong. How can you say that? How in God's name can there be nothing wrong? How? She's paralysed, bloody well paralysed. Can't move a muscle… there *has* to be something wrong.' He shook a stiffened forefinger under the doctor's nose. 'I'm telling you that it's bloody damned incompetence. It's not good enough and I demand a second opinion.'

The calm demeanour of the Ugandan doctor remained unshaken.

'Of course sir, it's your privilege,' he said, 'If you would like to speak to my associate, Dr Sheehan?' He moved to press the intercom bar on his desk. Cocked his head, birdlike, enquiringly, 'Doctor Sheehan?' he repeated.

'Doctor Sheehan?'

'An Irish lady, she examined your daughter when she was brought into the casualty department. Very thoroughly.' he added as an afterthought.

'Huh! Alright then I'll see her, this Doctor Sheehan.' Simon Ashley-Jayle grudgingly conceded. Were there any English doctors left in the country? He wondered angrily. There are too many damned foreigners in the NHS. It was all the fault of those bloody Tories for letting them into the country.

Now when he came to power…

Doctor Sheehan was petite, attractive and competent. The long hours she spent in the casualty department had seemingly given her an inexhaustible but weary patience with the frailties of the human race. She answered Simon Ashley-Jayle's questions in a soft lilting Irish brogue. Yes, she had examined Cynthia thoroughly and no, she had not been able to find a physical reason why the young woman was partially paralysed. She offered a tentative suggestion.

'Could it be there is an emotional reason for her condition? It may be that there is something she is unwilling to face up to… a personal problem perhaps? Exam stress? Trouble at home? Has she had a falling out with a boyfriend? Anything…?'

It should have been difficult to become angry at the doctor's concerned and gentle approach. Simon Ashley-Jayle managed to achieve the impossible.

'Nonsense! Utter rubbish!' he exploded, 'There is nothing like that wrong with my daughter. She has never been deprived, never lacked for a damn thing. What are you trying to suggest? That she's mentally sick or something? You're all the bloody same, you quacks, just because you don't know the answer you hang a stupid label on her. I want her out of here. Do you hear me? I want her out. Now!'

There was little doubt that they could hear. The MP's rising voice resounded from the walls of the wooden-panelled office. The little Ugandan Asian raised his hands in the universal gesture of supplication.

'Please Mr Ashley-Jayle. Sir, it would be most unwise to move your daughter so soon. At least wait until we have completed our tests and checked the X-rays.'

'A-ah! Changing your opinions now are you?' His angered simmered for a few moments as he thought about the consequences of his words. How it would look if he, a Socialist politician were to move his daughter out of an NHS hospital and into a private ward. Should they find out, the press would crucify him.

'Alright.' he replied at length, 'She stays put for now... but I want a private room for her. I can pay, no problem there. A private room, do you hear me? The best one that is available.'

A silent nod of agreement passed between the Irish and the Ugandan doctor.

'We'll make the arrangements immediately.' Sheehan replied, 'Perhaps you would like to see your daughter now?'

The honourable Member of Parliament pursed his lips then gave a swift jerky glance at his wristwatch. He cleared his throat, made an excuse about the pressures of work and his lack of time... and declined.

He departed with indecent haste.

Doctor Sheehan, shrugged, raised her eyebrows and gave her Ugandan colleague the benefit of her non-medical opinion. 'Well! That's one problem the poor girl has... her father.' The little Ugandan Asian nodded in full agreement.

*

It was seven-thirty before Young Barnett Hall arrived at the hospital. The bus service from Briseley T'ill was infrequent and far from direct. He fumed impotently as the lumbering coach meandered around the countryside along narrow lanes to villages and rural stops where, it seemed to the impatient Barnett, there was a dearth of passengers needing any sort of service at all. The bus was never more than a quarter full. Even so Barnett squirmed with embarrassment as he tried to hide a large bunch of freesias from the eyes of his fellow passengers. He didn't need to bother, none of the other passengers paid the slightest of attention to them.

The Royal Infirmary is an old building, Victorian, rambling and partially modernised in a hodgepodge of styles both ancient and modern. Wooden signposts pointed the way to the numerous facilities making it easy for

Barnett to find the casualty department. Sliding aluminium doors sprang apart at his approach and silently closed behind his back.

By now most of the visitors were leaving, slipping away, exhausted of conversation and contrived bonhomie, hurrying home to their families and a delayed evening meal. Apprehensively Barnett wandered around the ward without seeing anyone who remotely resembled Cynthia Ashley-Jayle. Eventually a sister took pity upon him and asked whether he needed any help. He did. She consulted a register and informed him that Miss Ashley-Jayle had been moved into a private room.

'Room 3B.' she said, mildly disapproving, 'Follow me!' Her ample proportions struggled valiantly within the confines of her crisply starched uniform as she strode briskly along the corridor. 'Are you a relative of Miss Ashley-Jayle?' she asked

'No. I'm just a concerned friend. Does that matter?' he hastened to add, 'I *can* see her can't I?'

'Oh yes, of course. She hasn't had many visitors at all. In fact just the one, her father... and he didn't actually see her to speak to. He only stayed for a few seconds.'

'He's not around now?' Barnett asked nervously.

'Oh no. He came, managed to create quite a furore, stopped for about five seconds and then hurriedly departed.' She managed to convey extreme dislike without putting her opinion into words.

Arriving at the door of 3B the sister flung it open and sailed into the room like an imperial galleon in full sail.

'There's a visitor to see you.' she announced cheerfully. Her plump capable hands patted the pillows and straightened out an invisible crease in the immaculate white bed sheet. 'Flowers?' she demanded of Barnett, 'I'll put them in water for you.' Then she hovered like a dragonfly in the background, tactfully arranging the freesias, discreetly chaperoning her charge without making it obvious.

Cynthia lay flat on the bed. A single pillow supported her head. Her long blond hair fanned out against the startling whiteness of the covers and her dark violet-blue eyes staring disinterestedly at the ceiling.

'Hello.' asked Barnett, 'How are you?'

'Rotten.'

'Rotten? Oh! I'm so-o sorry.'

'Why?' The word came out, snappy, bitter.

'Why? Because of the accident, I'm so sorry about the accident. If it was my fault...?' He was puzzled. Her dark blue eyes turned towards him, cold and alien, surveying him with cool disdain.

'Were you there, actually at the scene when it happened?' Cynthia asked.

'No. I didn't even know there'd been an accident until much later.'

'Then why should *you* be bothered? What's it to you?'

Barnett made a small helpless gesture as he tried to explain.

'You and I, we were together. Don't you remember?'

'Remember what?'

'Before the accident.   In the pavilion? We... we... we had a bit of trouble, an argument. You were very angry when you left. You do remember... don't you?' His head cocked questioningly to one side as he waited anxiously for her answer. A flicker of interest showed in her eyes, slightly less flatness in her voice as she replied.

'Remember what? I keep telling everyone I can't recall anything since Sunday. Why won't you... why won't *anyone* believe me? Nothing! Not a damn thing. It's all a blank. I went out for a ride in the morning, early. I can remember that. Then church, the morning service and that boring old fart of a vicar stammering his way through the service in his god-awful squeaky voice. It was all so rotten... rotten and boring. I hated every minute of it.' A note of panic crept into her final words.

'I'm sorry, I really am.' Barnett sympathised. 'You really don't remember me at all do you? Our argument... what happened between us. It's because... because of... *that* you had the accident. It's *my* fault. All... my... fault.' he repeated weakly.

'What does it matter whose fault it is?' she shouted back at him, 'It's too damn late... too damn late for me. I don't want your sorrow. I don't want your pity. I don't want you here. Just go will you. Bugger off!'

Barnett clenched his fists in anger. His knuckles gleamed white. The colour drained from his face. Speechless, he turned abruptly and hurried out slamming the door with a resounding crash.

Silently the sister crossed to the door, checked that there was no one outside and closing it firmly again, turned to face her patient. She waited, surveying her with a curious mixture of compassion and disbelief. Eventually she asked softly.

'Now wasn't that a silly thing to do? Losing your temper with that nice young man?'

'No!' Cynthia's head snapped angrily to one side.

'No-o? Listen to me young lady. You may be rich. You may be pretty and you may be clever. Your father may be important, a Member of Parliament and all that, but just think of this, apart from your father, who didn't even bother to come into your room, that young man is the only person who has been to see you. The *only* one.' She leaned over the hospital cot studying her patient's averted face then gently traced a soothing finger down one peach-like cheek.

'The only one,' she repeated gently, 'you should think about that.'

*

Barnett rested his forehead against the cold metal of the bus shelter and kicked dents in its metal panels.

Damn her!

Damn him-self!

Damn the whole flaming world!

He felt totally inadequate and extremely foolish. So much for his good intentions. *You soft-hearted fool,* Barnett berated himself. So much for humiliating himself, for visiting her, for trying to apologise and make friends again after their encounter and as for buying flowers, now that had been embarrassing from the beginning. It was bad enough on Mother's Day when everyone else was buying them and barely anyone noticed. Not to mention the cost. They had not been cheap. It was a waste of his hard-earned cash. *The nasty bitch doesn't deserve friends,* he told himself as he resumed kicking the bus shelter panels.

'I wouldn't say that's a good way to treat a pair of expensive shoes.' The words were spoken lightly, breathlessly. It was the sister.

'Oh yeah! What's it to you?' snarled Barnett.

'Nothing. But I've just run all the way after you from the hospital and I must be quite mad.' panted the ward sister. Her generous bosom heaved heavily, expanding and contracting, threatening to break from the moorings of her tight restricting uniform. 'You might at least listen to what I have to say.'

'Sorry,' Barnett smiled an apology, 'None of it was your fault.'

'Nor yours.' came the breathless answer, 'But about the girl... what she said. Please, ignore it. She is still in a state of shock. So would you be in her position. She is also very frightened and lonely. You may find it hard to believe... but she *needs* you. Honestly.'

'Needs *me*!' Young Barnett Hall was amazed. 'I'm just *not* her type. Never!'

'Well, that's where you're wrong. *Her* type, as you put it, are the wrong type. They're uncaring, thoughtless and totally selfish. She may not know it but it's someone like you that she *does* need. Someone to care.'

'It didn't exactly sound like it, did it?'

'No. That's true. But please, don't let that mislead you. Don't be put off.' She looked at the watch pinned to the starched front of her uniform, entreated him, 'I have to get back to the ward. Please... I beg you, call in again. She really does need your help.'

Barnett stared after her retreating figure. *You fool!* He admonished himself, *Mug! Lumbered yet again.* He kicked viciously at a metal panel, looked at his shoes and stopped. The sister, she was right, it was foolish to ruin a pair of perfectly good shoes.

Opening Spell

A foretaste of the coming season.

The fixture secretary's dream had finally come about and it was a perfect day for the opening match. Every year he arranged the opening match for the third Saturday in April. Invariably the game was either rained off, cancelled because the ground was unplayable, or due to a backlog of postponed football fixtures the cricket club found it had insufficient players to raise a team.

But this year it was perfect. The weather was fine, the ground fit for play and there was a surplus of players from which to select a team. What more could a secretary desire? His little bureaucratic heart filled with joy. The world was a wonderful place and nothing could go wrong. Nothing. Could it...?

The old captain arrived first. Erected on the main road for all to see and pointing the way to the ground was a notice board. It bore the painted heading '**Briseley T'ill Cricket Club'**. An arrow indicated to visitors the unmade bumpy footpath leading to the playing field. Near to the bottom of the notice board a second caption read; '**Today's Visitors'**, with a space to write in the name of the opposing team. A third caption read; '**Play to commence at 2:30pm – Promptly!'**

The reality of village cricket was that it seldom did. It should have done but for various reasons it failed to happen. Predominant amongst the many whys and wherefores was the lunchtime closing of the Cock Inn. Seduced by the flavour of the excellent local brew it took a little while for players to make their way from the bar to the venue where play was due to begin.

But then, when has rural life ever been punctual? It moves at its own sedate pace and refuses to be ruled by watches and clocks.

Armed with a piece of white chalk, George Burke wrote on the notice board in neat and elegant script beneath the visiting team caption. "**Kirk Loscoe Cricket Club"**. Then pocketing the chalk he set off to unlock the pavilion, sort out the playing kit and make their visitors welcome.

George stood on the pavilion veranda enjoying the sight of the smooth green expanse of turf as it swept away towards the distant boundary, rising slightly and ending with the steep embankment of the railway line. A warm breeze blew lightly from the southwest: featherlike fingers of air brushing his weathered cheeks. White cumulus clouds, soft and fleecy, drifted high across an expanse of blue sky.

It's going to be a perfect afternoon for cricket, mused the old player.

*

Adrian Hutton arrived with the Mole twins. He sat cross-legged in the back of the tinny old mini van as it bumped its way along the lumpy track to the playing field. At just fourteen years of age Adrian Hutton was a product typical of his generation. He was already taller than his parents at five feet eight inches in height and was fast developing into a wiry athlete. The thrill of being selected to play in the first game of the new season reflected in the eager look upon his young face. Adrian knew he was unlikely to be called upon to bowl. He would probably be asked to bat at number eleven and would most certainly spend his afternoon chasing leather around the boundary. It mattered not. Because for this game he had actually been selected to play. It was better than being the twelfth man who occasionally played but more often than not, didn't. It was better than being asked to score and far better than being dragged in as a last minute replacement to cover for a dropout. Today he was one of the selected eleven, an original choice, a member of the side on merit…and so proud.

On the old captain's instructions Adrian collected a polythene bag of white plastic boundary flags and paced his way around the perimeter of the field, inserting a flag every ten steps. George Burke set up the wickets, screwing the stumps firmly into the turf. He placed metal markers for the use of the bowlers neatly behind each set of stumps. Meanwhile Norman and Lenny Mole opened up the score-box, unscrewing the wooden shutters that had secured its windows against vandalism and the winter weather. They transferred crockery and an electric tea urn into the makeshift kitchen at the rear of the pavilion.

John Shackleton drove onto the field and up to the veranda in his estate car. Raising its tailgate he unloaded a large cardboard box and carried it into the kitchen. It contained bread, butter, lettuce, tomatoes, watercress, radishes, onions, cheese, six tins of luncheon meat and a selection of fancy cakes. Fresh produce from the village store owned and run by his wife, Josie. Later the ladies would arrive to prepare the cricket teas.

Mildred Burke was first on the teas roster. At every Annual General Meeting there was a lot of discussion about the teas roster (always a thorny subject) and agreement would be reached that there be an equal sharing of the duties involved. Every season the roster commenced in good faith and every season just as quickly fell apart. It failed miserably. By the end of each season an imaginary scorecard of the roster would read - Home matches 20. Mildred Burke 15. Others 5.

The political machinations became too complicated. If a player was unavailable or not selected to play then it was unlikely that his wife, girlfriend or mistress would be willing to prepare the teas. In such times of trouble the committee turned to Mildred.

At 2.35pm the opposition arrived. The rest of the Briseley T'ill players arrived close behind.

'A fine thing,' muttered George Burke, 'when the visitors manage to get here before players who live on the doorstep.' George thought it inexcusable.

All three Barnett Halls were present. Old Barnett, whose hair was now sparse and had turned to a rusty grey, was the Briseley T'ill umpire. Young Barnett's father was the incumbent captain. At forty-one his hair, like his body, had lost its youthful fire. Grey flecks toned down his once fiery thatch. But the athleticism lost by his body was more than compensated for by his fine cricketing brain and experience. He sought out his opposite number and introduced himself.

'Barnett Hall.'

'Tom Slater. Hi!'

'Are your lads all here Tom?'

'Oh. Aye. I reckon so. We know our way here by now. How many years is it?'

'More than I care to remember Tom,' Barnett senior replied with a sigh, 'Today has to be the best start to the season we've ever had. Don't you think?'

'Couldn't be better.' Slater acknowledged with a nod.

The fixture was long standing on the card of both clubs. It reached back over decades and was eagerly anticipated by both sides and always resulted in a closely fought game. The captains studied the immaculate strip of turf and ruminated on its condition like satisfied cows chewing their cud.

'It looks very good.' Slater commented, 'A new ball of course?'

'Yeah! Your call.' Hall senior produced a fifty pence coin from his hip pocket and flipped it high into the air.

'Heads.' called Slater, watching closely as the coin pitched edge up, rolled in a circle and finally came to rest in his favour. 'Mmm. New ball eh,' he reflected briefly as though the turn of events was unexpected, then decided, 'I think we'll field.'

Back in the dressing room the Briseley T'ill captain announced to his team 'Batting lads. Pad up George, you're opening with Young Barnett. Tim, you're number three, Shack, four and Snowball, five. OK?' Then he went in search of Lenny Mole to ask him to score. Given the choice he usually asked Lenny for although he was slow and methodical, the taciturn young man had neat and accurate handwriting. He also batted late in the order.

George Burke, Barnett and Tim Taverstock delved into their respective bags for their equipment. As dedicated cricketers each one possessed their own bat, pads, gloves and protective guards. George Burke took extra precautions for at the age of fifty he found that the inevitable knocks to be associated with the game came harder to him than to the younger players. Bruises took longer to fade. Cuts longer to heal.

Inside the sock of his left leg George inserted a foam pad to give additional protection to his tibia bone, it bruised easily despite the sturdy batting pads he wore. With age, wasting flesh had left the bone painfully exposed and being a right-handed batsman his left leg was the one that took most punishment. A lightweight high-impact polystyrene thigh pad covered his hipbone and a pink plastic box slid into the elasticised pouch of his jockstrap.

George pulled on batting gloves and as a final crowning glory perched a brand new cricket cap upon his head. The cap was bright red, a birthday present from his wife, Mildred. It sat like a cherry on a cake.

They walked out together in the bright sunlight, an oddly disparaging pair at opposite ends of the age scale. Yet, consistently, they formed successful opening partnerships. Barnett was the hammer, aggressive and powerful, a player full of grace and glorious strokes, always forcing the pace. George was the patient one, watchful, a rock in defence, a sturdy anchorman around which the team built its innings. Opposition bowlers hated his stubborn defence and were always anxious to winkle him out.

'D'you reckon we should appeal against the light?' asked Burke, a cheeky twinkle gleaming in his eye.

'Light?'

'Yeah! Too damn bright ain't it? T'aint what I'm used to... not in April.'

After the gloom of the changing rooms the bright sunlight was fierce, hurtful to the eyes, causing them to squint painfully. They walked slowly out to the wicket allowing time for their pupils to adjust so they were not dazzled by the glare.

'I don't recognise the opening bowler,' Barnett commented, 'New player is he? Any idea what he's like?'

'Name o' Staywood,' answered Burke, 'New chap, fancies 'issen a bit, I'm told. Did y'notice 'is boots? The ode-fashioned type wi' steel toecaps. I 'eard as 'e's a newcomer t'village.'

'Fast, is he?'

'Dunno! We shall see, won't we? We shall see.'

The visiting umpire went by the name of Bert Plumtree. Like most umpires he was a former player and adversary who had played against Burke for decades. He knew him well. He looked at his cherry red cap in astonishment.

'Good grief George!' he exclaimed, ''Ave you 'ad a mishap? Yer looks like one o' them tarts, Cherry Bakewells, ain't they called?'

Un-offended, Burke grinned and gave his cap a jaunty wiggle.

'New cap, Bert. D'yer like it? It's a present from Mildred

'A bit early in the year for poppies,' said the umpire dryly. He nudged Burke in the ribs with his elbow, 'Gotta new bowler in team for you. Never seen 'im play afore but 'e don't half talk a good game. We'll soon find out. Captain's opening' wi' 'im.'

*

Staywood, the bowler under discussion, was indeed about to perform. His warming up exercises alone looked frightening. His arms wind-milled like the blades of a helicopter that was dangerously out of control. He paced out an enormously long run up, stopping just short of the boundary rope by a few steps, only feet from the pavilion. Little George Burke looked on in amazement.

'Will ''e need pavilion door openin'?' he cheekily asked Plumtree.

Young Barnett, who was about to face the first delivery of the aspiring demon bowler, took guard carefully. He asked for leg stump. Drew a neat line in the turf with the spikes of his boot to mark his position. He settled comfortably into his stance. Head up. Eyes level. Relaxed, ready and still, a textbook stance.

Just inside the boundary the new bowler began his run. He gave a little hop, then a skip before setting off on his excessively long run up to the wicket. It culminated in a frenetic leap as he turned into his delivery action. The bright, hard, shiny ball pitched halfway down the wicket, an attempted bouncer that barely rose above stump high. Its direction was wildly off target as it arrowed across Barnett and travelled ever wider down his leg side. The Kirk Loscoe wicketkeeper gave vent to a despairing curse and threw himself sideways in a vain attempt to stop the delivery.

Young Barnett Hall never bothered to move.

The ball flashed over the boundary rope, passed through the protective fencing and came to rest halfway up the railway embankment. Bert Plumtree turned to face the pavilion and signalled. First he extended both arms to indicate a wide ball and then waved his right arm to and fro across his body, informing the scorers to record four extras. His bushy eyebrows climbed high upon his forehead as he turned beseeching eyes to Heaven. Faintly the words he uttered like a prayer were heard.

'Glory be to God, and to all who fancy they're fast bluddy bowlers!'

To a man the Kirk Loscoe players stared fixedly at the ground, or at the sky, or at the tight green buds breaking into leaf on the distant willow trees. Not a word was spoken. Meanwhile the ball was reluctantly returned to Staywood who stared at it as though the inanimate object was responsible before polishing it vigorously down the front of his flannels. He strode back once more towards his marker.

He turned to run in again, started with the same little hop and skip, the overlong run-up, the frenetic leap into the air, the wild misdirected delivery. Another wide. This time the ball failed to make contact with the pitch at all. It hurtled, head high towards the first slip as lethal as a bullet. The fielder, with a finely tuned sense of preservation in mind, took immediate action and threw himself to the ground.

Deep on the boundary the third man fielder, now alert to the situation, broke into a gallop. He raced around, shot out a despairing boot only to succeed in deflecting the ball. It rattled into the boards of British Rail's fence with alarming ferocity to disturb the woodlice and knock rotting pieces from the fence.

Mildred Burke, busily organising the kitchen, heard the distant impact. 'What was that?' she cried out, 'Are we winning?'

'Who can tell?' came the dry reply, 'Our lads haven't touched a ball yet.'

The umpire repeated his earlier signals. Tom Slater, the Kirk Loscoe captain, frantically signalled at his bowler to slow down. Dismay showed on his weathered face.

'Sorry Skip!' the offender apologised breezily, 'Bit rusty. Need to find my direction.' Six further deliveries sprayed around the batsman. None of them was near enough to trouble him or to threaten the wicket. They were just close enough to save Bert Plumtree the embarrassment of having to signal further wide balls. He called "over" with a sigh of relief before marching hurriedly to the square leg position, personally doubting whether Staywood had ever had any direction to find.

Dewhurst, the other opening bowler was a different kettle of fish, reliable, medium paced and accurate. George Burke played out his six deliveries with care. His bat was straight with very little back-lift as he played each ball into the ground, solid, dependable and safe, without a hint of fireworks.

Tom Slater was on the spot. To remove an opening bowler from the firing line so soon was tactically unthinkable. After only eight deliveries he could hardly suggest that the player "*take a rest.*" Lobbing the ball back to the bowler he suggested, 'Try one more,' He nodded down at the pitch, 'T'is a bit slow for a bowler like thee, lad. Try tekking it steady, OK?'

'Right Skip!' the unabashed Staywood replied and strode away to his distant marker. A marginally better over followed. One ball even pitched in line with the wickets, remained straight and would have hit the stumps, except that its length was regrettably short. To Barnett, a consummate batsman, it was a friendly delivery and with effortless grace he swung his bat down the line, picked up the ball on the rise and despatched it over the pavilion roof. Loud applause rippled from the spectators on the veranda.

On the field of play there was acute disillusionment amongst the Kirk Loscoe team. Bill Parsons, the wicket keeper, muttered dark curses under his breath, casting doubts upon the validity of the bowler's parentage. The left side of his freshly laundered flannels carried an unbecoming green stain, the result of a frantic dive to his left. The following swallow dive to his right had lacerated the skin of his elbow. Tiny droplets of blood oozed through the ruptured skin.

Barnett leaned on his bat and smiled sweetly at the fuming keeper as he sadly shook his head.

'He's a *very* dangerous bowler.' he commented.

'Not where you're effing standing,' snarled Parsons bitterly, 'Seems t'me the safest place to effing be is in front of the bloody stumps!' He vainly tried to manoeuvre his arm into a position where he could lick clean the injury to his elbow. It's a physically impossible task.

Barnett took two further boundaries from the over. A square cut for four followed by an onside drive which split the field and raced over the outfield. Fourteen runs from the bat, eight extras, a total of twenty-two on the scoreboard... and the game still in its infancy.

The Briseley T'ill players lounging on the veranda were delighted. Adrian Hutton hung black metal squares painted with white figures onto a row of hooks. The scoreboard was simple, primitive but effective. It displayed the total score, the number of wickets as they fell, how many overs had been bowled and the score from the previous innings. For economy purposes the metal plates were numbered on both sides and loosely stacked in a wooden case. Adrian organised the plates into neat piles. Odd numbers were painted on one side, even on the other. He kept the scoreboard ticking over efficiently, just being involved in even the simplest way increased his enjoyment of the game.

Tom Slater placed a comforting arm around his wayward bowler. A stranglehold would have been a more suitable reflection to his frame of mind.

'Take thee a rest lad.' He suggested in his North Midlands accent as he directed the man to a fielding position deep on the boundary. Staywood heaved an exaggerated sigh and muttering unrepeatable commendations upon the vagaries of cricket captains, trudged away. He spend the remainder of the Briseley T'ill innings simmering, a growing resentment that in the latter stages of the match exploded with resounding repercussions.

Young Barnett Hall and George Burke progressed steadily. George, with little prods and pushes, nudged the ball into space and took quick singles. At every opportunity he allowed Barnett the strike so the powerful, younger man could attack the bowling and push the score along. Barnett punished the loose deliveries unmercifully and presented a straight defensive bat to the good ones.

The total reached seventy without loss. That early competitive edge had deserted the Kirk Loscoe fielders. Unexpectedly the game changed direction. There was a sudden growing roar, a rush of displaced air, then with a loud *swooshing* sound one of British Rail's finest yellow perils tore along the track.

Afterwards Barnett could have kicked himself when he realised the folly of his mistake. As the bowler ran in to bowl the train raced across his line of vision. Its noise distracted him and the moving background momentarily drew his eyes away from the ball. His steady concentration was broken. Barnett knew instantly what he should have done. Backed off, or put up a hand to stop the action. It was basic common sense really, a spur of the moment decision that every cricketer needs to make. His swinging bat missed the ball; it clipped his pad, was deflected and shattered the wicket.

'Owzat!' A concerted shout went up from the Kirk Loscoe players. It was an unnecessary appeal but a natural one. Their spirits soared cloud high.

Barnett's heart sank, then as he walked from the field of play and reflected upon his performance, lifted. In his first match of the new season he had performed remarkably well. The players lounging on the veranda clapped him in. Their applause interspersed with comments offered condolences, advice, sympathy and congratulations at his fine innings.

'Well played Barnett.'

'Hard luck lad. Well played.'

'Forty-nine, just one run off your half century. Bad luck!'

'Should have stepped back lad. Stopped the play.'

'Tough luck Barnett... going like a bomb!'

The young opener acknowledged the plaudits with curt nods of his flame-thatched head. He smiled wryly at the thought of missing out on the first half century of the season. He checked his score in the book, looking over the shoulder of Lenny Mole at the neat row of figures. His score of forty-nine included six fours and one six.

Lenny Mole completed writing in the details. B. Hall (jnr.) bowled Dexter 49. First wicket fell at seventy. Time out: 4:12pm. The writing was very precise, his figures round and clear, the point of the pencil pressing firmly into the paper, easy to read, accurate. Lenny's bookkeeping was immaculate, yet surprisingly he earned his living working with animals.

*

In the cool interior of the changing room Barnett stripped off naked. He towelled down his lean perspiring body. A shower would have been ideal but the only washing facility was an old white washbasin that was lined with surface cracks and stained a mottled yellow. It possessed a single cold water tap. When the faucet was turned on the water pipes rattled and shook and water jetted out in erratic spurts. The plug was missing from its chain. Barnett splashed the cold running water onto his face and neck before drying himself and pulling a fresh white shirt over his head. He combed his mop of unruly hair into a semblance of order.

After each innings it was his habit to sit quietly in a corner and go over every aspect of his performance in his head. He would analyse any mistakes he'd made and evaluate the reason for his dismissal. In this way, he reasoned, his game would develop and improve for as much as he enjoyed his playing for the Briseley T'ill cricket club, his home village, Barnett had ambitions for greater things and fervently desired to move up to a higher level. Today's little disaster was obvious. The express train flashing by the ground so unexpectedly, its approach unheard until the last few seconds due to the sound being swept away by the wind. Usually there was some warning and the umpires would hold up play until the distraction had thundered by.

Oh well. Barnett mentally shrugged aside the occurrence. There was no point in dwelling on the past.

The past? A picture formed in his mind, clear and stark of a young woman lying flat in a hospital bed. A picture of blonde hair that fanned out over a snow-white pillow, of dark blue eyes, angry and bitter, turning black with inward despair. Despite the sister's eloquent plea Barnett had still to return and visit Cynthia Ashley-Jayle.

A battle raged within him. On one side, guilt and his conscience urged him to go. Yet a reluctance to lay his feelings on the line again held him back. Another battering of his ego he did not want... and yet...

The dressing room door crashed open breaking into Barnett's introspective thoughts. Tim Taverstock stormed into the room, hurling his bat and gloves into an untidy pile. The rage of failure showed upon his face.

'OK. What happened?' asked Barnett. Knowing Taverstock's style of batting he already had a good idea but thought it wiser to ask and allow the player to give vent to his frustration, like taking the whistle off a steaming kettle.

'Shooter!' replied Taverstock fiercely, 'First one of the bloody season and I have to be the one who gets it. It pitched short, went onto the back foot to hook, what bloody happens? Never bounced. It shot along the ground. Didn't have a bloody dog's chance.' He flopped down, dispiritedly unbuckled his pads, reached for a towel and began to wipe his face and then paused. He flung the towel to one side in disgust.

'Never even worked up a bloody sweat.' he grumbled to himself.

'Well, hard luck.' Barnett commiserated, knowing that left alone for ten minutes Tim Taverstock would soon recover his good humour and overcome the disappointment of his failure. The man was an eternal optimist and before long his ready smile would flash out once more from beneath his flamboyant Zapata-style moustache. In his mind the fatal delivery would become increasingly potent, a deadly unplayable ball that no one could have defended. Only then would he be happy.

Barnett ambled onto the veranda, settled himself into a deckchair and rested his boots on the rail. Ted Decker sat relaxed in the next seat. When asked, his version of Tim Taverstock's dismissal was the one Barnet expected. 'The daft beggar hit across a straight one.' said the policeman. *Typical of Tim,* thought Barnett, *Vast potential but not a shred of patience.*

Out on the pitch George Burke and John Shackleton faced a torrid time. Boosted by their success the Kirk Loscoe bowlers had taken fresh heart. Tom Slater pushed fielders into catching positions, close to the wicket, pressuring the batsmen. He urged his bowlers to greater effort. Hostility reigned.

One sharply rising ball crushed George Burke's fingers against the handle of his bat. He snatched his hand away in pain, shook it, swearing softly under his breath as he strove to keep the pain from showing on his face. Histrionics had never been his forte. In cricket, George reasoned, rolling about in agony, real or otherwise, only encouraged the bowler to greater aggression.

John Shackleton ducked under an obvious bouncer, pitching short, the ball was easily read and evaded. Not so the following delivery which lifted unexpectedly from a full length. He tried in vain to sway out of the way but the ball, swinging late in its flight, followed his body. It clipped the edge of his bat, deflected into his ribs and carried through to be caught by the wicketkeeper. The Kirk Loscoe players took to the air like a squadron of Harrier jump jets, loosing a concerted roar of appeal.

Out! And suddenly the Briseley T'ill team were in trouble at 73 for 3 wickets.

Snowball Jackson's reaction was typically West Indian. Take the fight to the enemy. Ask no quarter, give none. He only faced six balls. Played the first one carefully, hit the second for six where it was recovered from the railway embankment, then failed to connect with the third and fourth. He gave the full meat of his bat to the fifth, a huge six that cleared the railway embankment altogether. Precious time was lost searching for the ball. His concentration broken by the delay Snowball was cleaned bowled by the final ball. It was a clever delivery, deliberately bowled from a yard behind the crease, cunningly flighted to appear identical to its predecessor but arriving fractionally later. Everett Jackson's flowing stroke was a shade too soon. His follow through completed before the stumps were rattled.

Briseley T'ill were now 85 for 4 wickets.

It needed a captain's inning to restore sanity to the proceedings and the captain duly obliged. Barnett senior played with the studied calm of long experience. He stroked the ball into spaces with finely controlled shots. Drooped a deadening bat on the lifters and punished the loose ones with imperious drives into the covers. And all the while little George Burke prodded, poked and nudged his way to thirty useful runs. By the time Bert Plumtree lifted off the bails to indicate tea the score had reached 152 for 4 wickets with Barnett Hall senior scoring exactly fifty.

In the home changing room speculation was rife. Half the team wanted to bat on, the other half advised a declaration, pointing out the need for time in which to dismiss their opponents. The equating voice of Ted Decker swayed the argument in favour of a declaration.

'It's a fair total lads.' he said, 'We don't want to kill the game altogether. If they can knock them off then they deserve to win. I believe we can bowl the beggars out. What say you Lenny?' He looked at the big fast bowler.

The tall, lean, dark-haired young man was as reticent as ever. He smiled a brief, lop-sided smile as his shoulders twitched in the faintest of shrugs. His acknowledging "Yeah!" came out more as a grunt than a spoken word.

*

Mildred Burke received unexpected help preparing the teas. Helen Argosy arrived at the pavilion, part dragged, part coaxed there by her cricket-obsessed son, Jason. At first Helen hung about, separated by a few yards from the rest of the spectators. She felt unreasonably shy, almost an intruder. Her son, devoid of similar inhibitions, quickly befriended Adrian Hutton and became involved in operating the scoreboard.

It was Mildred who spotted Helen first. She waved a friendly hand, called out a greeting and offered her a cup of tea. Ever since the accident a tenuous bond had formed between the two women, unspoken and invisible and barely recognised until now. A bond formed by a shared experience.

The tea was strong and hot, brewed in a small brown pot with scalding hot water from a large electric urn. There were also two large aluminium teapots, each one holding around a gallon, sufficient for thirty cups of the strong refreshing brew, a pot for each of the thirsty teams.

Helen sipped her tea and silently admired Mildred's organisation. Thirty teas had been requested and thirty thick, large white plates lay ready. On each platter, a slice of ham, a slice of luncheon meat and a large tomato. Bowls of lettuce – Webbs – crisp and crunchy, slices of cucumber, radishes, pickled onions, grated cheese and small round baby beetroots. A sprinkling of watercress decorated each plate. Mildred was halfway through buttering the bread and still had to layout the fancy cakes upon the elderly and wobbly cake-stands.

'Is there anything I do?' offered Helen. The older woman paused reflectively, remembering occasions when proffered help had proved to be more of a hindrance.

Unlikely this time, Mildred decided in her mind as she quickly assessed the younger woman. 'You could set out the tables. T'would be a great help. You'll find tablecloths in my basket. Knives and forks underneath, they're wrapped in paper napkins. Lay out sixteen places at the long table, that one's for the visitors, and fourteen for the home team. Best to stack the cups at the end, it makes it easier to pour the tea. The players can pass the cups around themselves.'

'Got it.' said Helen positively and set to work. It was strange but once she was actively involved she felt less of an intruder. It was never easy slotting into a new community. There were problems in a town but it was even more difficult in a small tightly knit village environment.

She laid out the thirty place settings on the trestle tables. Once covered by Mildred's snow-white tablecloths they looked quite respectable. The food looked tasty and appetising, but the seating…? She struggled with long rickety benches and wobbly folding chairs. Many of the seats had missing slats and one chair had lost one of its legs. Helen snorted in frustration as she struggled to set up a workable arrangement.

'Don't 'e worry about the seats,' advised Mildred, 'Let 'em sort themselves out.'

Suddenly the room was full of men. Full of white flannels, open-necked sports shirts, clumping spiked boots and bodies glowing with healthy perspiration. They squashed onto the narrow rickety benches, their elbows knocking together and their knives and forks rattling noisily against the thick white plates. Tim Taverstock was the lucky player who drew the short straw; left with the three-legged chair.

'Cor! Just my luck,' he grumbled good-naturedly, 'T'ain't my day is it? Out for nowt. Now I'm left the chair with three ruddy legs. C'mon chaps move along the ruddy bench.'

'Not likely, I'll finish wi' Ted's fork up me nose.'

'Shove up!'

'Not me, find another place.'

'Serves yer right for gerrin' out fer nowt.'

'T'was a bloody snorter, that ball. Best one I've ever faced. Best of the match.'

'Rubbish! You just missed a straight 'un.'

'Straight 'un? It kept low, a real grubber.'

'Oh shurrup moanin' and pass the salad cream.'

'Oh God! Who's drunk my tea. This buggers got sugar in. I hate sugar.'

'That 'uns mine you daft bat. You've just drunk yourn.'

'More tea?' Helen moved around with the large aluminium teapot, offering seconds. She poured, two handed, refilling all the cups. The tea, by now well and truly stewed, came out like dark brown sludge but no one seemed to care or notice. She saw Ted Decker watching her, an expression of surprise and pleasure showed on his face at the same time.

'Hello.' he mouthed across the hubbub of conversation.

'Hello.' Helen mouthed back, 'Speak to you later.'

Back in the galley kitchen she spoke to Mildred. 'They're like little boys – full of mischief. It's not what I expected. Out on the field, dressed all in white, they look so elegant, perfect gentlemen. They're not a bit like that really, are they?'

'Lord bless you, no.' laughed Mildred, 'Boys they are to be sure. They'll never grow up, any of them. Just like Peter Pan, little boys at heart forever... and they'll never change. But cricket, now that *is* serious. Mark my words, once a man is hooked on cricket that's it. You'll get no change there. If you don't like it, then you just have to learn to lump it.'

'But it's only a game.' protested Helen Argosy.

'Only a game! That's right, to you and me it *is* only a game. A damn silly one at times, believe me, especially when they're dashing in and out between showers of rain. But a game... never!'

She smiled compassionately at the younger woman's bewildered face as she explained, 'It's like a religion with 'em. Gets into the blood stream. Seems as if they can't do without it. Worse than drug addicts they are. Take my George, not as you'd want 'im, he's been playing cricket for Briseley T'ill since 'e left school at fifteen. He's fifty now. You would think he'd have retired gracefully long ago and left it to younger men. But not 'im. Not George. 'E says as 'ow it keeps 'im young.' Mildred shook her head at the incomprehensible nature of men. 'It could be worse I suppose, though I find that hard to believe when 'e comes 'ome covered in bruises every other week.'

'Bruises!' There was alarm in Helen's voice.

'Lots of 'em. Plus the odd broken finger... and cut 'eads as need stitchin', pulled muscles. There's even been cases of concussion, as if they 'aven't enough daftness in their 'eads as it is. They're mad, quite mad, the whole lot of 'em Did you see that West Indian on the tele? One arm broken, in a sling, batted one-handed. What for I ask... what for?'

Helen shook her head, mystified. She didn't know what for.

'Glory!' postulated Mildred, 'Glory! Though I can't see much glory in a broken 'ead, damned if I can. Never did.'

'I never realised the game could be dangerous. It's so traditional, so English. Saturday afternoons, a game of cricket on the village green, it seems so harmless.'

'Harmless! You've a lot to learn young Helen.' Mildred sniffed, her nose twitched as she considered her words, 'We-e-ell, perhaps that's a bit over the top. I'm just trying to make my point. But men and cricket, put the two together and what do you get? Obsession.'

*

There was a shuffling of feet, the scraping of benches on the pockmarked floor. Barnett Hall senior's greying head peered tentatively into the galley kitchen.

'Lovely tea Mildred,' he called out, 'Don't know how you do it?'

'Practice!' Mildred informed him, but he had already gone. Her words filled the space where his head had been, the irony in her comment, unheard. Briseley T'ill's captain was already leading his men back onto the field of battle.

'What happens now?' asked Helen.

'We wash up... Oh! You mean about the match. It's our turn to field,' explained Mildred, 'Briseley T'ill scored 152 and then declared. Now Kirk Loscoe have to score more than us to win.'

'And how long will that take?'

'There's no way of telling,' answered the older woman, 'Could be they lose early wickets and shut up shop. Go for a draw. That's cricket... one never knows.'

'Oh.' Helen sounded deflated, 'Will the game go on for long then, end very late?'

'Lord bless you! Don't look so worried. There is a time limit, seven-thirty. She gave Helen Argosy a shrewd enquiring look, 'Is it that Ted Decker you're keen on?'

Helen gasped, 'How did you know?'

'S'easy, I'm not blind you know. I do notice things.' Mildred smiled knowingly as she brushed unruly hair from her eyes. Soapy washing-up water dripped from her reddened hands, tiny bubbles drifting in a descending arc. 'It's my experience that when an attractive unattached young woman takes an interest in cricket there has to be a man in it somewhere. Am I right?' She cocked her head to one side, birdlike, watching the young woman's face, waiting for an answer.

Helen flushed darkly, staring down at the thick white plates now shining and clean.

'Yes. You *are* right,' she admitted reluctantly, 'It is Ted Decker. I liked him from the first moment he spoke to me after the accident. Silly isn't it? Me, acting like a schoolgirl. After all I'm hardly a teenager... thirty-one and with a young son. And Ted, he... he's quite a bit older than me...' Her voice faded into uncertain silence.

'It ain't silly at all,' Mildred replied comfortingly, 'Age don't come into it much these days, do it? What's Ted? Forty-five... forty-six? It ain't nothin'. He's a good man is Constable Decker. A real gentleman he is, though I reckon you've a chase on your hands there. I've always thought it a terrible waste, a man like 'im being on 'is own. Do 'im good and you to get together a bit... if y'know what I mean?'

Then noticing the eager light awakening in the younger woman's eyes she added a note of warning. 'Mind you, you'll needs watch that sister of 'is. A right tarter that Beatrice, could be quite a handful that one.'

It should be very interesting to watch, Mildred mused, turning back to dry the pots.

*

The object of their interest was preparing to bowl. Edward Decker had not anticipated being called upon to open the attack. He was a slow bowler, an off-spinner and usually it was much later in the game that his services were called upon. But over his cup of dark brown tea Barnett Hall senior had brewed up a strategy of his own, an untried theory had been buzzing around at the back of his brain for two seasons. Like a small seed it had germinated slowly and now, he felt, was the time to try it out.

The strength of Kirk Loscoe Cricket Club lay in their number one batsman, Whitehead. He was unprepossessing to the casual eye, short and stocky with thick stumpy legs and an even thicker body. Built with a low centre of gravity, Whitehead had forearms of machined steel. His biceps measured a full twelve inches in circumference and were capable of enormous strength. He destroyed opening bowlers, driving their best deliveries back past their startled heads in a soaring trajectory that carried the ball clean over the boundary. A technique entirely his own... and unique.

His stance was a mere foot in front of the stumps with both feet well behind the popping crease. It looked inevitable that any back-lift would break his wicket, yet it never did for those steely hawser-like forearms needed no such movement. The bowler felt encouraged to flight the ball well up to the bat, a full length. Whitehead patted first one, then two and sometimes a third delivery firmly back along the ground towards his unsuspecting opponent. Quickly he would assess the pace and bounce of the wicket, never allowing time for doubts to creep in. Then he launched his attack. Seconds later a shell-shocked player would be waiting, head bowed in dismay, for the ball to be returned from its screaming flight.

It seemed a fluke, a chance in a million... until the next delivery. Demoralisation set in quickly. There would be an early shuffling of the attack. Normally eager bowlers crept away, trying to look invisible and none of them sought to catch the captain's eye.

Together, Decker and his captain placed their field. John Emmett and Young Barnett were sent to long-off and long-on respectively. Both men were fine catchers of the ball and took up positions very deep, their backs almost touching the whitewashed boundary fence. Next to the wicketkeeper, Jackson, George Burke was the solitary slip. The captain placed himself in the mid-on position. When complete the effect was one of two rings of fielders. A deep outer ring comprising six players all noted for their ability to catch the ball and an inner ring of five.

Nervously Decker paced out his run, just seven steps. He dropped the flat metal marker on the spot and fitted the ball between his fingers. His thumb supported it from underneath and his forefinger, slightly crooked, lay across the seam, the ridges of stitching giving him a firm and confident grip. He waited for the batsman to complete his preparations.

Whitehead and his jumbo-sized bat appeared to blot out the entire wicket. A single bail and a thin sliver of the off stump was Ted's only sighting. His first attempt to bowl became a non-event. There was a distinct lack of cohesion between his brain and his legs as he began on the wrong foot and arrived at the crease out of step.

He pulled to a halt.

'Sorry.' he apologised in general. The umpire gave him a startled look and raised a quizzical eyebrow. From the waiting batsman, wrapped in concentration, came a flat unblinking stare.

His second attempt produced an innocuous ball that pitched twelve inches outside the off stump. The bounce was even and it barely turned an inch. Two following deliveries were identical. His fourth turned slightly more in towards the stumps. All four balls were caught by Everett Jackson, who in turn, tossed the ball back to Barnett Hall. He flicked it, underarm, back to Decker. Everyone waited for the explosion. It was due at any moment.

That early tension had left the bowler's action. Easily and rhythmically Decker moved in to bowl. A cobra could not have struck with greater speed or venom. Whitehead's feet shuffled into line. His massive forearms flicked rather than swung his bat. In a movement that was all wrist and timing the ball was cracked away. It soared into the atmosphere, a diminishing black dot against the ceramic-blue sky.

Deep in the long-on position John Emmett's eyes were riveted upon the soaring dot. As it fell towards him he moved backwards until the white fencing rails pressed into the small of his back, preventing further retreat. Both his hands reached back over his head, his back arched painfully, but in vain. Agonisingly the projectile landed two feet behind him, crashed into the grassy embankment, rolled down the gradient and back onto the field of play.

Six. And yet he'd been so near...

A disconsolate Barnett Hall tossed the ball one final time to Decker. The expression on his face read; "You can't win 'em all. But Edward Decker had been hit for six before and a little tactic all his own came to mind. Upon reaching his run-up marker he deliberately took another stride. He turned, took a slow deep breath to steady his nerves and commenced to bowl. A full yard short of the wicket his arm came over and his hand released the ball a fraction of a second earlier in a high looping flight. To the batsman it looked a gift. Whitehead's feet performed a double chasse. Again he played the wristy, flicking cobra stroke. Too soon! The ball dropped short, bounced high and passed over the blade of the bat into the safe hands of Everett Jackson. In his eagerness to break the wicket, Snowball sprawled the stumps in every direction.

'How is dat?' he screamed triumphantly. Whitehead was hopelessly out of his ground, stranded by a full yard. Square with the wicket Bert Plumtree raised a weary index finger. In his capacity as an umpire Bert was strictly neutral but as a loyal Kirk Loscoe man he considered it far from the best of days.

The Briseley T'ill players all rushed to congratulate Decker and Jackson upon their combined success. No one thought to praise the captain for his strategy. A forgotten man, Barnett Hall shrugged philosophically, enjoying with inward satisfaction the result of his tactical ploy.

It was time to settle down the team. Their exuberance was premature. He clapped his hands to catch their attention. 'C'mon lads. Man in. We've taken *one* wicket, not won the game.'

And indeed they had not.

The match developed into a tense and dour struggle. It was as though the early loss of their match-winning opener doubled the resolve of the Kirk Loscoe players. Their performance proved gritty and stubborn, born of an inward strength. Decker bowled four more economical overs without further success. He was removed and replaced by Lenny Mole. The lean young man performed with mean aggression, whipping the ball down from his considerable height, achieving lift and pace from the unusually dry pitch. Every run had to be earned. Every stroke made with resolution. The Briseley T'ill players fielding with taut economy forced Kirk Loscoe to grind out the runs.

Wickets fell, but without a sudden flourish.

Norman Mole took a stinging catch to dismiss Tom Slater for twenty-five valuable runs. Adrian Hutton raced around the outfield with youthful athleticism to take, fully stretched, a plummeting ball. He glowed with pride at the well-deserved praise heaped upon his immature head.

Dependable John Emmett bowled with reliable consistency and was rewarded with two wickets, both clean bowled, when the batsmen lost patience and made false strokes. Inexorably the score continued to mount.

100 runs for 5 wickets.

Still the game hung in the balance. Evenly poised. With either side still able to win… or to lose.

Barnett Hall senior pondered upon his tactics. Time was running out for the match was being played in the old tradition, to a fixed time and close of play had been set at seven-thirty. In 1984 limited-overs cricket was still fiercely scorned by the traditionalists in both clubs, they preferred to leave the '*Cut and Slash*' game to less prestigious clubs.

There was no merit in just containing the runs; to win it was necessary to dismiss the opposing batsmen. The captain studied the two men occupying the crease. Of the two, Ashfaq, the Kirk Loscoe number four, had the greater talent. Pakistani by origin, he was one of the newer breed of Englishmen who played his cricket correctly and so far had shown no discernable weakness. His technique was correct, his defence sound and his strokes elegant.

Better to concentrate our attack on the weaker players, Hall decided in his mind. He had already noticed in Bill Parsons a tendency to stand with his weight upon his front foot. He also had the habit of *leaning* on his bat. The limitations of his style meant that while he could easily hook and cut short deliveries, in order to play forward to a full-length ball it was necessary to transfer his weight. That was when he ran into difficulties.

'Norman,' Barnett Hall beckoned over the second of the Mole twins, 'Are you feeling fully fit?' A broad smile creased Norman's friendly, chubby face.

'Sure.' he replied. Carefully Hall explained his plan to the young bowler. He knew that the heavier built twin was slower and less hostile than his wiry brother. Instead he possessed the redeeming virtue of greater accuracy. Ask Norman to bowl a certain type of ball and invariably he could and did.

At first all did not go strictly to plan. In cricket it seldom does. The redoubtable Ashfaq kept stealing the bowling. He would take a four and then scamper a single from the last ball of each over. It was intelligent cricket and the scoreboard rattled steadily as Jason Argosy hung the metal numbers on the rows of rusty hooks.

Finally with the score on 127, Bill Parsons faced an over from Norman Mole. First a straight delivery, slightly short of a length and Parsons played it back to the bowler. The next delivery was shorter, the batsman stroked his shot through the offside field and took two runs. Again going onto his back foot and across his stumps Parsons moved inside the third delivery and hooked it beautifully for four runs. Loud applause came from the veranda. Shouts of encouragement floated across the field to reach the ears of the two Kirk Loscoe men. The Briseley T'ill fielders looked in consternation at the rising score. It now read 133 for 5 wickets.

Barnett Hall gave the barest of nods in Norman's direction. His lips moved imperceptibly, 'Now Norman, Now!'

The young man ran up to bowl, even as his arm flailed over Bill Parsons was moving onto his back foot, the arc of his bat lifting high above his head. Norman's eyes were fixed rigidly on the base of the stumps, his direction perfect. He bowled a perfect yorker. Too late the batsman realised his error. He dabbed down desperately. The ball took the middle stump and sent it cart wheeling away. Snowball Jackson caught one bail, the other flew over the heads of the slip fielders and landed thirty feet away.

Jason Argosy squealed with boyish delight and rattled up a metal '6' against the wickets down. The tail end rabbits were left exposed and Briseley T'ill were back in the hunt. Now if only…?

Ashfaq tried his best. To steal a run off the final ball of every over was virtually impossible. The fielders cut off runs with the savagery of ferrets falling on a rabbit. John Slater, young and nervous, edged away from the pace of John Emmett and was bowled neck and crop. A magnificent throw from Lenny Mole ran out Dewhurst. Dexter swept with great power and greater intent, but far too soon. The ball bobbled from the back of his bat and was gently caught by George Burke.

The last man in was Staywood.

The Kirk Loscoe team, like a sickly choir, groaned in unison. Staywood had sat in stony isolation ever since the tea interval. He seethed with inward frustration. A pressure cooker of resentment, its lid screwed tightly down and ready to explode.

As he made his way to the wicket the scoreboard read 145 runs for 9 wickets. Eight more runs were required for a win. He had one delivery left to face. John Emmett's final ball was too good for everyone. It seamed off the turf, beat a madly thrashing bat, deceived the wicketkeeper and ran through for a bye.

'Yes!' bellowed Staywood and raced along the pitch.

'No, stay.' cried Ashfaq in desperation. As the senior, and by far the better batsman, he needed to keep the strike. Then. 'Oh Shit!' as the reckless dash by Staywood continued unabated. He set off... and scrambled home with inches to spare.

Bert Plumtree looked at his watch, then towards his fellow umpire. He held up two fingers and asked, 'Two minutes?' The other man agreed.

'Last over.' Plumtree called out to the players.

There was just one hour to sunset. From the west the sunlight slanted low over the pavilion roof. Staywood, crouching over his jumbo-sized bat, squinted into the fierce light and concentrated.

Just one good accurate ball, Lenny Mole told himself, *Just one*!

The harder he tried the less he achieved. Two lifted sharply over the stumps and smacked into Snowball's gloved hands chest high. Two more drifted off target and went down the leg-side. The fifth one swung away late in its flight. All beat the bat and missed the stumps. One ball left to go. Tom Slater buried his head in his hands and did not dare to look at his madly cavorting batsman.

It's muck or nettles. A grimfaced Lenny Mole told himself as he launched into one final superhuman effort.

Staywood's jumbo-sized bat was high above his head. Its virgin blade, gleaming white in the late evening sunlight, had yet to strike the ball. He saw the round object hurtling towards him, black against the sky. Took three running steps down the wicket and gave vent to a massive clubbing swing. Primeval in intent, willow met leather in perfect accord. It was the sweetest of sounds. High over midwicket soared the leather sphere, rising into the darkening sky. It passed over the boundary, cleared the willow trees and dropped towards the Sinkhole.

Both sides watched in disbelief. It was the greatest hit ever seen on the Briseley T'ill cricket ground; a full two hundred yards. No one, but *no one* had ever put a ball into the Sinkhole before.

They watched… and they marvelled.

The Killer also watched. A worried frown creased his features.

*

Cricket creates unlikely heroes. A player may be King one day and a Clown the next. Staywood achieved the reverse. He went from villain to hero in one brief moment. Instant glory! His six had saved the match. Four and a half hours of a closely fought battle had ended in a tie. Honours were even and both sides were satisfied.

Excited players thronged the ancient wooden pavilion. Their noisy chatter filled the building like the buzzing of bees in a hive. They stripped off their whites, blindly stuffing the sweaty garments into their sports bags, before racing off to the Cock Inn to celebrate with an eagerly sought after pint. The rival captains congratulated one another upon an excellent game, shook hands and arranged to share a jug of ale.

Decker sought out Helen Argosy, 'We're going to the pub,' he said, 'Care to join us for a drink.' She looked at his flushed, excited face and remembered the words of Mildred Burke. *Little boys at heart who never grow up.*

'I'd love to go… but Jason…?' Mildred was listening in.

'Lord bless you!' she interrupted, 'Don't 'e worry about 'im. I can take care o' the lad for a while. You go and enjoy yessen.'

The light of hope danced in Helen's eyes. An anxious tugging at his arm distracted the policeman.

'Mr Decker… Mr Decker!' The words carried a note of hysteria. It was the voice of Adrian Hutton. The young player sent to retrieve the match ball from the Sinkhole. His face was white from shock and his voice trembled and stuttered as he tried to speak. 'Mr D-Decker, p-p-please Mr D-Decker, c-can y-you c-come? I-In the S- Sinkhole…t-there's a b-body. A d-dead h-h-human b-body!'

Nightwatchman

An overnight guardian who, unexpectedly, may succeed against the odds.

Barnett missed all the drama.

As soon as the game ended he hurried from the field, changed rapidly, left his cricket gear in the boot of his father's car and slipped away quietly. He caught the bus with two minutes to spare. With any luck he would arrive at the Royal Infirmary soon after 8pm. Fortunately the hospital was flexible in its visiting hours. Officially 6:30 until 8:30pm was the evening rule, but Barnett knew the staff were tolerant and very understanding. Turning a blind eye was an unspoken and unwritten axiom.

During the latter half of the match Barnett's concentration had wandered. Every time he ran to field a ball a comparison flashed into his mind. He was fit and active, she lay immobilised and sick. *Is it my fault?* Barnett asked himself over and over again. No clear thinking person would blame him but that didn't ease his conscience. He felt the guilt, as heavy as lead and twice as poisonous.

The incongruous aluminium doors of the old Victorian hospital sprang apart as Barnett approached the entrance. It was shortly after eight-fifteen. Hordes of relieved looking relatives were already streaming out and he battled against the departing tide. With mounting trepidation he approached the door of 3B. As though on cue, out came the sister. She stopped short, cocked her head to one side and threw him a quizzical look, 'Well! Here's a turn up for the book. I didn't expect to see you again.'

'Oh! Why not?' asked Barnett in protest, 'It was *you* who asked me to come.'

'Took your time though!' she censured him mildly, 'Still, you *are* here. All these years and I never realised I had such an influence on men.'

'It wasn't that, I just couldn't get her out of my mind. She's so helpless while I'm still running about, enjoying life. I felt duty-bound to come. Tell me, has anyone else been to see her?'

'Not a soul.' The sister shook her head regretfully then held up an arresting hand as Barnett moved to enter the room. 'Wait!' she commanded.

'Eh!' he queried. Her grin was impish.

'Bedpan!' she answered shortly, 'Does a girl like to be caught with her pants down? Literally.' She pulled a solemn face and disappeared through the doorway of 3B. Barnett was still giggling when she reappeared holding a rounded object at arm's length and covered by a cloth. 'That's better.' she said to him, 'You don't look quite so fierce now.'

He laughed, the tautness of his apprehension easing. It was impossible to feel nervous about anyone with the mental picture now held in his mind's eye. 'Can I go in?'

The sister looked at the bedpan, suitably covered with a sterile cloth. With her free hand she pinched her nose, made a chain-pulling motion and winked solemnly at Barnett.

'OK. I think the air will have cleared by now. But please don't stay too long. Visiting time is almost over. My girls want to get away on time tonight. We've a hen party planned at the pub.'

'Boozing! Nurses?' exclaimed Barnett in mock disapproval, 'What is the world coming to?'

'We're only human. One of the nurses is getting married next week. Now, can we pass up a chance like that to celebrate?'

'Most definitely not.' he agreed.

'In you go then and remember… people aren't always what they seem to be. She's got a lot of guts, that girl, never complained once about her condition. So be patient with her. OK?' Barnett nodded his agreement and watched her sail away like a maternal galleon in full rig, her ample body still fighting the restraints of her constricting uniform.

She may be unorthodox, he thought, *but what a bonus for the patients.*

He knocked timidly on the door and went in.

*

The room was very much as he remembered it. Clinical, detached, with pale green walls, a highly polished floor and a tubular framed hospital bed on large castors. There were two bedside chairs, very hard and formal looking, hardly designed to encourage the visitor to a lengthy stay, a bedside cabinet and a single plain wardrobe. One addition, a portable colour television set stood on a Formica-topped table along with a vase of freesias. After ten days the flowers had withered and died. They looked a sad little offering.

Cynthia was no longer lying flat on her back. The backrest of the bed had been adjusted to an angle of forty-five degrees. Three pillows supported her comfortably in a sitting position. Her blonde hair was shining and clean, a touch of lipstick adding colour. Her dark blue eyes regarded Barnett with unabashed curiosity.

'Hello.' he greeted her.

'Hello.' she replied… and waited.

Now that they were face to face he couldn't think of a single word to say. A blank empty space lay between his ears. They stared at one another, both in the same boat, no common ground and no meeting point.

'Flowers look dead.' He said eventually, 'About time to throw them out.'

'No!' Cynthia snapped back too quickly, 'I-I want to keep them.' Barnett studied the dead freesias with an intensity they barely deserved.

'Suit yourself.' he replied.

There was another painful pause.

'I thought you wouldn't come again.' she ventured awkwardly.

'Oh!'

'Did you… did you bring anything with you this time. Like a present?'

'Present?' Barnett sensed aggression creeping into his voice, 'A present? No. I just brought myself.' He answered as though, for all the world, that was sufficient.

She gave a little high-pitched snorting sound, half laugh, half stifled sneer. 'You!' she questioned, 'Just you. No present, no flowers, no chocolates, no fruit… not even a single grape. You *do* know how to treat a girl well… don't you Barnett?' Her words came out all wrong. She had intended them to be jocular, ribbing him. But her intonation was too high and far too intense.

'I'm *so* sorry.' Barnett sneered sarcastically, rising and turning towards the door. There was a moment of shocked silence and then as he turned the handle she cried out, an anguished plea.

'Wait! Please… don't go. Oh God! Why do I make such a mess of everything?' Cynthia pressed both hands over her eyes, fighting hard to suppress her tears. Barnett crossed to the bed and stared down helplessly at the pathetic figure.

Pig, he reprimanded himself, *So much for your good intentions.*

He looked at her bowed head with its clean shining hair. Its perfumed fragrance tantalised his nostrils. An insatiable desire made him want to feel the silken tresses. To touch them, to stroke them, his tentative exploring fingers reached out and lightly followed the curve of her golden head. Cynthia's hand caught his fingers and crushed them against her cheek. Her head relaxed against the side of his body.

'Barnett.' Her voice came low and muffled.

'Yes.'

'I didn't mean to make you angry. About the present, I was just teasing, but with me it always seems to come out wrong. I upset people when I never intend to. I just put my words over badly. D'you know what I mean?'

'S'alright. Don't worry about it. I'm every bit as bad in my way, always jumping to conclusions, usually the wrong ones. I'm sorry too.'

For a while there was silence. Neither one wanted to be the first to speak and risk breaking their fragile truce. There was a tap on the door, its handle rattled and in sailed a mini version of the sister. A young nurse, barely twenty years of age, five feet of nothing, with a round chubby body and a black smiling face.

'Oh!' she exclaimed, stopping short at the unexpected sight of Barnett, 'Visiting time is over.' Her attempt to match the imperious tones of the sister failed. Barnett turned on his most disarming smile.

'Sorry. I was late arriving. The sister said I could stay on awhile. I'm on the bus you see... and it doesn't leave until after nine.'

The nurse clicked her tongue in disapproval. She looked at her wristwatch and frowned. Worried briefly on a decision.

'We-e-ell! I'm supposed to settle down the patients by nine-thirty.' She placed a tumbler containing a clear liquid on the bedside cabinet, fussed unnecessarily around the bed, all the while studying Barnett with appraising eyes. She decided he was not about to rape and pillage the ladies ward and finally conceded. 'Alright then, just a little longer. I'll pop back later.'

'Bless you.' Barnett said effusively, 'Enjoy yourself at the pub.' He winked knowingly. The black girl giggled, smoothed imaginary creases from her immaculate uniform and continued on her caring way.

*

Outside the twilight faded into darkness. It was uncomfortably hot in the room with the windows closed and the central heating still pushing out heat. Barnett was still perched clumsily on the low hard chair looking up at the bed. It was awkwardly high on its big metal castors. Cynthia patted the side of the bed.

'You look so uncomfortable like that, why not sit up here, next to me?'

'Is there room?'

'Just about, I could move over but you will have to help me.'

'Should I? Won't it hurt?' he asked, concerned. She shook her head.

'No. There's no pain. It just feels numb.' Cynthia pressed down with both hands, attempting to move to one side. 'Come on. Help me... Please?'

Nervously Barnett slid his hands under the covers. He slipped one hand under her body, just below her waist, and the other lifted her beneath her knees. Her flesh felt warm and firm underneath her knee-length nightgown. He lifted her without effort and moved her body eight inches to one side.

'See,' she said, 'there's plenty of room.'

Barnett backed towards the bed, perched his bottom on the edge and swung his legs half onto the counterpane, reluctant to soil its virginal white surface with his dusty shoes. It was a clumsy position.

'Oh Barnett!' in exasperation, 'For God's sake kick your bloody shoes off.'

He pressed first one big toe and then the other against the heel of the opposing shoe. They fell to the ground with a loud clump.

'Suppose someone comes in?'

'Then they won't see us.' There was a faint click and the room was plunged into semi-darkness. Cynthia had operated the light cord that dangled down over the bed. From the roadside lamps a dim orange light filtered through the Venetian blinds. She took his arm, pulled it around her body and nuzzled her head into his armpit.

'Mmm! Now *this* is cosy.'

'Uh huh!' Barnett was still tense. Listening warily.

'Can we talk Barnett?'

'But we already are... aren't we?'

'I mean really talk. Heart to heart stuff. Deep. Meaningful. Very few people have talked to me properly. They never have. I don't know why, especially not my parents, not my Father... nor Mummy when she was alive. They never had any time for me.'

'Perhaps it wasn't easy for them.'

'No, it wasn't that.' She lapsed into silence for a moment, thinking, 'I haven't lacked for material things, fine toys, nice holidays, expensive clothes, the very best schools. Private of course, Daddy wouldn't consider any other. He bought me a car on my eighteenth birthday. The insurance cost him the earth. And I have my own horse, Dapple. You should see her. She *is* beautiful.'

'I have.' Barnett replied with feeling. He remembered all too well the big strong mare charging down upon him like some medieval warrior steed. His undignified leap to the safety of the pavilion steps.

'Have you? I don't remember that. When did you meet Dapple?'

'It was at the cricket ground on the day of your accident. Frightened me to death it did. The less said about it the better.'

'Barnett, Dapple wouldn't hurt a fly.' Cynthia proclaimed defensively.

'You could have fooled me.'

'You're not frightened of horses... surely? Someone who lives in the countryside, it's impossible.'

'I may live in Briseley T'ill, in the countryside, but I actually work in an office. How many horses do you find wandering about in an insurance office?'

'Insurance! Oh God Barnett, not insurance. It reminds me of the words from a very old song. Something about, "There's no one has endurance like the man who sells insurance." Are you a man with endurance Barnett?' she asked cheekily. There was a scornful inflexion in her voice as she asked, 'What exactly do you do? It doesn't sound as though it can be very exciting.'

'It's not at the moment,' he admitted, 'I'm still being trained. But there is a lot of scope. Marine, aviation, accident, industrial, it's worldwide, *international* in fact. I have so much to learn and I'm finding it hard to decide which area to specialise in. One of my colleagues in the industrial section has to inspect those huge cranes you see on building sites. Can you imagine what it must be like to crawl out along the jib to check it for faults? He's really high up, two to three hundred feet.'

'Ugh! I couldn't do that. I'm terrified of heights.'

'So was I at first, but you become used to it.'

'Y'see! You could get used to Dapple if you tried. It's a question of proximity.'

'Proximity?'

'Being close. The closer you are the quicker you become good friends.'

'Ahh!' mused Barnett, 'Like this eh!' He wriggled further down the bed, his arm pulling her closer and his hand moving between her arm and body gently exploring. He concentrated all his tactile senses into his fingertips, moving them in tiny circles, lightly stroking and stimulating her senses. Cynthia drew in a sharp intake of breath as a tremor of excitement passed through her body. She eased her body over to one side until the soft contours of her breast moulded into his hand.

'Barnett.' Gentle mockery tinged her voice.

'Mmm...mmm.'

'You wouldn't be taking advantage of a helpless woman would you?'

'What me?' His voice was drowsy.

'Who else then? It feels like somebody is.'

'Mmmm!' Barnett closed his eyes. The lids felt so heavy, as though leaden weights were pulling them. Overpowered by the dry suffocating heat he was finding it difficult to remain awake. The tip of his tongue circled his lips, moistening them.

'Barnett, are you nodding off?'

'Mmm! Sorry. It's the heat. I'm so dry.'

'Well have a drink then. There's water on the cabinet.'

'Water!'

'Water, what do you expect…Champagne?'

'No. But… water. Ugh! Normally I'd be into my second pint by now.'

'Where do you think you are Barnett, the Hospital for Real Ale?'

Barnett eased himself up onto one elbow, careful not to disturb Cynthia and lose contact with the warm sensual touch of her body. He stretched across to the bedside cabinet. The glass tumbler gleamed in the reflected light. One swift gulp and the liquid had gone so quickly that it scarcely touched the sides. There was a short pause and then, 'YUK!' His cheeks were sucked in by the unexpectedly vile taste.

'Ugh! What in God's name was *that*?'

Cynthia turned to look. 'Oh Barnett you clown. You've just drunk my medicine.'

'It was vile.'

'Tell me something new. I have to drink it every night. Oh!' Her hand flew to her mouth as Cynthia realised the significance of her words. She began to laugh, a vibrating gurgling chuckle that welled up from deep inside. It went on and on, her first real laughter in weeks. It was as much an emotional release as an expression of merriment.

'It's hardly that funny.' Barnett complained, aggrieved.

'Oh… yes… it… is.' She spluttered between waves of laughter, 'You w-wait until m-morning.' Tears trickled down her cheeks. She fingered them away still shaking with unsuppressed amusement. 'You're… you're go… going to need a b-bedpan to-morrow. That stuff, it d-d-doesn't h-half open your b-bowels.'

'Aw Christ! That's all I need.' groaned Barnett. He flopped back onto the pillow, staring horrified at the ceiling. Slowly the humour of it dawned upon him and he began to giggle. It became contagious. The more he giggled the funnier Cynthia found it and giggled back. They even giggled at one another's hysterical merriment until their ribs ached with the effort. Eventually Cynthia gasped for a halt.

'Stop Barnett! Please stop, my ribs are aching so much that my tummy muscles are beginning to hurt me.'

'I'll rub them,' he offered and made gentle circular motions with his free hand on her flat stomach. He stopped, 'your tummy muscles...? I thought...?'

Stunned, they looked at one another in the half-light. Her dark eyes went round with wonderment and hope. 'If I can feel my stomach muscles, if they hurt when I couldn't feel them before, perhaps... perhaps... Barnett, do you think? Could it be...?'

Tentatively he moved his hand, pressing searchingly with his fingers.

'Can you feel that?' he asked.

'Yes.'

'And that?'

'Slightly, no, not now. Barnett, *BARNETT,* where *is* your hand going?'

'Just testing.'

'Yes, I know that... but what for?' He grinned impishly.

'Well! Shall we say, the situation?'

'It won't do you any good, or me.' She moved her hand to her stomach exploring the returning sensation for herself. 'But I can feel something. Do you believe, do you think I'm going to get better? Really improve, that I'll recover? I hardly dare to believe it.'

'Of course you will.' Barnett reassured her with a confidence he did not wholly feel, 'Of course. You are certain to recover.' There was a light in her eyes he had not seen before, a dawning hope.

'Having to lie here, helpless, for hours on end, I thought I... I... w-would never recover. As though I was being punished. As if G-God was punishing me. I blamed God, Barnett. I cursed Him. Asked, why me? Why pick on me? What have *I* done? I have thought and thought. There was nothing else to do and I'm still unable to figure it out. The doctor, Doctor Sheehan says that physically I'm alright. There's no medical reason for my condition but I still can't move, or feel, anything below the waist. Daddy said that the doctor told him it could be psychological, a mental block of some kind. He was very angry, my father that is, he made the doctors carry out all their tests again. But they still ended with the same verdict. Why Barnett, why?'

He shrugged impotently, unable to express in words the inkling of understanding that lurked in the deep recesses of his mind. Perhaps it *was* to do with the events that had taken place in the cricket pavilion.

Perhaps, but then again, why should that be so?

Human beings are very complicated entities he was discovering. Their minds worked in strange ways. It was incomprehensible to him, especially the minds of young women.

'I don't know.' he replied cautiously.

'Nor do I, but I mean to find out. The more I think about it the more convinced I am that it must be something that happened recently, just before my accident. But I can't remember. I can't remember a single thing. Two complete days of my life are a blank, just a large chunk of nothing. What happened? Tell me Barnett...please tell me what happened.'

'Er! – Well! – Er!' Barnett stumbled to find the words. There was a dry nervous lump in his throat, an obstacle to explanation. He was saved by the sound of footsteps approaching. 'Someone is coming.' he gasped.

'Just slide down the bed and lie flat.' Cynthia instructed him in a low voice. Luckily he was on the side of the bed farthest from the door. Cynthia began to breathe deeply and make little whistling noises with each exhalation of air. It was ludicrous. He was certain to be discovered if the night nurse came into the room. A hysterical giggle welled up inside his body and he rammed frantic knuckles against his teeth to stem the sound.

The door opened halfway. Framed against the light stood the little black nurse. She did not enter the room, just listened to the deep steady sound of breathing, checked the time with her watch, quietly closed the door and slipped silently away to her duties.

'Phew! That was close.'

The bed vibrated as Barnett's pent-up giggles exploded and pandemonium reigned for a while as he struggled to regain control. Finally, when their merriment had subsided he said, reluctantly, 'It's late. I'm going to have to go. The bus for Briseley T'ill leaves at 9:40. It's the last one.'

'9:40! You'll be lucky.' Cynthia pressed a button on her watch. Its digital display glowed green in the dark. It was just after ten o'clock. A groan escaped his lips.

'It's *seven* miles. Christ! I'll have to walk What a drag!' He stopped short, aware of her eyes watching him. Two round violet orbs in the half-light. Reproving.

'Oh God! – Sorry. I'm so damn stupid. Every time I open my mouth I say the wrong thing.' His feet fumbled around in the dark, found his shoes and wriggled into them. He squeezed her arm reassuringly, trying to make his voice sound convincing as he said, 'You'll walk again. I'm sure of it. Hope no one spots me sneaking out.'

'Hadn't you better put me back in the right place?' she suggested.

'Yes. Right.' Once again his hands slid under the sheets, gripped her body and eased her gently back into the centre of the bed. Cynthia's arm was around his neck. She pulled him close. Her lips brushed his cheek in a gentle caress.

'Thanks for coming Barnett. It didn't turn out at all as I imagined.'
He regarded her quizzically, eyebrows climbing up his forehead. 'No?'

'No. You are so totally different to what I expected.'

'Am I? How?'

'Don't you know? You're softer somehow. Quite unlike your image, all that red hair and aggression. Underneath it all there's a much gentler person. It's rather a nice surprise, unlike other men I've known.'

'What were they like?' he asked.

'The usual – you know!'

'No. I'm afraid I don't.'

'Come off it Barnett, of course you do.' Exasperation crept into her voice, a note of bitterness. 'Most men, they just have one thought in their minds – Sex! A bit on the side, that's how they regard women. They tell you that they love you when all they really mean is "Let's get into bed." Then it's Crash! Bang! Wallop! Thank you madam and goodbye. Next day they don't want to know you. You're just one more notch on their bedpost.'

He drew back, contemplating her expression. 'Is that what you thought of me?' he asked, 'That I was like that?'

'No. Oh no… not you.' Her angry expression faded as she spoke, 'That's what I mean when I say you are different. Very different.'

'How do you know that I wouldn't be that way in other circumstances?'

'Would you?'

'No but…!'

'There you are then. I don't know why you are the way you are, but for me it's a pleasant change.'

'Perhaps I had a good teacher.' he said carelessly. Cynthia made a little pouting motion with her lips. 'Did you now, and who may she have been?' she asked.

'Dai…!' he began, then stopped short at his incredible stupidity. Mentally he gave himself a short sharp kick up the backside. *Engage your brain Barnett, well before you speak,* he silently admonished himself. But it was too late.

'Day?' teased Cynthia, 'Now that's a strange name for a woman. It *is* a woman I hope. Day…? Could that be short for… let me see… Day? Day?… Daisy. Of course, that's it. Daisy, Daisy Kutter. Barnett, tell me it's *not* Daisy Kutter. It is, isn't it? Good grief! She's old enough to be your mother.'

'No she's not.' Barnett retorted hotly, defending her, 'Daisy's alright, and she's only thirty-three. I'm ni – er - twenty.' he replied, adding on a few months.

'Oh yes! She's alright Barnett. Everyone knows Daisy is alright. Every man in Briseley T'ill knows she's alright. They should. They've all been for a ride. Isn't that why they refer to her as the village bicycle?'

'That's unfair.' proclaimed Barnett angrily, 'and it's untrue. Just because she's a loving, caring person.'

'Loving! Ha! She's loving alright… very loving. We all know that.'

'Do you.' he replied flatly, 'Well I like her.'

His chin jutted defiantly. His statement, unequivocal. Even in the dim light Cynthia could see the glint in his eye and recognised the danger signals. Swiftly she changed tactics. Her voice became soft and concerned.

'Of course you do. Sorry Barnett. I should know better. You are a very loyal friend. Forgive me. I just can't resist teasing you. You know what a bitch I can be.'

He studied her pensively and said, 'I'm beginning to, but, sorry, I *have* to go.' He bent and kissed her quickly, half on the mouth and half on the cheek, a friendly kiss that did not commit him.

'Come again.' she pleaded.

'I'll try.' Then he was gone, a shadow slipping away through the darkened wards.

*

Cynthia Ashley-Jayle lay motionless staring at the ceiling. Strange thoughts wandered through her mind. Thoughts about a virile young man who could lie alone in the darkness beside a young woman clad only in a skimpy nightdress and not try anything on. What was wrong with him? Was he gay? If what he had implied about Daisy Kutter was true then it was certainly unlikely. Daisy's appetite for sex was well known throughout the village. As for her, she would soon sort her out. Cynthia had never been one to share her playthings with others…she was not about to start now.

*

It was a long walk back to Briseley T'ill. Barnett's muscles ached. The first few matches of a new season always brought on a crop of aches and pains; stretching ligaments that had lain dormant throughout the winter months.

The night air was cold. A touch of frost was in the air again and around the moon a misty halo glowed. He was glad of the moon; away from the garish city lighting the lanes were dark and poorly lit. There was just the occasional lonely lamppost, an iron relic of long gone days.

He remembered a short cut he could take, illegal, but lopping off the miles. Across the fields, over the railway embankment and out below the cricket field, then skirting around the Sinkhole and back onto the road again by the old cottages.

It would save him a lot of time.

From the top of the railway embankment Barnett spotted an unexpected sight, some kind of tent arrangement over the Sinkhole? Also there were metal stakes with fluorescent orange tape running through loops and fencing off the area.

How strange! Barnett thought, his curiosity aroused. He went to investigate. A tall black shape loomed behind him. An arm crooked around his neck. Hard muscles bulged, pulling back his head. His body arched backwards, painfully, helpless in an iron grasp.

In the moonlight there was a silvery, gleaming, metallic flash…!

*

There was no doubt about the body. The frost, the wind and the sun had dried out the viscous black mud. The natural supply of water to the Sinkhole, by stream and drainage, had dwindled to a mere trickle. Wide cracks had opened in the crusty surface of the ground. Even the covering of grass cuttings had dried to wispy brown strands, been scattered and blown away by the wind.

Adrian Hutton had found the lost ball quite quickly. As he bent to recover it his eyes had picked out the shape of a hand. It lay at the bottom of a gaping crack in the earth about eight or nine inches down.

Once he had confirmed young Adrian's gruesome discovery Edward Decker headed for the nearest telephone. It was at the cottage of Helen Argosy.

'What happens now?' she asked as he put the receiver down.

'We wait. They're sending a murder squad. Should be here within half an hour. I have to go back and guard the site. Keep folks away.'

'Aren't you supposed to be off duty?' she asked. Along with the sense of shock and fear there was disappointment in her voice.

'Yes. But in a situation like this…' he shrugged, 'Sorry about the pub.'

'There'll be other times. Will they be able to do much? It's almost dark.' Helen pointed out.

'Probably there's very little they can do tonight. Although they may bring portable floodlights. The most likely thing will be to fence off the area and keep people away to prevent any contamination of the crime scene. Then there'll be a thorough search as soon as it's daylight, take photographs, comb the ground for clues, search for the murder weapon and recover the body.'

'You think it *is* murder then?'

'What do you think? How could it be anything else?'

The answer was so obvious that Helen did not bother to reply. 'Do you know who it is?' she asked.

'Not yet, although I'm fairly certain it's a woman.'

'A woman! How horrible. I can't believe it. Murder! Here in Briseley T'ill. It doesn't seem possible.'

'It's possible.' Decker replied with a heavy sigh, 'It's possible anywhere and at anytime, just unexpected. All the years I've lived here, and now this.'

He paused a moment contemplating the awful effect that Adrian Hutton's discovery would have on Briseley T'ill. Shock waves would ripple through the village and touch everyone. Particularly himself, for Decker suddenly realised the full significance of the muddy edging spade he had found in the storage shed. The caked-on mud, dried on the outside but still sticky underneath, could mean only one thing, the tool had been used recently. Used to bury the body. Used by someone who had known where to find it and had known where the key was hidden. Which had to mean that it was someone connected to the cricket club. A member, or a player?

It was probably someone who had been there today.

And much worse, he, Police Constable Edward Decker, had, unknowingly, cleaned up the spade. Had scraped off the mud with meticulous care, polished the blade until it gleamed and then re-hung the tool back in its rightful place. He had in all innocence destroyed the one piece of evidence that might have provided a clue to the identity of the murderer.

*

The first police car arrived in a crescendo of flashing lights and screeching tyres. It came to a halt, slewing at an angle across the road and bumping jerkily onto the grass verge. A young uniformed officer shot out of the front seat like a blue projectile and smartly opened the rear door. With heavy dignity a bulky figure eased his body from the confines of the rear seat. Detective Inspector Moxon closely resembled an egg that had failed to hatch. His clean, bald and shining head flowed without interruption into a rotund body apparently without the benefit of a neck. Perhaps God, in a moment of forgetfulness, had failed to give him one. The Inspector had also drawn the short straw when it came to looks and physique. His disagreeable face sat upon narrow shoulders that rounded into a comfortably proportioned lower half.

Decker met him on the footpath leading past the cottages.

'Name?' the Inspector snapped at him without preamble.

'Decker sir, Constable Edward Decker.'

Moxon's small piggy eyes examined the policeman sullenly, taking in his grey flannel slacks, opened-neck shirt and the cricket sweater casually fastened around his shoulders, its long sleeves tied in a loose knot.

'Uniform?' he snarled meaningfully.

'I was off-duty sir when the discovery was made. The lad, young Adrian Hutton, discovered the body shortly after the match ended. I telephoned in as fast as I was able.'

Moxon's egg-like head barely nodded in acknowledgement. A curt and wordless gesture of one hand demanded to be directed to the site. Decker led the way.

Although the sun had dipped below the skyline a clear sky and an early rising moon meant there was sufficient light to see by. They picked their way along the footpath, carefully avoiding the roots of the willow trees that protruded out upon the path in one direction and in the other vainly sought out the pathetic trickle of water flowing towards the deserted Sinkhole. Moxon turned puzzled eyes towards Decker.

'No one?' he questioned, 'No gawping sightseers? How'd you manage that?'

'Just luck sir. By good fortune only three people know so far; Young Hutton, Ms Argosy and myself. After the match ended everyone else rushed off to the pub.'

'Luck!' repeated Moxon sourly, 'We're going to need more than bloody luck. And who might *Miz* Argosy be?'

'She owns the cottage by the road, where I telephoned from.'

'And you're certain that no one else knows?'

'Not as far as I know sir. No. I warned the boy to keep quiet. Then sent him home. He was very shaken. Absolutely terrified. Looked as though he was going to be sick. Much too frightened to say much I would think.'

'Let's hope you are right.' Moxon replied grimly.

Decker knew he had been fortunate to keep Adrian Hutton's dreadful discovery from becoming common knowledge. In the hubbub of excitement at the end of the game only himself and Helen Argosy had heard the boy's words.

As a breed cricketers can be very self-centred. They are so full of their own esteem as they relive every moment of the glory they've enjoyed. Each player recounts his own particular contribution to the game, over and over and over again. And with each retelling of the events the decibels increase and their enthusiasm expands.

The three of them had slipped away unnoticed. Helen took the boy to her cottage. Decker headed towards the Sinkhole to confirm the truth of the boy's story. By the time he returned to telephone in, the cricket ground had become deserted as a stream of cars and players 'tally-hoed' in search of the Cock Inn.

Moxon stood on the hard crusty mud and surveyed the screen thoughtfully. His nose wrinkled as the sweet sickly smell invaded his nostrils. Half aloud he muttered his thoughts. 'Only nine inches down, it's bloody amateurish. Asking to be found!'

'No sir. I would say, unlucky.' Decker ventured.

Moxon's egg-shaped head came up slowly, piggy eyes viewing him with distaste.

'Unlucky? How do you figure that, Constable?'

A younger man might well have been inhibited by the Inspector's obvious dislike but Decker answered him placidly, 'Local knowledge sir. This place isn't called the Sinkhole for nothing. Over time everything that goes into it does exactly that, it sinks – or rather did. There are thousands of disused lead mines all over the Pennines. Many date back to Roman times. It's believed there's an old shaft below the Sinkhole. It was probably flooded and collapsed in centuries ago. Look around you, sir, you'll see we are at the lowest point. All the natural drainage and the streams flow down towards the Sinkhole. The water seeps down through the mud and disappears below ground. God only knows where the water comes out again. All the debris and rubbish rots down quickly and is washed below ground, it vanishes. Layers of silt build up and cover everything. Only this year, the drought last back end, the long dry winter, there's been very little rain; freak conditions really have altered things. Normally you wouldn't be able to walk on this area. It's like a bog.'

'Really!' mocked Moxon, seemingly unimpressed by the information.

'And the way the body was discovered,' continued Decker, 'Chance in a million. I've never seen a cricket ball hit so far, certainly not on this ground. It was incredible. Pure chance that it landed where it did, right over the spot. Yes, our man was dead unlucky. He certainly picked the right place.'

'Our man,' mused the Inspector, 'you don't happen to know his name I suppose?'

'No sir, not yet.' Decker replied evenly.

'Not yet.' mimicked the Inspector. There was a nasty glint in his eye. 'Not yet. Bloody cocky for a country copper aren't we Constable Decker?'

'No sir, I don't think so.'

'*No sir, I don't think so.*' Moxon mimicked him again. 'Are you always so bloody obsequious? How long have you been in the force - twenty years? Twenty years and still a bloody constable, you're hardly brimming over with ambition are you... or ability?'

The policeman remained silent. His problems were his own affair, both past and present. He saw little point in inviting further antagonism.

*

A back-up vehicle had arrived with a specialist team of men with tools, a canopy, steel posts, orange fluorescent tape and lighting. With the speed of long practice they fenced off the area and erected the tubular steel frame to support the canopy. In the harsh glare of portable arc lamps they set about exhuming the body from its brief, un-consecrated grave.

The Inspector watched with impassive features as his specialist team worked with delicate care, seemingly unaffected by their gruesome task. Not so Decker. For all his years of experience he had only once before been in a similar situation. Then it had been an intensely personal one and long buried memories came flooding back. He felt sicker by the minute as each trowel-full of earth was cautiously removed and examined. Long tentacles of nausea crept through his bowels, turning the contents of his stomach into a churning liquid mass.

A severed portion of yellow plastic-coated washing line was put into a polythene bag. The mud, which had dried hard, almost like a plaster cast, was lifted away from the victim's face. Decker recognised the features, closed his eyes and turned away.

Decomposition of the flesh had not begun. He recalled accounts of bodies, some of them centuries old, being discovered in peat bogs. Cadavers, long dead, murdered or slain in battle, which had lain awaiting recovery and had been found in perfect condition.

'Well!' asked the Inspector, 'Perhaps you will be good enough to tell *me* who it is. With your local knowledge...I assume you know.'

The vomit curdling in his throat prevented Decker from speaking. He swallowed, forcing back the bile as he consciously took a grip of himself. 'It's the nurse, her name is Kutter... *was* Kutter. She lives in the village, close to the church, has... *had* a cottage there. Her full name is Daisy Kutter.'

'A nurse?' queried Moxon, 'A nurse, in a small village like Briseley T'ill, and nobody missed her? Nobody wondered where she was? Didn't she have a routine, a regular round, patients to visit? Strange isn't it that no one missed her?'

Decker explained, 'Normally you would be right sir, but it's just after Easter, a Bank Holiday weekend. Daisy, that is Nurse Kutter, made a habit of visiting her mother during the holiday. She lives in Yorkshire. It was such a regular occurrence that people came to expect it. They knew it was likely that she'd be away. So they didn't miss her... well, so far they hadn't...' he finished weakly.

'Relatives?'

'Just the one sir, as far as I know.'

'We shall need her to make a formal identification. Find out her address Constable.'

'I doubt there would be much point sir.' Decker informed the Inspector as tactfully as he could, 'Old Mrs Kutter is in a nursing home for the terminally ill, a hospice I believe they are called. From what I have heard her mind has gone. It's impossible to get a word of sense out of her. Senile dementia, the doctors call it.'

'Damn and shit!' swore the Inspector. The hostility in his eyes seemed to be directed at the unfortunate Decker. It was as though he held the policeman personally responsible for the murder, the inconvenience to himself, as well as the decrepit Mrs Kutter's damaged brain.

Daisy Kutter's mortal remains were zipped into a plastic body bag, loaded onto a stretcher and carried into the waiting vehicle. Decker had been wrong in his assumption that little would be done until daylight. Despite his slothful physical shape Inspector Moxon was no slouch. Speed was of the essence. The sooner this sordid little village crime was solved the better.

'I'll want some one on watch here tonight.' Moxon informed Decker.

'*All* night sir?' that certain some one asked.

'All night Constable, until our murderer returns.'

'But…!'

'All night.' Emphasised the Inspector, 'Don't worry, I'll be back to join you. You see, unlike your trusting self, I *can* imagine the news creeping around the village, spreading like couch grass. And who knows what curiosity will bring us? Now cut off and change into uniform.'

*

Beatrice was furious. Dinner was spoilt. A brown concentric ring of dried gravy encircled the china plate. The fact that Decker wasn't hungry was irrelevant. Providing an evening meal was a part of Beatrice's campaign to make herself indispensable. She ignored the fact that Decker had earlier partaken of a cricket tea.

'What do you mean, "You've got to go on duty." Why?' she demanded

'There's an emergency.'

'What emergency? Have the Russians landed? Surely you can sit down for five minutes and eat some food after all the trouble I've taken to cook it.'

He looked at the congealed fat around the rim of his plate, the dried up peas and the lumpy potatoes. His 'No.' was emphatic.

'Well that's nice after the effort I've put in. Thank you very much!' she ended bitchily. Methodically Decker fastened the buttons on his tunic. He replied slowly, trying to keep the anger from his voice.

'*I* did not expect a meal. I don't want a meal. I don't *need* a meal. And, I can manage my own affairs perfectly well.'

'I presumed…'

'That's the trouble. You presume too much Beatrice. Now I have to go. I have a job to do and I have no idea when I will be back. OK?' And with that parting shot he closed the door quietly, but firmly, and departed.

The bubble of Beatrice's rage collapsed. Once alone her veneer of confidence disappeared. Fear and loneliness invaded her face, piling on the years, adding cruel, prematurely aging lines. She cried bitter tears of frustration.

*

It was well after eleven and the cold was beginning to penetrate. His thick blue serge uniform and heavy soled shoes fought a losing battle against the misty rising dampness. His bones began to ache.

A light bobbed along the footpath. It was Helen Argosy. She brought him a flask of hot coffee. Together they stood in the shadow of a willow tree, its canopy of wispy branches curved out and over them, screening and stretching to the ground, Mother Nature's own perfect gazebo. The plastic cap of the Thermos served as a cup. They gulped the scalding coffee in turn, passing the cup between them, hands touching, entwined together around the warm plastic.

'The secret is out.' whispered Helen.

'How?'

'How! You can't keep a secret for long in a village. You should know that, especially with police cars screaming about all over the place. Mildred, she brought Jason home, thought at first that we had slipped off to the pub together. Then after finding out we'd never even been there she brought Jason back to my cottage. Once she saw the police cars there was no stopping her curiosity.'

'Exactly how much does she know?'

'Just about everything, I tried to say very little but it was damn nigh impossible. Jason was fagged out… fast asleep. We carried him up to his bedroom. It's at the back of the cottage. Do you know that it's possible to see everything as clear as a bell from his window? Well you know Mildred, she's a lovely person, but word will travel around the village like a dose of salts. Sorry.' Helen finished apologetically, pale shadows of moonlight falling across her serious upturned face.

'Don't worry. It can't be helped. Sooner or later everyone was bound to find out. Much as I hate to admit it but Inspector Moxon was right.'

'Moxon? Is he the one in charge, the fat bald-headed one? I watched him from the window. He isn't my cup of tea.'

'Nor mine.' Decker answered with feeling.

'Ted, is it alright if I ask you a question?'

'Sure. Fire away.'

'Who was killed? It *was* a woman wasn't it? I could tell that when they carried the stretcher past the house. But who Ted? Who was it?'

There was infinite sadness in the dull flat tones of his reply, 'It was someone we all knew, the nurse… Daisy Kutter.'

'The nurse! Oh God! How awful. Wasn't she supposed to be on holiday?'

He nodded in reply and posed a question, 'Yes. How did *you* know'

Helen thought for a moment before replying, 'Back at the accident, you remember, when that girl came off her horse, well, before the ambulance arrived, someone, I can't recall who, suggested calling for the nurse. Mildred – Mrs Burke, said she was away on holiday. She'd gone to visit her mother.'

'That appears to be what everyone else thought, the reason why nobody missed her. I tried to tell the Inspector but he didn't seem impressed.' There was depression in his voice as he added, 'He doesn't like me.'

'Why not? What have you done?'

'Nothing. You know how it is. He's a big city cop, an Inspector. I'm just a country bumpkin in his eyes, a mere constable. He doesn't rate me.'

'That's only because he doesn't know you yet.' Helen comforted him supportively, 'It's unlike you to be down. Is there a particular reason?'

He stared into the empty plastic cup. A kaleidoscope of long suppressed recollections flashing through his mind. Like an ancient film, reviving flickering pictures on the window of his soul. 'Memories,' he whispered sadly, 'just memories.'

'Memories! What sort of memories?' she asked gently.

When he answered the words came slowly, reluctantly in a painful peeling away of his lifelong protective shell. 'It's all happened to me before. Many years ago when I was just a young constable I was married. Few people know that, it isn't their business anyway. She went to a night-school class, just one evening a week. One night on the way home she took a shortcut through a park. Just once, it was one time too many. Some evil bastard attacked her. She was found raped and strangled. It wasn't like she was a real person when I had to identify her. All her life gone! All her wonderful vitality missing! It was like touching a cold marble statue, dead and stiff... and empty. It's their personality that makes a person what they are. Take that away...extinguish life and we are all just lumps of meat. When... when... I recognised Daisy... saw *her* body, all life's meaning drained away, empty, it shook me, brought everything flooding back.'

'Oh Ted! I'm so sorry. I didn't know.'

'Of course not, how could you? This is the first time I have ever told anyone, the very first time. My God! All these years it's been bottled up inside me. I've kept my feeling clamped down tight, afraid to let go, afraid to let myself care too much... for anyone. What a waste of my life it's been.' He stared bleakly into space.

'You've told me.' Helen prompted softly. Decker looked into her upturned face and saw the concern in her eyes, the understanding. 'You too?' he asked.

'Yes. Jason's father, we never made it as far as getting married. In fact *he* never even knew about Jason, never knew I was pregnant. It was strange how we met. I was on a march – CND – mostly students and other young people. It was peaceful and orderly until a crowd of yobs started trouble, throwing bottles and bricks at the procession. Panic set in. I was knocked down in the crush and very nearly trampled upon but this young army officer dragged me clear. He pushed me into a doorway and shielded me with his body until the trouble had passed. I didn't like soldiers on principle. You know what young students can be like…all very left wing and anti-establishment. We talked. John tried to make me see the other side of the argument. He never became angry; always so calm and bloody precise…logical in his answers. It was a strange relationship we had. Half of me loved him and the other half was against what he did, against what he stood for. Then he was posted to Northern Ireland. John never discussed his work. I never ever realised exactly what it was he did. The day the results of my tests came through to confirm I was going to have John's baby was the day he was killed. It was in Armagh, defusing a bomb. It was booby trapped… and exploded.'

'That's terrible, absolutely dreadful.' Deep concern showed in his weather-beaten features. A fiercely protective emotion towards Helen welled in his breast. Decker couldn't remember when last he had felt this way. It had to be many, many years ago.

'I never understood your situation,' he confessed, 'Thought you were one of those terribly modern young women, all independence and feminist. Keen to make your own way in the world and that men were an encumbrance.'

Helen stopped him from speaking, leaning forward and pressing a slender finger against his lip. 'I was a bit like that,' she said, 'but people change, grow up and mature. It's fine being independent when one is twenty and surrounded by fellow students. As a person grows older, somehow friends drift away and one becomes isolated… lonely. The struggle to earn a living *and* support a child doesn't leave time for friendships. It's difficult.'

'But attitudes *have* changed.' said Decker.

'True. All the same how many men want to saddle them-self with a dead man's child? It takes a special kind of person to do that.' She leaned towards him. In the pale moonlight Decker could see her eyes were closed, her lips ready and waiting.

Now you fool! Kiss her now, an insistent voice told him.

Over her shoulder the headlights of a car swept in an arc towards him. It was Moxon returning. Damn! Every time they were making progress, fate intervened. Decker's strong capable hands held her arms and moved her gently away.

'Later.' he whispered hoarsely, 'The Inspector is coming.'

Helen's eyes partly opened. Through narrowed slits she regarded him with controlled fury as she spoke in ultra refined tones.

'Sod your Inspector, Constable Decker. Are you going to kiss me?'

So he did. A trifle surprised at himself... and only just in time.

On her way back to her cottage Helen Argosy passed the approaching Inspector Moxon. She waved the empty vacuum flask in his face by way of explanation.

'Goodnight Inspector.' she called out airily.

Despite the dreadful events of the day there was lightness in her heart and step that had not been there before.

*

Time passed slowly. The temperature dropped. Decker had welcomed the coffee but now its effect was becoming pressing. He fidgeted from one foot to the other and concentrated his mind on controlling his bladder.

Moxon's hard elbow jabbed him in the ribs. The Inspector's rigid forefinger pointed at a tall lean silhouette on top of the railway embankment. Hidden by the shadow of the willow trees the two policemen watched a dark figure scramble down the steep slope, climb over the picket fence and carefully approach the Sinkhole. The unknown paused by the canvas obviously puzzled, studying the unexpected array of equipment.

'Now!' shouted Moxon, 'Grab the bastard!'

Daisycutter

Daisycutter: A ball, which upon pitching, fails to bounce normally, gathering many wickets on rural cricket grounds.

'Got him.' enthused Inspector Moxon as he sat at the breakfast table. 'Got the little bugger! He's our man alright. I can tell. What's more he's shit-scared, literally. Hasn't stopped going all morning. Nerves y'know. It gets to 'em in the end no matter how tough they think they are. Smells to high heaven in that there cell, it's enough to turn your guts.'

The Inspector spooned a generous helping of thick-cut marmalade onto his morning toast. His stomach was not easily turned. Cereals, bacon and eggs, numerous slices of thick wholemeal bread and three cups of strong sweet coffee had already disappeared down his throat. His small piggy eyes surveyed Decker from between rolls of puffy flesh.

'You're not convinced are you?' continued the Inspector, 'I'll soon have 'im coughing. Mark my words. Nine out of ten murders are domestic. Husband kills wife. Wife poisons husband. Frustrated lover strangles mistress. It happens all the time. It's obvious, young Hall there was 'aving it away with the district nurse. Finds out he wasn't the only one – Bang! Blows 'is top. A 'crime of passion' the Frogs call it. You said yourself it was a local man. Proves it!'

Not to me it doesn't, thought Edward Decker, but he kept his thoughts to himself. Moxon didn't have a shred of hard evidence. He presumed too much. As, in much the same way, he had presumed upon Decker's hospitality. Thrown off balance by the Inspector's early arrival the unwary policeman had invited Moxon in, contemplating offering him nothing more than a cup of coffee to start the day.

Moxon, with the confidence of rank behind him, assumed control. He seated himself at the breakfast table and proceeded to trough with porcine pleasure. Beatrice had not helped. Impressed by his rank, his uniform and anxious to prove herself a competent hostess, she clucked around the fat man like a broody mother hen. A dismayed Decker saw his carefully planned household budget destroyed at a single sitting.

'You'll be wanting to question Young Barnett?' suggested the Constable, in the vain hope of heading off further gastronomic excesses by the portly Inspector. Small wonder he was so strangely shaped, with his head and body running into one, the man did bear a close resemblance to Humpty-Dumpty.

Moxon sucked noisily on a piece of gammon wedged in a gap between his teeth and contemplated.

'Naw! Not yet. Let 'im stew awhile. Thought we'd go and nosey around the nurse's place. See what sort of state it's in. Pick up some clues. Right?'

'Right sir.'

But Moxon showed no sign of immediate action. His eyes flickered around the tables searching for further edible delicacies. 'Do yourself nicely here,' he hinted, looking about the room and nodding in the direction of Beatrice.

'Middling.' Decker answered stiffly, and of his sister added pointedly, 'Beatrice, my sister, she isn't always here to cook. She's just visiting.'

*

Young Barnett Hall was baffled. What did it all mean? Alright, so technically he had committed an offence by cutting across the railway tracks. Perhaps it had been foolhardy... and it was trespass. But hardly serious enough to warrant a night spent in the cells. Cell, to be precise. There was only one. A boxlike room, four feet six inches by nine feet long. It was exceedingly small with white emulsion on the otherwise blank walls, a tiny window set high at one end, a hard narrow bed and a portable chemical toilet. He regarded the toilet with particular horror. It smelt abominable. The medicine prescribed for Cynthia Ashley-Jayle worked exceptionally well. Barnett acknowledged that somewhere in the confines of the Royal Infirmary was hidden a budding 'Lily the Pink' and his, or her, medication was undoubtedly efficacious in every way.

Poor Barnett sat on the edge of the hard narrow bed and pressed his hands against his tormented stomach. Fresh griping pains stabbed at his intestines every few seconds. Involuntary movement recurred within minutes. He tottered on rubbery legs back towards the obnoxious loo. Why did that stupid egg-shaped man, the over officious Humpty-Dumpty of a police inspector, seem to regard it as significant?

Significant - of what?

And why was Ted Decker so distant towards him?

When would some one tell him what was going on?

*

Daisy Kutter's cottage was at the lower end of Briseley T'ill, the same part of the village as the church and the cricket ground. Approaching it from the east one first passed under the railway bridge. The cricket field lay on the left, the ground sloping away down towards the Sinkhole. Fronting the ground were two cottages. One was occupied and owned by Helen Argosy. An elderly widow, who was deaf and almost blind, lived in the other. There was a rutted and bumpy track leading into the field. A five-barred gate sealed the way. Visitors to the ground parked their vehicles on the grass verges of the road.

Fifty yards further on, sited on the opposite side, stood the church. Its main approach was from the west. Two splendid Yew trees cast majestic shadows across the gravelled drive leading to the Norman arch framing the west door. In solid English oak, the door had featured in the background of countless wedding photographs.

Tucked in between the churchyard and the stream was Daisy's cottage. The tiny parcel of land upon which it had been built lay to the west of the church. The design of the building was simplicity itself and therein was both its beauty and its practicality. Oblong in shape, the rear northern wall of the cottage sat on the boundary of the cemetery, a sensible farmhouse wall some twenty-four inches of solid stone, built to keep the weather out and the heat in. No windows overlooked the cemetery, rather like flowers seeking the sunlight, they all faced south. A high privet hedge enclosed a handkerchief-sized lawn. Late spring flowers pushed upwards from the carefully tended and fertile beds, remnants of crocuses, fading daffodils and newly opening tulips all thrusting towards the sunlight.

Decker led the way through a white, painted wicket gate, closely followed by the Inspector. Moxon's driver, a WPC, carefully locked the police car and brought up the rear. How typical of Moxon, thought Decker, as only then did he realise the Inspector had left his driver to sit alone outside the police station house while he had scoffed heartily in its kitchen.

On the journey to the cottage Decker had worried vaguely how they would gain entry to the building. Ought they to have a search warrant? Did they need one? A vivid pictured flashed into his mind of the unscrupulous Moxon prising open the door with a tyre lever. To his surprise the door stood ajar.

A strange groaning sound, deep and distant, emanated from the upper floor and dangling limply from the ceiling was a leg.

'Oh my God!' gasped Decker, fearing the worst.

The sound stopped and a familiar voice called out to him. The leg was withdrawn and replaced by a black shining face, hanging head down, white teeth gleaming like ivory in an inverted smile. 'Hi der partna'! 'Ow is de great bowla today?'

It was Everett Jackson. The West Indian was working on the upper part of the staircase. His pronounced Barbados accent had the trick of lifting the second syllable of words giving them a lilting musical ring.

The gradual renovation and modernisation of Daisy Kutter's cottage by the West Indian was a labour of love. Few, if any, in the village understood why the man devoted so much of his free time and energy to such a profitless enterprise. They whispered, wondered and speculated, added two and two until it made five and totally failed to comprehend Snowball Jackson's motivation.

They believed and feared the worst... and were completely wrong.

Inside, the cottage was a revelation. Jackson had converted it to open plan with the solitary exception of the kitchen, sited at one end of the building. He had dispensed with an under-stair cubby-hole, ripped out the old panelled staircase and replaced it with an open tread one in warm gleaming Luan mahogany. A plaster interior wall had been removed to open out the building and generate a feeling of spaciousness.

God spreads his gifts around in a random fashion. Everett Jackson, a black immigrant, was poorly educated, barely able to read and write. In a way Beatrice had been right for in repose Jackson's features were downright ugly. When he moved he walked with a loose and shambling gait. But the skill that lay in his hands was sheer poetry and the evidence was all around.

A rebuilt fireplace, lovingly hand-crafted in stone, inlaid carpets set in a surround of Danish beech-wood flooring and polished brass fittings on newly fitted hardwood doors paid silent tribute to his ability.

'I'm fine.' Decker replied, but the tone of his voice belied his words.

The West Indian came slowly down the staircase, an anxious look in his eyes as he searched the policeman's face for the truth. 'Is der something wrong man?' he asked.

Decker's nod was barely perceptible as he tried to convey a warning signal by the expression in his eyes.

'Who is this man?' snarled Moxon, pushing past, 'and what is he doing here?'

The Inspector directed his question at Decker, a third party. He totally ignored the black man when challenging his presence at the cottage. Everett Jackson had experienced just about every possible refinement of prejudice in his life. He refused to become riled and answered simply in his calm bass voice.

'I is jest workin' man, jest working.'

'Working? On a Sunday eh! Double time I suppose?' The sarcasm in Moxon's voice was pointed, calculated to provoke. 'Is this what they mean by the black economy? Ha ha! Black economy, get that constable?'

The sharp point of his elbow took Decker in the ribs. The policeman grunted which Moxon mistakenly accepted as a laugh and looked towards the WPC for approval.

'Sir!' she replied uncertainly, a faint smile ghosting her lips.

'When de jokes is ova' perhaps someone will tell me what is de matter.' Everett Jackson pleaded. Ted Decker looked for a lead. Did the Inspector want him to reveal the truth yet or not? And if not, when? Moxon's eyes travelled around the room. He seemed to have lost all interest in the black man as he moved casually about, weighing, feeling, attempting, to sense the ambience of its late occupant. A long awkward silence stretched interminably between Decker and Jackson.

'For God's sake!' Moxon snapped tetchily, 'Tell the man. Then we can get on with our investigation.'

'Investigation! What investigation?' Everett Jackson pounced on the word, 'Tell me Ted... Please. What on earth is de matter?'

The policeman found his eyes riveted to the floor. It required a conscious effort of will to force his gaze to meet the black man's worried face.

'It's bad news about Daisy.'

'Daisy? What about Daisy?'

'She's dead.' Decker replied bluntly. His reply was far from the one he intended but the sympathetic words he so dearly needed just would not come. They were lost in the horror of confusion in his mind.

'Dead! Dead! She can't be. She away in Yorkshire man. Gone t'see her Mum. She done told me so. Due back tomorrow. Left me de key to get in an' out. She is... she is... ain't she Ted?' The look of disbelief on the black man's face slowly dissolved, replaced by creeping acceptance in the face of Edward Decker's insisting and sorrowful expression.

'I'm so sorry Everett, but it is true. You must have heard something. Didn't anyone voice their suspicions in the pub? There must have been rumours? Last night? I can't believe word didn't get around. No?'

'You know me. Ah din stop long at de Cock. Jest had one pint and den ah left. Guess ah never heard no rumours man.'

'So you didn't hear about the discovery at the Sinkhole, the body that was found. It was Daisy, murdered, her body had been buried in the mud.'

It would have very difficult for Decker to give the news to a stranger but to a close friend of long standing he found it ten thousand times more devastating. The inhibiting presence of Inspector Moxon did not help. Decker heard his own voice, stilted and stumbling, as if it belonged to a stranger, tripping over his words and sounding like some alien official mouthpiece.

He watched helplessly as a part of Everett Jackson died. The lively sparkle in the man's eyes faded to a listless stare. His restless energy, his motivation evaporated as rapidly as rain falling on desert sand. His features crumpled like used wrapping paper. 'Ah tink ah go 'ome now.' he murmured softly.

Inspector Moxon, apparently wandering aimlessly around the room, had in reality been listening carefully and observing the black man's reaction. He looked directly at Decker and nodded, encouraging the policeman to hurry Jackson out of the way.

Everett paused in the doorway and turned stricken eyes towards his friend. 'Daisy... murdered? Who would do a ting like dat? Ain't right, it jest ain't right. Dere's no justice in dis world, none at all. None at all.'

His black head wobbled loosely from side to side and as he walked away the man's loose-limbed walk looked even more disorientated than ever.

*

'We are looking for a motive.' Moxon instructed Decker, 'A connecting link. Look for letters, a diary, appointment books, cards, anything to connect the deceased to a possible killer. And be careful. I don't want your ham-fisted paw-marks all over the place. And you,' he turned to instruct the WPC, 'Check her clothing. Look for anything obvious that's missing. Things like bra's, knickers, under-slips...there are some kinky people about...try and work out if it's all there. OK. We'll start upstairs.'

The layout of the building on the upper floor was simple. A small landing lead onto three rooms, two spacious double bedrooms and a bathroom with a toilet, a bath and a separate shower. There was nothing unusual, nothing untoward.

A workman's canvas holdall left behind on the landing by Everett Jackson was carefully examined by Inspector Moxon. He used a short stubby ballpoint pen to sort through the bag, turning over tools, poking them aside and checking each one carefully. Once again there was nothing to catch his attention, no indication that one of them may have been used as a weapon.

At 10am the church clock struck the hour. A hollow booming chime echoed through the cottage. The unexpectedness of it startled the Inspector and the WPC.

'Holy Bells!' he swore appropriately, 'I wouldn't fancy that bloody racket every hour. How the Hell do people sleep at night?'

Decker hid an amused smile.

'With difficulty, sir,' he replied, 'Except, that it's no longer a problem. There was a time when the chimes rang out all night, every hour, on the hour. A full set of chimes. Can you imagine it? That was until Snow… er… Mr Jackson modified the mechanism. Now they only chime once every hour, and then only between eight in the morning and ten at night.'

'Did he now… clever sod! What exactly does our black friend do?'

'Just about anything and everything.' replied Decker, 'Officially, a bit difficult to define. You'd have to call him an odd-job man. He trained as a welder, I believe, before he came to England and Briseley T'ill. He does all kinds of work, whatever people want. House repairs, joinery, some gardening, casual labouring on the farms at harvest time, a spot of welding for the local garage. He's even been known to dig graves at the church. You name it and he does it, always provided it's manual work. Anything clerical is beyond him. He can barely read and write. But he gets by.'

'Grave digging?' mused Moxon, 'Do you think our black friend may have done a spot of grave digging on his own account? Say, in your precious Sinkhole?'

'Everett? No-o-o. Not Everett. Never. I can't believe that.'

Moxon shot him a look that clearly meant that he personally could believe anything. Their searching continued. The policewoman reported that nothing obvious was missing from the wardrobe of the late nurse. Her dresses, slips, stockings, underwear and one uniform were all there.

'Only one uniform?' the Inspector checked, 'She must have possessed more than one, otherwise when did it ever get cleaned? Hmm! It sounds that very likely she was wearing it when she was killed, right Decker?'

'Yes sir.'

'So, she may have been killed when returning from a sick visit… perhaps?'

Decker found some corroborating evidence. Her appointment diary showed she had a visit booked for 7pm on Thursday. Against the booking was a name. It was that of Rowena Mole. Decker turned the page over to the following day. It was Good Friday. A comment had been scrawled across the page, 'Free! Whoopee!' followed by a row of exclamation marks.'

'What do you think of this sir?'

'Mmm! It's a starting point.' agreed Moxon, 'Let's check if she kept that appointment.'

'There's no problem there,' replied Decker confidently, 'It's the night Rowena Mole died.'

Suddenly the telephone rang.

Its loud strident call startled all of them. No genteel trim-phone bleep for this instrument. A robust and noisy bell fitted to the skirting board ensured it would be heard at anytime and anywhere in the little cottage.

Decker reached to answer it.

'Wait!' commanded Moxon. His stubby forefinger pointed at the policewoman indicating her to take the call. 'Just give the number and then listen. OK?'

She nodded her understanding and looking very nervous, hesitantly lifted the receiver. The Inspector pressed his head close to catch the conversation.

'Eight double one zero.' answered the WPC softly. The voice came over the wires clearly. Even Decker, two metres away, heard the low sibilant whisper.

'Kuttter,' snarled the voice, 'Listen. I know all about your tricks, all about your affair with Young Barnett Hall. It's hardly good for your professional standing is it? Having it away with a patient. Oh dear! Naughty! Naughty! Wouldn't it be really nasty for you if word leaked out? Know what I mean? So just take your aseptic little hands off him – OK?'

A click, followed by a continuous purring tone and the anonymous caller had gone. Moxon's lips pursed in thought as he looked at Decker and asked. 'You hear that?'

He nodded in reply.

'Recognise the voice?'

'I can't say I do.' Decker replied with a shake of the head.

'No? Likely it was disguised anyway. But a woman I would say, definitely a woman.' A thin smug smile distorted the Inspector's porcine features, 'What price now on our redheaded friend? Eh constable?'

*

Mrs Hall was a woman of routine. Every Monday, without fail, she did the washing. From mid April until mid September a large percentage of her weekly wash was comprised of cricket gear. White flannel trousers, white shirts, white socks and white underwear, there would be two pairs of each belonging to her husband and her son. There were also two items, smelly, sweaty and disreputable, which she never deigned to mention. Once, long ago, they had been new. Aeons ago when they arrived packed in smart green boxes and discreetly labelled, "Cricketers Support with Guard.'

Mrs Hall hated having to wash them and even more she resented displaying them on her washing line to dry. She tried to camouflage their presence with clusters of strategically placed handkerchiefs. Prior to '*The Wash*' came another unchanging ritual, '*The Soak*'. It was part of her upbringing that all white garments endured a soak for at least twenty-four hours. Her mother had taught her the rule and the ritual had to be observed... even on Sunday mornings.

Men! She grumbled at her husband. As he washed the family's saloon she rescued from its boot the sports bags of her husband and son and tipped out their contents onto the kitchen table. Her nose wrinkled at the smell of stale perspiration. She dropped rumpled flannels, creased shirts and discoloured socks into a bucket of cold water.

Mrs Hall paused.

A cricketer's jockstrap has an elasticated pouch designed to take a plastic guard to protect the player's manhood. But the bulge in Young Barnett's support was soft and giving. Jean Hall's searching fingers discovered the silky texture of a pair of black lacy ladies knickers. She stared at them with unbelieving eyes. There was a note of anger, mingled with one of trepidation, in the voice that called out to her husband.

'Barnett. Barnett. What's going off?' She asked, 'And where is Young Barnett?'

'Erm...Yes... erm... er... well, it appears he's at the... er... the police station.'

'What!'

'Er,... yes... er... last night. Ted Decker phoned me about midnight. He said, "No need to worry. Barnett was at the station. It's just a misunderstanding, the lad's alright." And he, Ted, would call around this morning to explain.'

Right on cue there was a knock at the door and through its glass panel the outline of two burly figures were visible.

'Oh my Lord!' exclaimed Mrs Hall. She immediately sensed that something was dreadfully wrong. Her intuitive female mind smelt trouble.

Moxon was trouble.

His beady little eyes missed nothing. As he entered the kitchen his searching gaze homed in on the washing and picked out the black lacy underwear. He knew immediately it did not belong to Jean Hall. She was too old… and the wrong generation.

'Now who in this house would wear those?' he mused.

*

Rumour swept through the village of Briseley T'ill like a brushfire. At the morning service there was a distinct lack of concentration upon matters spiritual. An undercurrent of whispered conversation prevailed. The Reverend Price struggled to maintain control, his nervous tension reflected in his tremulous vocal chords. Once outside the church the speculation increased and became rife. Many curious faces turned towards the little cottage adjacent to the church, the home of the deceased nurse. Wild imagination fuelled their fantasies as the rumours grew and spread. A body had been found in The Sinkhole. *Stark naked.* The victim had been a young woman. She had been identified as the nurse, Daisy Kutter and it was said that she had been brutally raped and her throat cut from ear to ear.

The rumours suggested there had been sex orgies at her cottage, a ménage a trois that involved Everett Jackson and Young Barnett Hall. A man was helping the police with their enquiries. Barnett was already being held in gaol and probably other men were involved. But who were they?

An anonymous caller had tipped off the police and rumour hinted that the unknown voice (cunningly disguised) had been that of a woman. But whose was it? The call had been short and to the point, too short for the police to track its place of origin. Rumour followed rumour, the truth, if it had ever existed, became more and more distorted. The few known facts were twisted and embellished as wild tales of death, sex and suspicion stalked through Briseley T'ill.

Other strange and inexplicable discoveries came to light.

In the hip pocket of George Burke's ancient and yellowing cricket flannels Mildred discovered a brassiere. It too was black and lacy, matching the knickers secreted into Young Barnett Hall's jockstrap.

An unsuspecting John Emmett pushed his hand inside one of his muddy boots as he prepared to whiten them. His fingers encountered a pair of black nylon tights bundled into a tight wad. His wife raised startled eyebrows as he drew them out.

'What the Hell!' she flared… and that was just for starters.

An under-slip fell from the inside of Tim Taverstock's cricket shirt. In the kit of nearly every player an article of female clothing was found. Between husbands and wives, players and their partners, tension and suspicion grew. Malignant and cancerous it spread like an unseen poison.

Word filtered back to Ted Decker. Much of it came through Beatrice. He was amazed at the amount of information she gathered in. For one so lately arrived in Briseley T'ill her antenna was incredibly efficient. She related the scraps of information to him with malicious glee.

*

Moxon arrived early on Monday morning, looking for breakfast. He beamed at Beatrice expectantly. She fed him bacon sandwiches flavoured with scraps of gossipy news. He listened benignly for as long as the food lasted, then rose abruptly.

'Time we left Constable,' he said, 'Are you ready to go?'

'Where to sir?' Decker enquired.

'Ever been to a Path Lab? No. It's quite an experience I do assure you.' Sadistic amusement twisted the Inspector's lips into a gargoyle smile. His narrow little eyes watched Decker's face closely. 'We are going to watch the autopsy. It should be fun!' he added with the air of one about to go to a party.

They were driven into the city, Decker sitting quietly alongside the Inspector, pale-faced, with his eyes fixed rigidly on the road ahead. Moxon secretly enjoyed and revelled in the obvious discomfort of his subordinate.

Yet in many ways the experience was less unpleasant than he had feared. His lowest point came when the victim's stomach was opened up and its contents examined, then the sudden smell of foul gaseous air made his insides heave in revolt. Hard lumps of bile clogged in his throat. He perspired with a cold and clammy sweat from the effort of controlling and forcing back the vomit. At that moment in time Decker loathed Moxon with a fierce intensity. Was it really necessary that he, Decker be present to witness the final degradation of a former friend? Of a fellow human being. A person he had respected.

The one redeeming feature was the pathologist himself, a tall silver-haired, distinguished figure who calmly proceeded about his gruesome profession with an air of dignified, clinical detachment. Having heard from former colleagues of the callous and uncaring manner adopted by some police pathologists Decker hadn't known what to expect. He had feared the worst, unnecessarily as it turned out, for what he experienced was a man at the top of his profession who, as well as being proficient, managed to convey feelings of respect towards the sad remains of the deceased nurse.

His precise and dignified voice calmly and quietly related the details of his examination into a tape recorder. Later the recording would be transcribed into a written report and passed to the police.

The pathologist peeled off his protective rubber gloves and dropped them into a pedal bin. He scrubbed his hands with the meticulous care of the medical profession, glancing as he did at Decker with gentle sympathy. His elegant hand gestured towards a door.

'Shall we all go into my office?'

Moxon, as impatient as ever, charged in like an enraged bull. 'Well!' he demanded, 'What can you tell me?'

If the Pathologist felt a sudden and immediate animosity towards the Inspector it did not show. He hid his feelings perfectly as he politely asked, 'What do you need to know? My full report will be on your desk later this afternoon, if you will allow my secretary time to transcribe it.'

'Hurrump!' Moxon cleared his throat, 'That's my problem, all that high-faluting medical jargon, it's bloody Greek to me. What I need is a few basic facts. Simple straight forward facts in yer simple straight forward basic English.'

'In layman's language?'

'Exactly! Not that I can't already guess.'

'A-a-ah!' sighed the Pathologist, deciding to pursue a form of subtle torment of his own, 'In layman's terms, just what do you suspect, Inspector?'

'Rape!' blurted Moxon, plunging, bull-like, into the China shop again, 'or... she got pregnant and tried to pressure the lad. He panicked, seized the nearest weapon to hand, a knife and stabbed her to death.'

'Just once?'

'Once was enough.' retorted Moxon, 'Wasn't it?'

'Is that usual... in a crime of passion?'

'No. But...!'

'And the blood? There would be a lot of blood when the carotid artery was severed. A veritable fountain. Was there any sign of blood?'

At last the gentle hints penetrated. Something was wrong. There had been a complete absence of blood in Daisy Kutter's cottage. In fact everywhere had been spotlessly clean. Untidy perhaps. Lived in. Used. As any home should be. But there hadn't been any sign of a disturbance, of violence and certainly there wasn't a trace of blood to be seen anywhere.

There has to be an answer to that, thought Moxon. If she hadn't been killed at the cottage, then where? Somewhere there had to be a patch of blood-soaked ground and signs of a struggle. People, victims of violent crime, seldom gave up their life without a struggle. The Inspector was certain of the fact. Past experience had taught him that, if nothing else.'

But wait! None of the garments found had shown traces of blood. There was no soil on them, none of the black viscous mud. They had all been clean and undamaged. Why was that? Moxon considered. He looked thoughtfully at the Pathologist, wondering, what is the crafty bastard's angle? Is he playing with me, like a fish on the hook? Reluctantly he was forced to concede and ask the question.

'Alright. Just what are you implying?'

The Pathologist sat back in his chair, his eyes roamed across the ceiling as he savoured the moment. He pursed his lips thoughtfully before answering.

'Something very unusual must have happened.' he said, 'First, just to put the record straight, the deceased was not pregnant. She couldn't have been. It's impossible. At some juncture in her life, probably about eight to nine years ago at a guess, she had a problem that resulted in damage to her fallopian tubes. There was no continuity between her ovaries and...' He paused, noting the glazed look that had spread across Moxon's face, '...to use an old fashioned expression, Inspector, Daisy Kutter was barren, and being a nurse she would fully understand the reasons why.

'Secondly, she was certainly not raped. There is no sign of sexual interference. If there had been I would have expected to find signs of bruising, violent marks, but there were none, also a complete absence of semen in the vagina. Nothing, in fact, to indicate recent sexual activity of any kind.'

'What! Nothing?' Moxon interrupted.

'Nothing,' the Pathologist repeated smoothly, '...to indicate *recent* sexual activity.' He paused again, a faint smile breaking through his professional demeanour, 'That is not to say she didn't enjoy an active love life. She obviously did. I believe it's commonplace in this day and age for a young single woman to enjoy a healthy and active love life. Quite right too, otherwise why did we bother to invent the contraceptive pill? Eh!'

Jesus Christ, Moxon cursed under his breath, *When will he get to the point? Why are these academic types all the same? Why do they have to go twice round the house just to open the bloody door?*

'Thirdly, and most unusual of all was the manner in which she was killed. There is just a single wound, just one incision at exactly the right spot. Don't quote me on this Inspector,' he warned Moxon, 'it's purely supposition on my part but I believe that whoever our murderer is, he was... is... an expert. He knew precisely where to strike. There isn't another mark anywhere on the body. Finally, there is the question of the blood...'

'The blood?'

'Well! The lack of it really, the victim's body was virtually drained.'

'What!' exclaimed Moxon sarcastically, 'Next you'll be telling me we're looking for a flaming vampire.'

'Not quite that Inspector Moxon,' answered the Pathologist with patient resignation in his voice, 'Nothing so dramatic. The human body has a remarkable capacity for healing itself. Even after a fatal wound blood begins to clot. The fibrinogen and blood platelets cling together, they struggle to stem the flow.' The glazed expression returned to Moxon's podgy face, this time it was ignored as the Pathologist persisted with his explanation. ''In this instance, little or no clotting followed, as though a conscious effort was made to drain off every last fluid ounce. It's reminiscent of the manner in which certain animals are slaughtered. The carcass is suspended, head down while still alive, then its throat is slit open to encourage as much blood as possible to drain away. It's done to make the meat white.' he concluded.

The Inspector's head seemed to sink even further into his squat oval body as he mulled over the information in his mind.

'Wouldn't all this take some time?'

'Most certainly.' replied the Pathologist, 'Which indicates that your murderer was a very cool customer, cool and calculating. A professional wouldn't you say?'

'A professional killer in a tin pot little village like Briseley T'ill? To murder a nurse? Why? It just doesn't make sense.'

'No Inspector, it doesn't make sense. Fortunately for me... that's your problem.'

*

A sullen silence pervaded the drive back to Briseley T'ill. Moxon was coming to terms with the fact that Young Barnett Hall did not fit the Pathologist's hypothesis of the murderer. It was hard to accept. He brooded on the information. Still, he had been right about one thing – Nurse Daisy Kutter and her free and fancy ways – the whore! That could mean that a lot of men were involved... and they would all lie. It was going to be difficult, a damn sight harder than Moxon had ever envisaged.

There was another problem that troubled Moxon; the current shortage of police manpower. So many officers were tied up by the political problems running rife that he was going to have to rely on Decker's local knowledge. As much as Moxon resented the thought he was far from stupid. Hard logic dictated his course of action. It was time for a change of tactics.

'Well, Constable, you heard the Pathologist. What do you make of his theory?'

Decker was surprised. Inspector Moxon was asking for his opinion? Had a miracle just occurred? His brain was already buzzing with possibilities, full of lots of little disassociated facts and happenings that were coming together, beginning to make sense. But as yet it was all too insubstantial for him to form a conclusion.

He replied slowly and carefully.

'This theory of a professional killer, I can't entirely agree sir. I can't see the sense in that at all. It's illogical. But, look at it this way. Instead of a professional killer, how about a killer who is a professional, but in another way.'

Moxon's head turned towards Decker, a wary look in his eyes. Decker explained.

'Take for example a vet. His normal job involves the treating of animals, fighting disease and sickness. But every so often, when the situation demands it, what happens? He has to put an animal down. Kill it. It's another aspect of his job. An unpleasant one but no one thinks it odd do they? People just accept it as normal. My point is that a man like that would have the knowledge. He would know how to put someone away quickly and efficiently.'

There were the faint beginnings of a newfound respect in the look Moxon gave the village policeman. Much as he hated to admit it, the man had a point.'

'Mmm! It sounds feasible,' Moxon conceded gruffly, 'Anyone in mind who fits the bill?'

'There's no one I can think of immediately,' Decker replied, 'Two vets live locally, one in the village, the other has a place about two miles away. Then there's the doctor. Nah! He's much too old and doddery. There's a surgeon, a chap by the name of Brice-Moore, has a big house near to Briseley Manor. Strewth! Ashley-Jayle, he's another, an outside possibility, ex-army captain, highly trained. Was in one of those specialist mobs that operated in the Middle East. Adan or the Oman, I believe.'

'A likely candidate?' prompted the Inspector.

'Frankly no.' said Decker, shaking his head, 'If what I think happened is correct then it's somebody close to, or within the cricket club. Very likely a playing member who was at last Saturday's match.'

'What!' cried out Moxon, his head jerking around on his thick stubby neck, 'How in God's name have you deduced that?'

'By the manner those underclothes turned up.' Decker explained, 'If you've ever been in a cricket changing rooms then you'd know. It's chaotic. There's never enough room. Sports bags lie everywhere. Everyone battles for a bit of space. Pads and bats are scattered about the floor. Boots, socks, shirts and sweaters lie all over the place. A dozen sweaty men are trying to get washed, parading about bollock-naked. It's crazy, a wonder anyone ends up with their own kit.

'Then everyone rushes off to the bar. It would be the easiest thing in the world for one man to hang back, dispose of the evidence by stuffing a garment into each player's sports bag. It rids him of the evidence and at the same time creates confusion by throwing suspicion onto everyone else.'

'Huh!' Inspector Moxon grunted by way of agreement.

'Then of course there's the spade.'

'The spade! What bloody spade?' blurted Moxon, ungrammatically.

'The edging spade, we use it at the cricket ground. On the Wednesday after Easter there was a work session at the ground. Preparation for the new season began, mowing, rolling, the usual thing. When we came to put the mowers back in the store shed I discovered the edging spade. It was caked in mud. I thought at first that it had been put away dirty at the end of last season. But no! Underneath, the mud was still tacky. At the time it didn't mean anything, now of course, it's obvious. Whoever buried the body used that spade to dig out the grave at the Sinkhole.'

'Jesus Christ!' exclaimed Moxon, 'Why the hell didn't you mention this before? Let's get the damn thing tested for prints.'

At that precise moment Ted Decker longed for a red emergency button. A Bond-style button that would operate an ejector seat and fling him clear of Moxon's car. He did not want to be around when Moxon's wrath exploded, and explode it surely would just as soon as he learned exactly what it was that Decker had done.

*

Young Barnett made a determined effort to exercise. It was difficult in the restricted space of his cell. With his arms at full stretch he could touch both the sidewalls with ease. The exercise he attempted was one of his own devising, to strengthen the left side of his body. Cricket is an unnatural game. To satisfy the purists and to bat at the highest level demands one plays sideways on. It places abnormal stress upon the spine and body muscles. Ligaments and joints are twisted in ways that nature never intended.

Barnett stopped, aware of being watched. The cell door was open. A stocky individual with sullen red features that seemed to flush all the way from the top of his balding head down to his thick bullish neck and probably beyond was gazing at him with an expression of baffled fury.

Hello! Barnett thought, *Humpty's back.*

'Right Ginger,' barked Moxon, 'Let's you and me get down to business.' If there was one gibe guaranteed to make Barnett angry it was reference to his flame red hair. Ginger, he considered the ultimate insult.

'My name is Barnett.' he said through gritted teeth, 'I've been held here for thirty-six bloody hours. When is someone going to tell me what the hell is going on?' His wiry young body bristled with anger. The medicinal compound had run its course and quite apart from his baffled rage, he was hungry.

'You don't know?'

'Don't know what? Alright, so I was taking a short cut across the railway tracks. It's illegal, so what? It's hardly the crime of the effing century is it? Just a bloody short cut on my way home.'

'Watch your language laddie,' warned the Inspector, 'Just tell me where you've been and what you were doing.'

'Again! How many times? I went to the Royal Infirmary and was on my way home. I missed the last bloody bus didn't I? Had to bloody walk. Seven miles… seven bloody miles it is. It's a long way. I was only taking a short cut.'

Moxon turned, seeking confirmation from Decker who was hovering in the corridor just behind the Inspector's right shoulder. The policeman nodded to confirm his agreement.

'Why did you go to the Royal?'

To see a friend… a young woman, she's very sick.' He appealed past the Inspector directly to Decker. 'Tell him Mr Decker, please, you know I've been to see her more than once.'

'That's right.' The policeman affirmed, his head nodding in agreement.

'But why did you approach the Sinkhole?' pressed Moxon.

'The Sinkhole? – Curiosity. I wondered what was going on, there'd been nothing there earlier in the day. I saw that tent thing and the orange tape. Couldn't make out what it was about.'

'There was something there earlier,' said the Inspector, 'It just had not been discovered. Know what I mean?' His small eyes narrowed, watching Barnett's face intently, waiting for the slightest telltale sign. There was nothing, just a complete lack of comprehension.

'A body... a woman's body. Someone you know.' There was still no sign of understanding. 'Name of Daisy Kutter?'

Now there was a reaction, a slow painful dawning of light.

'Daisy... Daisy Kutter. What do you mean?'

'She's dead Barnett. Dead. Murdered. Her body was buried there... in the Sinkhole.'

He took a long while to absorb the words. The blood slowly drained from his face leaving it strangely pale and drawn, his youth and vulnerability cruelly exposed. His words of protest were so faint that they were barely audible.

'No! No! No! Oh Daisy... Oh God! No... why? Who in the world would want to harm Daisy? All she ever did was to help people.' His anguish was obviously genuine. The Inspector waited until the young man had regained a measure of composure. In a friendly voice he asked, 'What was she to you Barnett, a girlfriend? A lover perhaps... Eh?'

'Ye-e-es! No... Yes... I... I... can't say.'

'But you must Barnett,' suggested the Inspector gently, 'We have to know the truth. It will be so much better if you tell us, give us your own story. So much better than some garbled tale from a vicious old biddy don't you think? You wouldn't want us to hear it from some old hen making up her own version. No. Of course you don't. C'mon lad, you can tell me. I'm your friend.'

Listening in Ted Decker doubted whether Moxon was a friend to anyone, but he had to admire the man's change of tactics. He was showing just the right amount of sympathy to encourage the distressed young man to open up.

Patiently they extracted Barnett's story. They heard all about his first tentative involvement with the nurse, his unexpected shyness and total lack of experience with the opposite sex. 'Daisy, she taught me so much.' he confessed reluctantly, 'I thought because I was nineteen that I knew it all. But I didn't, in fact I found that I didn't know very much at all...that was until she taught me. Daisy showed me how and what to do. Then we got on like a house on fire.' Barnett ended on a note of pride.

'So you were both willing parties to what took place.' Moxon suggested, 'She didn't take advantage of you? You weren't coerced in any way?'

Barnett shook his head and looked puzzled at even being asked such a question.

'Were you in love with her?' the Inspector asked. The young man shook his head vigorously as he explained that it had never been like that with Daisy Kutter. She was a free spirit, he told Moxon, a generous woman who cared deeply for her friends but never committed herself to any one particular person.

Even the cynical Inspector Moxon became convinced of the young man's sincerity.

'When did you last see her?' he asked.

'About a week before Easter.' Barnett replied without a moment of hesitation, 'I had a therapy appointment on the Thursday before Good Friday but it had to be cancelled. Mrs Mole took a turn for the worse. I guess she was a far more urgent case than I.'

'So as far as you know, Nurse Kutter kept her appointment with Rowena Mole?'

'Yes. Is that all?'

'It'll do for now lad. Thanks. You're free to go if you wish.'

'What! I'm free?'

'As a bird lad, as a bird. That other business – you can forget it. Just a misunderstanding.'

Typical Moxon, thought Decker, no apology forthcoming. The tension sighed out of Barnett as he visibly relaxed. Moxon threw in a final question, casually.

'How do you get into the tool-shed at the cricket ground?'

'The key... it's on a hook,' replied Barnett easily, 'Over the door, tucked up under the eaves.'

*

They met in the Cock Inn at lunchtime, an accidental meeting. The Killer was already there, dressed in his working clothes with a pint glass, half empty, on the table.

The old inn reputedly dated back over three hundred years. It was a low squat building with a roof of grey slate, head-cracking low doors, dormer-type windows on the upper floor and small poky windows at ground level. By the doorway the remains of an old iron boot-scraper peeped through the recently added tarmac. The step down into the bar had worn hollow with the passing of countless feet. Flagstones, laid years before damp proof courses had been invented covered the ground floor throughout the building. There was a large open log-burning fireplace, soot-blackened beams adorned with horse brasses that hung from mouldering leather straps, old brass lamps and an array of rusting farming tools clinging precariously to the whitewashed walls.

Atmosphere, the townies called it.

Barnett blissfully ignored the atmosphere. There would be 'atmosphere' when he arrived home… a hostile one! What he needed most was a swift half of bitter to boost his faltering nerve before he faced his mother. Dutch courage was what he needed. Mrs Hall was a small woman, a wispy scrap, but Barnett had few doubts about the size of the strip she would tear off him. Two nights away from home, involvement with the police (however innocent) and when she discovered how deeply embroiled he had been with Daisy Kutter. Phew! He hardly dared to think about that.

'Lo Barnett.' murmured a familiar voice, 'I didn't expect to see you in here.'

He turned, recognising the tall lean figure of a fellow player.

'Fancy another…?' Barnett offered. The man shook his head. He seldom wasted words.

'Off work?' he asked, fishing for information, having heard already where the young man had been.

'Work! Christ! I just wish I were. You wouldn't believe what I've been through.' Barnett flopped onto the bench seat beside the other man and with a complete lack of inhibition launched into a catalogue of the last thirty-six hours of his life. His audience of one listened intently. Not a flicker of emotion crossed the man's face nor did his black eyes betray his thoughts. He waited until the end of Barnett's rambling narrative before asking a question.

'This Inspector Moxon, what's he like?'

'Thickset, porky, got a balding head. A really fat little pottle pig of a policeman. Ha! That's very apt that is – Pottle Pig, that's what I'll call him, Inspector Pottle Pig. He's shrewd though. He asked me a lot of questions, some of them seemed nonsense… at first.' Barnett swirled the dregs of bitter around his glass, tossed the contents down his throat and rose to leave.

'Do you know?' he said, 'He asked me how to get into the store-shed at the cricket ground. Now why would he want to know that? Hell! Do you think this business is going to mess up our cricket?'

When Barnett had departed the man sat thinking quietly. Why had Moxon asked about the store-shed? Could he have worked out that the grave had been dug with the edging spade? Fingerprints! On the handle and shaft? He never wore gloves, scorned them, working out of doors meant that his hands were hard and tough. So what about fingerprints? It was natural for his to be on the spade... after all he had used the tool legitimately many times when working at the ground. But if his prints were the last ones on the spade it might be wiser to be rid of the implement altogether. Better to be safe than sorry.

*

'Tell me more about Daisy Kutter.' Moxon said to Ted Decker, 'How well did you know her? What was her relationship with this black fellow – Jackson?'

'Everett Jackson, I can tell you a little about him and about Daisy. She once told me how they met. It's a fascinating story.'

'You were close to her yourself?'

'Fairly, it's inevitable in a small community,' explained Decker, 'We all know one another's business to a degree. Being a policeman has its drawbacks, makes a difference, there's always a certain amount of reserve to a relationship. In much the same way that people react to a vicar. They hold back on swearing and act as though sex doesn't exist as if it's something a clergyman wouldn't know about. You know the kind of thing. But Daisy, she was special. The entire community trusted her, they told her just about everything. She responded to people, to everyone. She was a rarity, the type of woman who was liked, and got on well with both sexes, women as well as men. A most unusual woman.'

'Mmm! Perhaps someone told her one secret too many.' mused Moxon, 'Then came to regret it. And Jackson?' he prompted, putting the conversation back on track.

'She met him in Birmingham,' Decker continued, 'Quite out of the blue. It seems she was on a nursing course. On the last day, a Friday, she went shopping at the Fiveways Centre. A black man approached her. It was Jackson. She said that he immediately struck her as different, quite unlike the other down and outs begging for a handout. Even in dire straits there was an air of quiet dignity about the man.

'Apparently he said, "I know I'm only a black man miss and you are a white lady, but can you let me have ten pence for my bus fare. I'm trying to reach my friends and I haven't any money left." Daisy was terribly upset. She told me that the look on the man's face, such abject humiliation and tortured pride, cut through her like a knife. Being Daisy she could not let it go at that. She took him to a café for a hot drink and some food.

'The poor sod was ravenous. He hadn't eaten for three days and didn't know where or who to approach for help. To cap it all Daisy brought him back to Briseley T'ill and put him up at her cottage until he found a place of his own. He's been around ever since. At least six or seven years.'

'So you wouldn't consider Jackson as a suspect?' asked Moxon.

'Never! He was totally devoted to her.'

'Well, somebody killed her, someone close, you said so yourself. So who Constable, who?'

Decker shook his head. The question in his own mind wasn't just who but why. Why would anyone want to murder the nurse who, by all accounts, was admired and respected by all? He was unable to think of a single person or what possible motive they would have. Neither greed or money or revenge sounded feasible. Hatred? Jealousy? Perhaps the latter reason was the most likely one. There had been the anonymous telephone call at the cottage. It had hinted of jealousy. But whoever the woman had been she had not known that Daisy Kutter was dead.

'How well do you know the Mole family?' asked Moxon, 'There's three of them aren't there, a father and two sons?'

'Correct.' Decker answered the latter part of the question first, 'I've known Jack Mole ever since I came here, and the boys, Lenny and Norman. Rowena as well until she died.'

'Good! Then you had better be the one to visit them. Let's get back to checking facts. Find out about that last visit. What time the nurse left the house. Whether she said where she was going? It won't be easy coming so soon after a bereavement but it has to be done. OK?' He waited for Decker to agree then continued, 'Do you have a list of club members?'

'I can soon make one out, but for the moment I rescued the team-sheet for last Saturday's match from the notice board. Will that help?'

The sheet with its printed heading, 'Briseley T'ill Cricket Club' was limp from exposure to the elements, torn and tatty around the edges, but still clearly readable.

'Good.' exclaimed Moxon with mild surprise, 'It will do for a start. Me, I'm going to have a poke around that store shed. See what I can pick up. Then I must collect the lab report.' The Inspector looked Decker up and down, taking note of his formal uniform before making a suggestion the Constable did not expect. 'Change into civvies, casual clothing, it could help people to relax, help them to open up a little more. Chat to them casually and keep your eyes and ears open. OK?'

'Sir!' replied Decker smartly.

'We'll meet tomorrow, first light, have a confab over coffee. Right?'

'Breakfast?' hinted Decker, tongue in cheek.

'Why not.' Moxon replied with a watery smile.

The seeds of mutual respect were beginning to sprout.

*

Entering the Mole's house and its kitchen was like stepping back into a time warp, - the nineteen-thirties. There was green paint, large cracked white tiles, all badly crazed with age and brown linoleum. Upright taps, like twin sentinels stood over a white butler's type sink. Nothing about it had changed over the last half-century.

The house was at the end of Warren Terrace, a row of pre-World War One terraced houses with just sufficient space to the end plot to allow the Mole's to squeeze on a garage. It was a timber and asbestos shanty that leaned crazily against the end wall of the block and in all probability contravened the building regulations. Decker regarded the byelaws as outside his province (unless otherwise advised). Nor was he particularly interested in the battered grey mini-van owned by the twins. Whether it was roadworthy was a question better left unasked. Its tyres bordered from bald to the minimum legal requirement and its silencer hung dangerously low. The security of the van's rear doors owed more to a length of yellow plastic washing line than to the vehicles rusting hinges.

Decker gave the mini-van a cursory glance as he walked by. There was something about it that struck a chord, an insignificant detail that registered in his subconscious mind but deemed as unimportant at the time. He had followed Moxon's suggestion and dressed casually in a tan open-necked shirt, toning slacks and a club sweater in Lovat green which bore the motif, 'Briseley T'ill Cricket Club' Ted Decker knocked on the kitchen door, turned the handle and stuck his head inside.

'Hello there.' he called out.

Old habits die hard. Everyone in the village did the same, aware that Rowena Mole, confined to a wheelchair, was unable to answer the door easily. He remembered too late. Rowena was dead. Not only dead, she was also buried. In the changed circumstances it would have been proper to knock and wait, as he would have done at any other house.

'Jack? Jack Mole. OK if I come in? It's Ted Decker.'

It was dark in the kitchen and after the bright April sunlight took some time for the policeman's eyes to adjust to the gloom. An open fire burnt in the old-fashioned kitchen range. The man staring into its flickering flames was a mere six years older than Decker. A man, who less than three weeks ago had burned with a vital inner energy, who had walked tall in the community. Now the fire was out, his shoulders bowed by an unimaginable burden while his lack-lustre eyes stared with disinterest into the flames of the old range. Prematurely Jack Mole had aged by twenty years.

Decker was shocked by what he saw, by the drastic and sudden change. The torment in the man's eyes went far deeper than the natural grief of bereavement. Something else was there. Suspicion? Fear?

The policeman sensed that an invisible barrier had been raised. He found it difficult to lay a finger upon but it was there in the guarded answers to his questions.

'Jack.' he repeated, 'May I come in?'

'Suit yersen Mister Decker.'

'Mister Decker? It's always been Ted before.'

'Aye! That's as maybe.'

'Jack, I've called as a friend. It's an unofficial visit. I'm worried about you.'

'Worried! What d'you know about worry? Eh! Eh!' Jack Mole's voice rose with emotion. 'What d'you know about worry and death and sickness? What do you know? Year in year out, 'aving to look after someone who is helpless, crippled, stuck in a bloody wheelchair and slowly dying inch by bloody inch. Getting wus day by day. What d'you know you clever-arsed bastard, eh? What do you know?'

The man's eyes went wide in their raging appeal. They demanded what the policeman was unable to provide... an answer to his grief.

'Jack! Ja-ack! You can't blame yourself. It was no one's fault that Rowena became ill. You did more than enough for her. As much as any human being could.'

Decker's commiserations went unheard. His sympathy, lost. John Mole was so deeply enveloped by his grief and anguish that the words just failed to penetrate.

'It was my fault.' Jack Mole's voice dropped to a hoarse whisper, 'It was my fault. I was missing when Rowena died. I was away. It wouldn't have happened if I had been present.'

'No Jack, no.' replied Decker, 'How can you say that? It was fate, just fate. We humans don't decide such things. It just happens. How could you have prevented Rowena's death even if you had been there? It would still have happened when it did. It was fate Jack, just fate!'

Jack Mole slumped down into his chair. His eyes concentrated upon the glowing coals, seeing, yet unseeing. They were looking for a world that had disappeared. And all the while his hands twisted and turned in a perpetual washing motion, like Pilate, only without the soap and water, trying to clean away the guilt.

Decker waited. He seemed calmer now.

'I'll make tea.' suggested the policeman. He filled the kettle at the mottled white butler's sink. How strange, he thought, that the house has never been modernised.

The Moles were a relatively young family. The twins were both twenty years of age. Rowena had been thirty-nine when she died and John Mole, a comparatively young fifty... until recent events had taken their toll. Yet they had never spent time or money on modernising the house. Three wages were coming in with nothing to show for it. Why? Even the little mini-van was a wreck. Yet Decker knew they were not riotous spenders and that they had never lived extravagantly. So where did all their money go? Decker couldn't think of an answer. It was a mystery that niggled in his mind.

The house was always clean, spotless. Once it had been nicely decorated until the ceilings and wallpaper took on the yellowish look that comes from the smoke of an open fire. Almost every other house in the terrace had central heating... but not this one.

There were no fitted units in the kitchen, no ceramic tiled walls, no fitted carpets, not even a modern double draining sink unit. Just an old-fashioned white butler's sink with separate straight old taps. Standing guard like ancient sentinels to a bygone era.

Decker filled the one concession to the nineteen-eighties, an electric kettle, from the taps. The water jetted out fiercely from the orifice and swirled foamingly into the container. In Briseley T'ill, high water pressure caused the pipes in almost every house to moan and vibrate as it surged through the pipes. He found the teapot, a square white china pot with a recently chipped spout. It had become badly stained and he emptied out a number of old teabags. They gave off a faint odour of mildew.

Disgusting, Decker thought, since Rowena's death, neglect has quickly set a foot in through the door. Personally fastidious, he scalded the pot thoroughly before infusing the tea. A row of milk bottles stared him in the face. Too many were still being delivered for a family now reduced in numbers. He had to search to find a bottle that was fresh. When he tipped some of the bottles upside down their contents did not move.

Ugh! Decker shuddered in disgust.

Apathy and grief he could understand. Self neglect to a point. But the change in John Mole was unaccountable. Most characters in extreme adversity remained steadfast, their basic temperament stayed unchanged. A change as drastic as the one affecting John Mole required more than the bereavement of his wife. After all, Decker considered, her death was not unexpected, Mole had had years in which to prepare himself for it.

He probed further, making conversation along casual lines for a while, small talk, irrelevant gossip about events in the village and connected to the cricket club, before gradually turning his questions to more serious matters. He explored, how over the years, the Mole family had re-arranged their working lives around Rowena's illness. She had never been left alone for any length of time. John Mole spent the greater part of his time in her company, departing for work after five o'clock to work an evening shift from 6pm until 2am. Lenny set off for the abattoir in the early hours, finishing work in the afternoon.

Once Norman had worked factory hours in the hosiery trade until short time and finally redundancy had cost him his job. There had been an unhappy period for him on the dole until a takeover bid had revitalised the firm. Norman, a genial giant of a man, well over six feet tall and weighing in at fifteen stones, had been remembered, telephoned and offered a part-time position working in the evenings in the re-organised despatch department. His hours were from 5 until 10pm and his work involved arranging overnight deliveries. It was short time but supplemented by an extra payment for unsociable hours. As a bonus there were frequent occasions when he was required to work additional hours to cover for staff on holiday.

'Is Norman about?' asked Decker as he handed Jack Mole a cup of tea. He avoided the man's eyes, concentrated on the pale blue china cups, noticed the tremulous hands, heard the faint chatter of the cup as it rattled in its loose fitting saucer.

'Norman? Out walking.' Mole muttered briefly, 'What for d'you want 'im?'

'I though he may be able to help me with some information.'

'Information? What kind of information? Can't you ask me?'

'Yes Jack, I could, except that you said yourself you were absent when Rowena died.' Jack Mole, head bent low, looked from beneath lowered brows. It was a hard suspicious look, antagonistic almost and inexplicable to the policeman.

'No! I was not... nor was Norman.'

'So there was just Lenny and the nurse?'

'Aye. That's it, until the doctor arrived. But it was too late by then. She'd already gone. There was nothing he could do for Rowena. Nothing.' He added bitterly, 'Except write the death certificate.'

'This would be about… what time?'

'Eight-thirty, Nine.' Jack Mole replied, then in a sudden burst of anger, 'I should have been there. If only I'd been there everything would 'ave been alright.'

'Alright Jack, alright.' soothed a puzzled Decker. There it was again, that look, the wary suspicious look of a fox, cornered, searching for an escape route! Why? And how might Jack Mole's presence have made any difference to Rowena's death? It was common knowledge that she had died suddenly of an embolism. A possibility that was always likely as a side effect of her treatment. In his heart Ted thanked God that he didn't have to make such decisions. Between life and death. Between the crippling pain that Rowena suffered on the one hand, and on the other, prescribing pain-killing drugs with their unknown side effects. How could any sane man hold another responsible?

The spark of resentment in Jack Mole had died. He slumped back into his chair again, fingers picking aimlessly at the worn leatherwork and his barely audible voice endlessly repeating.

'I should have been there. I should have been there…'

Decker realised that further questioning would be futile. He had lost his man. Jack Mole was drowning in his own self-pity, sunk without trace in a sea of apathy and remorse. There had to be another way to check. Someone objective. Of course, there was the Doctor. He would know. Decker squeezed the man's shoulder in a comforting gesture and let himself out of the house.

Outside the air was fresh and clean. He blinked in the bright afternoon sunlight and with a light breeze ruffling his hair set off briskly towards the surgery. The road through the village had a gradient of one in twenty. Although the Doctor lived close to the centre of Briseley T'ill it was still half a mile to either end of the drawn out winding village. Decker enjoyed walking, the feel of his muscles stretching and flexing as they took the strain of the gradient. The brisk movement pumping the blood vigorously around his body, helped to stimulate his brain. Thoughts flashed across his mind in a constant stream of little pictures. He found abstract thinking to be a problem but things visual came to mind with the clarity of pictures taken by a camera. Little fragments of conversation floated through his brain, a phrase here a word there. What had Jack Mole meant when he had said he could have stopped it happening? Stopped what happening? Certainly not Rowena's death. Perhaps the man was speaking of another event. Perhaps he was confused and the two events were inexplicably entangled.

As Decker's broad shouldered back retreated a tall figure stepped through a gap in the roadside hedge. It was Norman Mole. His usual genial features were sombre. Worried eyes stared after the receding figure. His dark curly hair, damp from perspiration, clung to his moist forehead. He was dressed in casual clothes, a dark blue donkey jacket, thick heavily woven trousers and sturdy brown fell boots.

Over the crook of his arm hung his favourite gun. He snapped the weapon shut. Lifted it to his shoulder into the firing position and sighted along the barrel. His fingers closed around the trigger.

'Cr-r-r-rack!' Norman made the sound with his mouth like a small boy playing at soldiers. 'That's the end of you Mister Policeman.' he snarled, then burst into giggles of childish amusement.

Stumped

The end of an innings as the wicketkeeper seizes an opportunity to remove one of the batsmen.

In every pavilion in the land reside mementoes of long dead matches. They bear mute testimony to past deeds at every level of the game of cricket. Old cricket caps, in brash and lurid colours, hang pinned to the walls. There are time-blackened cricket balls mounted upon inscribed plaques to remind one that in 1906 Joshua Smith took 9 wickets for a mere 10 runs (including a hat-trick) against the club's keenest adversary: Kirk Loscoe Cricket Club – or some such similar feat. Sharing pride of place, and no less in importance, hang ancient bats, the edges of their blades cracked with the dryness of age and their handles, stripped of their rubber grips, exposed as bare cane.

If they could speak, what tales they would tell of the mighty deeds performed by their former owners. Many of the players are long dead, forgotten by all but a few of their former colleagues. Perhaps their sole and only claim to fame remains recorded in the dusty pages of past scorebooks. Does any cricketer worthy of his salt discard a favourite and cherished bat? Or lightly toss aside the ball with which he turned in his all-time greatest performance? Never! It is a part of the cricketer's magpie mentality, part of the magical memories of the great game.

Pavilion lockers are stuffed full of shattered stumps, broken bails, splitting cricket balls, cracked bats and totally useless old pads that have seen better days. Old leg guards have horsehair stuffing bursting from seams that have split, rusting buckles and missing straps. They smell of mildew, stale sweat and caked flaky whitening and over the damp winter months have accumulated a musty pungent odour. It is the eternal smell of cricket from club to county level.

The pavilion at Briseley T'ill Cricket Club is no exception. It suffers from the same magpie mentality and nothing is ever thrown away. At the end of one season, in a burst of untypical activity, the Committee resolved to clean out the pavilion and over-packed the storage shed. The following spring, finding it well nigh impossible to locate the mowers beneath the pile of rubbish, they had moved almost every item back into the dressing room lockers.

Everything? Almost, but not quite. One of the items left behind was an incomplete set of old stumps. Of the original set of six just four had survived. One had a long sliver of wood split away from the top half. The remaining three were whole except for the metal ferrules used to finish off their ends. Only one stump was complete in every detail as the manufacturer had made it with a steel band capping the top of the stump and a pointed cone of steel covering its point. It made a lethal weapon. A cricket ball striking the top of the stump at seventy to eighty miles per hour could send it cart-wheeling out of the ground. It posed a terrifying threat to the wicket keeper or to any other fielder who had the misfortune to be in the line of its trajectory.

Which is why cricket stumps are now entirely made of wood.

These particular stumps had been saved because they made a useful tool with which to search for lost balls. They fitted comfortably into the hand, ideal for thrashing down long grass, stinging nettles and probing into muddy hedge bottoms in the search for a lost 'cherry'. Just inside the door of the storage shed was an empty oil drum and behind it, a plastic bin in which the ancient stumps had been left.

Carelessly discarded, they rested with their points uppermost. Mounted neatly on the wall above was a row of tools dangling from pairs of nails hammered into the joists to form crude supports. A three pronged garden fork, a grass rake with long slender tines, a device to aerate the ground…*and the edging spade.*

The meticulous Decker had secured each handle into place with a twist of plastic coated wire to prevent them from falling accidentally. For immediately below the tools stood the plastic bin of stumps, points uppermost, like the killing stakes at the bottom of a tiger pit. Waiting.

*

He made his way across the fields to the cricket ground unobserved, blending in with his surrounding naturally, a typical countryman in his working clothes making his way along the hedgerows with a billhook in one hand. Who would notice him or pay the slightest attention? No one.

Without seeming to hurry he covered the ground effortlessly. The key to the storage shed lay hidden in its accustomed place under the eaves. It turned easily in the recently oiled padlock. When he had returned the edging spade to its position, how long ago was that, seventeen, eighteen days, a lifetime ago, he remembered the blade had been caked in mud, the clinging viscous black mud of the Sinkhole. But now... its blade was clean!

It was gleaming, shiningly, spotlessly clean. The stainless steel looked like new. Only one type of person polished a blade to that degree of perfection. Someone with military training, or a policeman; Constable Edward Decker!

He smiled, a brief sardonic smile. The irony of it touched his sense of humour. Saved by the law! There was no longer any need to remove the edging spade. If there *were* any fingerprints to be found on its handle... they wouldn't be his.

His keen ears caught a sound carried by the wind. A squeal of protest from the rusting hinges of the gate into the cricket field. Another person was coming. He closed the doors of the storage shed and screened from view by the pavilion made his way into the changing rooms. Through the windows, hidden by the protective net curtains, he observed the arrival of Inspector Moxon.

Droplets of perspiration beaded the fat policeman's balding head. His body, which had never been designed for prolonged exertion, laboured heavily up the gradient towards the pavilion. For once Moxon had foregone the convenience of his police car. His intent had been to arrive at the ground unheralded and to poke around quietly, undisturbed.

He peered up at the eaves, searching for the keys. Failing to find them where he had expected, a slight frown wrinkled the pale skin of his glistening head, then, noticing the padlock dangling unsecured from its hasp, he tried the doors. They offered only slight resistance, impeded by tufts of grass growing against the woodwork.

Moxon wore lightweight leather-soled shoes. It was many years since he had pounded a beat, most of his work being done from the comfort of his official car or from his office. Other men's legs did the donkeywork.

Derv from the oil drum had soaked the ground just inside the doors. An amalgam of smells: oil, petrol, rotting grass and fertiliser granules met his nostrils. Sticky bottles of weed-killer, partly used, lined the horizontal joists of the shed.

Moxon's eyes sought out the edging spade. Trying to avoid stepping on the oily ground he leaned over precariously and attempted to lift down the spade. It stuck, held firmly in place by Decker's twisted length of wire. Furiously Moxon jiggled it about but without result and the twist of wire was inches out of his reach. The Inspector reached across, took one of the old stumps from the plastic container and poked vigorously at the wire.

Still it held. There was only one way to release the spade and that was by climbing high enough to disentangle the twist with his fingers.

If he used the oil drum to stand upon then he would be able to reach easily. Several billets of wood lay about the shed floor. He piled three one upon the other to make a step then tested the drum with his hand. It wobbled slightly on the uneven ground.

Apprehensively he clambered up. There was nothing solid or convenient within his reach to hold and steady himself by. His position was most precarious, but the spade might yet reveal a clue. The faintest smudge of a fingerprint could still linger.

If it did... *he wanted it.*

*

The man in the changing rooms was curious. Moxon was out of his sight in the shed. What was he doing? And why? His curiosity over-rode his sense of caution. He *had* to know. His rubber-soled boots, soundless on the pavilion steps, gave no warning to the Inspector. Moxon, tugging impatiently at the plastic coated wire, suddenly became aware of another presence. His head jerked around violently. In the moment his eyes registered the newcomer, Moxon's body lost its balance. The smooth leather soles of his shoes skidded on the greasy surface of the oil drum. Frantically he strove to regain his footing. His feet, in a series of rapid steps, scuffed and slipped on the oily metal. Like a rat pounding a treadmill, working hard, totally in vain. The drum rocked and wobbled, crashed over onto its side. A final despairing thrust of his legs sent the drum spinning away.

It seemed that for a brief moment his body defied gravity, hanging in space, weightless. One hand grasped the shaft of the edging spade. The other clutched uselessly at the air. His head jerked back in a reactive movement, exposing his throat. Down he plunged. Rapidly down... onto the killing shafts of the tiger pit.

The steel-clad tip of the one complete stump took him in the throat. It skewered through his windpipe, piercing cleanly through his neck, splintering his vertebrae on its way and ended protruding from the back by several inches. A ghastly gurgling sound came from the stricken man. His toes beat a rapid tattoo, brown leather-clad feet pounding the oil-soaked earth. Then all movement ceased. Rich, dark blood flowed in a stream into the bin, down the outside of the plastic container and mingled with the spilt diesel oil soaking into the barren soil.

Close acquaintance with violent death was an everyday part of the Killer's life. He viewed it dispassionately. But for once even his cold and distant demeanour was disturbed. He drew back... shaken!

The accident had happened so suddenly, so unexpectedly, without warning. As soon as the policeman's feet began to slip he had sensed disaster. Seemed to know in advance what was about to happen and yet was powerless to prevent the fat man's terrible death.

Coherent thought fled from his mind. He pushed frantically against the doors, fighting to close them, to shut out the dreadful sight. The dead man's foot, in its ridiculous brown leather shoe, prevented the door from closing properly. It lay across the threshold. He never thought to move the leg. Could not bear to touch it.

Fury mounted in the man. How dare he be dead? How dare he? He pounded the door as though the inanimate object were some recalcitrant child refusing to obey him. He sobbed out his futile anger until, exhausted, his body twisted, slumped against the door and sank to the ground.

In his irrational mind the man sought to re-construe the facts. To turn them into a formula his brain could accept. The body was just an animal, another animal, like the one he had killed before. It was a pig, a pale, dead, pig-like carcass. It was natural to kill pigs. Natural... that's right... perfectly natural.

*

Barnett called at the Doctor's surgery on a sudden impulse. At the time it had seemed like a good idea. Fretting away the minutes in the waiting room his nerve began to fail. What on earth had led him to make such a rash and impulsive decision?

He sat alone in the sparsely furnished room. Sat amid the tatty out-of-date magazines upon the comfortless wooden chairs. Given half a chance he would have slipped out but he was the solitary occupant of the dingy waiting room and the benign eye of the middle-aged receptionist rested upon him, friendly and curious. It restrained him as effectively as any straitjacket.

So why, he asked himself, had he called at the surgery? Even to himself his motives were vague and confused. Was it to put off the moment of truth? To delay having to face his mother, or could the doctor advise him? Perhaps help to sort out the many doubts that clouded his mind.

Now if only the receptionist were to be called away perhaps he could still slip out unobtrusively. Too late! His luck was out. The previous patient, a bent arthritic pensioner, emerged from the consulting room at that very moment, a prescription clutched firmly in his gnarled and twisted hand. He left Barnett to his fate.

'Mr Barnett Hall.' The receptionist called out formally, 'Will you go in please.'

The die was cast.

'Hello Young Barnett,' the doctor greeted him, 'What can I do for you?'

Barnett shuffled his weight between one leg and the other, hoping for a chasm to open and swallow him wholesale. He began with a 'Hmm!' progressed to an 'Er!' and then dried up completely.

The Doctor recognised the symptoms, he eased him into a conversation gradually.

'How is the leg coming along?' he asked, as though Barnett was unique, a strange monopod creature that hopped rather than walked.

'Um! – Um! S'alright!'

'Muscles recovered their strength? Just about back to normal?'

'Er... er... yes. Yes.'

'Well enough to score some runs last Saturday I hear, a very fine innings young man. It was my pleasure to watch part of it.'

'Did you?' Barnett answered, relaxing marginally, 'I hope you enjoyed the game.'

'Certainly. A fine dramatic finish I believe. Unfortunately I was called away just before the end. It's one of the penalties of my profession. I'm only ever a fleeting spectator I'm sorry to say.'

Barnett nodded as though he understood the demands upon the elderly practitioner.

'Is there another problem?' asked the Doctor, 'I gather you had a slight contretemps with the law?'

'Yes! No! Well! Sort of... umm.' He shrugged, a vague indeterminate twitch of the shoulders.

'Not police brutality then?' suggested the Doctor in dry solemn tones.

'No. No.' replied the young man quickly. *Now there's a thought. If only he had, then he could have returned home expecting some sympathy.* 'It's... er... personal.'

'It usually is.' replied the Doctor, a hint of sarcasm creeping into his voice. He was losing patience and said, 'I have a stream of patients coming through my door, every one of them with personal problems. That's what it's all about, ill health. It's very personal to the one suffering.'

A flash of anger flared in Barnett, then as quickly died, stillborn.

'Sorry. I'm confused. So much seems to have happened to me in the last few days. I feel guilty, yet I'm not. It's help I need, your advice. I thought perhaps...' His words dried up again.

The Doctor looked at Barnett and sighed within himself. It was so many years, so long ago that he had been the young man's age that he'd forgotten what it was like; the growing up, the struggle towards maturity. One day believing you were an adult then the next finding out that there was still a long way to travel. That one could still be vulnerable and exposed.

'Guilty?' he asked, 'About Daisy, Nurse Kutter?'

'Oh no! It's not about her, that's nothing to do with me. It's about another matter entirely.'

Now it was the Doctor's turn to be surprised. He'd jumped to a wrong conclusion. He concealed the fact behind his bland medical face and asked, 'What is it then?'

'It's – it's sexual.' whispered Barnett, plunging into unknown waters.

'A-ah! Too much... or not enough?' A faint twitch at the corners of the Doctor's mouth would have given the game away to an acute observer but Barnett was too intense, too deeply conscious of his problems to notice. He answered seriously.

'None at all, it's gone!'

'Gone?' The GP's eyes looked into the top corners of the room, searching for Barnett's vanished libido. 'Gone?' he repeated, 'How do you mean, gone?'

'It's gone!' cried Barnett, in despair, 'the urge. That... that... Phwo-orrr!'

He clenched his fist and made an unmistakable upward gesture.

*

Revenge is sweet, whatever they may say to contradict, revenge can be very, very sweet. The Doctor savoured the moment. For years vague rumours had reached his ears. There had never been proof, nothing positively said, just suggestions, slyly passed, or if not always in words then in pitying looks and gestures. He was many years older than his wife. Twenty-one years to be precise and he had never been able to fulfil her desire for a child. But he suspected that someone had.

It had all been long ago when she was still in her twenties and he, a hard working general practitioner, had slogged day and night to build up a viable livelihood. He'd known all along that he'd failed to pay her the attention that a loving husband should.

From the very beginning he'd doubted that the baby was his own. The little boy reared as his son had a different genetic pattern. Russet hair instead of black, blue eyes in place of brown, a lithe athletic body instead of the stocky frame possessed by the Doctor and his ancestors. The child also differed from his mother. She was small-boned and petite. The boy grew tall with a strong and sturdy physique. He was intelligent and charming. A boy to be proud of, and the Doctor *was* proud, as proud as a father could be.

The Doctor wrestled with his conscience. Conscience won. He had never been a vindictive man. There wasn't an ounce of malice in his entire body.

Barnett was subjected to a long thoughtful gaze. He watched the Doctor anxiously for a comforting sign. Finally the practitioner spoke. Slowly and carefully he chose his words.

'Barnett, my boy,' he began gently, 'I have treated your family for many years and have known you since the day you were born. I very much doubt that there is anything *physically* wrong with you at all.' The Doctor's head slowly shook from side to side in contemplation of similar consultations. He continued, 'You would be surprised how many times I've hear about similar problems... sexual ones. Well! Let me tell you that it is *never* as straightforward as one may think. So many factors can affect a man's performance, poor health, anxiety, stress at work and worry. It may be as simple as the other person being unsuitable, sometimes our bodies recognise what our minds fail to appreciate. Then, there is tension, it may be that at the particular time the... er... *event* took place, or rather *didn't* take place, you were overwrought. Maybe another time, in a more relaxed situation... Bingo! It will all come together.'

Young Barnett failed to look convinced.

'Give it time Barnett, give it time, then if all is not well, say one month from now, come back and talk to me again.'

Barnett was shepherded towards the door so professionally that he was scarcely aware of the fact until he found himself outside and in the waiting room again.

The solitary figure of Ted Decker was perched upon the self-same chair recently warmed by Barnett's less substantial buttocks.

'Barnett!' the policeman greeted him.

So immersed in his own thoughts was the young man that he failed to hear the greeting and his eyes failed to register the sturdy presence of the officer. Decker shrugged off the apparent snub. Barnett's problems were his own and the policeman had more serious matters to consider.

'The Doctor is free now.' the receptionist informed Decker. He acknowledged her words with a faint smile, tapped lightly with the back of one knuckle on the woodwork and eased his bulky frame into the consulting room.

'This *is* an unexpected pleasure,' remarked the elderly doctor as he peered myopically over the top of his spectacles, 'To what do we owe the pleasure – business or is it a social call?' His fingers turned over Decker's medical record card which on one side bore details of his date of birth, full address and National Health Service number – and on the other paid silent tribute to his state of health by remaining stubbornly blank.

'Business,' replied the policeman. Then as the other man's eyebrows lifted in enquiry, he expanded upon his answer, 'Police business. Official. It's to do with the death of the nurse, Daisy Kutter.'

'Ah! Yes, of course.'

For a moment the Doctor's professional demeanour slipped. A look of sheer helplessness, very brief, appeared on his face before his training reasserted itself and restored his bearing. 'A terrible business... terrible... if there is any way I can help then of course I will. Anything, anything at all.'

'I'm sure you will,' Decker sympathised, 'My immediate concern is to piece together the last hours of Nurse Kutter. Am I correct in thinking that the last time you saw her was on the day that Rowena Mole died?'

The Doctor's brow furrowed as he thought carefully before replying.

'Ye-e-es! That would be, let me see, just before Easter, on the Thursday before Good Friday, around nine o'clock in the evening. Rowena died at approximately eight pm. It was very sudden, totally unexpected. Daisy was with her at the time. She visited her on a regular basis. Rowena's condition had started to deteriorate rapidly, so much so that she required constant care, to wash her, help her to dress and undress. One minute she was sitting on the edge of her bed and the next, gone! She just keeled over and died. Daisy Kutter tried desperately to revive Rowena. She tried the kiss of life, heart massage, but it was all in vain.'

'And you arrived at nine?'

'Roughly.' nodded the Doctor, 'It could have been a few minutes either way. I went there as soon as I received the call.'

'Was anyone else there then?'

'Erm! No... that is to say I didn't see anyone else. Lenny was there when his mother died. In fact it was Lenny who made the call to me. It took me some time to understand what he was saying. At first his words were garbled and incoherent. I put it down to shock, poor lad! Then Daisy came on the phone and explained what had happened. Naturally I went as quickly as I could, but it was far too late by then.'

'What happened to Lenny?'

'Nurse Kutter said that he rushed out while she was on the telephone. She said that he was in a very disturbed frame of mind.'

'I can understand that. The Moles have always been a very close-knit family, the sudden death of his mother was bound to upset him deeply.'

Decker paused, regarded the Doctor thoughtfully before proceeding. He chose his words carefully, 'It's common knowledge that Rowena Mole and Jack were never married, that they were first cousins. Well! What I wondered was, this business of interbreeding, is there any truth in it? Has it affected Norman and Lenny? Would you regard them as retarded? You know what I mean, are they ten pence to the shilling?'

If Decker expected a straight answer he was doomed to disappointment. He waited patiently for a reply. The Doctor, hunched over his clenched hands, stared pensively at a prescription pad lying on his desk. Writing failed to appear. No moving finger traced out a solution to his problem. He peered over half-moon spectacles at the policeman, shaking his head in doubt. 'You tell me,' he replied enigmatically, 'Do I know what thoughts are in another person's mind? I'm a General Practitioner. I examine bodies. I look for physical symptoms, try my best to recognise them and make as accurate a diagnosis as I possibly can. It's the best I can do. For the most part I may examine one of my patients once or twice a year, often a great deal less, as you know yourself.' He looked reproachfully at the policeman.

'But the Moles, Rowena, you must have visited her many, many times. She was *your* patient,' continued Decker. His voice pressed for an answer. 'If anyone was close to the family, it was you, or Daisy Kutter and I can't ask her can I?' Somebody killed her, probably soon after Rowena Mole died. And so far you are the last person I know of who saw her alive. Either you, or one of the Moles.'

There was anguish in the Doctor's eyes as he replied, 'Do you think I don't know that. I'm not stupid. But why? I can't think of a single reason why the Moles, or anyone else for that matter, would want to kill Daisy Kutter. She was their friend, as well as being a damn fine nurse to Rowena. There is no reason.'

The Doctor spread his hands in appeal, 'It was Easter. I never thought, never questioned her disappearance. Everyone in the village knows that Daisy visits her mother every Easter. It was one of those routine things she did. She was a very caring person.'

'Mmm! That's true.' The policeman nodded agreement, then continued, 'Just take me through the sequence of events after you arrived at the house.'

'Well, Daisy met me at the door. She looked pale but composed. Rowena had a bedroom on the ground floor. She hadn't been able to climb stairs for years, so what had originally been a dining room had been converted into her bedroom. Rowena lay across the bed. She looked... peaceful, like someone who had fallen asleep, except that her clothing was rumpled due to Daisy Kutter's efforts to revive her. There were red marks, blotches around the heart, again due to the battle to save her life. I carried out my examination and deduced that she had died of an embolism. In the circumstances it was the obvious cause of death...and the pathologist's report confirmed my diagnosis.

Decker's look required the Doctor to elaborate.

'It's fairly common. The drugs that made her life bearable probably contributed towards her death. It's a regrettable side effect.'

Decker reflected that every job has its downside. With all the drawbacks of his work at least he was not required to weigh the balance of another human life.

'So you didn't see Lenny or Norman or John Mole?' he continued.

'No. And that *was* odd because usually there was always one member of the family there. Norman, of course, would have been working his late evening shift. He was due home around ten-fifteen. Jack Mole worked until much later. Because of the situation at home he worked a permanent evening shift. And Lenny, well! God only knows where he was, probably wandering around in a state of shock. He could have been anywhere.'

The Doctor paused. Decker could visualise the events tracing across his mind. The man facing him suddenly held up an arresting finger. 'No! Wait a minute, that isn't how it was. I'm sorry, I've been misleading you. That is how it *should* have been but not how it was. I remember now, Daisy said she tried to contact Jack's firm, to ask them to send him home. When she rang there was only a security man on duty. He said that because it was Easter the firm had closed down early. Some still do you know.' The Doctor looked earnestly at Decker as though he feared the policeman would doubt his words.

'I do know.' Decker said, nodding sententiously, 'But if what you tell me is correct then where the hell did Jack Mole get to... and what happened to Lenny?'

The words of Jack Mole came back to him, haunting his mind. *If I had been there it wouldn't have happened!* If he had been - where? And what would not have happened? A theory had been taking shape until the Doctor's words opened his mind to wider possibilities.

The policeman was rising to leave when the physician came up with a new suggestion. 'Of course he could have gone to Marston Grange.'

'Marston Grange?' The name vaguely rang a bell. 'Where and what is Marston Grange? And why should Jack Mole go there?'

Mild exasperation crept across the Doctor's face. He was a benefactor and trustee of Marston Grange. It offended his sensitivities when anyone was unaware of its existence. 'It is a home for the severely handicapped and disabled. He could have gone there to visit his daughter.'

'His daughter! What daughter?' The news was a bombshell to Decker's ears. He stared in bewilderment at the Doctor. That worthy person was busy casting his mind back over the years, sorting out the sequence of events. Eventually he explained.

'Of course, it was before your time. Long before you came to Briseley T'ill. It isn't the kind of thing people want made public. So it's hardly surprising that you are unaware of what happened.'

Whatever it was, Decker wanted to know now, and said as much.

'It all harks back to Rowena's father, Sebastian Mole, a vicious man. Just about the meanest, vilest individual you could ever come across... or would wish to know. Generous people blamed it on the war but I never thought so. He was vicious from the day he was born, the most convincing argument for original sin that ever walked on two legs. The army trained a lot of men to fight...and to kill. But I believe he enjoyed it. Being a commando suited Seb Mole down to the ground. Huh! It's ironic. He returned a hero, and far, far better men died.

'Rowena was born in 1946, a part of the post-war baby boom. You may have heard what it was like just after the war? Difficult! The housing situation was impossible, so they all lived together in one big old house with the old lady; Seb and Frank Mole's mother.' The Doctor looked accusingly at Decker. He shook his head angrily as though it were all the fault of the policeman.

'It never works! Living with in-laws, packed in together, tight and smelly, like a row of sardines. It puts unnatural pressures on people. Is it any wonder that there were problems? There was old Mrs Mole, her two sons; Seb and Frank, both their wives, little Rowena and young Jack, seven people in a three bed-roomed house? It was far too many.' The Doctor paused momentarily, the mist of old memories in his eyes, then he asked Decker a rhetorical question.

'Do you know what was so strange? I'll tell you. From the very beginning young Jack took a fancy to the baby girl. It was eerie. One just does not expect an eleven-year old boy to become attached to a baby... least of all a baby girl... but *he* did. It was as though he assumed responsibility for her life and he never relinquished it until the day Rowena died.

'Looking back the trouble really began when the old lady passed away and the house had to be sold. Mrs Mole was a shrewd old biddy, she didn't leave a penny to her sons. She had them weighed up all right. She left it all to her two grandchildren, fifty-fifty, split right down the middle. Young Jack would have been twenty-seven by then. Rowena was only sixteen so her share was put into trust until she reached the age of twenty-one. Either that or until the day she married, whichever came first. That was the cause of the trouble.'

'How was that?' asked the policeman who had listened attentively to the older man.

'The inevitable happened.' said the Doctor with a shrug, 'Rowena became pregnant by young Jack Mole of course. There was never anyone else in her life. Her father was furious. He could see his source of income disappearing overnight. He couldn't touch the capital left in trust to Rowena by her Grandmother, but she was allowed the interest it earned. That money kept the family solvent. Despite his "War Hero" tag Seb Mole couldn't hang onto a job for long. Quite apart from his violent nature he was an idle slob and frequently drunk.'

Decker would have preferred a shorter version of events but concealed his impatience behind a bland expression as the Doctor continued his story.

'Young Jack wanted to do the honourable thing and marry Rowena. It never occurred to him that they couldn't. He's always been a responsible, level-headed lad. By this time the two families were living apart. Jack had used his share of the legacy to buy a small house of his own.'

The Doctor's head shook in reflection as he contemplated what life had been like back in the early nineteen-sixties. 'Two thousand pounds! It doesn't sound very much today does it? But then it was a small fortune. In a rural area like Briseley T'ill you could buy a decent little house for around a thousand. Seb Mole managed to get a council house. God knows how, but his name must have carried a bit of weight.

'To give young Jack his due he didn't shirk the issue. He went straight round to see Seb Mole and told him outright. My God! That was a mistake. The man went berserk. He lashed out at young Jack with the first thing that came to hand. It happened to be a batten of wood. Jack tried to fend off the blow with his arm. Parried it partially but it still gashed open his skull and knocked him sprawling. Rowena leapt in to defend him. That didn't stop Seb Mole. He punched her to the ground as well then set about kicking the pair of them. Most of his rage was vented against Rowena. It was sickening. Deliberate. He was out to destroy the baby. Time after time his boots thudded into her body. Every vile kick was deliberately aimed at her stomach. My God! How I loathed that man.'

Ted Decker had never seen the Doctor so upset. The memories he had conjured up were twenty-three years old, yet they still had the power and intensity to make him tremble with suppressed fury. With a great effort of will the Doctor shook away his anger. One hand pushed his spectacles up onto his forehead as he massaged his eyes and temples with slim, bony fingers. He shook his head in apology.

'I'm sorry, I'm sorry, I shouldn't let it affect me, but that man, that evil man...' His body heaved one long deep sigh then he was back in control of his emotions and continued in a carefully restrained voice. 'When the baby, a girl, was born there were complications. Poor little mite. Perhaps it would have been better if she had died there and then. But no! We have to play God don't we? Preserving life is a doctor's duty. It is a very noble sentiment... *in theory*. In practice it can impose a crushing burden, particularly upon young unsuspecting parents.'

'What was the matter?' Despite himself Decker had to ask the question. He was being drawn into the story, could feel a futile rage building up inside against a man he had never known, never met, and would never meet.

'The child was brain damaged, very badly and she had spinal problems. To tell the truth I did not expect her to live for more than a few hours...but she did...and still does...if you can call it living! For twenty-three years she has survived against all the odds. She can't see properly, can't speak at all, probably doesn't hear properly and has no real control of her limbs. She will *never* be able to walk. She just lies helpless and yet somewhere, somehow, there is a spark of intelligence locked away in that pathetic broken body. The only person to have made any sort of contact was Daisy Kutter. It was as though there was a form of telepathy between them. I can't pretend to know how it works but it does. I watched them together many times and in an inexplicable way the child could sense Daisy's presence, became more animated, more alive.' The Doctor tried very hard to express with his hands a sensation he was unable to put into words.

'Daisy was a brilliant nurse. She was more than just intelligent. One can possess every qualification in the book but still lack that extra something, that caring quality, that understanding, that compassion for people.'

Decker realised that he finally had the answer to the question which had puzzled him for years, the enigma of the Mole's deprived lifestyle when, with three adults bringing in a respectable wage, they lived in such abject poverty. The cost of keeping their daughter at Marston Grange must have been a crippling burden. Then later, when Rowena's illness had taken hold, the increasing strain would have proved intolerable.

Could it be that the motive for Daisy Kutter's murder went back further than he had ever imagined, and if not the motive itself, then the seeds of her destruction...?

'What happened to Seb Mole?' Decker asked suddenly. The man could not have been all that old when, as a young policeman, he had first arrived in Briseley T'ill. Yet he had never met him.

'He died,' replied the Doctor, adding with macabre humour, 'In fitting circumstances. Just about as squalidly as he had lived.'

'Would you care to tell me how?' asked the policeman.

'Certainly. I don't see how it's going to help you, but if you want to know, so be it. There's a public house on the Kirk Loscoe road, "The Navigator". Do you know it?'

'Yes. It's quite a pleasant place.'

'Well it is now. It used to be a dump with a terrible reputation. In those days it was run by a peculiar old couple, they didn't care two hoots for the place or the kind of clientele they served. The Navigator used to stand on the banks of a canal. The canal passed under an old stone humpback bridge. I suppose that years ago it was a thriving business when the river barges passed that way. It was a good stopping place. Over the years the canal fell into disuse. Parts of it were filled in, other parts just left to become stagnant and the usual thing happened; people began to use it as a dumping ground. All manner of rubbish rotted in the stagnant water. It became foul. I protested about it to the local health authority as well as the parish council. Pointed out what a danger to health it was becoming, which it was, but very little was done.

'As I've said, the pub was badly rundown, a disgrace. It did not even have proper toilets, just some quite disgusting chemical loos at the bottom of the garden. If you have ever smelt a chemical toilet then you'll know what I mean.'

The Doctor's face wrinkled in disgust at the pungent memory.

'There wasn't even an outside light so you can imagine what it was like on a dark wet winter's night. Rather than venture into the darkness customers used to nip under the old bridge and urinate into the canal.'

'Ugh!' Decker's face expressed revulsion, 'All of them?' he asked.

Amused, the Doctor removed his spectacles and leaned back into his leather-bound chair. 'Enough of them, you didn't see any members of the fair sex there. No self-respecting woman would go within a mile of the place. It was a pub for villains. Frequented by every deadbeat drunken dropout in the neighbourhood. That's why Seb Mole went there. It was the only place he could go. All the decent landlords had barred him long ago, what with his violent temper, his rows and his never-ending brawls. The Navigator was the one place left that would serve him a drink. God knows why the place stayed open... or how? No one ever seemed to pay, it was all on the slate.

'Your predecessor, George Turnbull, was frequently called out. The pub was the bane of his life. The only good thing about The Navigator, George would say, was that it kept all the local villains under one roof.'

'How does this relate to Seb Mole?' interrupted Decker, who was finding the Doctor's long-winded revelations beginning to pall.

'That's where he died.' came the reply, the tone of his voice implying that the policeman was slow to grasp the meaning of his words, 'He drowned. Fell into the canal while in a drunken stupor and drowned in the muck and slime he helped to create. The general opinion was that he was so drunk and incapable that he hadn't the wit to drag himself out again. It seems that his feet became entangled in the springs of an old bed frame. He couldn't keep his balance and fell face down into the water. Well, that's the theory. I had my doubts but...' the Doctor shrugged expressively, 'neither George Turnbull nor anyone else was going to probe too deeply. We were all of the same opinion. Good riddance to bad rubbish!'

An intercom on the Doctor's desk crackled into life. There was the sound of a throat being cleared followed by the slightly exasperated voice of the receptionist announcing that the next patient was *still* waiting for her appointment.

'Excuse me.' The Doctor's gesture managed to convey an apology while at the same time conducting Decker towards the door, 'If I can be of further help...?'

As the policeman edged his way out of the surgery he was brushed aside by the entry of a short stout woman who bristled with impatience.

Partly because he was dazzled by the bright sunlight and partly because he was deep in thought, his mind still locked in contemplation, Decker completely failed to notice the trim figure of Helen Argosy standing in his path. She passed one hand slowly before his face.

'My God!' she cried out in mock dismay, 'Have you gone blind, or have I become invisible?' The top of her head was just below the level of his chin. He looked over and beyond her diminutive figure.

'That's funny, I could swear I heard voices.' Ted replied, peering into space. There was music in her laughter, a symphony of happiness. She punched his arm in a light friendly gesture.

'Ted Decker, you're a silly sod.'

'Madam!' he feigned an officious manner, 'Do you realise that striking an officer of the law is an offence? I shall be forced to take you into custody.'

'Yes please.' Helen held out her hands with a giggle, 'Put the 'cuffs on officer.' Impulsively he put a strong arm around her slender young shoulders, turned alongside and pulled her body close to his own. 'That won't be necessary ma'am, but if you will accompany me to the station.' They walked in quiet harmony, matching footsteps as though they had spent a lifetime together.

'I saw you coming out of the Doctor's,' Helen said seriously, 'You *are* alright?'

'Fine. It was business, the investigation. I needed to crosscheck a few facts.'

'The investigation! Oh yes, I almost forgot. Seeing you out of uniform I thought you were off duty.' Her voice dropped a level, and he, quick to sense her disappointment, apologised, asking,

'Why, did you have something in mind?'

He'd always regarded her as a very self-confident person, so poised and sure of herself until she asked rather nervously.

'I thought... that is... if you were free... erm... you might... that is, would you like to come to dinner tonight?'

He was almost on the point of refusing. How could he when he sensed the effort her invitation had cost? He looked into her anxious grey eyes and nodded slowly.

'Yes. I'd love to come.'

'You would!' hurriedly, then realising she may have sounded too eager Helen continued calmly, 'What time? Does seven-thirty suit you?'

'Mmm! That should be fine, always providing that nothing drastic crops up... like our friend, Inspector Moxon.'

'Oh him!' she replied disdainfully, 'I don't like that man and I never will.'

'Fortunately you don't have to.' Decker replied wryly, 'But until half past seven I still have a job to do.' Reluctantly he disengaged the arm she had linked through his and stood back. 'Until later...?'

'Until later then.' and then she added as though to be absolutely sure, 'Will you let me know if... should... anything else crop up?'

'I will.' He reassured her.

She looked at her Swatch, which had a dark face and the faintest shadow of a hand, 'Heavens!' she exclaimed, 'It's time I collected Jason.' Helen quickly pressed two fingers to her lips, lightly touched them against his mouth, turned and briskly headed towards the village school. He watched her trim figure until she turned into the schoolyard and was lost to sight.

*

His enquiries took him in the opposite direction, to Marston Grange. Meeting Helen Argosy lifted his spirits. He was amazed at his good fortune and found it hard to believe that a woman, so young and good-looking could be attracted to him. It made him nervous. Underneath his air of solid dependability Edward Decker was a shy man. Vices he may have, but vanity had never been one of them. He failed to appreciate that his quiet diffident manner was attractive to a certain type of woman.

*

Barnett was ravenous. His stomach made strange noises like a tortured soul lost forever in a dark echoing cavern. It was close to forty-eight hours since last he'd eaten anything, yet Barnett trudged reluctantly in a homeward direction.

A vision of food arose before him - of Sunday lunch. Of his father poised, knife in hand, over a large joint of roast beef, of the rasping sound of blade on steel as he honed the carving knife. He pictured the thick slices of succulent meat falling before the keen blade as Barnett senior expertly carved. The beef oozing mouth-watering juices and a hot enticing smell lay upon his dinner plate surrounded by crisp brown potatoes, small green peas, tender baby carrots and slender young parsnips topped by a lake of rich brown gravy was cooked to perfection as only his mother knew how.

To Barnett it was a gourmet's dream

Then he remembered he was twenty-four hours too late. His depression deepened. His mother was certain to be upset and when roused her tongue had the sting of an angry wasp. *Oh God!* Barnet groaned under his breath as he resigned himself to a torrid fate.

He could not have been further from the truth.

Jean Hall had first been annoyed, then downright angry, then anxious, then worried sick and finally relieved when she heard that her one and only son was safe, sound in wind and limb, and on his way home.

She resolved to welcome him like the prodigal son. Better! The prodigal son would have felt rejected by comparison with the warmth of her embrace. A piping hot casserole waited in the oven. The table was set, ready and waiting. Barnett's father had been bustled off to work and his grandfather, Old Barnett, had been despatched to his allotment. The stage was set.

Jean Hall would ensure that her son was pampered, cosseted and well fed. She wouldn't allow a single angry word to pass her lips. Her warmth and sympathy would overwhelm him, then she would wheedle out the truth far more effectively than any confrontation.

Given the opportunity, in another time and place, Jean Hall would have made an excellent psychologist.

Wicket Maiden

Wicket Maiden: Once more the batsman fails to score but the bowler succeeds

Edward Decker approached Marston Grange with trepidation in his heart. He could simply check and confirm that John Benedict Mole had been there on the evening of his wife's death. Always assuming that the matron or a member of her staff recalled the visit, the exact date and the time. If he was really lucky there might also be a record, a visitor's book, or was that too much to hope for? The human memory is notoriously inaccurate Decker had discovered on more than one occasion. He needed to be absolutely certain of the date and time.

But was it necessary for him to see the daughter? He knew he would ask permission for despite himself he had to satisfy his curiosity. He had to see for himself the offspring that John and Rowena Mole had kept hidden away for more than twenty years. What would she be like...?

How is it possible, he asked himself, *to know a man and his wife for over twenty years... two decades, and yet be unaware that they had a daughter?*

He knew the man, knew his wife and his two sons, Lenny and Norman. Countless times he had met them, talked, drank, played sport with the family and enjoyed convivial evenings, yet not once had he suspected, not once had there been a hint of the skeleton in the Mole's family cupboard.

*

Marston Grange was screened from the road by trees. Its presence was nowhere near as impressive as its name implied having started life as a plain three-storey Victorian house to which had been added an assortment of annexes and extensions as and when the need arose and funds permitted. There was a large area of land at the rear of the house surrounded by a wall three metres high in crumbling red brickwork. An atmosphere of decay hung like an acrid mist surrounding the building.

Decker pressed firmly on the doorbell and waited patiently for a spirit to appear. He seemed to be waiting for hours though in reality it was less than a minute. A thin ghoul of a woman with lank unwashed hair and a vague harassed face let him in. She clutched a crumpled sheet to her body having been interrupted in the middle of changing a bed. The sheet had a yellowish tinge and smelt of urine.

'I'll fetch Matron.' replied the ghoul in answer to his request to see the person in charge. She hurried away leaving Decker alone in the gloomy reception hall. He tried not to breathe deeply, loathing the all-pervading odour, a mixture of unwashed bodies and disinfectant, accentuated by the suffocating heat.

'I'm sorry about the temperature.' A soft gentle voice apologised, 'It's necessary for our patients. They are all bedridden. They need the warmth.'

The voice was at odds with its owner.

Decker was completely taken aback by the woman facing him. She was huge, at least two metres tall with broad shoulders and strong capable hands. He guessed her age as being around sixty, but still fit and active despite her grey hair and the tired lines around her clear blue eyes.

'I'm Mrs Janna, the Matron.' Her gentle voice offered the information, 'What can I do to help?'

'Police.' he replied briefly, handing his warrant card to be examined, 'I'm investigating the death of Nurse Daisy Kutter.'

'Nurse Kutter. Ah yes, how terrible. I don't quite understand how *I* can help.' Her English was impeccable but Decker, who always listened to voices carefully, caught the faintest hint of an accent. *Dutch... or German perhaps?* Just a suggestion came through.

'One never knows,' explained the policeman, 'I have to check on every possibility. Perhaps we could speak in private...?'

'Of course,' she nodded her acquiescence and lead the way to her office. Once seated she regarded him pensively and asked the obvious question, 'Surely you can't suspect anyone here?'

'No! No!' replied Decker with a vigorous shake of the head, 'Nothing of the sort. It's simply a question of confirming the whereabouts of certain people at a particular time. Merely a question of elimination you understand.'

She smiled in understanding. It was a faint shy smile and he had an overwhelming feeling of a small self-conscious girl fighting to escape from an ungainly body. He warmed to her instantly, quickly appreciating that her voice rather than her physique was the clue to her real nature.

Experience had taught Edward Decker to leave vital questions until later. It was far more effective to insert one into the middle of a seemingly casual conversation than to ask it outright. For reasons best known to themselves even the most reliable, honest and straightforward of people failed at times to answer truthfully.

'Forgive me for asking but do I detect a slight accent?' asked Decker putting on a disarming smile and trying to sound casual.

'That's very sharp of you. Very few people notice my accent so quickly. I've been in England for many years so I tend to forget.'

'It isn't that noticeable,' he hastened to assure her, 'Is it Dutch or...?'

'German.' Mrs Janna replied quickly, 'I come from Dusseldorf, on the Rhine.'

'I know the place.' replied the policeman enthusiastically, 'I was there as a young man...' then added reflectively, '...a *very* young man. I was only eighteen, doing my National Service. If I remember correctly it was a beautiful city. I loved it there but unfortunately there was a rule, no fraternisation. We weren't allowed to talk to the German people with the exception of those who worked for the military. I got on well with the few I came into contact with but it was very frustrating for a healthy young man not being able to meet any girls.' He looked at her sheepishly, 'Forbidden fruits, you know, it made them all the more inviting!'

His words obviously struck a chord in her memory for she smiled sadly and there was mistiness in her clear blue eyes. Wistfully she replied, 'I think I know what you mean. But... er... aren't we wandering off the point?'

Decker's ploy to disarm her hadn't worked as planned. He spoke briskly, asking, 'About Nurse Kutter, I wonder, can you recall the last time you saw her? I believe she came to Marston Grange on a regular basis.'

Mrs Janna nodded in the affirmative. 'Yes, they came twice a week, on Monday and Thursday evenings. She usually arrived in the early part of the evening, about seven o'clock and always with Mr Mole. They had a special arrangement for her to treat his daughter.'

'Treat?' Decker's puzzled face sought clarification.

'Elizabeth, Mr Mole's daughter requires regular physiotherapy,' the Matron explained, 'It is never going to cure her you understand, but it helps to prevent her muscles from atrophying, poor child.' The massive head shook in sympathy. 'John Mole, that man is a saint. He has never given up hoping, not once in twenty-three years has he ceased to pray and work for a miracle. It's not to be, I fear, but he won't give up.'

'Doesn't Marston Grange have its own physiotherapist?' asked Decker.

'Good Heavens no! I wish to God we had but our funds just do not run to such a luxury. Someone permanent like Daisy Kutter would have been a Godsend to the home. Physiotherapy treatment is expensive. She was very well qualified you know, quite apart from being a State Enrolled Nurse she held a degree in physiotherapy and she also specialised in neurological problems as well as orthopaedics, not to mention her treatment of sports injuries. Oh yes! We did not *always* see eye to eye, Nurse Kutter and myself, but I have to admit she was superb at her job.'

Edward Decker nodded sagely at the Matron's glowing tribute as though he understood every word. He had seen the letters after Daisy Kutter's name on the neat brass plate screwed to the brickwork of her cottage. The significance of the letters: SEN, MCSP, SRP, Grad Dip Phys, escaped him, but that remained his secret.

'In fact,' continued the Matron who welcomed the opportunity to unload her problems upon a responsive ear, '...we have a very tight budget to work to. I'm the only qualified person who is employed full-time at Marston Grange. The rest of the staff are willing helpers and in their way, concerned for our patients, but...' her hands fluttered in the air signalling a meaning she tactfully avoided putting into words, '...shall we say, less than one desires!'

Putting it bluntly, thought Decker, *it's a thankless, depressing job that few would want.* He personally wondered how anyone could stand it for longer than five minutes. All the more credit then to the Matron and her loyalty to her inadequate staff, such devotion was rare.

'So the last time you saw Nurse Kutter would have been the Thursday before Easter?' prompted the policeman.

Mrs Janna evaded the trap. She was positive in her reply.

'No!' she said sharply, 'Mr Mole came alone on that occasion. But she did telephone. She rang soon after eight o'clock to break the bad news of his wife's sudden death.'

'Did he rush back home?' suggested Decker, assuming that would be a normal reaction to such devastating news.

'Oh no!' replied the Matron, 'He wanted to go but Nurse Kutter wisely suggested that he stay with Elizabeth to avoid distressing her, and in any event it would allow time for the Doctor to call and certify the death, as well as enable Daisy to compose Rowena Mole's body. That way she thought it would be less upsetting for John Mole when he returned to his home.'

'Mmm!' mused the policeman, tucking his chin into his chest as he wondered where to go next. The problem was quickly solved.

'Shall we go and see Elizabeth?' invited Mrs Janna, rising from her chair, 'I'll introduce you to her, I think she'll take to you.'

'But... I thought... isn't she severely handicapped?' The apprehension showed in his voice as he recalled the Doctor's description of Elizabeth Mole's disabilities.

'So she is,' answered the Matron, disapproval in her voice, 'but she is still a human being. Come and judge for yourself.'

Decker expected to be shown into a sparsely furnished hospitalised room, one reeking of disinfectant-laden air and uncomfortably over-heated. Instead Mrs Janna lead the way to the rear of the building, passing through a large airy conservatory and out into the garden. Most of the area was turf with a scattering of well-stocked flowerbeds. Tall mature trees cast their mottled shade across the neatly mown grass. It looked a pleasant restful place, a peaceful haven from the world.

'Elizabeth loves fresh air. The garden is her favourite place.' chirped the Matron.

An image, preconceived, had formed in Decker's mind. One of a stunted deformed body huddled grotesquely into an iron-framed cot with high restricting sides; a picture of wildly staring eyes and a loose slavering mouth.

He was totally unprepared for Elizabeth.

Mrs Janna lead him down the gently sloping grounds to where an alloy-framed sun-lounger was positioned between two flower beds in the shade of a mature flowering cherry tree.

'Constable Decker, meet Elizabeth Mole.' Introduced the Matron.

She was beautiful. A young woman, who in other circumstances, would have shattered the hearts of a myriad of young men. A halo of golden hair cascaded over her shoulders to fall halfway to her waist creating an illusion, like sunlight falling upon a mountain waterfall. Her skin was crystal clear and healthy, tanned to a light golden brown by the fresh air and sunshine. The faintest bloom of peach-like down covered her smooth rounded cheeks. Hazel eyes, with a mixture of blue, green and brown in their iris, looked out over classically high cheekbones and a slender aquiline nose. Someone had touched her mouth with a delicate shade of pink lipstick. Carefully outlining the perfectly shaped contours of her lips. She was dressed in a pale turquoise short-sleeved blouse and white shorts that revealed slender but shapely limbs.

'Not quite what you expected... is she?'

There was piquant humour in the gently spoken question. Mrs Janna took Elizabeth's right hand and pressed its palm against her mouth.

'Elizabeth, I've brought someone to see you.'

'I was told that she's deaf.' Decker remarked with a puzzled shake of his head.

'All sound is vibration,' explained the Matron, 'It's a method Nurse Kutter tried out. It seems to work. We know that Elizabeth can't hear much normally, if at all. But she can sense vibrations and the movement of your lips. Here, you have a try.'

She pressed the young woman's hand into Decker's own and guided it towards his mouth.

'Hello Elizabeth.' he mumbled awkwardly, hardly expecting a response. To his surprise and dismay he felt his hand gripped by slender fingers and tugged towards her face. Her lips fluttered against the palm of his hand and he realised that she was sniffing vigorously with all the curiosity of a young puppy.

'There. I knew she would like you.' said the Matron, satisfaction in her voice, 'She knows that you are different... a man. She always responds more to a man's touch than to any of ours.'

'How does she know?'

'The same way any woman knows,' explained Mrs Janna, 'by instinct. Surely *you* can tell the difference between the touch of a man and that of a woman?'

'Of course, but...?' He remembered his recent parting from Helen Argosy, the feather touch of her fingers against his lips. The tingle of excitement that passed through his body as though an electric current was being transmitted. The soft warm pressure of her arm linked with his own. Of course he knew.

'Just because she's handicapped doesn't stop her from being a woman,' explained Mrs Janna, 'She has the same feelings, the same needs, the same emotions as any other young female. She's alive. ALIVE! A human being who needs love, affection, warmth, all the feelings that a normal attractive girl craves...' Her gentle voice was impassioned in its plea. Elizabeth Mole engendered strong emotions.

In her father, in the Doctor, in the gentle phlegmatic Matron and now, Decker had to admit, in himself.

Elizabeth held the back of Decker's hand against her cheek and rubbed her soft downy flesh against his skin. The movement was feline, animal and sensuous, demanding both his attention and affection. He felt himself becoming uncomfortably warm despite the gentle afternoon breeze. A turmoil of emotions gripped him and wrenched at his heart. Tenderness and pity were mingled with anger and affection... and finally frustration because he knew there was so very little that he could do to help. His face cast a desperate plea for assistance towards the Matron.

She rescued him, gently loosening the slender fingers from his hand, all the while smoothing and caressing the girl's hair and face to reassure her as she murmured, 'There there Elizabeth, there, there.'

As soon as her patient was calm Mrs Janna signalled to the policeman that they should leave. Unlike many tall people who stoop in a vain endeavour to disguise their height, the Matron walked erect with her head held proudly high. Even though he was sturdily built Decker felt dwarfed and insignificant by comparison. She walked back towards the house with a strong regimented stride, military in her bearing. Then, suddenly aware she was being observed, Mrs Janna made a conscious effort to walk in a relaxed feminine style.

The incident triggered off a chain of thought in Decker's mind that later he regarded as ludicrous. On her own admission Mrs Janna failed to see eye to eye with Daisy Kutter. She was a big strong woman, used to handling inert flaccid bodies, with her training as a nurse and detailed knowledge of the human body she would know precisely the spot to strike a fatal blow.

Why had he assumed that the killer was a man?

If his estimate of her age was correct she would have been born around 1924. That would make her fifteen, or sixteen, just prior to World War Two. Born in Germany with blue eyes, fair hair, Teutonic looks, a proud member of the Master Race.

Wasn't it Adolph Hitler who had claimed, *Give me a child until the age of five... and their minds are mine for life. No!* Decker mentally shook away the invasive thought. It was too ridiculous for words. He glanced at his wristwatch and was surprised to see that the time was nearly five o'clock.

'Could I use your telephone?' he asked the Matron.

'But of course you may. Use the one in my office if it's private...? Her question hung in the air, a speculative look upon her face.

'No. No. It's quite alright, I just want to warn my sister that I won't be home for a meal.'

'That's a relief,' sighed the Matron, adding with sly humour, 'I thought for a minute you might be sending for a Black Maria.'

*

Beatrice answered the telephone with astonishing alacrity. She must have been poised, just waiting for it to ring, thought Decker. To his surprise she was not at all upset when he informed her that he wouldn't be requiring an evening meal and that he would be home late. *Very late,* he emphasised.

'It's alright, I've seen the news.' Beatrice answered in her superior voice.

'News? What news?'

'On the tele. It's all over the place. Trouble in the coalfields caused by the striking miners. Like a battlefield.' she informed him with excitement rising in her voice, 'They're calling in reinforcements from other areas. It's chaotic... absolutely chaotic!' Then added anxiously, ' You will take care won't you?'

'Yea! I'm alright.' He reassured his sister, wondering what all the fuss was about, 'Have you heard from Inspector Moxon? Has he rung? Are there any messages? No! You sure? Right then, bye.' And he hung up.

Decker looked at the Matron and gave an expressive shrug, 'Sisters! Sorry about that. She's such a fusspot.'

'That's alright.' The wistful note was back in her voice, 'It must be nice having someone who cares.' From such a large and powerful looking woman the sentiment sounded incongruous. Decker suspected there was a yearning emptiness in Mrs Janna's life. It was one of those quirks of nature. Whereas the tiniest of women would be attracted to a giant of a man, it seldom, if ever, worked in reverse. Quite probably, thought the constable, Mrs Janna enjoyed his questions. Enjoyed someone, a man, taking a personal interest in her life. He resumed his questioning.

'You mentioned earlier that on occasions Nurse Kutter and yourself failed to see eye to eye. What would that be about?'

The Matron crossed to the window that looked out over the sunlit rear garden, a vantage point from which she was able to keep watch over her charges. After a few moments of careful consideration she replied in her quiet gentle voice.

'Nurse Kutter had quite radical ideas about the rights of handicapped patients. She argued that they should be allowed to live as normal a life as possible. That they should experience every aspect, as far as it was possible, that they should be able to express their emotions, form attachments, touch one another, explore their feelings, like sorrow, and anger... and love. She argued that there is so much emotion and frustration within them, bottled up, and that there should be an outlet.

Mrs Janna turned from the window and looked earnestly into his face.

'I care about our patients Mr Decker. I love them and care for them to the best of my ability but Daisy Kutter said that it was not enough. That they should be allowed to experience everything... even sexual love.'

It was a devastating recommendation.

'And you disagreed.' suggested the policeman.

'Naturally! It's irresponsible, totally irresponsible. One only has to think of the consequences.' She beckoned him towards the window. It provided an excellent view of the garden and all the patients enjoying the afternoon sunshine were clearly visible. Pointing at Elizabeth Mole she continued, 'What do you imagine the consequences would be to someone like Elizabeth? How could one gauge her reaction? How could one know for certain that she would not be terrified or traumatised by a physical action that she is unable to understand? How on earth could anyone explain its meaning? How?' she asked the policeman.

Unable to provide an answer Decker simply shook his head in sympathy.

'Just suppose for one minute that a patient like Elizabeth became pregnant... it is possible you know, she is capable of bearing a child. Her condition is not genetic, it's the result of physical abuse, not hereditary. Would she know what was happening to her body? How could one explain to her? What would become of the baby? How could she ever learn to care for the poor little mite?'

'Do you suppose Nurse Kutter ever discussed her ideas with John Mole?' he asked. Clearly the possibility had never occurred to Mrs Janna for her voice lost its gentle tones and became vociferous as she exclaimed.

'I hope to God not! John Mole would have gone berserk. He dotes on that girl. His life has been spent shielding and protecting her from the real world. He's built a safe haven for her, here. This place is her refuge. He keeps her safe and protected at Marston Grange and not another soul is allowed near her. No-one!'

'No one?' asked Decker in astonishment, 'No one else at all? Not even her family? Her brothers?'

Mrs Janna was emphatic. 'Not a single person. He is quite adamant about it. From the day Rowena Mole became too sick to see her daughter there has never been another visitor. In fact I doubt whether John Mole's sons have even been told that they have a sister. I don't think they have any knowledge of her whatsoever.'

'But... but... why? What *is* the point?'

'I wish I knew. At first I thought he was so ashamed of the girl that he didn't want the outside world to know. But I was wrong. He loves her deeply, so much so that it has become an obsession. He knows that her whole life is totally dependant upon him. Inexplicably, that fulfils him.'

'My God!' Decker did not normally blaspheme, in fact he rarely swore at all. He suddenly realised that friends he had known for decades were complete strangers. It also occurred to him that he had discovered a motive. A motive so powerful it could tip the balance of a man's sanity.

John Mole would have been crushed by the news of his wife's sudden death. If, at that inopportune moment, he was mistakenly lead to believe that his daughter had been violated as well, then the shock could have driven him beyond the bounds of reason. He would have cracked.

*

Decker thanked the Matron for her time and made his farewells. As he strode purposefully back towards the police station his brain buzzed with possibilities. One theory concerned Mrs Janna. It was an unlikely theory, but possible. Her formative years had been spent in Nazi Germany at a time when the concept of breeding a master race was prevalent.

Ideals learned as a child, even misconceived ideals, remained in the memory forever. There had been a policy of exterminating the mentally sick and handicapped. It was not fantasy but a fact. It had happened. The very idea of interbreeding with a handicapped person would have been abhorrent to a woman raised under those evil and discredited ideals.

Could it be that Mrs Janna's dedication and devotion to her wards was in reality an act of atonement? Decker had no doubt that she was genuine, a caring person. But could she, prompted by a subconscious belief, inadvertently have made a suggestion to John Mole that had triggered off a violent reaction? It was possible.

The timing was right. He could have arrived back home after nine o'clock, after the Doctor had left and Daisy Kutter was alone with the body of his wife, Rowena. He was a local man with local knowledge. He knew about the Sinkhole and as chairman of the Briseley T'ill Cricket Club his presence at the ground would not arouse suspicion. It would pass unnoticed or be accepted as perfectly normal. John Mole was slighter shorter than his sons but easily tall enough to reach the key hidden under the eaves of the pavilion. He would have known where to find the edging spade that Decker believed had been used to dig the makeshift grave in the Sinkhole.

Motive and opportunity… John Mole had both.

So why am I unconvinced? Decker asked himself.

A sudden gust of wind ruffled his hair. Decker looked at the sky with a countryman's eye. There were dark clouds gathering in the Southwest over the distant Pennines. The breeze was stronger. Unless he was mistaken a storm was brewing. There would be rain before morning. It was long overdue, but coming.

Too late for the Killer!

His watch showed 6:30pm. There was just time for a shower, a shave and a change of clothing. And time for pleasant anticipation as the charming company of Helen Argosy beckoned him.

He pushed all thoughts of murder from his mind.

*

At the Royal Infirmary the Sister burst into room 3B and tossed a copy of the Evening News onto her patient's bed.

'That young man who came to see you,' she said without preamble, 'the one with the red hair. What was his name?'

Cynthia Ashley-Jayle, propped up by three pillows, was listlessly leafing over the pages of a woman's magazine. The last three days had been interminable. Her only relief from boredom being the attention of the buxom Sister, regular checks by the small black nurse and twice daily visits by the doctors; a morning examination by the Irish one, Doctor Sheehan and a later visit by the funny little Ugandan with the bandy legs. The prospect of a visitor cheered her immensely.

'You mean Barnett, Barnett Hall. Is he here?'

'Barnett. So that's his name. No, I'm afraid he isn't.' There was a warning note in the Sister's voice that Cynthia failed to heed.

'Huh! Trust him. I expect he's completely forgotten me.' grumbled the girl, 'He hasn't been for three whole days.'

'Perhaps you should look at the paper.' suggested the Sister, a finger pointing accusingly at the front page, 'I think you'll find that he is otherwise engaged.' Cynthia Ashley-Jayle stared at the Sister, a puzzled look in her dark violet blue eyes.

'Engaged? What do you mean...?' Casually her gaze flicked towards the newssheet, caught sight of the headlines... and stared, transfixed.

'**DISTRICT NURSE MURDERED.**' read the caption, then, in slightly smaller print, '**LOCAL MAN HELD FOR QUESTIONING.**' There was a picture of Daisy Kutter, fresh faced and smiling, taken some years previously, also a smaller, fuzzier print of Barnett in an open-necked sports shirt. It looked as though it had been lifted from a group photograph.

Horrified, Cynthia studied the article. The information was brief but significant. She read, '*Police investigating the murder of District Nurse, Daisy Kutter, aged 33, whose body was discovered at the Briseley T'ill cricket ground on Saturday evening, intercepted an anonymous telephone call which provided vital information. A local man, Mr Barnett Hall, aged 19, is being held for questioning at the Briseley T'ill police station.*'

The article went on to give general background knowledge of the nurse. It was clear that at this stage of their enquiries the police were revealing very little and the reporter had needed to pad out his story with every scrap of detail he could find.

The blood drained from Cynthia's face. Her vindictive call had landed Barnett in serious trouble. Quite possibly herself as well if they were to discover that she was the one who had perpetrated the threat. Frantically she sought to recall her exact words. To the police it would so easily have sounded like a blackmail attempt.

'Do you realise that *I* allowed that man in to see you... Twice!' The Sister's voice was fraught with anxiety, 'Alone! You were alone with him. Jee-sus! There's no telling what could have happened.'

'Don't be silly,' retorted Cynthia scornfully, 'Barnett wouldn't hurt a fly. He's harmless... a gentle person.'

'Gentle? Ha! How can you tell? He's got a temper that one. I've seen it. It matches his hair, red and fiery. Didn't he lose his temper right here, in this very room, and that was over nothing. Now if he was really provoked...?'

'He's not! He's not! I know he's not like that.' stormed Cynthia angrily. She was convinced. But *how* did she know? How? At a time in the past she knew Barnett had been intensely provoked... almost beyond reason... and by herself?

Yet he *had* restrained himself. There had been no real violence. She was certain of the fact. But how did she know? There was a dark curtain across her mind shutting out the light of knowledge. If only she could tear it down... and remember. If only...!

The Sister pointed an accusing finger at the newspaper headline.

'Then why have the police arrested him?' she asked with telling sarcasm in her voice, 'Do they normally arrest people without good reason? No. It says they had a tip-off, inside information. They know what they are doing.'

Desperation touched her mind. Tears of anguish filled her eyes. Barnett had tried so hard to befriend her and she had betrayed him. It was unforgivable.

'But they don't know the facts. They are wrong, wrong. The tip-off was a mistake, a mistake, it's all a dreadful, dreadful mistake...' Cynthia's voice tailed away in forlorn despair. Who was going to believe her now? She fell silent, suddenly looking much older, wretched in her guilty knowledge.

The Sister watched her quietly, a shocked expression slowly dawning on her normally cheerful face.

'I believe you know something,' she addressed her patient thoughtfully, 'I think you know who made that call. You do... don't you?'

The evidence was clearly written on Cynthia Ashley-Jayle's face.

'It was *you.*' accused the Sister, 'Mother of God! IT WAS YOU. In Heaven's name, why? Why?'

The violet blue eyes blinked rapidly, their lids tightly closed in a vain attempt to stem the flood of tears that coursed forlornly down her cheeks.

'It w-wasn't l-like that,' she sobbed, 'I d-didn't know that D-Daisy K-Kutter was dead. I th-thought it was h-her on the t-telephone. I was so angry with B-Barnett because he c-cared more about her th-than m-m-me. I wanted to warn her off.'

Cynthia lapsed into silent tears as waves of emotion shook her body. Pity flooded the Sister's heart. She still remembered the passion and intensity of her youth. Once, just once in her life, there had been a moment when her heart had ruled her head, when her common sense had failed her. She remembered it well. Remembered writing a vindictive letter to the fiancé of a young man with whom she had fallen in love. But, unlike Cynthia Ashley-Jayle, the Sister had stopped short in her act of folly. At the final fence her nerve broke. Try as she may she had been unable to push the sealed and stamped envelope into the letterbox.

'You know what you have to do now?' the Sister advised her patient, 'You *have* to put things right. You have to tell him... and the police.'

Sheer panic paralysed Cynthia's vocal chords. He head rolled from side to side in negation as every trace of colour drained from her cheeks.

'Best to do it now,' urged the Sister, 'before any more damage is done. The sooner the better it will be.' Matching action to her words she bustled out of the room, quickly returning with a local directory and a plug-in telephone. There was a jacking point close to Cynthia's cot and the Sister pushed in the square ended connection until its little plastic catch clicked into place. Thumbing energetically through the directory she rapidly located the number of the police station, murmuring to herself lest she forget, 'Police... police... police. Briseley T'ill. Here it is. It's Oh one, oh, one, oh. That's easy to remember. Right young lady, get on with it!'

She plonked the instrument on the side of the bed, its push buttons significantly facing towards Cynthia. A grim little nod of her head urged the girl against delay.

'I can't! I can't!' came the despairing cry, 'Please don't make me... Please.'

The Sister's patience snapped. She put her face close, invading the frightened girl's territory. In a voice that hissed with anger she told her coldly and distinctly.

'Miss Ashley-Jayle, you are a miserable, spoilt, little brat. You *are* going to make that call and I am going to make sure that you do.' She thrust the telephone receiver into the frightened girl's hand and stabbed at the buttons with a rigid finger.

*

At the Briseley T'ill police house the telephone rang. The only person there was Beatrice Layland. Her superior voice sounded official. The caller was unaware to whom she was speaking and assumed it was a policewoman. Beatrice strained to hear the distant voice that sounded as though it was speaking to someone else in the background. As her ear became attuned to the pitch she caught the words. '...can't, I can't, What shall I say?' Then a second voice, firmer, with a positive ring, speaking in the background said,

'Tell the truth. Just tell the truth. Start with your name.'

The first voice returned, still nervous, still hesitant but clearer.

'H-Hello. Hello. Th-th-this is Cynthia Ashley-Jayle sp-speaking. It's about th-the y-young man held for qu-questioning. You know, Barnett. Barnett Hall. Well! It's not him. Y-you're h-holding the wrong man.'

'We are?'

'Y-yes. He didn't do it. Y-you have to let him go. You must. P-p-please.'

'Calm down.' instructed Beatrice, positively enjoying her position of authority, 'There is nothing to worry about I assure you. Mr Barnett Hall has been released.'

'He has?'

'Most certainly, I do assure you. Mr Hall was released earlier today.'

'Oh... oh! Thank God!' The heartfelt relief surged in a wave over the telephone. It clicked and changed to a continuous purring sound.

Beatrice lowered her receiver and briefly wondered whether she had done the right thing. Should she have let on that Barnett was free? She gave a careless shrug. In any event it was too late now. She had also gleaned a piece of information that would make very interesting gossip.

*

'Was that as bad as you expected?' asked the Sister as her charge replaced the handset. A smiling Cynthia shook her head, 'He's free,' she explained, 'the police released him earlier today. It's wonderful, wonderful news and I didn't even have to mention that I made the anonymous call. No one need know that it was me, not ever.'

'Maybe… maybe not.' The Sister subdued her euphoria all too quickly, 'Some-one is certain to put two and two together. Just don't count your chickens too soon. How will it sound if your young man hears the truth from another person? How do you think he will react to that?'

'Oh no! I hadn't thought of that.' Bemoaned the girl, 'What can I do?'

'I think we can easily solve that problem,' said the Sister, 'up until now the onus has been on young Mr Barnett Hall to make the moves. Why don't *you* call *him*? Invite him to pay you a visit. I think I can arrange it so that you're not disturbed. And… erm… what about you buying him a little gift to say thank you. Something special…?'

Cynthia was instantly taken with the idea. It caught her imagination. Her condition had not improved since Barnett's last visit. From the waist down she was still paralysed. The hopes raised then had failed to materialise into a permanent improvement. It was as though the trauma and aftermath of her accident were inexplicably linked with the young man. Without knowing why she sensed that her recovery depended upon her relationship with him.

'Please help me. Please.' she asked the Sister

*

For almost an hour Jean Hall listened patiently to Barnett's rambling, stumbling explanation. She did not criticise or comment or interrupt the flow of words that poured in a torrent from his lips once the dam of his reserve had been breached. Every now and then she made soft encouraging sounds, little murmurs of sympathy and friendly nods of her head to signify agreement, even when, secretly, she disapproved.

Barnett kept to himself the more intimate details of his relationship with Daisy Kutter, nor did he reveal how his new association with Cynthia Ashley-Jayle had begun. Perhaps the details he left unsaid gave away far more than he appreciated. At least, thought his mother, he was showing a sense of responsibility towards the Ashley-Jayle girl. What did concern Jean Hall was his apparent lack of emotion over the murder of Daisy Kutter. It was as though a steel trap had closed and shut off that part of his mind forever, a defence mechanism to protect his sanity.

'Barnett.' Jean Hall addressed her son, ' I can't pretend to like what has happened. I'm deeply upset, but I want you to know that you have my support, and my love. I don't like the Ashley-Jayle's, I never have and I never will. But I do understand why you feel an obligation to the girl. In fact I'm proud that you do. It's a worthy sentiment

Barnett was both surprised and relieved at his mother's attitude. He had expected a dressing down and the unexpected sympathy caught him off balance. His mind was still in a whirl of confusion over the events of the last three days. Death was new to him. Immediate death, losing a friend as close as Daisy Kutter, was an experience he'd never before encountered. Added to that the fact that it had been the result of violence, undoubtedly murder, had left him in a distressed state of mind. His apparent lack of concern was because he was still trying to come to terms with his real feelings for the dead nurse.

Six months, Daisy Kutter had predicted. In six months time, Barnett, she had said, you will have forgotten me and moved on to new pastures. It's what happens when one is growing up. I just hope and pray that I remain a happy memory for you, a learning curve in your life that you will look back upon and remember with affection.

She was so wise... and practical, mused Barnett. It would have worked out the way she predicted except that she had been murdered and he could not imagine who could have done it... or why.

Now, he would never forget her.

*

There was a far-off ringing sound. The Hall's telephone rested upon a window ledge just inside the entrance hall of their semi-detached house. Jean Hall hurried to answer its demanding call. 'It's for you Barnett,' she called, 'from the hospital.'

Barnett's heart slipped into his boots. His first reaction was to fear the worst.

'Hello.' he said weakly, expecting to hear the Sister's voice, 'Hello, who is speaking?' At first the voice failed to register.

'Hello? Hello? Barnett it's me. Barnett, are you there?'

'Oh my gosh! It's ...it's...'

'It's me, Cynthia. Are you alright? Your voice, it does sound queer. That is you Barnett, isn't it?'

'Yes. Of course it is.'

'Oh! Thank God for that. Are you sure you're alright? You sound so odd.'

'No. I'm alright.' he lied, 'I'm fine. How about you?'

'About the same. Listen, forget about me for a moment. I read in the paper about Daisy Kutter…Oh God Barnett. I'm so sorry, so sorry about all those awful things I said about her. I didn't mean any of them. Honestly. I didn't mean a word. Please forgive me Barnett… Please.'

The distress in her voice was genuine. It cut deeply into his heart.

'It's OK… OK.'

'Oh! How I wish it were. How I wish I could call back all those terribly cruel words. How can I ever forgive myself? You will forgive me Barnett, please say that you will. Please… Please.'

Coping with a near hysterical woman was a new experience. Being an only child, one without sisters to torment him, left him ill prepared. Lost for soothing words to say he kept repeating, 'It's OK… Ok…' on a descending scale until his voice became inaudible. It must have worked for Cynthia gradually became calm and rational, asking, 'When will you come and see me again? I'd love to see you… and there's something I have to tell you, in person. I need to speak to you face to face.'

'You *want* to see me.' he said, amazed, 'You're asking *me* to call in and visit you.'

'Of course I want to see you.' Cynthia was flattered by his response. It restored her self-confidence. 'How soon can you come?'

Barnett was on the point of saying tomorrow, when his real world came crashing back. Tomorrow was Wednesday. He had already missed two whole days away from his job. Heaven only knew what his employer was thinking. He hadn't even telephoned the office to offer an explanation. There was the distinct possibility that he no longer had a job. In the light of recent events, facts reported in the newspapers, who could blame them? He gulped down his dismay and suggested tactfully.

'Friday… Friday evening. I'm certain to have a lot of work to catch up on. But Friday, definitely Friday, say about eight o'clock.'

'Fine, that will be fine.' Cynthia replied, fighting to keep disappointment out of her voice. Two clear days would give her time to choose a gift. 'Yes, Friday will be fine.' she finished brightly, 'Bye.'

'Bye.' Barnett managed to squeeze in quickly before the telephone cut off.

*

'I suppose *that* was the Ashley-Jayle woman.' Jean Hall's face registered disapproval. She preferred an end to their association; the opposite seemed likely.

'Why do you hate her?' Barnett asked bluntly.

'Hate? Did I say hate? Have I ever said I hated the girl?'

'You don't have to put it into words,' snapped Barnett, 'It's obvious, I can tell.' Then seeing the hurt expression on his mother's face his fiery temper quickly subsided. He was instantly sorry. How could he explain that words were unnecessary, that his mother's body language revealed her true feelings? Young Barnett knew he should apologise. Teenage pride and arrogance ruled.

'Anyway,' he continued, 'I'm going to see her again. I've promised, and nothing will stop me from going.'

Jean Hall sighed wearily, agreed, 'OK. I understand that, I wouldn't want it otherwise. But please, don't get in too deep again. That's what concerns me. She is so much older than you. You're still a boy... just a boy.'

Even as she spoke Jean Hall realised the futility of her words. Barnett towered over her; he was almost six feet tall, lithe, athletic and powerful, a flame-haired Adonis. When was the last time a nineteen-year-old accepted parental advice?

'Don't worry.' He assured her, 'I can handle it. Just wait and see.'

Can you my son? Her silent thoughts ran, *Can you?*

*

Edward Decker decided to drive down through the village to Helen Argosy's cottage in his little old Morris Minor. It was the only car he had ever possessed, the only car his meagre salary as a police constable could run to. Its dark green paintwork still had its showroom lustre. Decker washed it religiously every week and applied a wax polish two or three times a year. He seldom travelled far and after twenty years the vehicle's speedometer showed just over sixty thousand miles. Under its rounded bonnet the engine and its accessories were spotlessly clean. There wasn't a speck of rust in sight and the little car's chromium plated hubcaps and fenders were as bright and shiny as the day they were manufactured.

The green Morris Minor was Decker's pride and joy. What he failed to appreciate was that in its pristine condition the car had increased in value many times over. In fact, it was now a collector's item.

Before leaving the police station Decker showered, shaved and changed into a clean shirt. He checked with Beatrice to see if there were any messages and was both surprised and puzzled to learn that Inspector Moxon had not been in contact. When Beatrice mentioned the telephone call from Cynthia Ashley-Jayle he simply nodded, smiled to himself and refrained from discussing the matter with his sister.

Well, he thought, *that was one small mystery solved.* He hadn't attached much importance to the anonymous call in the first place. But Moxon, he had expected to hear from the porcine Inspector. That *was* strange. It was inexplicable.

Beatrice, who was perplexingly quiet, switched on the television to catch the latest news. It focussed on political problems and the continuing violence in the Midlands coalfields. Pictures flashed onto the screen showing hundreds of beleaguered police officers fighting to contain a surging mass of striking miners. Their numbers ran into thousands, supplemented by the flying pickets from the Yorkshire and collieries in the north-east of the country.

It was possible, Decker surmised, that Moxon had been called away to assist on matters more pressing. As he watched, the cameras concentrated upon an injured police officer being lead to safety, blood streaming from a head injury.

Decker thanked his lucky stars that he was not involved.

*

Arriving precisely one minute early, Decker made a neat 'U' turn and parked his car on the grass verge outside the semi-detached cottages that fringed the Briseley T'ill cricket ground. Helen Argosy must have been on the lookout for she appeared, on cue, at the front door as he arrived. Her son, Jason, peered at him shyly from behind her slender legs, excited and full of curiosity. Helen welcomed him with an affectionate hug and looking past him exclaimed rapturously, 'It's a Morris, a dear little Morris Minor. How lovely. How long have you had it?'

'Oh years! It must have been around seventy-three, or four when I bought her. Do you like it?'

'Like it? I love it. It's gorgeous.' She ran her hand over the shining paintwork, shook her head in disbelief at its superb condition. 'It's what I've always wanted, an original little Morris Minor. They are so reliable and easy to work on. And there's so much room around the engine. Say, can I look under the bonnet?'

Her enthusiasm was infectious. He laughed good-naturedly, lifted the bonnet and exposed the engine. Helen pulled her son close to the vehicle and pointed out its components, naming each one in turn. 'Look Jason, that's the engine, that bit's the rocker box and that is the sump. Those silver things with the black wires attached are the spark plugs and the black wires, called leads, go back to the distributor, and that lead goes to the coil. See!'

Jason stood round-eyed in wonder, soaking in the mysteries of the internal combustion engine. His piping six-year-old voice exclaimed.

'Cor! Brill! Can we go for a wide Mummy? Can we?'

'Ride darling… Rr… Rr… ride. Say RIDE.' His mother automatically corrected the boy's speech impediment. Her eyes sought Decker's face in silent enquiry. He smiled good-naturedly.

Upstaged by an old car, he thought and teasingly replied, 'So it's my car you're really after and I believed it was my fatal charm.' Decker switched his attention to the boy, 'Alright young Jason, I'll take you for a drive. We'll all go for a drive, that's a promise. But it will have to wait. At this moment I think your Mummy has other plans. Am I right?'

'Absolutely. Come on Jason, I promised Mr Decker dinner, and dinner he shall have.' Helen made a mocking curtsy and indicated towards the cottage. 'This way sir, I'll show you to your table.'

Ted Decker offered his hand to the small boy. He seized it eagerly and together they followed Helen Argosy into the tiny cottage. Picturesque country cottages may be delightful to observe from without, the policeman soon discovered, but are the very devil to negotiate on the inside. He narrowly avoided a low stone lintel, failed to notice a downward step into the dining kitchen, stumbled and then caught his head a resounding crack as he straightened up and came into painful contact with an oaken beam.

'O-o-o-oh!' Helen sucked in her breath in dismay. She rushed to his side, steered him into a chair and, greatly concerned, examined his head with gentle fingers.

Decker sat motionless, relaxed in the chair with his head tilted slightly back and his eyes closed. He could feel the warm pressure of her slender body pressing against his shoulder as she bent to examine the injury.

It was a moment to savour. He would have traded far more than a bump on the head for a moment such as this. The fragrance of summer flowers invaded his senses. Every tactile nerve sent tingling messages racing through his body as Helen's gentle fingers traced across his scalp.

'Well! The skin's intact.' She murmured thoughtfully, 'You may have a lump though… but I think you will live.'

Decker opened one eye. He could see the soft curve of her mouth, a faint crease in the bloom of a cheek that softened into a dimple when she smiled and the beginnings of laughter lines at the corners of her grey eyes.

'Live?' He faked a groan, 'Live... oh no. I think it's terminal.'

'Terminal! It was just a slight bump, nothing more.'

'I wasn't thinking of the bump.' He opened both eyes and chuckled deep inside, 'It's the treatment that could prove fatal...'

'Oh!' Helen pulled away sharply, 'You're just an old fraud. It was all a trick to get my attention.' Although her words chided, a sudden warm certainty filled her heart.

'Mr Decker. Mr Decker.' Small fingers tugged at his shirtsleeve as Jason's voice piped a question, 'Do you need a plaster? We've got lots and lots of plasters. I can stick one on for you. I can, I ever so good at it. Honest.'

Ted ruffled the small boy's hair affectionately. 'I'm sure you are Jason,' he replied, 'You're probably the very best sticker on of plasters in the whole wide world, but I'm alright. I don't think I'll need one.' He beckoned the boy closer and dropping his voice to a whisper, confided, 'I think that you and I should have a little arrangement, a *secret* arrangement, just between you and me. OK?'

'A secwett awwangement? Oo-er!' lisped Jason, 'What sort of awwangement?'

'Well, just between ourselves, when we are alone, and so no one else in the whole wide world knows about it, you can call me Ted. It will be our very special secret, just between you and me, alright?'

'Cor! But you're a gwown-up. Mummy said I should always call gwown-up people by their pwoper names... like *Mister* Decker.'

'Quite right too, so you should Jason and that's what I want you to do when anyone else is there, but when we are alone together, it's Ted. Our secret. OK?'

'Oh, alwight then.' Jason replied looking a little apprehensive.

Helen returned to the table carrying a steaming platter of meat. 'Hello.' she remarked, 'What's all the secrecy about?'

Decker tapped the side of his nose. He gave the boy a slow conspiratorial wink.

'Oh! Nothing much,' he said airily, 'Just a man to man discussion.' Then breathing in the aroma, he closed his eyes and skilfully switched the conversation, 'Let me guess. Roast lamb with mint sauce, yes?'

'Right first time! Roast lamb it is, with mint sauce, new potatoes and fresh garden peas. I hope you like it.'

'Like it? It's one of my favourite meals and it looks delicious.'

*

It was a delicious meal, simple and uncomplicated. Enjoyed in a friendly relaxed atmosphere. It was a perfect situation for their relationship to develop easily. Decker made certain to include the little boy in their conversation, drawing him in skilfully and speaking and treating him as an equal. He even invited Jason's opinion on the Briseley T'ill cricket team and paid close attention to his reply. In response Decker gained a new admirer and unwittingly became the boy's hero.

'Where did you learn about motor cars?' Ted asked, 'So many women learn how to drive but haven't a clue about what is under the bonnet. Yet you sound like an expert.

'From my Father,' explained Helen, 'He has a repair shop, his own business. I grew up with cars, mainly old bangers. My Dad never had the capital to expand in a big way, he just has a small country garage. It's too small to warrant a dealership but he manages to earn a good living. He's a steady reliable mechanic. People trust him, rightly so. He doesn't charge the earth so they know they are not being ripped off. The only problem is my mother.'

'Your mother! Why? What do you mean?'

Helen hesitated before replying, she was naturally a loyal person. 'Well! I suppose she is a bit of a snob. She hates the fact that her husband earns his living by getting his hands dirty. She hoped for something better, a white collar-type man. She just can't see that my Dad is happy doing what he does. He does it well and he enjoys it. I think that if I had been a boy it would have given my father a lot of satisfaction if I had followed him into the business. Erecting a sign that said "Argosy & Son" would have made his day. But I was a girl and even Dad had to agree that the motor trade was an unsuitable choice. So I went to the College of Art, my second great love, and truth to tell it's a career I have never regretted.'

Until that moment it had not occurred to the policeman to ask Helen how she earned her living. Obviously she had to support herself and the boy. Looking around the cottage he realised it's contents were far from luxurious. Everything was clean, but worn. Second-hand, guessed Decker, noting the threadbare patchiness of the carpet, the plain but serviceable dining chairs and table and the sagging upholstery of the three-piece suite.

'Are you some kind of artist then?' he enquired.

'Artist? Well you could say that.' She gave him a bemused little smile, 'You really don't know what I do... do you?'

'No,'

She searched under the cushions of the settee, found what she was looking for and tossed a popular daily newspaper into his lap. 'Look at the back page,' she instructed him, 'That's me – HAG.'

'HAG?' Puzzled he turned over the paper, searched the rear sheet and finally realised the meaning of her words. With the evidence staring him in the face he still found it hard to accept that the brilliantly drawn cartoons were the creation of the lovely young woman facing him. He read out aloud.

'Winnie the White Witch, by H.A.G. HAG! Why HAG?'

'They are my initials,' explained Helen, 'with the addition of my mother's maiden name which was Gardner, Helen Argosy Gardner. H.A.G. It's subtle don't you think? One of the Oxford definitions of a witch is "an old hag." Clever! Yes?'

'Mmm.' he mused, 'If *my* memory serves me correctly another definition refers to a hag as an ugly old woman.' His eyes languidly assessed her from head to toe. 'Now, would I say you were an ugly old woman? Oh no, quite the opposite in fact. You are definitely a woman, but young and very beautiful.'

Helen blushed with embarrassment at the compliment. She scolded him. 'And you Ted Decker are just an old smoothie.'

The old smoothie smiled to himself with pleasure. He was normally very reticent and found it hard to recall the last time he had paid a lovely woman a compliment. It was years ago, far too long. Hopefully there would be opportunities in the future.

'How on earth do you think of new ideas?' He asked her, 'every day? It must be very difficult. I'd be lost just trying to think up one.'

'The hardest part was creating the character. That took me a long, long time. Once the idea for Winnie came to me I sat down and plotted out her characteristics. On one side I listed her attributes and on the other her less desirable idiosyncrasies. I set out to create a character for children to enjoy, instead Winnie caught the imagination of adults, much to my surprise, and she has ended up being popular with everyone.'

'Have you always drawn, created other characters?'

'Yes. I started when I was only six years old. Mostly cats and dogs to begin with, you know how children love animals. It just carried on from there. Winnie was my breakthrough. I could scarcely believe my good luck when the newspaper accepted my preliminary sketches. One day the telephone rang and this gushing woman burbled down the line, "Darling this, Darling that." And could I come to London, *immediately* and bring my portfolio of ideas. So I did. They offered me a six-month trial period to be followed by a contract if the strip became successful. Winnie has been going for just over a year now, God bless her little broomstick, and for the first time in my life I have been able to earn decent money and stand on my own two feet. It's great!' Helen paused, a little breathless in her excitement, proud of her achievements, glowing with satisfaction.

Decker shook his head in admiration. *She is someone special,* he told himself. Charming, attractive, intelligent and talented. Was it any wonder that she was getting to him? *No! It was more than that,* he admitted to himself, *I'm falling for her. Falling in love. Me, Ted Decker… at my age!*

'You look pensive,' she said, 'what deep thoughts might you be thinking?'

'Erm… er.' Her perception embarrassed him. He could feel his skin on fire as the blood rushed to his face. 'Nothing… nothing at all.'

'Nothing? You can't fool me Ted Decker, you wicked man, just you wait.' She chortled with mischievous laughter, a hidden promise of pleasure to come in her demeanour.

Hoping to divert her attention Decker addressed the boy. 'How about your ambitions Jason? What are you going to be when you grow up?' To his surprise Jason answered without a seconds hesitation.

'A stwonomer.' He said.

'A what?'

'Astronomer.' explained Helen, 'He wants to be an astronomer. He's crazy about the moon and stars. That's why he has the top room, there's a dormer window, it's perfect for his telescope.'

'Would you like to see it?' burst in the boy, 'Please Mummy, can I show Mr Decker my telescope? Please. It's ever so good. Honest. Oh!' Jason's little face became quite serious, 'Oh blow! Look, it's clouding over. We won't be able to see a thing. Quick, before it's too late. This way Mr Decker.' He tugged at the policeman's hand pulling him towards the staircase.

'Alright Jason, steady up,' said his mother, 'Just for a few minutes, and then it's off to bed. It *is* past eight-thirty already.' Helen looked towards Decker, 'Will you humour him while I tidy up down here?'

Eagerly Jason led the way up two flights of a steep stairway. Although referred to as a cottage the building had been built on three levels. Jason's room lay under the roof and was a spacious area for one small boy to occupy. His room had sloping ceilings and a dormer window that looked out in a south-easterly direction. The rear of the cricket pavilion was in view and beyond it the playing square. Further still, partly screened by the line of willow trees, was the Sinkhole. He judged it to be about four hundred yards from the cottage.

A rising wind tossed the trailing branches of the trees. Dark clouds scudded across the evening sky, riding in on the wind. Occasional spats of rain splashed against the windowpanes. In the distance the sound of an unlatched gate or door banging reached their ears as it was caught by a sudden gust.

'That's my telescope.' Jason said proudly, 'Super, isn't it?'

To Decker's untutored eye it looked to be a magnificent instrument, mounted on a sturdy metal tripod with an accessory tray, all manner of adjustable micro dials and mysterious declination circles that meant nothing to the policeman. He made a low whistling sound of appreciation. 'Incredible!' was his only comment.

'My Gwandad bought it for me.' The boy informed him, 'It was a Chwistmas pwesent... the bestest ever!'

'There's no doubt about that Jason. How does it work?'

Ted Decker's perception of a telescope was of a long tube. One placed an eye to one end and looked out of the other. With luck and a bit of fortuitous focussing, objects then became nearer and clearer.

Jason's astronomical telescope was far more complicated. He sat on a low stool, carefully consulted a chart, place his eye against the viewfinder and made microscopic adjustments to the angle of the instrument which to the policeman seemed negligible. Finally Jason was satisfied. He looked so serious and adult that Decker found it hard to remember that the boy was only six years old.

It took a few seconds for his eyesight to adjust. At first there was just a hazy light, then, as his focus sharpened, Ted realised that he was looking at a magnified section of the moon's surface.

'Can you see it Mr Decker... Ted?' Jason reverted to a small boy again. 'Can you see it? That's the Sea of Tranquillity. Oh dwat! It's clouding over, that would happen.'

For a few precious seconds Decker had had a close up of the dead airless sphere that is the Earth's closest neighbour. It looked cold and inhospitable, yet man had been there and stood upon its surface, one quarter of a million miles away. It had been a lonely adventure, probably the loneliest adventure that man would ever undertake in his exploration of the emptiness that is space.

He marvelled at their courage.

The silent sphere disappeared under a blanket of cloud. Decker shivered and pulled back from the telescope. There was so much out there that was unknown, so much for an eager young mind to explore. He could understand the fascination.

'Did you see it?' Jason asked again, 'Did you manage to see the Sea of Tranquillity?'

He smiled at the boy's enthusiasm, 'Just in time young shaver, just in time. What did you call it? The Sea of Tranquillity, I shall have to remember that.'

*

They stood in silence for a while, looking out at the darkening sky. Man and boy together, watching the clouds that raced like a tidal wave across the moon, catching glimpses of its soft effulgent light whenever there was a break in the overcast heavens.

'Jason, do you see other things at night, or are you too busy looking at the moon and stars?' Why he asked the question Decker never fully understood. It came out of the blue. 'Do you ever use your telescope to look at people?'

'Sometimes,' answered the boy thoughtfully, 'Mostly I see foxes, I have seen an owl, and a badger, twice I've seen a badger.' There was a long pause and then he added, 'Once I saw two men. They were playing a game, I think… like… like at the cemetwy.'

Decker sucked in his breath sharply, 'Game? What kind of game? What do you mean Jason?' His question was a natural but unfortunate gut reaction. The little boy withdrew into a frightened silence. Gently he pressed Jason for an explanation.

'How long ago Jason? How long since you saw them playing the game?'

'Mmm… er… ages… ever so long ago, ages and ages, I think.'

Decker almost gave up in despair. He knew that to a child time is infinite. An hour seeming as long as a week, a week as long as a month, while a month, to one so young, takes as long as a year. He tried another approach.

'How long ago Jason? Were you looking at the moon that night? What was it like? Was it a full moon? Could you see it clearly?'

'Ooo, Yes.' answered the boy without hesitation, 'It was weally big and bwight as bwight.'

Decker made rough and ready calculations in his head. The present moon was waxing, just about three quarters from being full. That would mean that the last full moon had fallen around three and a half weeks ago. He counted back on his fingers. The last full moon had fallen at Easter, on Good Friday. Of course! How stupid of him to forget, the dates that determine Easter depend upon the lunar phases. There is always a full moon just prior to Good Friday, or within two to three nights of the holiest day in the Christian calendar.

He asked the boy one more question.

'How often does Helen... your Mummy let you stay up to look at the stars? Every night? I mean, you have to go to school next morning don't you?'

'Oh yes. Mummy is very stwict. She only lets me stay up weally late when I'm on holiday. She says that I need my sleep, that boys who miss their sleep don't gwow. Do you go to bed early Mr Decker... Ted? 'cos you're very big!'

'Sometimes Jason, sometimes I go to bed early but there are times when I have to work all night. Policemen do.'

'Just like stwonomers.' Piped the boy, 'They work at night, every night. I want to be a stwonomer and work all night. It's more fun.'

'I'm sure it is Jason, I'm sure it is. You are a very clever young man. Tell me, when you saw the two men playing the game, did you tell anyone about it? Did you tell your Mummy?'

'No-o-o! I felled to sleep and forgot all about it until the lady's funeral.'

'Mrs Mole's funeral?'

'Yea! That lady. Why do they buwy people in the gwound? And why did she die? Was she vewy, vewy old?'

'No Jason, she was not very old, just very poorly. Poor Rowena, so poorly that the doctor was unable to make her better.'

'Oh!' Jason thought about it quietly for a few minutes, then added, 'When they put her in the gwound, that's when I 'membered the men. I twied to tell Mummy but she said it must have been a bad dweam.'

*

My God, thought Decker, fighting to contain his excitement, it all fitted together. The last time Daisy Kutter had been seen alive was on the eve of Good Friday. She must have been murdered the same night that Rowena Mole died a natural death. Now he had a witness, probably not a very credible one but a witness non-the-less. The question was, how much credence could be placed upon the evidence of a six-year old boy? Who would believe him?

Four hundred yards was a long way. Was it too great a distance over which to recognise a person? He thought back to the night he had stood watch by the Sinkhole. Helen had said that the scene was clearly visible from Jason's window. But then she had known he was there. It is much easier to recognise a familiar figure than that of a stranger.

'Jason,' he asked the boy another question, 'How clearly did you see the two men? Do you know them?'

'Mmm, p'raps, can't 'member very well. I *might* know them.' he replied vaguely.

'Try Jason, please try and remember. It could be important. What were they like? Where they short, tall, fat, thin...?'

'I think... I think... Mmm... I think they were tall, big, very big. One was sort of fat, and the other was thinner. He looked like a spider, the thin one.'

Decker sensed the boy was losing interest. He was obviously tired and fighting hard to stay awake. The policeman tried one further tactic.

'Will you be coming to the cricket match on Saturday?' he asked. The boy nodded eagerly. 'Would you like me to bowl at you in the practice net?'

Jason's eyes shone with joy.

'Cor! Would you, with a weal cwicket ball?'

'A *real* cricket ball?' exclaimed Decker, 'They are very hard you know. You'll need to put some pads on.' Jason's eyes rounded with excitement.

'Cor! I'll be a pwoper batsman, won't I?'

'Indeed you will Jason, indeed you will. Now, better pop into bed, before you fall foul of your Mum. Sportsmen need their sleep... and so do astronomers.'

The boy peeled off his clothes, changed into pyjamas and snuggled down into the single pinewood framed bed just seconds before his mother, Helen Argosy, appeared in the doorway.

'How did you achieve that?' she asked, taking in the scene, 'It takes me ages.'

Jason, unable to contain his excitement, burst out, 'Ted... Mr Decker said he's going to bowl at me in the cwicket nets on Saturday. With a weal cwicket ball. I can go Mummy, can't I? Please.'

Helen's look towards the policeman was a mixture of gratitude and alarm.

'Will he be alright? It won't be too much bother, will it?'

'It will be a pleasure,' he answered truthfully, 'and I'll take good care he comes to no harm.'

'But won't you be playing?' she enquired. Decker shook his head.

'No. I didn't put my name forward for selection this weekend. Officially I'll be on duty, the investigation?' He raised his eyebrows, trying to convey a hidden meaning to his words. Helen looked puzzled, momentarily, and then caught on. What Ted was trying to tell her was that he would be on duty, but in plain clothes and to all intents and purposes his presence at the game would be as a good clubman and supporter.

Helen bent over her son and kissed his head fondly, 'Goodnight Jason, time to settle down.'

'Goodnight Jason.' Decker echoed, adding conspiratorially, 'See you on Saturday. If you should see anyone you recognise, you know, either of the two men you saw through the telescope, you'll tell me?'

Jason nodded sleepily. His eyes were firmly closed, the Sandman already weaving his spell.

*

Helen led the way down the narrow staircase to the first floor. It consisted of just two rooms. There was a small austere bathroom with a toilet. Its walls, in uneven plaster, had been painted with plain white emulsion, relieved only by a square of nine tiles backing an old iron-framed washbasin.

The second room was used by Helen as both a bedroom and a studio, a large room that had been inexpertly converted by the removal of an inner wall. Decker noticed an uneven ridge in the plaster that ran vertically from the floor to the ceiling where the wall had once been.

'Well!' exclaimed Helen, 'It's time to start earning your supper.' If he had been watching her face carefully he might have chosen other words as he replied.

'Anything,' he said eagerly, 'anything I can do to help. Just name it.'

'Anything?'

'Mmm. Sure.'

'Well… er… How do you feel about taking your clothes off?'

'Eh!' His jaw sagged at the unexpected request, 'All of them? That's a bit blunt isn't it? I know times have changed but…' Helen's laughter bubbled out like a mountain spring. Her slim frame shook with merriment.

'Your face Ted Decker,' she chortled, 'If only you could see your own face. It's a picture, it really is. What do you think I'm asking you to do?'

'Well... you know…?'

'Ted Decker! Really!' She tried hard to keep a stern expression and a reproving tone to her voice, but failed miserably. 'I want you to *pose* for me, that's all.'

'Pose? Me! I wouldn't know how. What as?'

'A genie.'

'A what?' His voice oozed incredulity.

'A genie…as in Aladdin and the magic lamp. You know, the spirit that appears from the lamp when it's rubbed.'

'I know what a genie is, but why me? What's it all about?'

'I'm stuck.' admitted Helen, 'I've been trying for days, but I just can't get the body right. It's a new character I plan to introduce into Winnie the White Witch. I thought you might have the right body shape. You see I'm fine when it comes to drawing a young person, but that isn't what I need. After all, this genie… Well! It *is* supposed to be over two thousand years old.'

'Oh! Thank you for that.' Decker exclaimed, the sarcasm heavy in his voice.

'No. No. Please.' placated Helen, 'It's just that a fine mature body will look so much better. You do understand, don't you?'

'No! But I'm trying.'

*

Posing was harder than Decker had anticipated. Parts of his body that had never bothered him before began to itch. He felt an irresistible urge to move. He tried to engage Helen in conversation but this disturbed her concentration. She preferred to work in silence, her pencil flying rapidly over the sheet of cartridge paper clipped to her drawing board.

He tried letting his mind dwell on other matters. Detection, he discovered, is all about thought and imagination. About collecting facts, forming theories and sifting through them time and time again in his mind until what he knew was fact and what he thought of as probable came together and made sense.

Brief pictures flickered into his brain like the jumping frames of a hand-cranked bioscope. An image of the body, Daisy Kutter's body wrapped in a black bin liner and secured by a length of yellow plastic covered washing line. Is it normal for a person to cut a piece from the end of a washing line? Unlikely, for then it may end up too short for its proper use. Somewhere, he recalled, he'd seen a similar length of yellow plastic line used for an unusual purpose. Where, he asked himself, and was it of any significance? Maybe, then again it could have been a coincidence and meant nothing.

The Killer had to be connected to the cricket club. All those items of clothing distributed amongst the players equipment. Had that been deliberate, a ploy to cast suspicion upon others, or had it been a case of seizing an opportune moment to dispose of incriminating evidence?

Upon first examination it had appeared to be a clever idea, until one appreciated that in truth it served to limit the number of suspects to a specific group, the members who had played in, or were at, the match.

The guilty party, Decker decided, was cunning, but far from clever. The evidence showed that he (or even she) lacked the ability to think events through to their ultimate conclusion.

*

'You can relax now,' said Helen, 'I've finished. What do you think?'

'Mmm-mm!' Decker grunted a reply. Sitting half naked for the best part of an hour, with the room temperature steadily falling, had left him stiff in his neck and shoulders. Decidedly chilled, he rolled his head around and flexed his shoulders in slow tentative circles.

'Oh! Poor you,' cried Helen in concern, 'you must be perished. Here, let me give you a massage.' She pulled him across, sat him on the edge of her divan bed, kneeled behind him and with gentle rhythmic movements kneaded the muscles and sinews of his shoulders, neck and upper spine.

It was wonderfully relaxing.

'Do you like it?' she asked, looking over his head at her handiwork. 'I knew you would be just what I needed, a perfect model for my genie. Do you see what I mean now? A youthful physique would have been wrong. Too skinny, I needed someone substantial, someone mature.'

He was impressed by her skill. Helen had completed four pictures in just under an hour of concentrated effort. They depicted a tall muscular giant of a genie rising up out of a cloudy bottle. His massive arms were folded authoritatively across a broad chest and his head was tilted in an arrogant attitude as he scowled down at the timid quavering figure of Winnie the White Witch. There was just the right amount of detail, sufficient to create interest, unspoilt by fussy elaboration.

'It's very good,' he said, 'almost too good. Are people who read comic strips really that critical?' It wasn't the comment Helen expected. She had to think for a moment before replying.

'No. I don't suppose they are... but *I* am. I set myself a standard when I started. What other people do, or think, is their concern. My aim is to be the best. Why shouldn't there be just as much artistic merit in a cartoon as in any other art form?'

'Good for you,' agreed Decker, 'and why not? I expect more people follow Winnie the White Witch than have seen the Mona Lisa. Eh?'

'Alright Ted, there's no need to go over the top,' Helen said laughing at the exaggerated praise, 'But it's a lovely compliment. Thanks.' She ceased massaging and wrapping her arms around his body gave him a warm affectionate squeeze. Her head relaxed against his shoulder and he felt soft lips brush against the nape of his neck. Little shivers of excitement travelled down his spine. Her lips gently worked their way across his neck and nibbled at the lobe of his ear. Her voice murmured softly.

'What was that you said earlier about taking me into custody? Yes please!'

'But there has to be a charge.' He pointed out, 'What could it be?'

'How about molesting an officer of the law?'

'But I haven't been molested.' Her hands went on a journey of exploration, searching out dark untapped erogenous territory. A deep throaty chuckle accompanied her reply.

'Perhaps not yet...but give a girl time!'

'Oo-er! A-Ah! Phwor! Can two play this game?' he asked.

*

The wind gusted stronger. Jason slept uneasily. The sound of a gate or door banging repeatedly in the near distance penetrated his sleeping mind, disturbing him. The wind veered around, blowing in from a north-easterly direction. The banging noise grew louder. Crash! Slam! Bang! Slam! CRASH! SLAM! BANG!

Jason tossed and turned in his sleep but there was no escaping from the increasingly violent sounds. Crash! Slam! Crash! Bang!

Suddenly he was jerked wide-awake. It was pitch black. Disorientated by the sound invading his room, a lurking black monster of the night. CRASH! SLAM! BANG! SLAM!

'Mummy!' he screamed, 'Mummy! Mum-me-e-e!'

For a few brief seconds there was no response, then the landing light clicked on, closely followed by the sound of footsteps pounding up the steep, narrow staircase.

'Jason... Darling... What's wrong?' A mother's concern for her child was overwhelmingly evident in Helen Argosy's voice. All else was forgotten. She rushed to his bed and swept him up in her arms, clutching the small boy protectively to her naked body. 'Darling! Darling! Whatever is the matter?'

Bang!... Slam!... CRASH!... SLAM! The sounds vibrated in the bedroom, the reason for Jason's terror, self-evident.

'The noise,' he sobbed, 'It fwightened me. It woked me up.'

'It sounds like some damn fool has left a shed door undone.' cursed Ted Decker, hesitating in the doorway, 'I'd better go out and fix it.'

'Would you?' Helen flashed him a look full of appreciation, 'I'd be so grateful.'

Jason, secure in his mother's arms, quickly recovered his composure and his curiosity.

'Mummy,' he asked, 'Why has Ted... Mr Decker got no clothes on?'

'Oh Lord! Ted, take my bathrobe, it's behind the bedroom door,' Helen cried out after the departing policeman, 'and there's a torch on the dressing table, it's by the bed.'

The flimsy bathrobe, in vivid pink, offered poor protection against the elements. It flapped and fluttered in the wind. The rain, falling steadily now, quickly penetrated the flimsy garment. It lashed against and stung his skin sending cold shivers over his body. Seconds earlier, he recalled, his shivers had been those of anticipation. That his expectations would have been fulfilled he had no doubt. But could he have lived up to them? Would he have matched up to Helen's expectations of him? There was a doubt in his mind that was hard to banish.

Maturity, he decided, is a two edged sword. It had brought him confidence, resilience and dignity. It had enabled him to brush aside Moxon's condescending insults as easily as a mild case of dandruff falling on his broad and powerful shoulders. Sex was another matter. In that respect the advancing years had caused his confidence to ebb away. The brash cockiness of youth was long gone. Could it be that Jason's timely cry had saved him from an embarrassing disaster?

Embarrassment! *I hope to God no one sees me,* thought Decker, suddenly aware of his bizarre appearance. At least he had had the presence of mind to slip into his boxer shorts. There had been time for little else. He'd eased his feet into slip-on shoes and rushed out of the house like a lunatic, just to secure a banging gate. That's love!

I'm mad, quite mad, he told himself. *Thank God it was dark, if anyone were to me... what would they think?*

He stumbled along the uneven footpath, the torch bobbing with each step, until he reached the gate. It was securely fastened with a U-shaped steel hasp mounted on the gatepost, a sturdy bolt acting as a pivot. A crashing sound from the direction of the storage shed drew Decker on. The driving rain lashed at his bare legs, His boxer shorts, soaked through and through, had become translucent. The bathrobe hung like a piece of limp wet rag. He might as well have been naked.

Rainwater trickled down his bare legs filling his shoes with water. Wearily he squelched across the outfield, up the gradient and towards the old pavilion and store shed. The offending door swung in an arc of ninety degrees. It crashed back against a wooden stop set into the ground and then slammed shut with a shuddering jar, almost, but not quite closing.

Decker could cheerfully have strangled the unknown culprit who'd left it open. He swore unmentionable oaths under his breath. Words he would never have spoken aloud against anyone. The feeble light from Helen's torch probed weakly ahead as its beam struggled against the stormy gloom. Decker was two strides from the door when the circle of light illuminated the sole of a brown leather shoe. A city shoe, with a thin leather sole and the high glossy shine of patent leather.

The country people of Briseley T'ill wore sensible footwear, sturdy green Wellington boots or robust brogues. They *never* wore patent leather.

A prickle of apprehension touched Decker's skin, a first feathery moment of foreboding. A pair of legs came into view. They were set rigidly in the position of a person running, a grotesque parody of movement for they would never move again of their own volition. Slowly, reluctantly, Decker swung the beam upwards until its light gleamed dully on the coned metal point of the killing stake. The one intact cricket stump had found its mark. He recognised the body even though it faced away from him. There was no mistaking that squat porcine shape.

The dead body of Moxon was balanced precariously, supported by the cricket stump that had pierced his neck and the large plastic container. One hand gripped the rim of the receptacle. Attempting still to lift its owner's body free of the fatal shaft, but in vain. All in vain!

'Holy Mother of God!' Decker recoiled in horror. His heel caught the edge of the toppled oil drum. It rolled away with a hollow sound. Its movement set off a chain reaction for the grotesque tableau before his eyes swayed and slowly toppled over like a badly constructed set in a theatrical farce.

But this wasn't farce. This was reality, a Theatre of Death. And Death, with grim humour, had played out a final scene with the unfortunate Moxon at centre stage. It had not even let him die with dignity for Moxon's face was set like some macabre gargoyle that had fallen from an old, old building. A face cast in stone, parodying life. His wide glassy eyes stared straight at Decker, the eyebrow lifted high, emphasising the mute appeal that lingered on. His mouth was twisted into an agonised grimace with his tongue poking through like some obscene member, coated black from blood that had dried.

Blood had flowed from both the victim's mouth and throat, covering his lower jaw and upper chest. It had trickled down the inner and outer side of the plastic container, drying into a coating, which in the dim light of the torch, resembled black tar.

The sudden shivers that wracked Decker's body were not caused by the rain or by the biting chill of the wind whipping away his body heat. It was shock. His hands shook so violently that he almost dropped the torch. A tight iron band closed about his chest, his ribs crushed inwards by a relentless force. He swayed, perilously close to fainting, fought to remain conscious. Finally he regained control.

His police training reasserted itself and his eyes searched out factual information. They recorded the deep circular groove in the earth where the oil drum had rested in its upright position and noticed the billets of wood Moxon had piled one upon another to form a step. There were smears of diesel oil on the soles of the dead man's shoes and scuffmarks on the side of the canister where Moxon's feet had pounded in treadmill fashion as he fought to regain his balance. Finally, as though in silent confirmation, one of the dead man's thick and chubby hands stretched towards the edging spade. Frozen in time by rigor mortis, still vainly seeking an object they would never reach.

A terrible accident had occurred. The signs were all there to be read. Though why the Police Inspector had taken such a fearful risk was beyond Decker's comprehension. The insatiable curiosity that had made Moxon such a good detective had resulted in his death.

*

Helen welcomed his return with a warm blanket and a piping hot drink. Once reassured, Jason had snuggled down and within seconds had fallen into a deep sleep. With the perversity of a small child he remained blissfully unaware of the subsequent events. Helen leapt to her feet at the sound of Decker bursting through the door. She held the blanket before her, ready to wrap its warmth around his rain-drenched body. The rain had plastered Decker's hair into limp dark shanks to his head. Droplets ran down his face and cheeks, dripping from the end of his nose and chin like a flood of coruscating tears.

'Phone.' he gasped, panting from his exertions, 'it's Moxon... in the store shed. He's ... he's... dead.'

'Dead? Moxon? What do you mean?' Helen stared with uncomprehending eyes, 'What did you say? What's happened? Ted, tell me.'

His chest heaved painfully, drained of oxygen. He sucked in great shuddering gasps of air as he battled to control his breathing. Slowly... slowly... breathe in deep and slow, hold it, then let the air out steadily. There, that was better.

His recovery rate was rapid, an indication of his overall fitness. Calmer now, he regained control of himself. Decker took Helen Argosy by the shoulders. He squeezed reassuringly with his strong capable hands.

'There's been an accident,' he said slowly, calmly, 'It's Moxon. I found his body in the store-shed. I need to ring Police Headquarters. Now.' He turned away towards the telephone and dialled carefully and deliberately. When he spoke into the receiver it was in a calm, matter of fact voice.

'I can't believe it,' muttered Helen Argosy half aloud, 'I just can't believe it. That Moxon, he came between us when he was alive... and now he has come between us from the dead.'

Was it always going to be like this?

Bouncer

Bouncer. A hostile ball used to intimidate the batsman.

Nigel Rowthorne had great presence: physically and intellectually. His aura of authority filled Helen Argosy's tiny dining kitchen every bit as much as his rugged frame. He had a reputation for cool efficiency, a natural air of dignity. He was a man who had never been seen to lose his temper in the most trying of circumstances. Attributes sorely needed in a county whose council actively pursued a policy of under-funding its police force.

It was undermanned, under-equipped, under-funded and under pressure. Yet Nigel Rowthorne handled an impossible situation with tact, diplomacy and unfailing good humour. Throughout the force he was held in the highest esteem, noted for his integrity, thoroughness and for treating each and every officer with equal respect. Nigel Rowthorne was a better man than the politicians deserved, held in respectful awe even by his enemies.

In difficult circumstances the response had been remarkable. Within twenty minutes of Decker's call the police had arrived. A small party to be sure, sadly depleted in numbers, but lead by the Chief Constable himself.

There were tired lines around his eyes and the white of exhaustion in his face, yet he managed a wry smile at the sight of his constable's unconventional attire. He listened, gravely attentive, to Decker's report, smiled apologetically towards Helen Argosy for the intrusion and agreed with the local man's assessment of the facts.

'Right.' said Nigel Rowthorne in his deep commanding voice, 'I'll take a look at the scene of the accident and then we'll leave Forensics to do their bit. Perhaps, Constable Decker, you could slip into something *less* comfortable... Eh!' There was irony in the Chief's voice as he inverted the popular expression. 'I'll be about ten minutes, then you and I can review what happened together.' Rowthorne glanced at Helen, 'If Miss... er?'

'Argosy.' Decker supplied the information.

'Miss Argosy, if you will permit us the use of your kitchen? Please. I need to have a personal discussion with you, Decker. Alright Miss Argosy?' The Chief Constable assumed agreement with the authority of one used to being obeyed. Helen nodded tacitly and stepped aside as the big man ducked under the low stone lintel and strode off into the darkness.

A dejected Decker faced the young woman. He shrugged helplessly, resigned to the ruination of their evening together. 'Sorry.' he said, 'What a mess.'

'Yes.' Helen agreed, 'I can't pretend that I liked Moxon, couldn't stand the man, but he never deserved to die like that. It's horrible. You *are* sure it was an accident.'

'About ninety-nine percent.' Ted nodded in reply, 'There's no reason to think otherwise. You know, all day long I wondered why he wasn't in contact. When I failed to hear from him I thought he might have been called away to help out with the riots, though it's hardly his scene. Can you imagine porky Moxon embroiled with flying pickets... and all the while...' A sudden violent shiver shook him from head to toe, cutting off his words as the image of Moxon's corpse slowly toppling over before his petrified gaze returned to haunt him.

Moxon's body with his head twisted back, the one outstretched grasping hand and the metal coned stump like a giant meat skewer protruding from the back of the Police Inspector's short squat neck.

'C'mon Ted,' Helen Argosy whispered quietly, 'The Chief Constable was right. Let me dry you off properly. I'll make another hot drink while you put some clothes on.' She led him by the hand, like a bewildered child, up the steep narrow staircase to her room.

*

Nigel Rowthorne stood on familiar ground. He didn't need to ask directions to the Briseley T'ill cricket field. As a boy he played there many times. Fifty-four years ago he'd been born in the village. Give or take a few houses it was the same now as it had been then. His progress through the echelons of the Police Force had taken him to many places before he achieved his lifetime ambition, a final accolade, being made the Chief Constable of his home county. His love for the Pennines remained constant, from the wild craggy escarpments to the gentler rolling hills in the South. He loved the beauty of the sparkling little rivers that seemed to dance down from the mighty Peaks, flowing through tree-lined valleys and into the heart of the sombre city. From there, at Police Headquarters, he controlled the twelve hundred men and women of the county's force.

The death of a police officer was a serious matter. Rowthorne, with his ingrained sense of responsibility, had made it his personal duty to investigate the matter. The area around the store shed had been taped off and portable arc lights set up to illuminate the scene. As yet nothing had been moved. The pathologist would confirm the finer details in his report but as far as the Chief could determine Moxon's death had in all probability happened exactly as Decker had surmised.

After all, Rowthorne's thoughts ran, the possibility of deliberately killing a man in such a way was remote. There had been no signs of a struggle. It was bizarre in the extreme to imagine anyone trying to murder a man in such a manner. The odds against succeeding would be millions to one against the victim falling onto the upturned cricket stump. Rowthorne made one final sweep of the scene with his eyes, ensuring that he had overlooked nothing, then, nodding affirmation to his men to carry on, he turned away. As he walked slowly back towards the cottage he considered what to do. His limited resources were already over extended. There was talk of police reinforcements being drafted in to support his beleaguered officers. The cost of policing the politically motivated strikes was running out of control. Already he envisaged a battle with the County Council, a fight for funds, just to maintain his force at its present level. Only God knew how that would turn out!

Two deaths, one certainly murder, would normally receive top priority. Every resource would have been concentrated upon the investigations. However the present situation was exceptional and contingency measures were needed. In his last report, Moxon had shown considerable regard for Decker's ability and his local knowledge had already proved to be invaluable. There was only one course of action left, provisionally, he would have to leave Constable Edward Decker in charge of the murder enquiry and trust that his judgement was sound.

*

It was midnight. Decker, dressed once more in his own clothes, sat across the kitchen table from his superior officer. Helen had made both men a mug of hot steaming coffee before excusing herself and tactfully withdrawing to her bedroom.

'Are you two an item?' asked Nigel Rowthorne.

'An item?' The expression was new to Decker, 'Sorry I don't quite understand.'

'An item, my teenage daughter tells me in the current vernacular, means that you have a close understanding with a member of the opposite sex. It's a modern expression, you've never heard of it?'

'No sir,' replied Decker, 'We *are* a bit behind the times in Briseley T'ill. An item, what an odd expression.' He paused to think before continuing,

'I... er... I've only recently come to know Helen, Miss Argosy. She moved into the village six months ago. She... er... she invited me for a meal, tonight, for the very first time. Then the banging noise disturbed Jason, it woke him up. He was very frightened so I went to find out the cause, and the rest you know.'

'Jason. Who is Jason?'

'A little boy, Sir, he's six. Miss Argosy's son. He's fast asleep now but the banging frightened him. That's why I went to look.'

'And ruined your evening off in the process. Tough!' The Chief Constable expressed sympathy, then enquired, 'Tell me, why the pink bathrobe? How did that come about?'

'Um! Er! It was the first thing that came to hand. Y'see.. erm... I'd been posing, for Helen, Miss Argosy, she's an artist.'

'Nude?' enquired Nigel Rowthorne with a hint of a smile.

'Oh no sir,' came the hurried reply, 'not entirely, I kept my trousers on.'

A little chuckle started deep in his throat, rumbled around in his chest and issued forth into a bellow of laughter. The Chief Constable rocked back in his chair until Decker thought it would pass the point of equilibrium and he would topple over backwards.

'Oh Decker!' he gasped between waves of laughter, 'That is quite the best excuse I have ever heard. A real gem!' Then quite suddenly he sobered and muttered more to himself than anyone present, 'Thank God I can still raise a laugh.'

'Sir, I *am* single,' complained the Constable in an aggrieved voice, 'and so is Miss Argosy, even though she has a son. She's a one-parent family.'

'It's alright Decker. No need to worry.' Nigel Rowthorne waved aside his concern, 'Your private life is your own. Now! Can we get down to more serious business, the Kutter case, we have a problem there.'

The senior man paused, considering how far he should go. It was a most unusual step he was about to take. It could rebound disastrously. But an instinctive feeling convinced him he had made the right decision. He was certain that Decker was a man to be trusted, a man he could rely on, a man who would not let him down.

'I'll be frank with you,' said Rowthorne, 'I can't replace Inspector Moxon on the murder enquiry. I should but...'

'I see sir,' replied Decker, 'I understand. I saw how desperate the situation is on television, on the six o'clock news, the riots and everything. I feel very uncomfortable about it all sir, all those young men involved in the violence, my colleagues, fellow policemen. And I'm here, safe in

Briseley T'ill. It makes me feel that I'm failing in my duty.' He shook his head in concern, nibbling at his lower lip.

'How old are you?' asked Rowthorne.

'Forty-six, sir.'

'Forty-six... mm! Now is that an age to be involved in violence and scuffles? Leave it to the younger men Decker. You,' he tapped the table forcefully with a stiffened forefinger, '...you, are more important here.'

'If you say so sir.'

'I do. You may find it hard to believe but finding the right man to police a rural area is a problem. All these young fellow want is to work in the big city. To be where the action is. They figure that it increases their promotion prospects, which is true to a degree. But a man like you, mature and sensible, who knows the people and the locality can be every bit as valuable. Moxon knew that and was grateful for your input.'

'He was?' Decker was surprised. Moxon appreciated *him.* The coarse vulgar Inspector Moxon, the man who had poured scorn and insults upon his head appreciated him. Wonders never ceased!

'He thought that you had a fair idea who murdered Daisy Kutter.' said Nigel Rowthorne, 'Was he right?'

'I have my suspicions,' Decker replied cautiously, 'Unfortunately, as yet, no direct evidence. At the moment it's just a theory. Despite an intensive search we failed to find the murder weapon. Simply, I believe because Daisy Kutter was killed elsewhere before being carried to and buried in the Sinkhole. Another reason why we failed to find the weapon is because the murderer still has it in his possession. He never threw it away, in fact won't. It happens to be his favourite tool, something he uses every day. Something quite normal to him, an object that if he went *without* it would look very odd.' Decker paused a moment, looking to Rowthorne, expecting an opinion. He was not disappointed.

'Fair comment.' mused the Chief, 'What else have you worked out?'

'The day and time Daisy Kutter was killed, approximately, and now I'm fairly certain I know *where* it happened. The last person to see the nurse alive was the Doctor. He went to the Mole's house to certify the death of Rowena. It appears that Mrs Mole just keeled over and died while the nurse was there, while in the act of attending to her needs. That happened about eight o'clock on the eve of Good Friday. There was a call to the Doctor who rushed to the house. But in vain, all he was able to do was certify Mrs Rowena Mole as dead. When he left around nine o'clock Daisy Kutter was still alive and well. No one else was there at the time.'

'Was there anything suspicious about Mrs Mole's death?' probed Rowthorne.

'No. It was always on the cards. Rowena was a very sick woman.'

'So when did Nurse Kutter die? And how did you work that out?'

'Well Sir, I can't be exact to the minute but I believe she was killed around ten o'clock. Later that night, or in the very early hours of Good Friday her body was taken to the Sinkhole by two men and buried there.'

Nigel Rowthorne gave the policeman a hard searching look. A tiny frown of concentration furrowed his brow, 'How can you possibly know that?'

'I've discovered a witness. Someone who saw the body being buried.'

'Good God!' expostulated Rowthorne, his voice booming out. Decker's eyes jerked towards the ceiling. He pressed a finger to his lips to signify the need for quiet.

'The boy, sir. You'll wake the boy.'

'Bugger the boy. Who is this witness? Why didn't he come forward before now?' The Chief Constable spoke in a lower key, just as forcefully, every bit as eager for details. The tiredness lifted from his face. A hunter's gleam lit up his eyes.

'It isn't quite that easy,' warned Decker, 'With respect sir, I doubt whether a jury would place much credence on his evidence. You see its Jason. Miss Argosy's little boy... and he is only six years old.'

'Oh!' Nigel Rowthorne's sudden enthusiasm collapsed. 'Six. We have a six-year old witness. A little boy who claims he saw two men burying a body in the middle of the night. As you so rightly say Decker, barely credible evidence.' He pondered on the news, one crooked finger stroking away the fatigue around his eyes, added further thoughts, 'What was a small boy doing in the middle of the night? Why do you believe him? He could have been dreaming for all we know.'

'No sir.' Edward Decker replied firmly, 'If it was any other boy, I would agree. It just so happens that Jason Argosy is a very bright young man and has a particular hobby. He had a reason to be awake when other children would be tucked up and sound asleep. Astronomy sir. Jason's Argosy's hobby is astronomy and his bedroom window looks out over the cricket ground and towards the Sinkhole. It's the place where Daisy Kutter's body was discovered.'

'But how can you be sure of the date? Little children can be very vague about time, particularly at that age.' Rowthorne argued.

'Because of the moon. Jason's special interest is the surface of the moon. There was a full moon that night. The boy said it looked very big and was very bright. It checks out because the last full moon was on the eve of Good Friday. Also Helen, Jason's mother, is strict with the boy. She will only allow him to stay up late at night during the school holidays. Being Easter, the schools were closed. It nails down the date and time as near as possible.'

'Mmm! This boy, Jason Argosy, is he able to identify the two men... Positively?'

'That I don't know Sir. He has good eyesight. On the other hand I estimate that from his window to the Sinkhole is a good four hundred yards. That is quite a distance for him to make a positive identification. Also the significance of what he saw meant nothing to him. He imagined they were playing some kind of game. When he tried to tell his mother about it she suggested, just as you yourself did, that it was part of a bad dream. He forgot all about the incident until Mrs Mole's funeral.'

'Rowena Mole's funeral! What happened there?' Rowthorne was curious. He would never have considered it suitable for a six-year old to attend a funeral.

'It was funny in a macabre sort of way.' Decker replied, 'Most of the village was there. Without exception people admired Rowena Mole. She was such a courageous woman, even though confined to a wheelchair she would never surrender, never give up the fight. I must admit I was surprised myself to see Helen Argosy there with her boy. I suppose being new to the village she saw it as an opportunity to show her solidarity and her respect with the rest of the villagers. To see, and *be* seen.

'It must have been strange and boring for the boy. Despite that he was very well behaved until right near the end.' Decker ended.

'What did he do, fall into the grave?'

'Nothing as drastic as that, it was what he said that was comical. As the coffin was being lowered into the ground the Reverend Price came to the words, "In the name of the Father and of the Son and of the Holy Ghost." Young Jason misinterpreted the words and piped up with his own version of the last part; "And in the hole 'e goes." It made the mourners giggle. Poor Helen Argosy was most embarrassed and shushed the boy to silence. But I remember his words, "...I told you they put bodies in the ground, Mummy, I *saw* it." Of course, at the time the words meant nothing to me. We put Daisy Kutter's absence down to the known fact that she visited her mother every Bank Holiday, including Easter.'

'I read Moxon's report explaining Nurse Kutter's absence.' Rowthorne replied, 'The question is, where do we go from here? Is the boy's mother aware of what young Jason said?'

'No sir.' Decker shook his head emphatically, 'and at this stage it may be preferable that she isn't told. She would only worry unnecessarily. You and I are the only ones who understand the significance of what the boy saw. It was quite by accident that I found out myself earlier this evening when the boy was showing me his telescope. I happened to ask him, quite by chance, what else he had seen on his nightly vigil. That was when he mentioned seeing the two men putting a body into the ground.'

'Mmm!' A degree of uncertainty showed in Rowthorne's face, 'It's a very tenuous link. I wouldn't like to base our case on the evidence of one small boy. A good defence lawyer would rip it to shreds. We need a lot more than that.'

'I agree sir.' replied the policeman, 'If it is at all possible then I would prefer to keep the boy out of it altogether. The slightest hint to the murderer of a witness could place Jason in terrible danger. That is unthinkable. But I have an idea, just the beginnings of a plan at this stage. There's more than one person involved who knows what happened. The murderer had at least one accomplice, and that is his weak point. All I need is for Jason to confirm my suspicions and pick out one of the two men he saw that night.'

'How do you propose to do that?' asked Nigel Rowthorne, 'and when? I need this case solved, the sooner the better. The force is getting a hammering from the media. It's meat and drink to them. All the violence resulting from the strikes shows us up in a very bad light. The press aren't concerned about presenting a balanced view. Bias works in their favour. It makes for riveting television. I need a success... and soon!'

'Saturday.' suggested Decker, knowing he was putting himself out on a limb, 'Saturday will be the crunch day. The murderer is connected to the cricket team. The club has a home game. Everyone who matters will be there, including our man.'

The Chief Constable studied his officer's face carefully. *'Trust your judgement,'* he muttered to himself, *'Decker is a good man.'* He's honest, hardworking and reliable. Also he had a degree of intelligence that surprised him. Decker used his imagination in a logical reasoning manner. Pray to God he was right.

'Are you sure of your man? There's no room for doubt in your mind?'

'No sir, the person I have in mind fits the bill. I wish it were otherwise. With all my heart and soul I truly wish it were.'

'Would you care to tell me who?' asked Rowthorne gently.

'Yes, I will.' Decker revealed his thinking in minute detail, the time and place, the strange condition of the body, the reason why there had been so little blood and the murderer so efficient in the practice of sudden death. The only question left unanswered in Decker's mine was "Why?"

Why? Why? Why?

The Killer's motive was as obscure to him now as it had been from the beginning.

*

Wednesday evening at 8pm was the usual time and day for the selection committee to meet. The committees' normal venue was in the cricket pavilion at the ground. It was currently unavailable due to the continuing presence of the County Police Forensic Department who still had to complete their careful analysis into the death of the late unlamented Inspector Moxon.

*

'It's a bloody nuisance,' grumbled George Burke, wiping away a layer of froth with the back of a scrawny hand, 'Banned from our own pavilion jest 'cos a prat of a Police Inspector kills 'issen fallin' off a bloody oil drum. 'Ow bloody stupid is that?'

'Aw! Shurrup George. You shouldn't speak ill of the dead. Anyway, yer knows as 'ow yer prefers the Cock Inn. It giss yer more suppin' time and we can pick team 'ere just as easy as at the ground.'

'T'aint just that.' answered George, who enjoyed grinding an axe, 'It's pickin' a strip, mowin', rollin' and marking out wicket. It all needs doing, and that takes time y'know.'

'Yes George.' Ted Decker's voice joined in the conversation from the corner of the room where he had been sitting quietly. He was a long-standing member of the committee and noted for his reasonable views. 'We still have Thursday and Friday evenings to prepare the ground. I'm sure we can manage it.'

'Huh! S'pose it bloody rains on Thursday, ain't many as ever goes ter ground on a Friday is there? They got better things ter do. Then wot?' George, the club's eternal pessimist, was hell-bent on creating imaginary problems. He felt it was his privilege as a former captain. The present incumbent of the post ignored his griping and forged ahead with the meeting. Barnett Hall senior wrote out a list of available players. On paper the club had twenty active members, but it was a rare occasion for all twenty to be available at any one time. The majority lived in or around the village of Briseley T'ill. Two very keen clubmen who had moved to live in nearby towns still remained loyal to the club and frequently travelled as far to a home game as they would to one that was away. The side was rarely the same from one week to the next.

Decker made a mental note of who was chosen. A nucleus of six or seven talented players formed the heart of the team. Certain names were always first onto the team sheet. It usually read; Barnett Hall senior, as captain, followed by Young Barnett, Tim Taverstock, Everett Jackson, (Snowball being the only genuine wicketkeeper in the club) The Mole twins, Lenny and Norman, John Emmett the builder and John Shackleton. George Burke, although present at the meeting, had declared himself unavailable at the weekend.

'How about you Ted?' asked the captain, 'Are you definitely out?'

'I'm afraid so. I'll probably be around, but only call on me if you're absolutely desperate. With the situation as it is I could be called out at a moment's notice. That would let the side down. Sorry.' The excuse came easily.

In truth Decker longed to be out there on the pitch. He longed to feel the summer breeze in his face, the sun on his back, the bite of his cricket spikes into the springy turf and the challenge of testing his playing skills against those of his fellow enthusiasts. It was a great game to play, whatever the level.

An even greater game demanded his attention, the game of life, death... and justice.

*

'Teas.' said the captain, having finalised the team sheet. It showed that young Adrian Hutton had been selected as twelfth man. 'Teas? Do we have any volunteers to prepare the teas?' It was always a thorny subject. Barnett Hall looked around the circle of faces. They stared back at him, expressionless, blank minds behind blank eyes. George Burke sighed heavily and after reflecting moodily, spoke out.

'I suppose Mildred will 'elp out if one of yer lot can collect 'er. I've got ter bloody work.' Finally the reason for his bad humour became apparent. George loved cricket. He was dejected at missing an opportunity to play.

Decker offered immediately, saying he could pick her up at two o'clock on Saturday. He also made the suggestion that perhaps Helen Argosy might be willing to help out. 'I could ask her...?' he murmured.

Thinly disguised smiles wreathed the faces of the committee members. George Burke's sharp little elbow nudged Ted Decker in the ribs suggestively. 'Got yersen in there orlright...Eh! I wor beginning t'wonder if'n yer still 'ad it in yer...What!'

George was seldom short of a ribald comment.

Decker kept his shrug nonchalant and diplomatically stayed silent. Let their imaginations soar, he thought, whatever he chose to reveal he knew the villagers would form their own conclusions.

If Helen were present then it would explain why the boy was there. Jason was mad about cricket. What could be more natural than for him to want to mix with the players at practice? But would his eyes and memory prove sharp enough to identify the nocturnal gravedigger and his accomplice?

*

On Thursday, after breakfast, Beatrice announced she was leaving.

'Oh!' exclaimed Decker. It was hardly an overwhelming expression of brotherly love. They were still strangers and had been for most of their adult lives and it was doubtful if the relationship would ever change. In his heart Decker knew he ought to regret her departure, perhaps express disappointment at her going but there were no feelings between them and less words. A vast gulf existed, a division of mind and thought. All they had ever had in common was the same mother and father.

. The news of Moxon's death had stunned Beatrice. Decker returned home in the early hours of Wednesday morning and had given his sister the news at the breakfast table. The depth of her reaction had astonished him. One moment she'd been happily pouring out a torrent of trivial gossip in her artificially bright voice and in a second the sound had gone, cut off as though her vocal chords had snapped with the dropping of her jaw. The colour drained from her face and she slumped heavily into a chair.

Beatrice Leyland fell into that unusually large category of people who had never experienced violence at a personal level. This was too close. This was intimate. This was a man she had spoken to less than twenty-four hours ago. A man she had cooked for, twittered and fussed over. A man she had expected to meet again. One she had taken a shine to.

Daisy Kutter had been foully murdered but she was a person that Beatrice had never met. To her it was an abstract event, a remote occurrence to express shock and horror and outrage, but still distant. Like an abstract oil painting that roused one's emotions but never quite touched one's soul.

'Where will you go?' asked Decker.

'Home, where I belong. It's empty and it's lonely since Reg died but it is still where I belong. I thought it would be different here, a village in the countryside, peaceful like, away from the hustle and bustle. I could make new friends, a new start. But I was wrong. It hasn't turned out as I expected.'

'I'm sorry about that, life seldom does.' Decker heard his voice say the words. Sorry about what, Daisy Kutter's murder or Moxon's tragic accident? Or the fact that his sister had been unable to adapt and fit into country life?

'I'll run you to the station,' he offered, 'What time is there a train?'

'There's one at 10:58. It's direct. I'd like to catch it.'

*

It was on the way to the station that a new thought came to mind. How had Daisy Kutter intended to travel to Yorkshire? She owned a car. He couldn't remember seeing it at her cottage. Where was it? Who would be likely to know? As a district nurse she made domiciliary visits every day. Some were close to hand but others involved considerable travel. Decker was reasonably familiar with Daisy Kutter's routine. She frequently walked to calls in the immediate vicinity, striding out in her distinctive bouncy way, full of vitality, her Gladstone bag swinging rhythmically with each step. Just to see her made one feel better. For calls further away she used her car. It wasn't a question of penny-pinching, but commonsense. Daisy firmly believed that the human body had been designed for movement. She followed the physiotherapist's dictum – "Keep it moving."

Therefore, it was likely, reasoned Decker, that the nurse had walked from her cottage to the Mole's house on Warren Avenue, a distance of around 800 metres. Say, about half a mile from her cottage next to the church at the northern end of Briseley T'ill. If she had planned to travel by rail then she was already halfway to the station and logically the sensible thing to do would be to take her travel bag with her when she visited Rowena Mole. Afterwards she'd continue on her way to the station. Daisy Kutter's schedule had been upset by the unexpected death of her patient.

It was an event she could not have foreseen.

What had happened to her luggage? Very likely there was just a single suitcase for the practical minded nurse wouldn't have lugged along excessive baggage.

Edward Decker escorted his sister onto the platform, settled her into a comfortable seat on the train and stowed her cases in the cubby-hole by the automatic carriage doors. 'Bye Beatrice.' he said, pecking her dutifully on the cheek. He stood on the platform as the train departed, waving halfheartedly as she slowly disappeared from view. Carried away, perhaps forever. He neither knew nor particularly cared.

*

Pokey Parker slid Daisy Kutter's travel bag across the station counter.

'About time too.' Pokey grumbled at Decker, 'It's bin 'ere weeks.' As he spoke he made the familiar gesture with his forefinger that, as long ago as junior school, had earned him his nickname. Each word brought forth a prod at the large tapestry-patterned holdall with the initials; "D.K."

'You could have reported it sooner.' replied the policeman wearily, 'Can you tell me who left it here? The grizzled little man who looked after the Briseley T'ill station momentarily froze. 'I don't bloody know.' he growled, wagging his finger from side to side in the absence of an object to prod. 'I just found it 'ere the night afore Easter. I ain't bloody paid ter go reportin' every bag 'as is lost. Got better things ter do I 'ave.'

'Alright Pokey, I'll take it and give you a receipt.' Decker decided to play down the situation, remembering the railwayman's reputation for incessant grumbling.

He sat in his car and examined the contents. What did they prove? There was clean underwear, two brassieres, panties, tights, a change of casual clothing; the type of comfortable jogging suit that physically active people seemed to wear continuously. A pair of white trainers, a bag of makeup, socks, handkerchiefs, a couple of clean towels, a portable hair dryer, a Ladyfem electric razor… and a packet of condoms.

Daisy had been prepared for everything and anything.

But what did it prove, the policeman asked himself again. Nothing.

Almost anyone could have left the bag unnoticed in the station waiting room. Daisy herself, or her murderer, his accomplice, or perhaps one of her many friends doing Daisy a good turn.

A friend?

Who amongst her friends was likely to know the whereabouts of her car?

Decker pictured all of the people with whom the nurse was acquainted, a sequence of little portraits flashing through his mind. The gallery was endless. Just one person stood out – Everett. He was the most likely candidate, the ever-present comfortable companion who demanded little and gave so much.

*

The eyes of the man watching Edward Decker were dark with concern. He had spotted the policeman's immaculate green Morris Minor parked on the station forecourt. It was a familiar sight to his eyes. Unaware that Decker's original reason for being at the station had been to see his sister safely onto the train, the man jumped to a wrong conclusion. Then, when he saw the constable emerge from the booking office carrying Daisy Kutter's distinctively patterned travel bag it confirmed his suspicions. The net was closing in!

Now he knew how the hare felt when caught in the wire noose. He tugged at his collar as though a wire loop was already cutting deep into his skin, starving his lungs of air, causing his eyes to bulge and his veins to burst in an agonising struggle to break free.

He was like the hare, a creature of nature. Simple. Uncomplicated. Outwardly strong and powerful, a big man, who, simply because of his size, was seldom challenged. Potential enemies took note of his stature and melted away. Yet he was a man who was easily led. His powerful body belied a weak and feeble mind. He'd always shied away from confrontation and trod the easier path of acquiescence. Now that path had led him into trouble, into deep trouble. To death, to destruction... and to murder!

He, who had never sought to harm another being, was now entangled in a growing mesh of intrigue and subterfuge. It was too much for him to bear.

One death, the first one, had been natural. He could have learned to live with that, learned to accept it and adjust his life... eventually. The second death had been violent, spawned of ignorance and obsessive secrecy. It should never have occurred and he should never have become involved. A misplaced sense of loyalty, the fatal flaw in his character, and a deep-rooted fear had been responsible. The fear had been with him for as long as he could remember. It dated back to his childhood.

For the life of him he couldn't recall its origin.

The third death had been an accident. That was an established fact and logic dictated that he was not responsible. The Police Forensic report confirmed it.

But calm rational thought had long departed. His mind swirled in a fog of confusion. Inspector Moxon's death was the final link in a chain of events driving his mind to the edge, sweeping him to destruction.

He *had* to escape. There was only one certain way...

*

Everett Jackson rented a council house at the top end of Briseley T'ill. He lived opposite the entrance to the village school where from time to time he acted as a stand-in caretaker, covering holiday periods and the rare occasions when the regular incumbent fell sick. Decker tried the doorbell, failed to hear it ring so hammered vigorously on the door.

An unusually grave-faced Jackson invited him in.

'Are you alright?' asked the policeman with concern. He had an uneasy feeling that the black man was on the verge of tears.

'Nope. Ah guess ah ain't.' sighed Jackson, 'Fact is, ah'm feelin' kinda shook-up. T'ain't evry day ah gets a letta. Truth is ah don't get many letta's at all. Ah… Ahh.' The pent up emotion became too great and the man's voice gave up the unequal struggle. He gestured helplessly towards the sideboard inviting Decker to see and read the letter for himself.

A brown envelope, with the embossed name of a firm of solicitors stamped into the sturdy manila, had been torn open. There were two letters inside, a formal one from the solicitor and a second one that had been sealed and addressed to Mr Everett Jackson. Decker read the solicitor's letter first. It simply stated that he had been requested to forward on the enclosed document in the event of his client's death. His client being the late Daisy Kutter and it was the contents of her letter that were the cause of the black man's distress. Decker recognised her neatly rounded handwriting immediately. It was identical to the notes scribbled in the nurse's diary.

Written with affection to a person for whom she had a high regard it was an intensely personal letter. Reading it made the policeman feel uncomfortable, as though he were intruding into another person's life.

Daisy recognised that there was a gulf between Everett and herself, a divide of race and colour. It was a gulf that both were unwilling to bridge in emotional terms. Their relationship had always been, and would have remained, a strictly platonic one.

That apart, there wasn't another human being in whom she placed greater trust or held in higher esteem. The nurse had an abundance of acquaintances: grateful former patients who all became her friends… up to a point. There had been many lovers, some more casual than others, some of them she had held in great affection, others had been no more than ships that passed in the night. But there had only ever been one man Daisy Kutter had trusted as a confidant, Everett Jackson.

Daisy's only surviving relative was her old and senile mother. She had recognised the possibility of accidental death, that, unlikely as it may seem, there was always the chance that she could predecease the old lady. In the absence of a natural heir Daisy Kutter, in her last will and testament, had decided to leave to her most trusted friend everything that she possessed.

'Phe-e-ew!' Decker whistled tunelessly through his teeth, unable to contain his astonishment. Had the late unlamented Inspector Moxon still been around he would have immediately elevated Jackson into the position of prime suspect.

'You do realise what this means?' Decker said to Jackson, 'When the will has been through probate and the legalities sorted out, you will be well off. Perhaps not filthy rich, but comfortable, very comfortable. It may take some time though, perhaps as long as a year.'

'Time! What da hell time matta? Ain't neva' gunna bring Daisy back is it? Not time. Not nothin'...' Everett's deep bass voice dropped by an octave with the depth of his emotion. 'Ah'd give all da time an' all da wealth in da world to bring dat woman back.' A tear escaped from the corner of one sombre brown eye and trickled slowly down the man's careworn face. He shook his head angrily at the futility of fate. The tear coursed sideways across his cheek before he dashed it to oblivion with the back of one hand. 'Why? Why she leave me da cottage? Why? Ah doan wan' no cottage. What Ah gunna do with it? Eh! What Ah gunna do with it?'

Decker looked sorrowfully at his friend, the pragmatism in his character coming to the fore.

'You could try living there,' he said quietly, 'Do what Daisy wanted. Have you thought what will happen if you don't? It will be occupied by strangers. Is that what she wanted?'

'No but... Aw heck man, how can Ah live dere? Evry ting Ah'd see an' touch, it would 'mind me of her.'

'Is that bad?' asked Ted, 'Wouldn't it keep her memory alive? Believe me Everett it *is* what she wanted. Just think about it, you and Daisy, between you, just about rebuilt that cottage. It was virtually derelict when she bought it. Now look at it... it's a little palace. I know Daisy put up the money but it was *your* skill that worked the miracle. All your time and effort, how much did she pay you for that?'

'Pay! Man, Ah didn't ask her for nothin'. What Ah did Ah done for lur..' He stopped short, gave a loose-limbed shrug of his shoulders. 'Ah done it 'cos Ah wanted to. Owed dat woman a lot, more'n a man can ever repay.'

'Let's say it was a partnership.' compromised Ted Decker, 'A partnership that was of benefit to both of you. You put in your skills and time and she put up the money. I'd say that makes you partners, and partners share things. There's no reason on this earth why you should feel guilty about accepting the cottage. Without your efforts it would only be a fraction of its present value. Think about it. Please.'

Some of the doubt in Jackson's face lifted. He smiled wanly and finally asked the reason for Decker's visit. 'Daisy's car? It's in Shackleton's garage with a burnt out exhaust valve. 'Appen 'bout four weeks ago. She always drive too damn fast. Ah told her but she neva' listen till it too late.'

'I found her travel bag at the railway station.' Decker informed him, 'Did she ask you to leave it there for her?' The black man shook his head. 'Would she have arranged for anyone else to leave it there?'

'Nah! Dat not like Daisy. Plenty folks willin' but she seldom asked for favours. 'Ow long it be dere?'

'Pokey Parker said he found it in the waiting room just before Easter. You know what an awkward old cuss he is, it could have been vital, it would have alerted us to her disappearance that much sooner if only he had bothered to report it. Then again, to be fair, I suppose people leave their belongings at railway stations all the time. How was he to know?'

'D'you tink it was left by the murderer?' asked Everett.

'Possibly, or an accomplice. Probably as a ploy to convince us that Daisy had gone to the station and left on the train.'

The black man shook his head in disbelief. 'It wicked man. Ah jus' doan figure no reason why anyone 'arm dat woman. Makes no sense at all.'

''It never does.' Decker agreed, 'All it does is create heartache all around. That reminds me, have you seen Jack Mole lately? He missed the committee meeting on Wednesday. He seems to have turned into a hermit. I've barely seen him around.'

'Yea. Dat's true. He sorta changed. Look terrible sick to me, and old like.'

'Perhaps you could call in and speak to him,' suggested the policeman, 'Jolly him along, try and persuade him to come to the game on Saturday. I need... that is, I'd like to talk to him informally.'

'Sure. Dat man gotta load o' trouble. Ah'll do my best Ted.'

So must I, thought Decker, *I must do my utmost to trap the bastard who murdered poor Daisy Kutter... without apparent reason.*

*

Death sat uneasily on the big man's conscience. Throughout Thursday afternoon he sat in the garden and brooded. The house held far too many memories for him to stay indoors. It was the place where death had stalked and although it was the only home he had ever known he knew that he would never feel comfortable there again.

Conscience turns a man into a coward, easily. Coupled with a fertile and overactive imagination it becomes destructive in the extreme. If only he was aware how fragile the evidence against him was? If there was someone he could turn to for guidance, a friend with whom to share the burden then he might have been able to see things logically. But there was no one. He felt totally alone.

The garden faced north, overlooking fields. In the near distance, less than half a mile away, he could see the Briseley T'ill cricket ground and the adjacent Sinkhole.

The village, built upon a hillside, rose from north to south. Its main thoroughfare curved in an arc to his left and the railway track, which bridged the road at the northern end of the village, swung in an arc to his right so that track and road formed an elliptical shape. Rather like an enormous eye set in the landscape.

A footpath ran from close to the bottom of the garden and meandered in a manner that was traditionally English across the open ground and towards the cricket ground. Players used the path in the summer months as a short cut and all the year round ramblers used it to assert what had become an accepted right of way.

It was along that footpath that he had helped to carry the body.

In his dreams, whenever he managed to sleep, the journey returned in a nightmare. He came home from work late in the evenings, exhausted, ready to collapse into bed and the arms of sleep. But sleep was denied him. Over and over his fertile mind would retrace the journey. His legs followed the same stumbling steps in the semi-darkness. The limp flaccid weight dragged at his arms until his muscles ached and his joints felt as though they were being pulled from their sockets. His breath came in the same short painful stabs. Plumes of mist hung in the frosty air and overall watched the fulsome moon like a sentinel. Its cold full light illuminated the scene, creating dark unearthly shadows, creeping black silhouettes of houses and trees and imaginary people. It was a globe of light that watched... and could not be extinguished.

In his nightmare it grew larger and larger, brighter and brighter, expanding until it filled the universe. It burned into his mind and probed into his very soul.

He would wake up dripping with perspiration. The pillows and bed-sheets were moist with the sweat of his body, damp and clinging. They enveloped him like a cold and clammy shroud. How he longed for... *needed...* the healing power of sleep.

That other great healer, the passing of time, also failed to minister to his needs, he felt as though the forces of nature were in reverse, serving only to accentuate his fears rather than to alleviate them.

There was no moon on this Thursday evening. A thick blanket of cloud shut out the dying rays of the sun. Dusk fell early. Drawn by the unseen hand of fate the big man moved slowly, trance-like, inexorably along the winding footpath. Down through the fields and past the Sinkhole. On across the cricket field to where the white-painted fencing separated the ground from the railway embankment. It was close to the spot where Barnett had made his short cut across the metal tracks.

Barnett had been heading in the opposite direction, towards the Sinkhole, towards the police and into the arms of Inspector Moxon and Decker. Ironically, towards safety. If only Decker was present now... if only...

The embankment was a steep climb, almost vertical. He dug his toes into the crumbling soil and sought purchase with his hands, grasping shrubs and tufts of coarse grass to lever his way towards the summit. Breathing heavily he finally reached the top. He eased his bulk upright and brushed the dirt from his hands.

A footpath of loose granite chippings ran parallel to the track for the benefit of the permanent way engineers. He turned north, heading for the bridge that spanned the main road through the village. Below him, to his left, lay the cricket field spread out like a map. He was able to look down upon the square, the pavilion roof and the cottages. Even the church spire appeared to fall below the level of his eyes. Had there been someone watching, a pedestrian out for a stroll or an ardent young astronomer, his outline, dark against the sky, would have been visible, barely discernable but clear enough to be recognised.

There was no one following his progress. Gathering cloud and the threat of further rain deterred would be strollers and for a budding astronomer there was nothing to be observed. He continued across the bridge, glancing over its low parapet to the road below, the same dark and winding road where Cynthia Ashley-Jayle had crashed to the ground in the fall from her horse.

Moving on a further two hundred metres he eventually came to a signal post and just beyond it, standing a short distance from the gleaming rails, stood a bunker formed by pre-cast concrete sections slotted together. The bunker was four feet wide by six feet in length with a flat sloping lid made of wood. It was hinged at the top and secured with a robust padlock. The time was nine o'clock in the evening.

At 21:12 the evening mail train was due to pass through Briseley T'ill station heading north towards its destination, Edinburgh and Scotland. It gathered speed on the down gradient before beginning a steady climb as it raced towards the Pennine range. Along this section of its route the express reached speeds in excess of ninety miles per hour. It thundered along the track, an unstoppable mass of raw power, hurtling towards its destination.

He chose his spot well, kneeling at the side of the bunker furthest from the approaching train. In this position, sitting back upon his heels with his head bowed forward, he was screened from the driver's sight. With the light fading rapidly an alert man might just spot the danger but would have no time for effective action.

He tried to pray, seeking desperately for words of consolation and forgiveness. The words failed to come. Those familiar childhood prayers, those phrases of supplication so painfully and laboriously learned had gone. Vanished. Blotted out by a curtain of despair. His mind was an empty void. Bereft of love, of knowledge, of consideration and of hope.

The roar of the big diesel drew nearer. Only seconds away now.

He murmured the only words that came into his head.

'I will lift up mine eyes unto the hills. From whence cometh my help?' Closer thundered the train. Closer. Almost there... almost there.

'My help cometh from the Lord... Oh God!'

Now! The moment had arrived. He straightened his body into an upright position. As he thrust forward his toes dug into the gravel footpath creating two long scar-like troughs. With one last desolate cry a single word screamed from his lips.

'M o t h e...e...e...er!'

His head fell across the gleaming rails. The racing wheels cleaved through the big man's neck with the ease of a guillotine blade. By a freak of fate the man's head was whirled around by the circular motion of the wheels and hurled forwards and upwards. Momentarily the driver caught sight of an object flying like a bouncing ball across his vision.

'What the Hell was that?' he called out sharply to his mate.

'What was what?'

'Like a football. Flew up in front, across the windscreen. Did you see it?'

'Naw!'

'Are you sure?'

'Of course I'm bloody sure. There was nothing I tell you.' The man shrugged broad shoulders, carelessly dismissing the incident from his mind.

The lifeless head fell where the track divided and wedged between a set of points. Within seconds the wheels of the locomotive, followed by those of a dozen carriages, had ground the skull to powder, scattering blood and gore and human brain in all directions. In similar fashion the big man's body, all sixteen stones of it, was flung into the air like some oversize rag doll to fall on the very edge of the embankment. It teetered there, limp and lifeless for brief seconds, then tumbled with gathering momentum down the steep slope. At the bottom of the slope lay a gully overgrown with shrubs, nettles and wild bramble. The corpse crashed through the foliage and came to rest at the bottom of the gully. As though they had been designed to obscure, the branches of the shrubs and bramble sprang back into place, effectively hiding all trace of the human remains.

They were to lie there, undiscovered, for many, many days.

The sound of the mail train faded into the distance. Silence descended, and with the silence, as though it offered them an invitation, came nature's refuse collectors. The carrion eaters, to suck and gnaw and nibble away at the remnants of flesh and blood that littered the track. Human refuse to be disposed of like any other.

By morning when the permanent way engineers made their regular daily inspection of the line there would be little, if any, indication of the tragedy.

'I will lift up mine eyes to the hills.' The big man had prayed. If only he had raised his head. Looked beyond the hills. Looked beyond his grief. Looked to the future. Looked for help. If he had realised that nothing in life is permanent. That change is all. If he had talked to a friend, a colleague, a policeman... Decker! If fear hadn't created a mental block and he had called out for help. It would have been at hand. Now it was too late. *The tragedy of Briseley T'ill continued...*

Straight Drive

Straight Drive: A forcing stroke to penetrate the field.

Contrary to George Burke's gloomy prediction, six members turned out on Friday evening to prepare the ground for Saturday's game. Despite being unavailable for selection, George was present. In the front line as a good and loyal club-man!

Being a member of a village team requires more than ability on the field for there is always the work of preparation. A pitch to roll, an outfield to mow, a wicket to be marked out and kit to be cleaned and made ready. One of the reasons Briseley T'ill had prospered as a club was due to the fact that it possessed a higher than average number of willing workers. It was a tradition in the village, handed down over the years, father to son, son to grandson. They passed on their knowledge and their skills.

There were times when it led to dissension. A keen batsman would shave the playing strip so close that it was bare of grass, aiming to produce a bland flat surface on which he might prosper. Bowlers, on the other hand, preferred a green wicket and so were inclined to leave more grass to encourage the ball to seam and swerve after pitching. George Burke, the old captain, had a solution. Craftily he always arrived early at the ground. He selected and mowed a strip before anyone else arrived to help. It pre-empted all discussion on a choice of wicket. As an opening batsman, George shaved the turf as keenly as a barber seeking to impress his first customer. By the time Decker and the others arrived he had completed his self-imposed task.

It was a strange kind of evening, warm and sultry. The sun beat down like a hammer on an anvil of cloud, generating heat that was trapped by the cloud close to the surface of the earth. It was headache weather without a trace of a breeze to freshen the air or alleviate the oppressive heat. A day to sap one's energy, befuddle the brain and drain the will to work. A day galloping towards a thunderstorm!

*

Decker spent a long and boring time writing up reports. His only relief was a call out to the next village to investigate a theft. He was certain that on the telephone the woman had reported her bicycle as missing. When he arrived the only part missing was its pump. One of the two small lugs holding the pump had corroded and fallen off. Decker doubted that her bicycle pump had been stolen. When he drew the woman's attention to the missing lug and suggested that the pump had simply fallen off she became angry. Furious at his theory, which made her look foolish, she rained abuse upon Decker and the police force in general.

Mrs Bannister was usually a placid woman. Her tirade surprised him. He put it down to the oppressive atmosphere that was fraying everyone's nerves and making them edgy.

By six o'clock Ted Decker was thankful to call it a day, change out of his uniform and head towards the cricket ground. A couple of hours spent in the open air, working physically, mixing and relaxing with friends, chatting about the sport he loved, would be refreshing. Also, he would take the opportunity to call at the cottage, speak to Helen Argosy and ask whether she would be willing to help Mildred Burke with the teas again.

His visit on Wednesday evening had turned from pleasure into a disaster. The circumstances had been outside his control but Ted felt the need to make amends. He called at a chemist's shop that sold toiletries and bought a small bottle of perfume as a peace offering. Being unfamiliar with Helen's taste he sought the advice of the assistant on the beauty counter. She was sleekly dressed with immaculate make-up. Swayed by her apparent sophistication he accepted her advise without question. It was a mistake. The assistant suggested an expensive perfume marketed under the name of 'Sultry'. To Decker it implied a warm and passionate nature. Undoubtedly it would be suitable.

He forked out his money and left the shop glowing with satisfaction.

By the time Ted arrived at the ground Tim Taverstock and John Emmett were already there. He recognised Tim's metallic blue BMW and the old and battered builder's truck that belonged to John. They had parked their vehicles at the side of the footpath leading to the cricket field. As he approached the ground Decker could see the distant figures of Everett and Lenny Mole walking, Indian file, taking the short cut across the fields.

Down that same winding path, surmised the policeman, the murderer and his accomplice must have carried the body of Daisy Kutter to the Sinkhole. One of them had diverted, briefly, to borrow the edging spade from the store shed. It had been a bright clear moonlit night and the Killer had taken a fearful risk of being seen. Perhaps he had had little alternative. The good people of Briseley T'ill went to bed early with just a few exceptions, those who watched late-night television and those who worked shifts. On the occasions when he had carried out a late night patrol through the village, checking doors and windows to ensure they were secure, Decker had rarely encountered another person.

He looked across to the dormer window of Jason's bedroom, then back towards the two men nearing the Sinkhole and the outer rim of the cricket field. There was a clear line of vision. The chances of being seen were remote… except that one small boy with an obsession for astronomy, and the moon in particular, had been on watch that night.

The two men caught up with Ted by the gate to the ground. Everett greeted the policeman with a beaming smile that split his black face and displayed a perfect set of strong white teeth. Even Lenny Mole, who was normally quiet and introverted, gave him a cheery wave of the hand and a nod of acknowledgement. He appeared relaxed and completely at ease, as though the terrible events of the last week had passed him by… untouched.

Was it really only a week since the body of Daisy Kutter had been discovered? Only fifty-six hours ago that Inspector Moxon had met his terrible death? The ground and its surroundings appeared so normal. So quiet. Life carried on. The iniquities of man were quickly forgotten. That was nature's way. It was only mankind that required justice: that retribution be made for its sins.

Decker was the man upon whose shoulders rested the responsibility for bringing the guilty ones to account. It was the one part of his job did not relish. Especially now, knowing as he did, that the felon was closely associated with the cricket club, a fellow player and a colleague. He hated the situation that had erected a barrier, an invisible wall of distrust, between his close associates and himself.

At first they worked in silence with only an occasional nod of the head to one another as they passed by. The throbbing noise of the machinery precluded conversation. The heavy beat of the single cylinder motor mowers, the whirling rattle of the cutting blades and the chugging sound of the battered old diesel tractor stilled their voices. Only when the mechanical work was completed were they able to speak in comfort, freed from straining their vocal chords above the hubbub.

George Burke broke the silence first, speaking to Ted Decker as they pulled on the handles of the heavy iron roller. Perspiration glistened on his brow, the result of the sultry atmosphere more than by physical effort. His words came in short broken gasps as his lungs struggled to take in oxygen.

'It's… bloody…'ot!' gasped George, stating the obvious, 'Reckon… we'm due… a storm.' His fellow players just grunted in agreement finding lengthy conversation too great an effort.

'You're probably right,' the policeman elaborated, 'but we do need the rain, though preferably after tomorrow's game. It should be a cracker. We always have a good match against Wingfield. I'll be sorry to miss out. It's my bad luck to have to be on standby tomorrow.'

'Is that because of Saturday's demo's?' asked Tim Taverstock, 'I saw a bit about it on the six o'clock news. There's a big rally planned with speeches and a march and everything, a lot o'trouble I expect. Is that why you're having to standby?'

'Sort of...' Decker's shoulders twitched in a dismissive shrug. It went against the grain, deceiving his friends but it was imperative that no one caught an inkling of his plans. 'Have we a full team?' he asked by way of a distraction, '...everyone available?'

Tim Taverstock replied. As the club secretary he made a point of telephoning every player selected to ensure they were available.

'There's just Norman Mole left to confirm. I haven't managed to catch him yet. It's a problem at times because he works an evening shift.' Tim looked at Lenny Mole, 'I take it he *is* OK Lenny?'

The tall bowler gave a quick nod of his head, 'I 'spect so. Norm loves his game too much to miss out against Wingfield. Fact is, I ain't seen 'im for a couple of days. Y'know 'ow it is!' He shrugged casually.

Decker thought that for Lenny Mole that was quite an oration. Could it be that the dark taciturn young man was emerging from his shell?

'How... about... yer Dad?' gasped out George Burke, 'Will 'e be 'ere on Sat'day... supportin' us?' More than any of the other players, George seemed affected by the oppressive heat. Again came the uncaring shrug of the shoulders.

'Dunno! He's barely said a word of late.'

Decker stared momentarily at Lenny Mole, then, flashed a concerned look towards Everett Jackson. The black man's eyes widened as he tried to convey a silent message of reassurance with a barely perceptible nod of his head.

'He needs ter get out more,' George Burke blundered on with well intentioned but tactless comment, 'Sort isself out. T'ain't no good broodin'. T'ain't wot Rowena would 'ave wanted, is it? She wor a fighter that gel. A proper fighter.'

'Oh shurrup George!' pleaded John Emmett, 'Everyone admired Rowena, and we all know Jack Mole. Just give 'im some space... eh! Alright.'

Burke's mouth tightened in exasperation, he loved to gossip. Realising he'd been insensitive he lapsed into a sullen silence.

The work at the ground was soon complete. Softened by the midweek rain the wicket rolled out evenly. Given a rain-free night and a drying wind the pitch would be an excellent batting track, firm, fast and true. On the other hand, if the storm that threatened broke over Briseley T'ill and the ground soaked by a heavy downpour, then it would be difficult to predict how the pitch would play. While underneath the soil would remain hard and dry its surface could well become greasy with soft patches in the hollows where the rainwater collected. Very few cricket pitches are perfectly flat and only the wealthier village clubs can afford the luxury of covers to protect a wicket from the elements.

As Decker made his way towards the cottage of Helen Argosy he was unaware how fate had decreed the part the weather would play in Saturday's events.

*

A small sad face stared miserably out of Jason Argosy's bedroom window. Ted Decker, catching a glimpse of the boy, waved cheerfully. There was no response and that surprised the policeman. Thunder rumbled faintly in the distance as he knocked on the door. He waited, patting his pocket to make sure he still had the gift-wrapped bottle of perfume.

Come on Helen, he thought, *where are you?* He knocked louder. Still the door remained stubbornly closed. A tiny worm of anxiety began to wriggle in his mind. Was everything alright? He hammered loudly on the woodwork until his knuckles tingled. There was the sound of feet clattering down the staircase. Of course, Helen had been hard at work in her bedroom studio, so deep in the throes of concentration that she completely shut out the world. He knew what she was like.

'Oh! It's you.' she said, standing squarely in the doorway, blocking his entrance, 'I've got a bone to pick with you Edward Decker.' It was the first time he had ever seen her angry. A little knot of irritation puckered the skin between her eyebrows.

'A bone? What do you mean? Has something happened?' he asked, bewildered by her attitude. It was completely out of character.

'Has something happened?' she repeated scathingly, 'Has something happened? Well might you ask! You and your bloody ideas. Of course something has happened. A bloody disaster, that's what's happened, and it's all your fault.'

'My fault? H-how? What? I don't understand. What's my fault? What am I supposed to have done? Tell me, please.'

'Didn't you say that Jason could practice in the nets on Saturday?'

'Well yes, but…'

'Well that's it. You know what children are like. Can't wait can they? Jason became so worked up and excited, he couldn't wait until Saturday could he? No. Swishing and flailing his damn little cricket bat all over the place. What happened? Do you know what happened? No. I'll tell you what happened. He only knocked over my pictures didn't he and ruined them. He sent a pot of paint flying and it ran all over my work. My precious work! It's ruined.'

'B-but… but… can't you do them again?' he stuttered out the question, completely taken aback by her aggression. It was so untypical of the Helen he'd come to know.

'You don't understand do you?' she raged, 'Hell's bells! It's *my* work. W.O.R.K. Work! I've got a deadline to meet. A DEAD LINE. If I fail to meet it then I've broken my contract. I could lose everything I've worked for… everything!'

Now he understood her concern. He appreciated the anxiety that was clouding her reason. Only too well he knew how one's judgement could be affected in moments of stress. It was highly unlikely that the publishers of Helen's work would cast her aside so lightly. They were onto a winner. Winnie the White Witch grew in popularity by the day. But how to reassure Helen Argosy at this moment was another matter.

'Can I help?' he offered, speaking in as calm and even a voice as he could muster, 'If you want me to pose again…?' Helen gave an angry little shake of her head. Her immediate rage was already abating, a balloon of emotion collapsing with the release of her pent-up feelings.

'No. That won't be necessary. Once I have an image in my mind I can always reproduce it. It just takes time. I… I've a lot to do…' Helen fidgeted anxiously, eager to return to her work. She glanced at the staircase leading to her studio, back towards Decker, then again to the staircase. 'I *need* to press on, to be alone, you do understand…?'

'Yes, of course. I'm sorry. I'll let you get on with it. Erm… I…' He knew only too well that it was a bad time to ask for a favour. The worst possible moment and yet it had to be now. There wouldn't be another opportunity.

'Was there something else?' she asked, formality ruling her voice. Her head cocked aggressively.

'Mmm! Well yes. Two things really.' Suddenly he felt quite miserable. Nothing was working out as he had planned. He slipped his hand into his pocket and drew out the gift-wrapped package and handed her the perfume. 'After Wednesday night's disaster I bought you a little gift, something to compensate. Perfume, I hope you like it. The other thing, well, I... erm... I wondered if you could... if you would... be able to help Mildred Burke tomorrow with the teas? Please!' His eyes made an eloquent plea, 'I'm sorry it's such short notice.'

She fingered the packet, exploring its shape, curious about his choice. 'Can I open it?' she asked. He nodded. Her fingers ripped apart the paper with the eager abandon of a small child on Christmas Day. Deftly she unscrewed the stopper and dabbing a few spots onto the back of one wrist, bent to sample its aroma.

'Oh!' Helen's face screwed into an expression of distaste. Quickly she tried to disguise her features, but it was too late.

'Is it alright?' Ted asked in dismay.

How does one conceal disappointment? Helen Argosy was too open-natured to lie.

'No. I'm sorry Ted, but it just isn't me. It's too... heavy, too cloying. It's, how can I describe it? It would suffocate me. I prefer a perfume that's light, fresher, something with a delicate fragrance.'

'Oh thanks!' Decker replied, sarcasm heavy in his voice, 'Thank you very much.'

Damnation, thought Helen, *Why do I have to make my feelings so obvious?*

'Ted. Please.' She said aloud, 'It isn't a problem. I can change it for one that I like. There's no need to be upset.'

He backed away from her, half turning to depart.

Oh God! Decker's thoughts ran, *why didn't relationships run smoothly.* He had forgotten what it was like, the ups and downs of a developing love affair. It was because he cared so much about her that he now felt so deeply hurt. 'About tomorrow,' he asked primly, 'will you be able to help? And you will let young Jason come, won't you?'

'We'll see.' Helen answered, unwilling to commit herself, 'we'll just have to wait and see. It all depends on meeting my deadline. Now I'm sorry but I must go.'

With an effort of will she did not feel, Helen Argosy closed the door in his face.

Decker stared morosely at the closed door. Dear God, was nothing going right today? Were all his plans to trap the murderer of Daisy Kutter falling by the wayside, all his efforts coming to nought?

Lightening stabbed down towards the earth, followed within seconds by the crack of thunder. The storm was breaking. Hell! Hell! Hell!

He made a mad dash for the shelter of his car.

Helen slumped with her back against the closed door. A single salt tear squeezed from between her eyelids. *You fool!* Helen rebuked herself, *you stupid damn fool. You could have handled the situation far, far better than that.* Poor Ted Decker, sent away with his tail between his legs. He never deserved that. And poor Jason, sent to bed in disgrace just because his natural exuberance had run away with him. Did he deserve to be punished as well? What was the matter with her? She had behaved like a totally different woman. It was time to take a firm grip on her life.

*

'You've had your hair done.' Barnett commented as soon as he entered the hospital room. 'It looks absolutely gorgeous, stunning.' He crossed to the bedside, kissed Cynthia Ashley-Jayle on one peach-like cheek and buried his nose in the silken fragrance of her hair. 'Mmm-mm!' he murmured, 'You smell like an angel.'

'How does an angel smell?' giggled Cynthia, thrilled by Barnett's unexpected compliment. She had taken great pains to look her very best. Making special arrangement for a hairdresser to shampoo and set her hair at the hospital had not been cheap. It had stretched her allowance to the limit.

'Like all the good things in life,' answered Barnett buoyantly, '...from Chanel perfume to the smell of fish and chips on a frosty winter's evening.'

'Fish and chips! I don't think I want to be compared to the smell of fish and chips. Chanel perfume, yes. But fish and chips!'

Barnett plunged his nose into her hair once more. He nibbled with his lips at the lobe of her ear. Murmured softly, provocatively, 'It's a very enticing aroma... to a hungry man. A-a-a-argh! I'm a hungry man. R-r-r-r-agh!' With a wolfish growl he pretended to bite at the smooth white flesh of her exposed neck.

'Oo-oo-oo! Barnett! Stop! Stop it.' Cynthia giggled and squirmed from his lunges, though without serious intent. 'Oo-oo Barnett. Stop it. What *is* the matter with you tonight? Have you been drinking?'

'Drinking? No-o-o. But I *am* intoxicated, with you. Why do you ask?'

'You're so... bubbly... so full of yourself.'

'So I am,' he replied positively, 'So... I... am. Do you know why? It's because I'm here with you, that's why. I've been through a horrible experience the last few days. Now it's over. I'm free again, I'm here with you and it's where I want to be.' Cynthia found it hard to believe.

'Barnett, do you really mean it? Honestly?'

'Yes.'

'Oh Barnett.' She sighed, wrapping her arms around his body and pulling him close. To his own surprise Barnett was genuinely pleased to be with Cynthia again. She was very beautiful with her dark violet blue eyes and her softly waved blonde hair shining like a halo of burnished gold against the snowy whiteness of the hospital pillows. Deep in his heart Barnett recognised the commonsense in his mother's warning. The difference in his background and that of Cynthia Ashley-Jayle was too wide a gulf to be bridged. Her father would never recognise him and he doubted that he would ever fit into Cynthia's circle of friends. Educationally and financially they were oceans apart.

Jean Hall had been clever during her heart to heart talk with her son. She had forbidden nothing and refrained from setting rules. Instead, gently and casually, she'd suggested to Barnett the problems and obstacles he was likely to face. His intelligence would do the rest.

For his part, Barnett decided he would take their relationship one step at a time. He'd expect little and enjoy it while he may.

'Barnett, your shirt, it's wet.' Cynthia's hands moved across his back feeling the clammy dampness of his creamy white cotton shirt.

'It'll dry.' he replied with the careless disregard of the young towards their own well-being. Current fashion, amongst the young, decreed that *real* men went jacketless and ignored the elements whatever the weather, a foolhardy way to prove their manhood.

'You'll be stiff tomorrow.' Cynthia warned, 'It won't help if you're playing cricket will it? Slip it off and hang it on the radiator. It'll soon dry off.'

'I can't do that. Suppose the nurse comes in. What will she think?'

'Aw Barnett! You can be a stuff-pot. She won't come in, nobody will, I arranged it with the Sister.'

'Did you now! And what did you have in mind?'

'I wanted us to be alone together. There's something important I have to tell you and, well, I bought you a present. I hope you like it.' She looked anxiously at his face. It was new ground for Cynthia. Rejection would be more than she could bear. 'Sister helped me choose it.' she added, as though to divest some of the responsibility. Awkwardly she felt under her pillow, twisting her arm to reach the flat package hidden there. The movement arched her back, pushing the fullness of her breasts against the silken white material of her nightdress. Barnett could see that she was naked underneath, see the firm outline of her nipples pressed taut and tantalising beneath the flimsy garment. In some confusion he turned away, peeling off his damp shirt in the process and fighting to control the floodtide of emotions that threatened to overwhelm his resolve.

'H-how are y-you?' he mumbled, 'I half expected you to have made more progress. After my last visit you seemed so much improved.' Cynthia turned down the corners of her mouth in a brave attempt at nonchalance.

''I was, but the improvement was temporary, it only lasted a few hours, then I slipped back... back to the way I've been since the accident.' A trace of a tear glinted in her eyes. Angrily she shook it away. Threw off the creeping self-pity. 'Help me Barnett. Help me to sit up. I want to see if you like your present.'

'Oh sure! Sure!'

Anxiously he moved to help, slipping his strong young arms around her back and beneath her knees. He lifted her slight weight easily.

'Over to one side, like last time,' she instructed him, 'so we can lie close together.'

He was conscious of her bare arm pressing against his naked chest as he eased her across the bed. It was covered in fine soft hairs that caught the light and reflected the same golden sheen as the hair upon her head. Barnett's breath caught in his throat, then exhaled in an appreciative sigh. He bent his head and lightly brushed his lips along the length of her arm. His gesture brought a shiver of pleasure from the young woman. She smiled softly, the light of anticipation in her violet blue eyes.

'Patience Barnett,' she whispered, 'Later. I want to show you your present first.'

He settled her comfortably in a sitting position, solicitously re-arranging the pillows to support the slender arch of her back. He kicked off his shoes and edged onto the bed to sit in close proximity. Cosy!

'Ready.' He said, screwing up his eyes like a small child and holding out both hands in anticipation. Pleasure and amusement reflected in Cynthia's eyes as she placed a small flat parcel on his outstretched palms. She held her breath, praying and hoping that her choice of gift had been the right one.

'It's a book!' guessed Barnett immediately. 'The Skills of Cricket.' He read out seconds later, 'Oh my God! It's magic... pure magic. It's what I've always wanted.'

'It is? You really like it?'

'Like it! I love it. I've never been given a coaching book before. It's a perfect gift.' He flicked over the pages with growing excitement, pausing to read out sections as he pored over the numerous action photographs of internationally renowned players. For a dedicated and ambitious young cricketer it was an ideal gift.

'How did you know what to buy?' he asked. Cynthia was tempted to be smug but confessed that the Sister had helped by making suggestions and that she had telephoned several bookshops before settling on her final choice.

'Look inside the flyleaf,' she urged, 'I've written an inscription. I hope you don't mind.' In a flamboyant hand, characterised by excessive loops and curlicues, Cynthia had inscribed.

To Barnett
Who proved to be a true friend.
With Love and Affection
Cynthia.

Barnett slipped a protective arm around her shoulders. He squeezed her arm with genuine affection, pulling her close into the safe custody of his lean athletic body. At that moment he'd have been willing to take on the whole world to protect her, a knight errant in white flannels.

'I don't know how to thank you enough.' he said.

Cynthia nuzzled into the hollow between his chest and arm. She turned the full power of her violet blue eyes appealingly towards his face. 'There is one way you could thank me Barnett. A very special way.'

'Anything, anything at all. Whatever you want, just ask.' was his naïve reply.

'Then make love to me,' she implored him with limpid eyes, 'Please... I want you so very, very much.'

'What!' Barnett's eyes popped wide with surprise, 'What! Here! Now! In the hospital, I couldn't do that, suppose someone came in?'

'No-one is going to come in,' she reassured him in a low voice, 'I've fixed it... and there is a key. If it makes you feel better you can always lock the door.'

'But... but...'

'Barnett... Ple-e-ase.'

Gingerly he turned the key, as gently, as softly as he could. To Barnett's ears the resulting click of the mechanism sounded unnaturally loud, a hammer blow on an anvil resounding through and through the lofty wards and corridors of the building. It had the power of a dinner gong calling the staff to their evening meal. He waited in nervous anticipation. All remained quiet and still.

Outside the sky darkened early as the dark thunderheads passed over the city. Streetlights flickered on with an orange glow, their sensors activated by the premature fall of night. A jagged flash of lightning split the sky. It was quickly followed by a thunderous crash as the storm broke overhead.

Faintly Barnett heard the distant sound of patients calling out in alarm. The voices of the nurses, calm and reassuring, soothed the fears of the nervous. Any sound they made would surely be lost in the ferocity of the storm and the nursing staff would be fully occupied attending to their charges.

Escape was out of the question. The nervous lump in Barnett's throat seemed to swell by the second, cutting short the air to his lungs. He was aware of his breathing coming in harsh gasps, short and painful.

Damn the doctor. He should have given him some pills. An aphrodisiac! Anything... anything at all rather than allow him to be humiliated in this way. How could he face the next half hour? How would he cope?

'Barnett! Why are you standing there? Is something the matter?'

'No. No. It's just... I... I want to be sure.' He unbuckled his belt and allowed his stonewashed jeans to fall to the floor, stepping out of them. As he slipped between the cool white sheets Barnett realised that somehow, while his back had been turned, Cynthia had managed to wriggle out of her nightdress and lever herself down the bed. Her white satin nightgown lay in a crumpled heap upon the floor. Beneath the sheets her slender body was now completely naked. His own body was trembling violently, a mixture of fear and excitement.

'You're shivering,' exclaimed Cynthia, 'surely you can't be cold.'

'No. No. It's... it's just... it feels so... so wrong. I'm finding it hard to accept, the idea of... of making love to... to... to one who is ill. Who is...'

'Paralysed.' bluntly Cynthia completed the sentence for him.

'Yes.' He replied miserably, 'Making love... sex... it should be for both parties, for both of us to enjoy. But this way it makes me feel... feel...' Frantically he searched for the right word, 'feel selfish, so self-indulgent. D'you understand? I mean paralysed as you are... how will it be for you?'

'Barnett. Oh Barnett. Don't you understand? Can't you see? It's what I want. Now. Before it's too late. Now, while I still look the way that I do and while you still find me desirable.' There was a passionate intensity to her pleading, 'You must know Barnett, must appreciate what happens to anyone who's forced to spend their life in a wheelchair. You're not blind are you? They waste away don't they? Their bodies and legs just waste and wither, become like sticks. You wouldn't want to make love to me then would you? No! Of course you wouldn't, no man would.

'Please Barnett. Please don't let me down, don't reject me.'

He was caught between a rock and a hard place with nowhere to hide. What had happened to his virility, the fabled procreative prowess of the Barnett Halls? Why now, he asked himself, why am I like this now? He had never had problems before. When he had been with Daisy Kutter he'd been as strong as a young bull - Alive, vibrant, powerful.

There had never been any doubts in his mind then. It had all gone wrong since Daisy had died. She had been the perfect lover. She had taught him so much. Making love with her had been a wonderfully exciting and exotic experience. A game played at the highest level, one full of joy and laughter, of teasing and expectation and of fulfilment.

My little soldier, Daisy had referred to his manhood. My little guardsman – a Grenadier guardsman – tall and strong – complete with Busby, she had said, a guardsman who had never failed to stand to attention when Daisy was in command.

'Oh God!' Barnett moaned in silent despair.

His powerful arms crushed Cynthia's body against his own. He pressed his full muscular length against her slender frame with fierce intensity, thigh against thigh, breast to breast. He was like a frustrated sculptor, a cosmic God trying to mould two frail human bodies into a single piece of clay. But still his body failed to respond.

Cynthia could scarcely breathe. Her ribs felt as though they would crack. Her arms were trapped against his chest and her full round breasts, painfully crushed.

'Easy Barnett!' she gasped, ' Just... ease... off... a... bit.' His grip slackened and his body fell away. Cynthia ceased the opportunity to take the initiative. Her hands moved below the sheets to Barnett's body.

'Oh my sacred aunt!' she exclaimed, 'Barnett, you *are* well endowed, like a young stallion.' She worked away in silence, her eyes closed in concentration, her hands moving tenderly in a steady rhythm while her soft succulent lips teased their way across his skin exploring and seeking out the sensitive erogenous zones of his body.

But still the response was minimal.

'You may be built like a stallion.' muttered Cynthia with growing frustration, 'One that's been bloody gelded. Damn it Barnett! What *is* the matter with you? What kind of man are you?'

'What do you mean what kind of man? There was nothing wrong with me until...' he paused, 'until... until... recently.' He'd been halfway to saying, 'Until the incident at the cricket ground.' Then decided against it. He wanted to put *that* traumatic event firmly into the past.

'Until when, until you became involved with me?' Cynthia flashed back at him, 'I'll bet you're going to tell me everything was alright with that bloody Daisy Kutter.'

'Well it was. It bloody was!' Barnett's fiery nature exploded into sudden anger. Daisy was dead. Dead! She had been so good to him, so kind, so generous, so caring and so true. The utter futility of her death outraged him. It was senseless. Senseless! Someone had to pay. Must pay. The anger boiled inside him like a tide of molten lava rising inside a volcanic crater. The pressure was building, the fiery fires of Hell ready to burst upon an unsuspecting world.

Cynthia's fist beat against his chest. Her blood-red finger nails clawed at the soft white flesh of his buttocks, 'Damn you Barnett Hall. Damn you! I hate that Daisy Kutter, hate her, hate her, hate her, even if she is dead. I don't care. I still hate her. I'm glad the police intercepted my call. I'm glad I tried to phone. Even though she was dead by then. I didn't know... I...'

'You what?' enraged, Barnett interrupted her flow of words, 'You what? You rang the police at Daisy Kutter's house. When? When did you ring them? What did you say to them? Come on, out with it. What did you tell them?'

He gripped her shoulders so fiercely that his fingers left livid red marks upon her pale skin as he bounced her violently against the bed. Cynthia's teeth rattled painfully as she tried to speak.

'I told... I told... her... that I knew all... all about her... and... and you. I said t-to k-keep her hands off y-you. Oh Barnett!' she wailed, 'I didn't know it... it... w-wasn't Daisy speaking. I didn't know it was a p-policewoman. How was I t-to know you would be arrested?'

Barnett found it hard to believe what he was hearing. He seethed with fury at the humiliation he had suffered. It was all because of Cynthia Ashley-Jayle that he had been arrested by the police, flung into that miserable little cell and confined for untold hours. Then subjected to an intensely personal interrogation by the objectionable Inspector Moxon and made to reveal the intimate details of his relationship with the nurse. Worst of all he'd had to suffer the degradation of being forced to use that revolting, evil-smelling chemical toilet in his hour of greatest need. It was too much.

The dark side of Barnett took control. The dark deep evil forces within him swept aside his inhibitions. Away went the restraints of civilisation as for brief minutes his animal instincts came to the fore. Wild, savage and unrestrained, animal instincts and animal ardour!

Cynthia felt the hardness surge into his body. The raw power excited her, overcoming her fear.

'Oh God!' she cried out, 'It... it's like... like a rod of iron. Love me Barnett... Love me. Now! Now! Take me! Take me!'

Her hands clutched at his loins and pulled him towards her. Barnett, his manhood returned, fired by ungovernable passion, drove straight into the warm and tender recesses of her welcoming body.

It was revenge. It was punishment. His was the arrow of retribution flying to its mark. There was a roaring in his head like the sound of waves pounding. The vibration of great crashing chords of music resounded in his ears, they swept him on with their power, thunderous Wagnerian chords, "Ride of the Valkrie" chords that carried him to victory and to triumph.

Time and time again he thrust into her with unbridled passion. Satisfying his own desires, his lust insatiable. Cynthia's feeling counted for little. At first she lay supine, her arms clasped around his body, her violet blue eyes tightly closed, little gasping sounds escaping from her lips, driven by the force of his exertions. Slowly her own desires became aroused. Her breathing quickened. The little gasping sounds turned into murmurs of ecstasy. Her arms pulled him closer as she smothered his face, his neck and his lips with fierce hungry kisses.

Simultaneously, it seemed, the straining couple on the bed and the raging thunderstorm reached a climax together. A blinding flash of light lit up the room as though a thousand neon tubes had flickered on. Every detail stood out stark and clear in the steely blue light. A brief second later the room was plunged once more into stygian gloom. An explosive bang followed as a thunderbolt struck home. All the lights in the Royal Infirmary failed. Frightened screams rent the air as terrified patients cowered in their beds. Pandemonium reigned within the wards. Even the calm assurance of the nurses was shattered as they clung to one another for comfort and support.

Barnett felt as though he was clamped between the jaws of a massive vice. There was a tight restricting band around his neck and his ribs were being crushed inwards with unrelenting pressure. He fought for precious air, vital life prolonging oxygen. Cynthia's arms were locked in terror around his neck. One forearm pressed tightly against his windpipe.

Crouched awkwardly, his elbows and knees taking the weight of his body, Barnett gently eased his fingers around Cynthia's wrist and carefully levered the pressure away from his throat. He sucked in a great gulp of air.

'Barnett,' she whispered in a frightened voice, 'don't let me go. Hold me. Hold me tight please.' Tenderly he smoothed her hair, stroking it away from her face with gentle fingers. He kissed her forehead, her eyelids and cheeks with soft reassuring lips. Made comforting noises in his throat. Her panic subsided. Her confidence began to return.

Their bodies were moist with perspiration, damp from the humidity and their physical exertions. Barnett pushed against the bed, easing his muscular frame away from the girl's slender body. It felt like peeling away Sellotape, as though their bodies had been moulded together from a single piece of clay.

There was a problem. Cynthia's legs were wrapped crushingly around his waist. Her legs were crossed at the ankles, tightly locked, her powerful thighs, their muscles developed by years of riding, gripped his body with bruising strength.

The significance of the situation did not dawn on him immediately. But Cynthia knew, her eyes watched his face, waiting expectantly for understanding to arrive.

'Help me.' he said, 'We're all of a tangle.' And then the light in his mind flashed on. 'A tangle...? Oh my God! Oh my bloody sainted aunt! Your legs...I've just realised... *your* legs, they're... they're wrapped around *my* body. You can move them. How? When?' Barnett's head slowly shook in disbelief.

It was a miracle and Cynthia was still trying to come to terms with what had happened. Words would come later but for the present her eyes mirrored the overwhelming joy flooding her heart.

Barnett found two bath towels in the bedside locker. He wrapped one around his middle, pulling the end tight and tucking it in to form a skirt. With the second towel he covered the girl's slender form and very, very gently patted dry the sheen of perspiration that glistened in the faint orange glow of the street lights.

Cynthia's eyes watched his every move with adoration. He could have been a latter-day Messiah and she a Mary Magdalene ready to worship and follow him to the ends of the earth.

Suddenly shooting pains wracked her body. Her legs twitched in agony. She flinched as a gasp of anguish escaped her lips. Barnett froze, an expression of deep concern upon his face. 'Have I hurt you?' he asked, 'I'm so sorry.'

'A-a-a-h! It's... it's... like p-pins and needles,' Cynthia wheezed out the words, 'Pain, shooting down my l-legs. A-ah! Pins and needles... only a thousand times worse. It's agony.'

'A doctor, I'll fetch a doctor, or one of the nurses.'

'No! No!' she cried out sharply, stopping him in his tracks as he made to rise from the bed. 'Don't go. Don't leave me. I'll be fine... I will... I really will. Please Barnett, stay with me.'

He hovered, tormented by indecision, wanting to remain and comfort her yet concerned that medical attention was a pressing need. She read his face.

'Barnett, stay. I'm alright, really, I'll be alright. It's just like cramp. I'm sure it is. If you could massage my legs a little I'm certain it will help.'

Barnett moved her into a semi-reclining position. He manoeuvred her legs so that the muscles were relaxed and with strong supple fingers commenced to knead at her shapely limbs. Techniques, used on him by Daisy Kutter, were fresh in his mind. He recalled the way she had stretched his limbs to exercise the wasted muscles and ligaments of his broken leg. If it had worked for him, he reasoned, very likely it would work for Cynthia. He copied the treatment religiously for almost thirty minutes until his arms and fingers began to tire. The amount of strength and effort needed was a revelation. It had looked so simple and easy when he had been the patient. Gradually Cynthia's body relaxed, the spasmodic twitching in her legs ceased and the pain disappeared from her face. He sat back on his haunches, drinking in the exquisite perfection of her body. 'How do you feel now?' he asked.

'Wonderful!' she answered and stretched luxuriantly back, pushing her toes to the bottom of the bed and reaching back with her arms. It was a feline movement, sensuous and revealing for her breasts popped from under the towel and the sight of their firm round beauty stirred anew the fire in Barnett's loins. He bent forward and kissed them tenderly, feeling her nipples harden and respond to his touch.

'Darling Cynthia,' he murmured softly in her ear, 'Can we make love again?'

'Now? So soon! You really can?'

'Just wait and see.' Barnett whispered impishly, 'Just wait and see if I can.'

If their first improbable union had been fired by rage and anger, an overture of Wagnerian dimensions, this time the symphony they played together was a gentler melody, a romantic lilting rhapsody of love. This time Barnett was in full control of his emotions and made love with the utmost delicacy and sensitivity, using his body to tease and tantalise, seeking only to ensure the satisfaction of his nubile partner. Love, not rage, dominated and patience controlled his passion. It was consummation on equal terms.

Over the city the storm abated. As the thunderheads rolled away the drumming rain eased to a gentle patter. Nature was matching the mood of the young lovers entwined together. In the hospital the lights flickered to life and normality was restored.

'Time for me to go.' whispered Barnett. He stroked her cheek, feeling its soft peach-like texture, reluctant to leave.

'So soon?' she murmured softly. There was fulfilment in her eyes, the dewy look of pleasure remembered on her face. 'If only moments like this could last forever...'

Barnett wriggled into his stonewashed jeans, slipped shoes upon his feet and pulled his cream-white shirt over his head. He picked up the satin nightdress, holding it out for the girl to put on. 'It's a sin to cover up such beauty,' he smiled ruefully as he helped her into the garment, ''I'd much prefer to be taking it off...'

'Barnett!' Cynthia feigned surprise, 'haven't you had enough, you ravenous beast?' There was genuine affection for the young man in her voice. She laid a restraining hand upon his arm. 'There's something I need to tell you, something we need to sort out before you go.'

He was intrigued by the seriousness of her voice, the earnest cast to her features. He perched on the edge of the bed, hanging onto the present she had given him, hugging the book to his chest like a small child.

'It's about us,' Cynthia began, 'you and I, our relationship. There's something you need to know.'

'Go on.' He looked grave, 'Tell me the worst.' Her violet blue eyes looked into his face, willing him to understand. Steadfast.

'I love you Barnett,' she stated simply, 'but I'm not *in love,* if you know what I mean. There's no doubt in my mind that you are the best thing ever to happen to me. The truest friend I've ever known. Perhaps the *only* true friend. But... Hell! What I'm trying to tell you is... there's... there's no long-term commitment. There can't be. You see, come September, I'll be off to France and then to Germany. I'll be away for two years. My father wants me to go to study their languages. It's his idea, part of his plans for my future.'

'And you?' he asked, 'How much say do you have in the matter?'

'Oh! It's my idea as well. I *want* to go. I'm really looking forward to it because eventually I hope to take over the family business and run it all by myself. One day, in the future.

'So you see Barnett my love, this can't last forever. Oh, sod it! Barnett, you know I'm just a selfish bitch. I want to have my cake and eat it. But we *can have* a few months, a few summer months to spend time together. We could have a summer romance, something wonderful to remember for the rest of our lives? Couldn't we?'

'A summer romance?' Barnett's face went sombre as he considered her proposal. Then his shoulders lifted in a shrug of Gallic proportions. 'OK... yes.'

You agree?'

A huge grin spread across Barnett's face. His relief was clearly palpable.

'Agree? You bet I agree. I think it's a wonderful idea. In fact the more I think about it the better I like it. It's like... like having the best of both worlds... for both of us. And when the summer is over, who knows? At the very least we can part as good friends.'

*

Barnett virtually skipped out of the hospital. He felt as light as air. Uplifted.

'Hello. Hello-o! Who looks full of the joys of spring?' a familiar voice passed comment, 'I trust you had a good visit?'

'Magic! Sister dear. Pure magic.' And he planted an impromptu kiss upon the startled woman's cheek. The Sister's face turned crimson as she sought to cover her confusion. 'Really!' she exclaimed, 'Behave yourself young man.'

'Ah! Sister dear, if only I could.'

The Sister tapped the book still clasped against Barnett's chest. 'How about your present? A good choice? Was it a nice surprise?'

'Perfect. Bloody per-r-r-fect! Oh yes, and thank you for the little tip about Cynthia's hair. I'd never have noticed it myself. You can't imagine how that one little compliment helped to set the mood, and oh boy, what a mood it was.

'Ah yes, by the way Sister dear, you may be in for a little surprise yourself.'

With those enigmatic words he flashed the Sister a dazzling smile, nodded farewell, turned and walked jauntily away.

Late Cut

Late Cut: A delicate shot that requires perfect timing.

Decker switched on the television to catch the one o'clock news. It made grim viewing. By coach and by car, parties of coal miners and their supporters were travelling towards the city to take part in a mass rally. The police were also preparing as additional officers from outlying forces arrived by the hour. They poured out of transit vans carrying their equipment; riot shields, batons and visored helmets. The television commentators all predicted violent confrontation. They spoke with barely suppressed excitement in their voices as though anticipating a major sporting event.

There would be bloodshed and violence with people injured, some seriously, some, perhaps, fatally. Many would suffer broken limbs, battered heads, their guts ruptured and their blood spilt. In the minds of the commentators it made for great television: the prospect of gore and brutality. Bugger the misery! Think of the viewing figures.

Edward Decker switched off in dismay. He feared that his fellow officers were in for a hard time. They would have more to handle than they could manage. It was a sombre thought. Of even greater concern, he reflected, was his own situation. When *he* needed backup, where on earth was support going to come from…?

It was likely he'd have to handle the whole messy business on his own.

*

Mildred Burke was ready and waiting for him with two large boxes of provisions at her feet. Decker helped to carry and load them into the boot of his Morris Minor. He loved the old car. Its sleek curves had character and strength. To his eye it was far more aesthetically pleasing than the flat square shape of contemporary vehicles when a man had to look long and hard to distinguish one model from another. His only regret was the shape of its boot. Even Decker had to admit that the sweetly curved lid restricted the amount of luggage one could take on a journey. Still, there was ample room for his cricket bag, and on this occasion, the two cardboard boxes of food fitted in quite snugly.

Ever the gentleman, Decker held the car door open for Mildred Burke. She fitted a shade too snugly into the passenger seat, her ample figure overflowing its austere upholstery. Mildred fidgeted her body into a comfortable position. An ominous creaking sound came from the seat's tubular frame.

He slipped the car into gear and drove the short distance to the cricket ground, turning neatly to park on the grass verge close to Helen Argosy's cottage. As he walked around to open the passenger side door and assist Mildred out of the car a small figure burst from the house and tore towards him. Jason Argosy was agog with excitement, as fizzy as champagne and about to spray himself in every direction.

'I'm weddy!' he cried out, 'All weddy to pwactice. Can we start now?'

'Whoa! Steady on young shaver. All in good time.' Decker put out a restraining hand. 'First we have to help Mrs Burke unload the teas and then we can think about a bit of practice. Now, about your mother, did she manage to complete her work?'

His question was answered as a smiling Helen Argosy stepped through the door and hurried to greet him. Without any hesitation she stretched up and planted a welcoming kiss upon his cheek. 'Ted, I'm so sorry about last night. I was in such a panic, terrified of missing my deadline. Please forgive me, won't you…?' She looked at him with such beseeching eyes that any lingering rancour he felt instantly melted away.

Mildred Burke, her ears flapping for a hint of gossip, smiled benignly and pretended to be looking elsewhere.

A lover's tiff, she thought, *so, there is something there after all.* She tucked away the snippet of information for future use. On a suitable occasion, with embellishment, it would make her the centre of attention.

Decker carried the tea boxes into the narrow galley-style kitchen at the back of the pavilion. He set them down on the Formica worktop, ready for Mildred to sort out. Three adults in the confined space was a tight squeeze. There was barely room to swing the proverbial cat. *Now if he were alone with Helen…!*

Brusquely Mildred bustled him out of the way

'Off you go to play.' She instructed him as though he were a little boy rather than a burly guardian of the law. 'Let the dog see the bone.'

Helen chortled in amusement at his discomfort. She tipped him a sly wink as he edged past her, whispering affectionately in his ear. 'See you later, after the game.'

'Yeah!' he replied eagerly, as momentarily he forgot the reason for his presence. 'I hope so.' Whether he *would* have an opportunity to spend the evening with Helen Argosy largely depended upon events that were unpredictable.

*

Decker rummaged in the wooden lockers of the old pavilion. He tossed aside old bats, tattered gloves and a selection of fusty smelling pads until he came upon the items he was searching for, a Harrow-sized bat and a pair of junior pads. Although a shade too large for the boy to handle comfortably they were the best he could do at short notice. He would have preferred to coach the boy using an old tennis ball. It was a safer method of teaching and eliminated the need for protection. It also allowed greater freedom of movement and was less tiring.

But boyhood pride was at stake. Jason was determined to emulate his idols. He waddled, stiff-legged down the practice strip, waving the cumbersome bat like a two edged sword.

'Centre!' piped his squeaky treble voice. He looked squarely down the pitch. Fierce determination burned in his eyes. Decker held the ball loosely in his fingers. Deliberately he'd chosen an old ball, one that had swollen with age and constant use, a ball with softened leather. He ambled three short steps and floated down a gentle delivery.

Most small boys have a single shot in their locker: a scything, agricultural sweep to leg. They try to hammer the ball with all the power they can muster and always in the same direction, to the leg-side. Jason's left leg moved smoothly forward as his bat pushed firmly at the ball and met it with a satisfying clunk. It was as near to perfect as a small boy with an oversize bat could manage.

The policeman was astonished.

Quite obviously Jason had observed and inwardly digested. Decker bowled a succession of deliveries, each one slightly quicker than the one before, all very straight and accurate. With studied concentration the boy played every one correctly.

Then Decker tossed up a loose ball, wide of the wicket, Jason seized his chance and swung at it with all the strength at his command. The bat was too heavy for his little limbs and the ball chipped into the air and returned in a gentle arc to be caught by the bowler.

'Dwat!' exclaimed Jason crossly, 'That means I'm out.'

'It would be in a match,' said Decker, 'But not in the practice nets.'

Disappointment faded from the boy's eyes. Eagerly he shaped up again, a frown of concentration once more upon his little face.

'Afternoon Ted.' The voice of the Briseley T'ill captain called out, 'What have we here? A budding star to be sure! What's your name young man?'

'Jason...Jason Argosy. Ted... Mr Decker said I could pwactice in the cwicket nets.' lisped the boy apprehensively.

'Did he now. That's fine by me. We'm allus on the lookout for new talent but you'll 'ave to grew a bit fust lad.' Barnett Hall senior nodded his approval and moved on towards the changing rooms. By now a stream of players were arriving at the ground. They strolled casually by, disappeared into the pavilion, changed into whites and re-emerged to stretch their limbs and loosen up before the game began.

A group of Wingfield players formed a tight circle and practiced their catching skills. The hard bright leather ball flew to and fro across the ring with shouts of derision directed at any player who dropped a catch.

Adrian Hutton, who was twelfth man, Lenny Mole and Young Barnett approached the practice nets, keen to warm up before the game began. Barnett picked up a spare ball and with an easy loose-limbed action bowled at Jason. Clunk! The boy met it squarely in the middle of his Harrow-sized bat.

'Well played!' Barnett shouted encouragement to the budding star. The tall figure of Lenny Mole approached the crease, his arm whipped over. To an accomplished player it was a medium paced delivery, one to be played firmly and defensively. But from Lenny's height and trajectory the ball lifted sharply off the pitch. It whistled inches over the small boy's head. Jason flinched perceptibly but bravely stood his ground.

A sneaky grin of amusement flitted across Lenny Mole's face. Decker was quick to step in. He turned an angry glare upon the powerfully build fast bowler. What kind of person would choose to put a little boy at risk...?

'Careful Lenny.' he snapped, 'You could seriously injure the lad.' He turned to speak to Jason, missing the contemptuous look that spread across the man's saturnine features.

'C'mon Jason, time to let the others have a turn.'

'Wight-ho!' chirped the boy, 'Will I be able to come again?'

'Sure! Of course you can. You did very well.' He guided Jason to a safe place, putting the netting between themselves and the players loosening up.

A strap on the oversized pads had chafed the skin of Jason's leg leaving an angry weal. Decker mentioned it as he helped the boy unfasten the buckles.

'It's alwight,' he replied brightly, 'Did I do weally, weally well?'

The policeman rumpled Jason's hair in a friendly affectionate gesture. 'You certainly did young man. Very well indeed.' He looked towards the nets which, by now, had seven or eight Briseley T'ill players milling around. 'Do you remember the other night when we talked about the two men, the ones you saw in the moonlight, playing the game? Have you seen them today, either one?'

The young cricketer slowly shook his head. Doubt was clearly on his face as he struggled to recall a picture of them in his mind. 'They look different now, in white. When I saw the men in the moonlight, they were just shapes, sort of black spidery shapes.' He looked disappointed, turning a crestfallen face towards the policeman.

'I'm sowwy Mr Decker... Ted. I *am* twying.' He wanted so much to help his newly found friend.

Edward Decker hid his frustration well. It had been a lot to expect of a small boy. There were alternatives, a game of bluff perhaps, and the need to keep his nerve!

*

In the middle of the playing square the two captains shook hands.

'Barnett Hall.' The captain of Briseley T'ill introduced himself.

'John McKenzie.' replied the captain of Wingfield. He bent and prodded the pitch with a horny thumb. The overnight rain had darkened the shaven turf so that it resembled a strip of brown earth. There was a fresh breeze blowing from the west that had dried off the surface. Lower down the soil remained hard and dry but the top inch had a texture like putty.

Barnett Hall senior flipped a coin in the air and John McKenzie called 'Tails!' vainly praying that it would fall the other way and save him having to make a tricky decision.

Sod's Law prevailed and the good lady, Britannia fell uppermost.

'Huh!' grunted McKenzie, 'Here was I hoping you were using your double-headed coin.' He spent a full sixty seconds stroking his chin and contemplating, 'We'll bat.' He finally decided. 'It's certain to cut up,' he muttered as he walked away, 'Certain, I can't see it getting any better...'

The captain of Briseley T'ill was in full agreement with McKenzie's decision. He kept his opinion to himself, knowing as he did the vagaries of the wicket and how it would behave under a drying wind.

*

'Do you see that man?' Decker said to Jason Argosy, 'He's John McKenzie, the captain of Wingfield Cricket Club. He has one of the finest throwing arms you will ever see. It wouldn't surprise me if he runs out at least one of our players before the game is over. When he throws, the ball comes in like a tracer bullet, low and flat, just over the top of the stumps. In one match I saw their wicketkeeper duck out of the way, he was so nervous. The ball flew from one boundary to the other before you could bat an eyelid.'

'Cor!' exclaimed Jason, suitably impressed.

*

In the changing rooms Barnett Hall senior counted heads, '…eight, nine, ten. Only ten! Who's missing?' He consulted the team sheet, 'Where's Norman Mole? Has anyone seen Norm?' He looked around a circle of blank faces. 'Lenny!' called out Barnett senior, 'Where the 'ell is Norman?'

The tall dark-haired bowler turned an impassive face to his captain, 'I dunno,' he muttered, his dark, slightly oriental-looking face showing a total lack of concern, 'I 'aven't seen 'im for a couple of days.'

'Oh Hell!' Barnett Hall senior considered briefly. Time was pressing, the game due to start in five minutes. Without Norman Mole the team would be missing a reliable bowler, but needs must. 'Adrian.' He addressed the fourteen year-old, 'Get changed… you're in.'

Adrian Hutton had already counted heads and realised they were a man short. He'd been sitting in the dressing room for the last five minutes with his kit at his feet, his fingers crossed behind his back and an ungodly prayer in his young heart that Norman Mole would fail to show up.

*

'Ted.' Barnett senior approached the policeman who had settled to watch the game with Jason Argosy from the relative comfort of the pavilion veranda, 'Do you mind scoring? Norman Mole hasn't turned up. Adrian Hutton was down to score. He's playing instead.'

'Sure. Any idea what's happened to Norman?'

'Gawd only knows!' came the exasperated reply, 'I asked Lenny who said he hasn't seen Norman for two days, *two whole days,* would you believe? His twin brother and he hasn't a clue where Norm is. A right funny bugger that one.' The captain walked away, stamping his feet and shaking his head at the peculiarities of the human species.

*

Despite being the last player to change Adrian Hutton was the first to emerge from the pavilion and follow his skipper out onto the pitch and into the glare of the afternoon sun. He was bubbling over with excitement. The light was painful to his eyes after the relative gloom of the changing room and the conditions outside were unusual. A prevailing wind blew from the southwest. High cloud covered most of the sky, diffracting the rays of the sun and creating a harsh light that reflected from the surrounding hills. Yet in the distance black clouds hung low over the Pennines, like malignant predators waiting to pounce, threatening to bring the game to a premature end.

Barnett senior considered his options. The Mole twins combined well as an opening attack. Lenny had fire and aggression. Norman was not as quick but far more accurate and steady. His replacement, young Hutton, could also bowl but the lad lacked experience and could not be expected to show the same degree of reliability. If in the later stages of the game he came under pressure the lad may wilt.

On the other hand, reflected the captain, the fourteen-year old is agile and quick in the field, a far better fielder than either of the Mole twins. Although big men their reactions were on the slow side.

There was the ever-reliable John Emmett to call on, the wiry builder had deceptive stamina and a willingness to bowl all afternoon should it be necessary. On a rain-affected wicket, the captain reasoned, the Wingfield batsmen would begin cautiously. He decided to gamble and open the attack with John Emmett from one end and young Adrian Hutton from the other. He would save his main strike bowler, Lenny Mole, for the latter stages of the innings.

*

'It's boring!' complained Jason to his fellow scorer, 'Why don't they whack the ball for six like last week?'

The match had been in progress for almost an hour. A mere thirty-five runs were on the scoreboard and the bowlers had still to take a wicket. Decker smiled sympathetically at the boy. There are times when cricket is a hard game to justify, he meditated, especially to the enthusiastic young.

'It's the state of the pitch,' he explained, 'there's no pace in it and the ball is keeping very low, skidding off the surface so the batsmen find it difficult to play good shots. When they do, the soft ground takes the pace off the ball. That makes it easy for the fielders to intercept and cut off the runs.'

As though to belie his words Adrian Hutton, who was into his eighth over, had a lapse in concentration and over-pitched. The batsman seized his chance with relish, swung hard and hammered the ball in the direction of the Sinkhole. Young Barnett Hall, his mind dwelling more on recent events than on the game, reacted slowly and the speeding missile shot between his legs. He quickly recovered, turned and hared frantically after it. Deep in the outfield a second player raced around the boundary to cut off the shot.

Far beyond the Sinkhole, beyond the distant hills, a break in the cloud cover let the sun burst through. It illuminated the scene like the back lighting of a theatre stage, throwing the running figures into stark relief. Black shadows against a brilliant light.

'There!' shouted Jason Argosy suddenly. He pointed dramatically with one finger in the direction of the Sinkhole. 'There! That's the man... that's what he looked like... the man I saw in the moonlight.'

'Barnett?... Barnett Hall?'

'No! No! The other man, with the long arms and legs, that one.'

In the peculiar glaring light the figure took on a grotesque appearance, with long thin gangling arms and elongated stick-like legs. Then a dark cloud rolled across the sun, cutting off its rays and the scene returned to normal. Two players in white were chasing after a cricket ball on a Saturday afternoon. What could be more English?

*

The cricket match, that most unpredictable of games, sprang to life. Sensing that Adrian Hutton was tiring, the Briseley T'ill captain turned to his main strike bowler. With a beckoning wave of his hand Barnett Hall invited Lenny Mole to bowl. For an hour resentment had been building up in Lenny's head. Why hadn't the captain asked him to bowl first? Wasn't he the recognised opening bowler? His aggression exploded against the poor unsuspecting Wingfield batsman. He pounded in with a lengthening stride, his body rocked back as he turned into the classical sideways on position of all great fast bowlers. In a blur of movement the ball was propelled with all the strength of Lenny's wiry body towards the stumps.

For the first time that afternoon there was real venom in a delivery. It lifted sharply from the pitch, rearing dangerously towards the startled batsman's throat; a deadly ball. The batsman's first reaction was one of self-preservation. His head and body arched violently back, one hand lifting involuntarily to protect his face. The ball struck the soft padding of one batting glove and flicked high into the air, dropping comfortably into the safe hands of the fielder at slip.

'Owzat!' A concerted roar went up. Bob Selby, thankful to have taken his first catch of the season, clutched the ball to his chest with both hands and beamed a satisfied smile at his team mates.

'Hoo – way!' cried Jason, 'A wicket! A wicket! We've got a wicket.' He rushed to the scoreboard to rattle up the numbers. Decker called out instructions to the boy.

'Thirty-five runs, one wicket, sixteen overs gone.'

'Tea for the workers.' Helen's voice distracted Decker's attention from the game. She offered him an inelegant white mug, 'How's the game going?' she asked.

'Better now we've taken a wicket. Otherwise, pretty boring.'

It was an opportune moment to speak with her as one unfortunate batsman trudged disconsolately back to the pavilion and another one strode optimistically to take his place at the wicket.

'Helen,' Decker's voice was low, confidential, 'I'll need to make a phone call, discreetly, preferably during the tea interval. Can I use the phone at the cottage?'

'Certainly.' Helen fumbled about in the hip pocket of her jeans and came up with the keys, 'Here! Take my keys and let yourself in. You know where the phone is.' Her curiosity was aroused, 'Can I ask what it's all about?'

He checked to make sure no one was within earshot before replying.

'Back-up. I need to send for support.'

'Support?' Helen's brows knitted together in puzzlement, then intuitively she guessed. Her hand flew to her mouth in shock. 'You mean *police support*. Why? What? Is it to do with the murder? It is!' Her eyes went wide with the knowledge, 'It is... you know something... you know who did it. Oh my God!'

Decker pressed a finger to his lips to signal discretion. He placed a comforting arm around her slim shoulders and drew her to one side, away from curious ears.

'Yes. I've had my suspicions for some time,' he whispered, 'Now I know for certain who killed Daisy Kutter. Don't worry, everything will be alright.' He squeezed her shoulders, sending a message of reassurance by his close physical contact. 'I won't make a move until the match is over. By then, hopefully, support will have arrived.'

'What do you mean – hopefully?' asked Helen with mounting concern, 'Surely they will send assistance, won't they?' She saw by the bleak look on his face that it was a forlorn hope. Anticipated the answer she dreaded to hear.

'It may be impossible. Did you see the news? No. Well, if you had you would have seen all the extra officers being drafted in from other regions. The county just hasn't got the manpower available to cope with the miner's rally. Let alone help me.'

'But surely, for a murderer? My God!'

'Look Helen, I'll be alright, I promise. There's just one thing, as soon as the game ends, make sure and take Jason back to the cottage. Safe. Out of harm's way... and *stay* put... both of you. I'll come round just as soon as I can.' Decker tried his hardest to dispel her apprehension but as she returned to help Mildred Burke set out the teas, Helen felt sick with fear for his safety.

*

Out on the playing field Lenny Mole wreaked havoc among the Wingfield batsmen. An hour of play had wrought damage to the pitch. Every ball, as it hit the wicket, had left its mark, taking off the top surface and leaving brown bare indentations. Slowly the drying wind changed the consistency of the turf. In places it had dried and hardened, but other spots remained soft and greasy. Batting became a lottery.

The Wingfield players didn't know whether the ball would skid through, keeping a low trajectory, or strike a rut and fly chest high. Those with courage moved into line behind the ball, played correctly and trusted to their reflexes to counter the hazards of a nasty knock. Those less brave stepped smartly two paces back and either made a defensive prod or swung vigorously with little judgement and a lot of hope.

Lenny Mole failed to steal all the glory. His aggression, allied to the state of the pitch, gave him a worthy haul of seven wickets for a meagre twenty runs. The reliable John Emmett bowled unchanged throughout and finished with the creditable analysis of twenty overs, six maidens, two wickets for twenty-nine runs.

The Wingfield innings closed on seventy-nine for nine wickets. Their last batsman was given out for failing to reach the crease within the allotted time. He never did appear and was later discovered in the primitive toilet at the rear of the pavilion. From behind its bolted door came a low moaning sound and a highly pungent odour.

A nervous disposition takes some players that way!

*

The Briseley T'ill team were jubilant and a mad rush from the pitch began as they headed for the tearoom. Barnett Hall senior, ever the tactician, blocked the way.

'Whoa!' he cried, 'Hold your 'orses. I want the roller on. We need to flatten out those ruts and ridges before the ground dries out anymore.'

'But won't that bring up the moisture?' Everett Jackson protested.

'Yea! Maybe it will, but if we roll *now* the pitch will have half an hour to dry off while we eat our teas.' The captain spoke slowly and emphatically, 'We are going to find it just as hard to score the runs as they did. At the very least this will give us a fighting chance. Alright?'

There were no murmurs of protest and willing hands helped to haul the heavy cast iron cylinder up and down the yielding turf. It *was* a gamble, but one well worth the taking.

*

Decker completed the details in the scorebook. His handwriting was not as clear and precise as that of Lenny Mole but it was legible. He gave the book into the care of Jason Argosy. 'Take it to the captain,' he instructed the boy, 'Scorers are entitled to a free tea. It's a tradition. I have a little job to do.'

'Wight-ho!' came the piping reply and Jason trotted off in search of a seat amongst the home players.

The policeman let himself into Helen Argosy's cottage, remembering to duck under the head-cracking beams and searched for the telephone. There were three jacking points in the building, one in the dining kitchen, another in Helen's studio/bedroom and a third on the top floor in Jason's room.

She plans well, thought Decker. He found the instrument plugged into the point near to the artist's bedroom window. A full five minutes passed before his call was answered. He waited, face impassive, fingers drumming nervously against the plastic receiver as he stared out of the window. *Come on! Come on! Where are you?*

A female voice answered. A voice loaded with tension. A voice fighting hard to stay composed. 'I'll do my best.' She promised, but he was far from reassured.

'How's it going at the rally?'

'Dreadful!' The unknown woman sounded on the verge of tears, 'Six officers have been hurt, one critical with burns. The bastards! Someone threw a petrol bomb.'

A petrol bomb! The prospect of being engulfed in flames was terrifying, too horrific to contemplate. He was unlikely to have to face that prospect. But would a knife in the hands of an accomplished killer be any less of an ordeal? He shivered involuntarily; someone in the future had stepped upon his grave.

*

A pathetic figure made its way along the shortcut, across the fields and towards the cricket ground. It was several seconds before the watching Decker recognised John Mole. Until recently the years of adversity had failed to grind him down. The John Mole of old had walked with pride, his head high, shoulders square, eyes contesting the world and all its problems. Decker heaved a sigh of sorrow at the man's decline. He clattered down the staircase, made certain to lock the door and hurried to intercept the approaching man. A serious discussion was long overdue.

*

Jason Argosy was in seventh heaven. He sat at the table encircled by his heroes. Everett Jackson, the gallant wicketkeeper to his left, on his right the captain of Briseley T'ill. Barnett Hall senior had the scorebook on his lap and was mulling over the details. Across the table sat Young Barnett Hall the cavalier batsman and hitter of sixes. He was tucking into a large plate of sandwiches and had become the butt of ribald comments from his fellow players. They, in some mysterious way, had found out where he'd been on the previous evening. The village grapevine could accumulate information faster than the KGB.

His performance in the field that afternoon had not passed unnoticed. Barnett had failed miserably to match up to his own high standards. Several times he'd been caught napping, once missing an easy pick-up, then he'd thrown in the ball and been yards off target and finally he'd reacted too late to a chance snick. There was no way his fellow players would let the captain's son off that easily.

'Bit off form today, eh Barnett? Did thee 'ave a bad night lad?'

'More like 'e had a *good* night. What! A bloody good night if you asks me.'

'They do say a bit of 'anky-panky leaves yer stiff in the mornin'.'

'Stiff! Bet 'e was a whole lot stiffer last night. Whoo-hoo!'

'Wotcher get up to Barnett to leave yer so knackered?'

Barnett chose to ignore the ribald comments. He kept his head down and concentrated on his salmon and cucumber sandwiches. Only John Emmett showed any concern and asked a serious question, 'Barnett, can I ask? How *is* the Ashley-Jayle girl? Is she any better?'

Barnett, his cheeks bulging with un-chewed food nodded vigorously in reply.

'She is… thank God for that.' The relief was evident on John Emmett's face, 'and her legs, are they alright? Can she move them yet?'

Barnett swallowed and cleared his throat.

'Yes.' a little smile of remembrance touched the corners of his mouth. He could still feel the power of her supple thighs. 'You could say that.' he replied.

*

John Mole was visibly startled when Decker's hand fell upon his shoulder. It was intended to be a comforting friendly gesture rather than a symbol of authority. The haunted wary look still lingered in his eyes but now the policeman detected something new: signs of resignation and acceptance. He sensed that the time was ripe for John Mole to unburden his soul.

'Jack. Mind if I join you?' Decker announced firmly, leaving no room for dissent. He eased his bulk onto the bench seat, edging close to the man until their bodies touched. Shoulder to shoulder, thigh firm against thigh. John Mole was cornered between the end of the bench seat and Decker's sturdy frame. He was trapped – or protected. Sheltered from prying eyes and ears.

The bench seat, made from varnished beech wood, was positioned some distance from the pavilion and set back from the boundary line in the shelter of the hedge. It was an ideal spot from which to watch the progress of the game. On hot sunny days the tall hedge provided shade and on cooler days sheltered spectators from the prevailing wind. No one would think it odd for the two men to sit there for it afforded a perfect view of the action. On such a mediocre day, with overcast skies and the prospect of rain showers, they were unlikely to be disturbed.

'Where's Norman?' Decker asked the question in a quiet matter-of-fact voice. 'He was down to play today. Norman loves his cricket. It isn't like him to miss a game.' He sensed the tension in John Mole, an inner trembling that belied his outward calm.

'He hasn't run away, has he?'

'Run away! What for? Why'd 'e want to run away?' Mole's head was turned, three quarter face, away from the policeman.

'Guilt?' came the suggestion, 'It's a powerful emotion, guilt. It's takes a very strong-minded person to live with guilt. Perhaps it became too much for Norman, perhaps he couldn't live with it any longer. Is that what happened Jack? Is that why he's run away?'

'No! No!' Jack Mole cried out in anguished tones, 'He hasn't run away, he can't have, he wouldn't, besides, his clothes are still there, all his clothes.'

'Well if he isn't around, where is he? Have you any idea Jack?' Decker probed gently, 'When did you last see him?' The old man was slow to answer. In the confusion that was his mind it was hard to sort events into their proper sequence.

'Tuesday? No, Wednesday, it must 'ave been Wednesday. The day after that Inspector of yours was found dead. Yes it was. I remember now because Norman became very agitated at the news. It was a terrible shock.'

'It was a shock to all of us Jack, but then there's been a lot of shocks of late haven't there? Poor Rowena dying like that, suddenly. That was unexpected. Such a cruel blow to you and your boys.' He paused for long seconds before adding, 'and of course there was the worst shock of all, the murder of Daisy Kutter.'

Decker felt the man's agitation increase. He felt it transmitted through the close contact of their bodies.

'No! No! You're wrong…you're wrong. It wasn't Norman, it wasn't. God help me… if anyone killed Daisy Kutter… it was me.'

*

'One leg please.' Barnett called to the umpire as he prepared to take guard. During the tea interval the wicket had dried out considerably, just as Barnett senior had predicted. The chances were that it would play fairly true for the first half hour until its surface became churned up by the action of the players' boots and the ball chipping out pieces every time it pitched.

Barnett had been instructed to look for quick runs, to push the score along while the effect of the roller lasted. He felt confidant and relaxed. His poor showing in the field had not been the result of stiffness or a lack of energy. It had been down to a lack of concentration. He was still in a state of euphoria, still living in the rosy afterglow of the previous evening.

He settled comfortably into his stance and waited. The Wingfield men were all well known to him and, equally, Barnett's reputation was known to them. John McKenzie was too experienced a captain to open his attack with an untried bowler. He knew that patience and a steady accurate attack was needed, then as time passed the natural deterioration of the wicket would do the rest.

He was happy to play a waiting game.

Barnett played out the first two or three overs carefully. He pushed a couple of balls into gaps between the fielders and each time took a single run. There was very little bounce and the ball struck the bottom of his bat as it skidded through. A loose delivery gave the young opener the opportunity he was looking for, Barnett picked out the over pitched ball early on, his bat lifted high and full, swept down in a clean arc and met the ball with perfect timing. It raced away down the gradient towards the boundary. He ran the first run quickly, turned and called his partner for a second, making his ground with ease. A quick glance convinced Barnett that a boundary was certain. The ball was travelling rapidly towards the ropes and the nearest fielder was thirty to forty yards away. Barnett stopped running, relaxed and wandered back down the pitch to tap down a divot with the end of his bat.

Deep in the outfield John McKenzie raced to cut off the shot. A lost cause to any other fielder except that at the lower end of the ground the turf still held a lot of moisture. The combination of soft earth and damp grass brought the ball to a premature halt six inches inside the boundary rope. McKenzie swooped like a predatory hawk, picked up the ball on the move, checked, turned and in a fluid movement sighted along his outstretched arm. His return came in like a cannonball, true and accurate. It hit the middle stump, sent the bails flying and left the wicket sprawled in every direction.

Barnett was still two yards out of his ground, and from then on, completely out of the game.

A concerted groan came from the players watching from the pavilion. It was followed by an outburst of pithy remarks.

'Wotta bloody stupid way to get out!'

'Gawd! That's all we need!'

'The silly sod! Got too cocky if you ask me!'

'Cocky? More like bloody arrogant.'

Arrogance... or supreme confidence, the dividing line is very thin.

*

The incident on the field momentarily diverted Decker's attention from John Mole's startling admission. He sympathised with Barnett's tactical mistake and generously applauded the brilliance of the Wingfield captain whose inspired action lifted the spirits of his team. Briseley T'ill now faced an uphill battle. They would need to fight like tigers if they were to win.

For long seconds Decker let John Mole's admission hang in the air unanswered, a technique used by clever interviewers as well as interrogators who wait... and wait... and wait again, until their victim feels compelled to speak.

'I said, if anyone killed Daisy Kutter it was me.' John Mole repeated, 'Me. Our Norman wouldn't hurt a living soul.'

'Did I suggest that Norman killed Daisy Kutter?' the question came softly, 'Did I?'

'No-o-o. But...' John Mole's voice was low and careful.

'Did I imply it? Did I? I don't think so Jack. In fact I know that Norman couldn't have murdered Daisy because at the time of her death he wasn't there. He was at work. He was on the evening shift that night. I know because I checked with the hosiery factory. The manager thinks very highly of Norman, says he's a good reliable worker, very conscientious. He told me that despite the following day being a Bank Holiday, Norman stayed late to ensure that an urgent export order was ready for despatch.'

The policeman leaned close and placed a consoling hand upon John Mole's knee. 'You're a good man Jack, a good man, but it's time for the truth. I know *you* couldn't have killed her either because you weren't there at the time. You said so yourself, only at the time I failed to grasp what you really meant. Do you recall? You said, *"If only I had been there she would not have died."* Those were your very words to me, but I thought you were referring to Rowena when at the time you were actually speaking about Daisy Kutter. Am I right Jack?'

A deep groan of anguish from the reaches of John Mole's tortured soul almost weakened Decker's resolve. Almost, but not quite, he steeled himself to carry on. The man was a friend. A man he respected, a man torn apart by inner conflict, torn by too much knowledge, by love and guilt and fear. Torn by fear of the past and an even greater fear for the future.

'I know what happened John. I know who killed Daisy. I know when and how and where it happened.'

'No! No! How can you know? There was no evidence. Nothing. So how can you possibly know?' The question came so quietly that Decker barely caught the words.

'But there is evidence Jack, there is,' continued the policeman, 'Very circumstantial I admit, and on that alone it would be difficult to prove my case. However, now there's a new factor – a witness. One who's identified the murderer, and his accomplice!'

'That can't be true. Y-y-you're bluffing.'

'Am I? We'll see. Let me acquaint you with a few facts Jack, then you can judge for yourself whether or not I'm bluffing. The last person to see Daisy Kutter alive was the doctor. That would have been at around nine o'clock on the evening of the Thursday before Easter, the day on which your wife, Rowena, died. He answered Daisy's call and when he left the house she was alive and well. We also know that she intended to travel up to Yorkshire that evening to visit her mother. There was a train for Sheffield from Briseley T'ill station that left at 10:05pm. Daisy planned to catch that train because her car was off the road. It's still in John Shackleton's garage with a burnt out exhaust valve.

'Someone planted Daisy's travel bag in the station waiting room to make it look as though she had been there, but she never made it, did she Jack?' Decker looked with hard questioning eyes into Mole's face. He continued relentlessly, 'She never made it to the station because she was dead by then. Murdered! She was ruthlessly and efficiently killed. In *your* house Jack. Probably in your very kitchen, because that's on the ground floor, next to the old dining room, the room you converted into a bedroom for Rowena.'

The last vestiges of colour drained from John Mole's face. His whole body was crumbling from within, shrinking, disintegrating, as the remnants of his world fell apart. Decker hated himself for what he was being forced to do. He felt like a menacing giant, like the towering genie in Helen's cartoon, battering down a weak and defenceless man. Perhaps Helen had caught an aspect of his character he had never known existed. Her perception went deeper than she realised.

'The pathologist said that Daisy Kutter was killed by an expert. Just one blow, he said, a single thrust to the carotid artery, a professional job. That puzzled Inspector Moxon. He could not imagine a reason for an ordinary nurse in a small country village to be murdered by a professional killer. He was even more puzzled by the absence of blood, but then he has always lived in a town. He buys his meat at a supermarket, all neatly packaged and sealed in cling film on a nice white polystyrene tray. No mess. No blood.

Easy! Like thousands of others he has never had to think about how it got there.

'But we know Jack, we know. We understand all about abattoirs and slaughter-men who spend their entire life despatching animals to provide beef and pork and lamb for the dinner table. We know all about it and we know someone just like that, an expert, a man who is very good at his job, a real professional. Your son... Lenny.'

*

Out on the cricket field Briseley T'ill were fighting back. Another wicket had gone down, that of Tim Taverstock who had batted patiently for half an hour and had scored ten runs. The Wingfield bowler dropped one short. Instinctively Taverstock moved onto his back foot to hook what should have been a rising ball. The pitch betrayed him and the ball was barely ankle high as it struck his leg.

'Owzat!'

Old Barnett Hall shook his head in dismay. He always wanted Briseley T'ill to win and remaining neutral every weekend constantly tested his sense of fair play. He raised a slow reluctant finger. Out! Some decisions were as hard on him as on the player concerned.

Poor Tim Taverstock, he thought, *out again in similar circumstances. Twice in a row now.*

Briseley T'ill were now two wickets down for a mere twenty runs. The meagre Wingfield total assumed new proportions, it was beginning to look like Everest! With only their captain as a recognised batsman to come the home team's position was as fragile as glass. A large question mark hung over the tail-enders, few of whom had ever been known to make a double figure score in their entire cricketing careers.

The captain's batting partner was Everett (Snowball) Jackson, who with considerable self-control, suppressed his West Indian desire to hammer every delivery clean out of sight. Instead he assumed the role usually played by George Burke, that of anchor man to the innings.

Slowly the score mounted.

*

'Shall we take a stroll round the ground.' suggested Edward Decker. He slipped a helping hand under the elbow of John Mole and eased him to his feet. 'There's something I want to show you.' They strolled around the perimeter of the field, two friends of long standing in conversation. A casual observer would not be aware of the tension within each man. To John Mole the solid figure of the policeman appeared like a rock, a solid immovable mass of granite. Honest and dependable. A person one could call upon in time of trouble – always assuming the trouble was within the law.

Decker had good reason for their stroll together. It provided him with the opportunity to manoeuvre John Mole into position. Sitting on the bench seat the two men had had their backs to Helen Argosy's cottage and the pavilion cut off the view of the Sinkhole. They walked slowly, pausing frequently to take in the action on the field. Eventually their circular tour brought them heading back towards the pavilion and facing in the direction of the cottages. To their left lay the Sinkhole, immediately before their eyes, a clear view of Jason Argosy's bedroom window.

Decker paused and laid a restraining hand upon his companion's arm.

'Take a look Jack,' he said, indicating the dormer window of the attic room, 'Can you see that window up there, the one on the top floor? From there you have a perfect view of the Sinkhole. There is a clear line of vision. That is where my witness stood and watched two men bury a body in the mud. There was a full moon that night. There always is at Easter, as a Christian you would know that, on the eve of Good Friday.'

*

On the pavilion veranda Adrian Hutton put down the scorebook and reached for a pair of pads. He was next but one in the batting order and had no desire to be caught unprepared. He called for another player to take over the duty of keeping tally. Volunteers were scarce. Only one man answered his plea. The tall lean figure of Lenny Mole picked up the book and settled himself comfortably next to Jason Argosy.

Decker caught his breath. His calculations had not taken into account the possibility of young Jason being in close contact with Lenny Mole. He should have considered it, knowing how enthusiastically the little boy liked to join in the action.

What if the boy was to blurt out the truth? If he revealed what he had seen from his bedroom window on that fatal Easter night...? If... Oh God! Just to think of the possible consequences sent a shiver down the policeman's spine. He may well appear to be a rock of all the ages to John Mole but inwardly a butterfly of apprehension fluttered within his bowels.

Furthermore, wondered Decker, *where the Devil is my backup?*

As accurate as the Wingfield bowlers were, sooner or later it was inevitable that one of them would bowl a loose delivery. Everett Jackson's patience was rewarded. The full toss was like a gift horse and the West Indian had no reason to examine its teeth. He gave full rein to his bat and smashed the ball clean over the pavilion roof.

'Six! Hoo-ray!' A delighted cry from Jason led the ripple of applause from the watching spectators. The dour action on the field had dampened their morale and there had been little reason to clap so far. It was the first boundary of the innings. Fifty runs were now on the board. Victory was a step closer.

A devious mistress, cricket, her promises are all too easily broken.

The Wingfield bowler kept his nerve, his line and his length. He bowled a slower ball. Everett, flush with success, aimed for an action replay of his previous shot. His leading foot was short of the pitch. This time the seam bit into the soft turf and the ball popped. It made contact just below the splice of the West Indian's bat reducing the power of the stroke. An easy catch dropped into the clutching hands of the fielder at mid-off. Elation turned to deflation. Jackson banged his bat against his padded leg in frustration and began the dismal trudge back to the pavilion.

*

'Is Lenny carrying his knife?' asked Decker. He knew it was a pointless question. The slaughter-man took it everywhere. It was part of his persona. He wore it in a tooled leather sheath attached to his belt. As the meaning of Decker's question dawned upon him a look of horror crossed John Mole's face.

'You don't think? I mean... Lenny? No. He wouldn't... he wouldn't... would he?' The man panted for breath as his agitation increased. 'Oh! My God! What are you going to do?'

'My duty.' replied Decker simply, 'It's my duty to arrest him. What other choice do I have Jack? But I *will* leave it until after the game. I'll try to be as unobtrusive as I can. But the knife Jack, *what about the knife?'*

'He will... have it... with him,' panted out Mole nervously, 'in the changing rooms with the rest of his gear. He wouldn't wear it on the field. Oh dear God! What a mess!' The man's distress was becoming visibly obvious. Decker drew him away from the watching eyes on the pavilion veranda and headed back towards the isolated seat on the boundary. He needed to play for time, at least until some form of backup arrived. Also, there were still a lot of questions to be answered...

*

'Owzat!' A fresh appeal from the Wingfield players rent the air. Everett Jackson's replacement had failed to survive for long. Bob Selby glanced at the grinning slip fielder clutching onto the catch. He gave a dejected shrug and began the dismal trail back to the changing room and the unwarranted advice of his team-mates.

It had been a beast of a delivery. A spot was developing just outside the line of the off stump where the pitch had been scuffed up by the bowlers' feet and the repeated impact of the ball. It had lifted viciously, taken Selby unawares and with little chance to get his bat out of harm's way.

The score was now fifty-four for four wickets, with still a long way to go.

Adrian Hutton was mature for a fourteen-year old. He was a natural athlete. Ball games came easily; football, tennis, rugby, cricket, he played them all equally well. The only quality he lacked was experience and time would soon cure that malaise. Through the long winter months Adrian had attended weekly coaching sessions. In years to come it was to benefit his game enormously. But indoor wickets are fast and true and unfortunately for Adrian an early season village pitch is a different beast. He played correctly, his back-lift was high, his left elbow pointed down the pitch and his trusty blade swung straight with a fine flowing follow through. If only it had made contact with the ball. He was still wondering where he had gone wrong when the sound of crashing timber reached his ears.

Fifty-four for five wickets, the rabbits were now exposed!

*

'It's a lot like life - cricket,' observed Decker, commenting upon the calamity facing the Briseley T'ill cricket team, 'just when you think you have got it beat, it kicks you in the teeth!' He turned to his companion on the bench. 'Isn't that how you feel Jack, as though life has kicked you in the teeth?' He spoke with sympathy and compassion to the shattered man.

'Aye! It has that,' replied John Mole in a voice lacking vigour, 'It's been kicking me in the teeth for a long time now. Seems like all my life.'

'But *you* will fight back,' the policeman encouraged him, 'It's something you've been doing all your life Jack. You have always refused to be beaten, in your personal life and on the cricket field. I know you better than you think. Know just how difficult your life has been.'

For the first time that afternoon John Mole's head came up. He turned his full gaze upon Decker's face. There was curiosity in his eyes and a hint of anger because someone had been prying into his background.

'Do you really?' he asked, ' Do you really believe you know it all? Perhaps there's even more to know than *you* realise. Tell me, we'll see just how much you've actually found out.'

'I know about Elizabeth,' replied Decker, 'I know about your daughter. I've been to Marston Grange. I've seen her, met her. In Heaven's name Jack, why on earth have you kept her existence a secret all these years? Why didn't you tell people about her? They would have understood. I can't believe you were ashamed of her. You... of all people.'

'No.' His reply came back short and sharp, 'Of course I'm not ashamed of her. Never.'

'Was it to protect her then?'

'Yes. Of course it was.'

'OK, I accept that. Who from? Who were you protecting her from, Seb Mole?'

It was an inspired guess by the policeman. One that struck home with unexpected force. Every vestige of colour drained from John Mole's face. His mouth worked soundlessly for several seconds before the words came out.

'Seb... M-Mole!' There was hatred in his eyes as he stuttered out the name, the same fierce hatred that Decker had seen in the Doctor's face. 'Yes! That's it. I *have* to protect her from Seb Mole.'

'But the man's dead.' replied Edward Decker, 'According to the Doctor he died over twenty years ago. He was drowned in the old canal, under the bridge. He can't harm anyone now. A *dead* man can't hurt anyone.'

'Can't he? That's what you think is it? Oh, he's dead alright, as dead as mutton, dead and buried these twenty long years. But... but... he came... back... he came back.'

Came back, thought Decker, *came back. Impossible. An enigma. What did the man mean?*

*

At the end of an over McKenzie walked in and studied the pitch. Unlike many captains, who place themselves close to the bowler, John McKenzie preferred to be in the outfield. He believed in playing to a person's strengths. His own strength lay in his brilliant fielding and powerful throw.

The Wingfield captain had quickly noticed the unpredictable behaviour of the ball whenever it pitched on the worn scuffed patch just outside the line of the stumps. A tactical bowling change was needed, McKenzie decided in his mind, left arm, around the wicket should do the trick. He instructed the player to use the full width of the crease to fully exploit the spot. An extra fielder was moved into the slips and a quiet word in the bowler's ear explained his tactics.

McKenzie placed himself in the third man position, deep, close to the perimeter rope. From there he would be able to cut off the boundaries. It was vital for him to keep a tight control of the game.

The new bowler took a little time to settle into his rhythm and find his direction. Barnett Hall senior was able to take full advantage of the lapses and add two more boundaries to the total.

Sixty-two for five. Only eighteen more were required for victory.

If he could retain the strike then there was a good chance of winning. It meant taking a single from the last ball of every over. Hall knew he had the ability to steal the singles always providing the supporting batsmen stayed alert and backed him up.

Tension destroys players. It wrecks their timing and confuses their minds. In the practice nets mediocre players flatter to deceive because there is no pressure upon them. But out in the middle, encircled by a tight ring of fielders even the very greatest players may waver.

Mike Selby was a bundle of nerves and as the game drew to its conclusion the tension grew in the players on the pitch and in those still waiting their turn to bat. It affected the supporters of both sides as they willed on their teams to win. The only person seemingly unaffected was Lenny Mole. He concentrated on the scorebook, laboriously and carefully, recording the details of the game in his neat handwriting.

It was the last ball of the over. Barnett Hall played it with supreme skill, pushing the ball into the gap between two fielders he deliberately weighted his stroke lightly so that the ball ran slowly from his bat and fell short of the field.

'One!' he called to Selby and commenced to run.

Mike Selby hesitated. Started. Stopped. Then started to run again. 'Yes! No! Wait!' he called in rapid succession. Seized by panic he dashed back to the safe haven of his crease. Barnett Hall senior was left hopelessly stranded three quarters of the way down the pitch. A Wingfield fielder, with great commonsense, picked up the ball, ran to the wicket and removed the bails. He hardly needed to appeal.

Sixty-two for six.

'Oh Cripes! That *has* done it.' moaned a Briseley T'ill player.

'Oh Cwipes!' echoed little Jason Argosy as he rattled up the falling wickets on the scoreboard.

*

Ted Decker wondered if John Mole was totally sane. For years the man had lived under an abominable strain, under the kind of pressure that would have destroyed a lesser man. Had recent events pushed him over the edge?

'John,' he asked quietly, 'I don't understand. What do you mean by "*He came back.*" How can a dead man return? That isn't what you mean is it?' He waited patiently, sensing he was on the verge of a breakthrough. *Gently does it,* he told himself... *gently... and all will be revealed.*

'They were twin brothers as well, Seb Mole and my father. Twins, like Lenny and Norman. Seb was the older, just as Lenny is the older, older by a few minutes. That's what makes all the difference... See!'

Decker didn't see at all. He was mystified by the man's words. He simply nodded as though he understood every word and waited.

'Chalk and cheese, that's what they were. Chalk and cheese, as different as chalk and cheese my father and Seb Mole, two halves of the same man. Peas out of the pod, one sweet and wholesome, the other bitter and corrupt. He was a lovely man my father, a lovely man, gentle and good. Too good for this world. Gentle and good, he never harmed a fly. Never!

'Uncle Seb was just the opposite, an evil man. Evil! He never cared a mote for a living soul. He was a vicious man who loved to hurt people. He loved to see the fear in their eyes, loved the power it gave him. He was so sick. Sick in his mind, sick in his actions. Sick! Sick! Sick!' John Mole spat out the words with such venom that traces of spittle dribbled from his lips and tracked down his chin.

'Calm down John, he's dead. There's no way he can harm you now. You, or anyone else.' Decker patted the man's arm comfortingly. Soothing.

'I wish you were right Ted Decker, I wish you were right.' Mole turned towards the policeman and seized his hand in a steely grip. Desperation gave added strength and the knuckles of his hand gleamed white beneath the skin. 'But it's in the blood... in the blood. It's all to do with the genes isn't it? That's the way it works, missing out one generation, and then coming out in the next.'

Decker was nonplussed. He shook his head at his failure to understand.

'Coming out Jack?' he asked, 'What's coming out?'

'Evil! That's what's coming out... in *my* Lenny. The evil he inherited from Seb Mole. The evil that makes him want to kill!'

'But he's your son Jack, *your* son. There can't be any doubt about it.'

'Of course he's my son. I know that. Only too well I know that. But he's not *all my* genes... not my genes. Rowena was Seb Mole's daughter, *his daughter*. But she's not... *wasn't* like him, just as Lenny's not like me. It's Seb Mole's way of getting revenge for what happened all those years ago.'

'You're talking nonsense Jack,' said Decker firmly, trying to restore a degree of sanity to the conversation, 'Surely Lenny and Norman were born long after the death of your Uncle Seb. Isn't that right?'

'Oh yes! Over two years later but that is what I mean about the evil coming back. The evil that was in my uncle... *is in my son, Lenny.* God help him!'

He spoke with such conviction, a religious fervour, that Decker was all but persuaded to believe him. 'Alright Jack, suppose you start at the beginning and tell me everything that happened.'

'I will! I will!' the man cried out. There was enormous relief in his voice because at long last he could unburden his soul.

*

The dark clouds that had lurked over the distant hills moved closer. The light was poorer now. Professional players would have headed for the shelter of the pavilion long ago. A few spits and spats of rain drifted in on the wind.

John McKenzie lifted his face as the cold droplets stung a sharp rebuke. Half an hour, he judged, half an hour at the most and then the approaching rain would drive everyone to the haven of the changing rooms. He needed a result, quickly.

Briseley T'ill had put up unexpected resistance in the person of Mike Selby. Sick at heart from the knowledge that he had been responsible for the dismissal of his captain, Selby concentrated his mind on stubborn defence. Every time the ball struck the solid middle of his bat his confidence increased. He also felt the cold sharp sting of rain upon his face. Should he play for time, or gamble for a win?

Wingfield's left arm bowler remembered his captain's instructions. He fixed his eyes firmly on the worn spot just outside the line of the stumps. It was an area roughly twelve inches square and, strive as he may, he had yet to achieve a direct hit.

In his quest for greater accuracy he shortened his run-up and cut back upon his pace. This time it all came together, the ball pitched exactly in the centre of the roughened turf. Mike Selby believed his moment had come. The delivery was wide of the wicket and there were inviting spaces behind the bowler into which he could blast the ball. He opened his shoulders and chanced his arm.

Rising sharply, the ball clipped the shoulder of Selby's bat, flew over the heads of the slip fielders and ran towards John McKenzie in the deep. 'Yes!' called Selby's partner and quickly set off down the track. Both men made their ground with ease, turned and looked for a second run.

'No, wait!' Spotting the Wingfield captain swooping in upon the ball, Selby opted for caution. Another run-out would certainly spell disaster for the team.

The sad irony was that Selby's caution exposed his batting partner who was dismissed the very next ball. Having found his range the Wingfield bowler produced an unplayable delivery that clipped the unfortunate man on the knuckles and carried into the safe hands of the extra slip.

One more to John McKenzie. Another wicket down for Briseley T'ill.

The total was now sixty-five for seven.

Lenny Mole handed back the scorebook to Adrian Hutton and reached for a pair of batting pads. The fall of another wicket would take him to the crease.

*

Most of the tension had gone from John Mole's body. It poured out of him with the flow of words as the stricken man came to terms with himself and the misfortunes of his past. An air of acceptance replaced his anxiety as he continued to talk freely to his companion.

'When the twins were born,' he went on, 'Rowena and I were delighted. We feared that her father's attack on her had left permanent damage. So when she gave birth to two perfect little boys you can imagine our relief. I think we first began to notice Lenny's unnatural aggression from around the age of three. He was always the dominating twin, whereas Norman was a placid little boy. I had trouble controlling Lenny, the more I tried to instil a sense of right and wrong the harder he resisted. Keeping discipline was tricky, especially so because little Norman always obeyed me while Lenny would do exactly the opposite of what I asked out of sheer devilment. The *only* person Lenny ever listened to and respected was Rowena. He would do anything for her, even going to extremes. What do they call it – an Oedipus complex – when a boy has an obsession for his mother?

'One day, when Lenny was about nine he overheard Rowena complaining about our cat, Sheba. She'd produced four tiny kittens and to tell you the truth we couldn't afford to keep them. In a moment of frustration Rowena said angrily that she wished they were dead. Lenny overheard her comment and before we realised what he was going to do he took them down to the bottom of the garden and slit their throats with his penknife.

'We were horrified. It made Rowena physically sick. I was so angry that I seized his penknife and threw it into the fire, gave Lenny a good hiding and sent him to bed in disgrace.

'There were other incidents that gave us grave cause for concern. In the early days we had refrained from telling the boys about their sister, believing they were too young to understand about her condition. We fully intended to tell them later, when they were a little more mature. As it turned out there never was a time to tell them. We feared the effect it would have on Lenny. That he would feel he was being supplanted in his mother's affections and he might resort to violence.'

'Couldn't anyone help? The doctor perhaps?' Decker asked.

'No. He's a good man and tried his best. But the simple truth is; he isn't qualified and was not capable of coping with a child like Lenny. The boy needed specialist treatment, a psychiatrist, or at the very least an expert in childcare. With Elizabeth already in a special home we couldn't possibly afford anyone like that.'

'Couldn't you have let Norman know about his sister?'

'What! And risk him accidentally letting the cat out of the bag. We just didn't dare take the risk of Norman letting slip a chance remark. You know how gregarious he is, there isn't a trace of guile in him.'

'That's true.' The policeman acknowledged. As big as he was there was a beguiling innocence about Norman Mole. He was a genial giant without a hint of aggression in him.

'Poor Norman,' continued Mole, 'He's always been in awe of his brother. Lenny was always leading him into trouble and then standing back to watch him take the blame. It amused him, yet in a strange way, after his mother, Norman is the only other person in the world Lenny seems to care about.'

'How on earth did you cope?'

'We prayed, and we watched, watched him like a hawk. Always fearful, always in abject terror of what he might do. Then when he was sixteen Rowena had an idea. She came across an advertisement in the local newspaper for a young man to train as a slaughter man. We saw it as an outlet for his obsession. A legal way, if you like, to satisfy his blood lust.'

'Perhaps Lenny never regarded it as evil.' Decker suggested with a flash of insight

'I don't believe he does,' agreed John Mole, 'Seb Mole was just the same. He could never see anything wrong in what he did, regarding himself as above the law. He had an utter contempt for law-abiding people.

'Fortunately for Uncle Seb the war came along and off he went to train as a commando. Killing people became legal, at least for him it did and suddenly *he* was a hero in everyone's eyes. He loved that. Loved the adulation and the publicity. Mercifully by the end of the war even he was sickened by death and destruction. He was still a vicious man, as you well know, foul mouthed and foul-tempered but I doubt he ever killed anyone after he came back from the war.'

Privately Decker thought that what the man had done to Elizabeth Mole as a result of his unwarranted attack on Rowena was a million times worse than murder. She, poor girl, had been sentenced to a lifetime of imprisonment in a useless body, alone and virtually unreachable.

'About Lenny,' the policeman reminded John Mole, 'He did kill Daisy Kutter. You can't deny that can you Jack? So what went wrong?'

John Mole closed his eyes as though a blinding pain had hit him. He would never be able to forget that night and its tragic consequences.

'You were right in your assumption that I wasn't there when it happened,' he murmured in a low voice, 'I *had* been there, but ironically, it was Daisy who sent me off again, out to look for Lenny because Daisy was concerned about him. Only he was still about, still there, still outside the house watching... watching her... and when I went off to look for him and she was alone, that's when he returned and killed her.'

'But why Jack, why *did* he kill her?'

'How can I make you understand?' pleaded John Mole, 'In his mind Lenny didn't kill a human being. He has this warped way of thinking, of rationalising what he does. I'm sure he believed he was doing his job, doing what he's trained all his life to do: slaughter an animal because that creature's time had come. God help us but we'd always taught him that there was no harm in doing his job properly. It was all a terrible misunderstanding, and my fault. What happened was all my fault.'

'According to the doctor, who heard it from Daisy Kutter, Lenny was very disturbed at the death of his mother. He rushed off into the night. Now you say that he came back. When? What exactly happened?' asked Decker.

'Well! As you know I was at Marston Grange when Daisy rang through with the news of Rowena's death. Even though I had been half expecting it, when it actually happened I was still shaken to the core.'

'Expecting it?' Decker interjected, 'You already *knew* Rowena was likely to die suddenly?'

'Yes and no! It was on the cards, a possibility. Oh Lord! How can I explain it without it sounding horrific? Please, whatever you do don't jump to the wrong conclusion. It's… it's just that in the last two weeks of her life Rowena's condition declined drastically. She was in ever increasing pain, so much that it was becoming unbearable to her. It was so bad that she couldn't bear to be touched. More and more drugs were being pumped into her and they were losing their effectiveness.

'Rowena had great courage… tremendous courage, but it was all wearing her down. She asked Daisy - No! She begged Daisy to give her something to put her to sleep – permanently. She *wanted* to die.'

'Daisy didn't…?'

'No! God no! It would have been against her training, against all her beliefs. But the problem was Lenny was there at the time. Lenny overheard what was said. He may have thought that the nurse had helped to bring about his mother's death. Especially with it being so quick. That may have been one of the factors that disturbed him.'

'One of the factors? There were others…?'

John Mole's agitation returned. His body writhed from the inward agony of self- torture, a man stretched on the rack of his own deception. His deception had been well intentioned, a sincere belief that his actions to protect his daughter were justified. His pain, non-the-less, was excruciating.

'He thought I betrayed his mother. Wrongly. I never betrayed Rowena in my entire life. She was the only woman for me. The only woman there has ever been. But that's *not* what Lenny thought.'

'Why? Whatever gave him that idea?' This was a new twist that Decker had not anticipated. John Mole's devotion to his wife was legendary. He was above suspicion… like Caesar's wife.

'For years Daisy Kutter accompanied me to Marston Grange on two evenings a week to treat Elizabeth. I never knew it but apparently at some time or other Lenny followed us there. He watched us go in and then come out a couple of hours later.

'God only knows what goes on in his mind, what he thought, but it seems he imagined the place to be a kind of brothel, a house of ill-repute masquerading as a residential home. Can you believe it?'

A picture of the old Victorian building came into Decker's mind. It was a very private looking place with its high walls of crumbling red brick. Isolated, well away from the village, on the Kirk Loscoe road.

Yes, Decker thought, *I can well imagine a young inexperienced lad like Lenny Mole forming a wrong impression.*

John Mole resumed his story.

'When I arrived home from Marston Grange I was in a state of total shock. Daisy, Nurse Kutter had composed Rowena's body and laid it out in clean clothes, her favourite clothes, a lovely silk dress that Rowena hadn't been able to wear for years. She looked lovely, so peaceful and calm. Without a trace of pain, just as though she were sleeping. I hadn't seen her look like that for many years. I couldn't cope and broke down in tears. You know what Daisy was like. She couldn't stand by and do nothing. She was always a caring person and understood people's needs.

'I was sitting on the edge of the bed, weeping over Rowena's body. Daisy put her arms around me and held me close against her body. Comforting me, that was all. We didn't know that Lenny was outside the window, watching... watching and misunderstanding, turning an innocent scene into something obscene. How were we to know?'

'How indeed,' Decker sympathised, thinking how trite and inadequate words sounded at such a time. The comfort of another human body, holding one close, was far more reassuring than mere words could offer. Far better, he thought, to make comforting noises. Solicitations are best left to the professionals, doctors and priests, people able to call upon celestial guidance.

'Daisy had planned to catch the train from Briseley T'ill station at 10:05pm. She knew there wasn't time to walk back to her cottage, wash, change and make it back to the station in time. She asked, would I object to her washing and changing here? Naturally I agreed, my only regret was that we lack a proper bathroom. I apologised for that but Daisy was unconcerned. She didn't have any inhibitions. After all, she said, she'd been visiting and treating patients in these old houses for years. A strip-wash over the kitchen sink is part of life hereabouts. When I went off in search of Lenny the last thing on my mind was thoughts for her safety. How could she possibly be in danger?'

The policeman simply shrugged in agreement and murmured soft noises.

'When I returned, an hour later, Daisy was dead. Her clothes were carefully arranged over the back of a chair and her body lay white and still on the floor, completely naked. It looked just like a carcass at the abattoir.'

John Mole's fingers gripped Decker's arm with unrelenting pressure. His voice became impassioned as he pleaded for understanding. 'You've *got* to believe me Ted, Lenny was out of his mind with grief at his mother's death. He was so crazy that he couldn't see Daisy as another human being. I'm convinced of that. He saw her as an animal waiting to be slaughtered. It was the only way he knew to expiate his rage. An animal, and that was how he killed her. He cut her throat with one quick slash of his knife and then held her naked body over the sink with the head down. Just like a stuck pig, holding her there with the cold water running to wash away all the blood as it ebbed out of her body.'

Edward Decker could feel the violent shudders once again passing through the man's fragile frame as the full mental horror of the terrible events etched into his memory returned.

'H-he m-must have re-remained there f-for ages... j-just letting the b-blood run. When I returned Lenny was standing at the sink, cleaning his knife and washing his hands as though e-everything was p-perfectly n-normal. Normal! God in Heaven! H-how can anything ever be normal again...?'

'It never will be Jack, it never will be.' The policeman stood up and helped the other to his feet. He walked him slowly past the pavilion and towards the gate, away from the field. 'Best go home Jack,' he advised, 'Best go home. You don't want to be around when I arrest your son.'

*

A loud appeal rang across the playing field. Mike Selby's stubborn resistance had finally come to an end. Wingfield's bowler had found the roughened patch once again. This time, instead of flying high, the ball kept low. A genuine daisy-cutter of a delivery that angled back off the pitch, shot under the player's stabbing bat and splayed the stumps in all directions. Decker heard the gasps of dismay from the players gathered on the pavilion veranda. The entire side watched, drawn by the mounting tension of a close finish to the game.

The score was now seventy-two runs for eight wickets. There were two wickets left to fall and eight runs were required for a win. The dark thunderheads rolled closer and the light continued to deteriorate. Players moved like flitting white ghosts on a darkening green background.

The tall lean figure of Lenny Mole strode from the pavilion, stepping briskly towards the centre of the field. In the fading light his tanned saturnine features contrasted sharply with the whiteness of his cricket shirt and flannels.

The butterfly in Edward Decker's stomach fluttered its wings. Despite his police training, in his heart, the policeman knew he was nowhere near to being a match for the strong young fast bowler. At twenty years of age, Lenny Mole was at his athletic peak. His supple body honed by constant physical work... and then there was the knife.

The knife!

Decker feared the knife. He imagined its keen blade slicing into his body, laying open the flesh. Seeing the spurt of bright red blood. His blood! A cold shudder racked his body. Police work and a fertile imagination made for uncomfortable bedfellows.

To tackle an unarmed Lenny Mole would be both dangerous and difficult. Armed with a weapon the balance of power was in the young man's favour leaving the policeman with little hope of success. He needed to secure the knife. Now was the opportune moment. Lenny was safely out of the way, on the field of play with every member of the club watching and willing him to succeed. With players and spectators alike engrossed in the closing overs of the game it was the perfect moment for him to slip, unnoticed, into the changing rooms and search for the weapon.

*

'Call me rash if you like,' said Barnett senior to John Emmett, 'but I think we have an outside chance of winning.'

'I wouldn't bet on it,' the builder replied, 'I'd say it was fifty-fifty, all down to luck. Yes?'

'No. I'll tell you why. Lenny is no great shakes as a batsman but he has one good shot. He can cut. He's tall and he has a long reach. If their left-arm bowler keeps on plugging away outside the off stump then it gives the lad a chance to play his best shot.'

'His *only* shot!' muttered John Emmett pessimistically.

In poor light a batsman has as good, if not a better than even chance, of sighting the ball than many of the fielders. At least he *knows* it will be coming towards him and is looking along the line of its direction. A player in the outfield has to pick up its direction off the face of the bat, often viewed against a dark background. John McKenzie watched his bowler run up to the wicket, saw his arm whirl over and a dark blur hurtle towards the batsman. He saw Lenny Mole move onto his back foot and across his wicket, saw the bat swinging down in a sabre-like chopping cut. He heard the impact of willow on leather. He moved rapidly to his right. Then stopped, bewildered. Totally deceived. In the rapidly fading light he had misjudged the direction of the ball.

It ran over the boundary yards away.

The score had reached seventy-six for eight. Just four more runs to win.

*

Decker heard the burst of applause in the dressing room. He froze. Did it mean a wicket had fallen? Was Lenny Mole already striding back to the pavilion? He waited. Heard the excited chatter of the Briseley T'ill players and guessed correctly that runs had been scored rather than a wicket fallen.

He breathed a sigh of relief. But where the Hell was the knife? It wasn't hanging from Lenny Mole's tooled leather belt. Quick. Think. In his sports bag? Naturally. Where else would he hide it for safety?

His fingers rummaged through its assorted contents. A spare pair of socks; none too clean, an extra shirt, a grubby towel. Sweatbands. Worn out bootlaces, chafed from too much use. A spare set of spikes complete with a key to screw them into the soles of cricket boots. A support bandage that had lost its elasticity, loose discarded chewing gum wrappers and a comb with half its teeth missing and the rest clogged with greasy dirt.

But no knife!

So where the Devil was it? In a panic his fingers poked around the corners of the bag once more. They encountered a hard tacky lump of gum that attached itself under the end of his fingernail. Ugh!

He wiped his hand across a rolled up towel, and felt a hard object inside. He shook out the towel and the knife in its leather sheath fell to the floor. A long sigh of relief escaped the policeman's lips as he bent to pick up the weapon. Two slits in the leather allowed a belt to be passed through the sheath and a band of leather with a press-stud secured the knife in place. Decker flipped open the press-stud and drew out the knife. It's slightly curved handle fitted comfortably into his hand. Viewed end on its long slim blade had a flattened diamond shape. He tested its razor sharp cutting edge against the back of one hand. The blade was keen enough to shave away the fine dark hairs growing there.

It was both a fine tool... and a murderously efficient weapon.

*

The boundary shot boosted Lenny Mole's confidence. He faced the following ball feeling completely relaxed and at ease. Again the delivery was outside the line of the stumps and aimed at the rough ground. The seam bit into the soft turf and the hurtling sphere of hard leather lifted viciously towards the batsman.

Lenny watched the ball onto the face of his bat and from his great height steered it delicately down to speed between the slip fielders and race away into the outfield.

'Yes!' called his partner and the Briseley T'ill batsmen raced through to add two more precious runs to the score.

Seventy-eight for eight.

Decker, with the sheathed knife safely in his blazer pocket, joined in the applause. Clapping vigorously helped to ease the mounting tension and settle the fluttering butterflies. But in God's name where were his colleagues? What had happened to the promised support? It was long overdue. The end of the game was only seconds away. He strained his ears for the "Bee-baw" sound of an approaching police siren. There was nothing, neither sight nor sound.

. *He was on his own!*

*

John McKenzie used precious time to re-organise the field. He moved his fielders into a tight circle around the batsmen. Wingfield needed to take two wickets without conceding a single run if they were to win. It was almost an impossible task but McKenzie was determined his team would fight to the very last moment. He shouted words of encouragement to boost their flagging morale and clapped his hands to sharpen their concentration.

'On your toes Wingfield,' he cried, 'And keep sharp!'

The spits and spats of rain turned into a steady drizzle. On the field the conditions worsened by the minute. Every time the ball was returned to the bowler, wet and greasy, vital seconds were lost as it was wiped dry and clean again.

Old Barnett Hall glanced across to his opposite number, the visiting umpire. He held out his hands, palms uppermost and shrugged his shoulders in a mute appeal against the weather. His fellow umpire nodded in agreement and held up a single finger. He mouthed the question, 'Just one more over?'

The Wingfield bowler noticed the interplay and determined upon one last supreme effort. He fixed his eyes firmly upon the area of worn and damaged turf, took a long slow breath to steady his nerves and launched one final time into his run.

Lenny Mole waited, motionless, his black eyes stared, unblinking, fixed in total concentration facing the bowler.

Wait for it, he told himself. *Wait until you see the ball in the air. Nothing else matters. Just watch it all the way.*

As he turned into his delivery stride the greasy turf betrayed the Wingfield bowler. His left foot slipped, only slightly, upon contact with the ground. His delivery fell short of the target area. The seam bit into the yielding pitch and the ball angled away towards the waiting slips.

Once again Lenny Mole stepped back and across his wicket. He allowed the delivery to come onto him. To the waiting slip fielders it appeared as though he had no intention of playing a shot. They started to relax. At the last moment Lenny's bat came down in a finely judged late cut. It was an exquisite stroke, played to perfection. A murmur of appreciation came from the knowledgeable few.

A fighter to the end, John McKenzie raced to cut off the speeding ball as the batsmen took their first run. Lenny made his ground, turned and in the fading light saw that McKenzie was still yards away from the pickup.

'Two!' he cried out, setting off to return. For a man as tall as Lenny Mole the sudden change of direction proved difficult. His feet failed to find purchase and slipped on the damp grass. He stumbled, recovered his footing and struggled to make his ground.

Those lost seconds gave McKenzie a fighting chance. He swooped upon the ball and in one fluid movement hurtled it at the distant stumps. It was a powerful throw. The energy sprang from his legs, his strong supple back, his muscular arms and shoulders. Five and one half ounces of compact leather rocketed in as lethal as a homing missile...!

From the pavilion it was difficult to see exactly what happened. In the fading light John McKenzie's throw was merely a dark blur. Lenny Mole was a distant figure racing towards the wickets, his long legs straining to cover the ground, his arm and body stretched forward as he thrust out his bat reaching toward the safety of the crease.

The tension and high excitement of the game's finish affected the accuracy of the Wingfield captain's throw. His aim was high and to the right of the stumps. Lenny Mole, his mind concentrated upon completing the winning run, failed to look up and see the ball hurtling towards him. He ran, full tilt, into it. There was a fearful crack as it struck him on the temple. His stride faltered. His legs began to buckle under him. Those watching fully expected him to fall, but a supreme effort of will carried him over the batting crease.

It was eighty runs for eight wickets. Briseley T'ill had won an incredible victory.

*

Out in the centre of the field Lenny Mole sank to his knees as though in prayer. He shook his bat high above his head in triumph. Concerned about the fearful blow to his head the Wingfield players crowded around him. There was an angry red mark near to his left temple but the skin was unbroken, there was no swelling and, as yet, little signs of bruising. John McKenzie slipped a helping hand under one elbow and lifted him to his feet.

'Well done lad!' he congratulated his opponent, equally as generous in defeat as he had been competitive in the game. With an arrogant gesture the Wingfield captain was pushed aside. Lenny Mole rose to his feet and looked down on his recent adversaries. There was nothing but contempt for them in his jet black eyes.

This was *his* victory. *His* moment of triumph. He scorned their congratulations as well as their concern for his well-being. He was a better man than any of them.

Hadn't he just proved it...?

*

'We've won! We have wo-on!' Jason Argosy's piping treble voice sang out a song of victory. He bounced up and down with excitement. As the teams walked from the field of play, prolonged applause greeted both sets of players every step of the way. The entire Briseley T'ill team gathered on the pavilion veranda. Mildred Burke and Helen Argosy joined them, both drawn by the excitement of the occasion and thrilled by the result.

Decker drew a happy smiling Helen into the shelter of his arms.

'Remember what I asked?' he warned her, 'to make sure and take Jason out of the way. Quickly. Please!'

'What now?' she asked, her smile turning to a look of puzzlement and then to one of concern at the gravity in his face.

'Yes. Now.' He glanced towards the approaching Lenny Mole, 'It *has* to be now.'

'Lenny? Lenny Mole?' Her anxiety increased with the realisation of what he was about to do. Her voice fell to a whisper, 'You're going to arrest him? Now! Here!'

'Yes!' he pleaded frantically, 'I *have* to. It has to be done. Please, do what I say.'

Decker pushed his way through the throng of players to the front of the pavilion and made his way down the steps and onto the field. Lenny Mole, still savouring his moment of glory, walked towards him. The cricket bat held high in salute, being waved triumphantly above his head.

What bitter irony of fate had decreed that Lenny Mole's moment of triumph would turn to dust so rapidly? That within seconds his arrogant smiling face would change to one of rage and his bat, raised in acknowledgement, could turn into a fearful weapon of destruction.

Please God, prayed Decker, *don't let me weaken now.*

There was sick fear in his stomach. Every ounce of his willpower was concentrated in controlling the tremble of his legs. The tall strong figure drew nearer. Decker had arrested men before, and women. Why now then were the formal words a jumble in his head?

Lenny Mole, I arrest you for the murder of one, Daisy Kutter. You do not have to say anything… taken down… used in evidence…

Just a few more strides… and then, face to face, they would meet.

A small figure shot past Decker towards the approaching giant.

'Hoo-way! Hoo-way! We won. We won.' cried a dancing Jason Argosy.

'Jason! No! Jason! Come back.' Helen's anguished cry went unheeded.

'Oh my God!' Decker watched in horror as the small boy flung himself to grasp the leg of the approaching Lenny Mole and try, enthusiastically, to pat his hero on the back.

Lenny wrapped his free arm around the boy, falling across his shoulders and encircling his neck. He pulled the lad into close contact as he strode to the pavilion.

Warily, slowly, Decker stepped out to meet the nearing pair. He felt the hard black stare of Lenny Mole's eyes boring into him with the intensity of a laser beam. Sensed the aura of arrogance and contempt that preceded the man like the evil vanguard of an advancing army.

He knows why I'm here. He knows what I'm about to do. The frantic thoughts raced through Decker's head. *The boy! What if he uses the boy as a shield… as a hostage? What if he threatens his life…?*

He saw Lenny's arm tighten around the boy's throat, pulling him upwards until his toes barely touched the ground. So easily he could snap that fragile slender neck or smash to a pulp that small fair head with one ferocious blow from the upraised bat.

Decker braced himself to move.

Unexpectedly the arrogance faded from Lenny Mole's eyes. A glazed blank look replaced it. His confidant stride became a stumble and his knees began to buckle. The massive bat, still raised in a triumphant salute, slipped from his grasp and tumbled to the ground. A thin trickle of bright red blood flowed from one nostril and with rapidly fading strength that turned his legs to rubber the wiry fast bowler crumpled to the floor.

Lenny Mole died from a brain haemorrhage before the eyes of his horrified team-mates. The life and vitality sighed out of him and there was little or nothing they could do to help.

With ironic timing the distant sound of a police siren reached the ears of the silent players gathered around the body. A flashing blue light was visible descending the winding road from Briseley T'ill.

Close of Play

Overnight the rain cleared as the prevailing westerly winds carried the storm clouds to the east coast, out over the North Sea and towards the continent. At 5:22am on Sunday morning the sun climbed over the horizon into a cloudless sky. There was a clean freshness to the air that offered the world a whole new beginning.

The morning sunlight radiated through the bright yellow curtains of Helen Argosy's bedroom window suffusing the room with warmth and light. It was going to be a glorious spring day. The raindrops, still clinging to the blades of grass and the leaves of the trees sparkled like diamonds in the dazzling light.

Soon after six-thirty Helen slipped from between the sheets and reached for her dressing gown. She stood for a few moments before the pinewood cheval mirror to admire her naked figure. Her stomach was flat and her breasts firm and round.

You're still in good shape my girl, she told herself, *for a mother of thirty-one… and a bargain for any man.*

The man in question lay sound asleep, oblivious to the fact that the bargain of his life was wide awake, buzzing with the germ of an idea and planning to turn it into reality. Helen pulled the dressing gown tight around her slim body and fastened the cord with a loose bow. She moved carefully and silently so as not to disturb the exhausted man.

Yesterday's dramatic events had left Ted Decker physically shattered. His outward veneer of rocklike strength hid a sensitivity that Helen was only now beginning to appreciate. It had been Decker who took control when Lenny Mole's death left his fellow players shattered and bewildered. Decker who'd consoled and reassured a desolate John McKenzie, convincing him that the whole concatenation had been an act of fate. Decker who had persuaded his fellow players to write out statements without delay while the events remained fresh in their memories. And it was Decker who took on the responsibility of telling John Mole about the tragic accidental death of his son.

That task had been particularly stressful to him after the time he had spent drawing information from the young player's father. Later the policeman had driven into the city to hand in the knife as evidence and submit a detailed written report of his own.

He also gave a description of, and information about, the missing Norman Mole, emphasising that the weaker and gentler of the twins was a threat to no one but himself. In his heart Decker feared the worst, that the unbearable pressure of guilt had pushed Norman too far and that the genial giant had taken his own life. Finally he'd driven back to Briseley T'ill, passing through the village to arrive on Helen's doorstep just before midnight.

She took one look at his white strained face and took control.

'There's only one place for you Ted Decker – bed!' She fussed around him like a broody mother hen. 'A warm bed and a hot drink is what you need. Off you go!' She pushed him up the narrow staircase to her room. He flopped down, too tired to remove his clothes. Long before she returned with a steaming mug of hot chocolate he was fast asleep.

Even in repose his face had character, Helen Argosy decided. There was strength in the firm line of his jaw, in his strongly chiselled features and yet, around the eyes and mouth was a hint of the gentleness and tolerance within.

The finest of bargains, she acknowledged, is one that satisfies both parties.

She unplugged the telephone extension and tiptoed down the staircase as softly as the proverbial church mouse.

*

The rattle of a teacup and the aroma of fried bacon greeted Decker's return to consciousness. He stared up at an unfamiliar ceiling, puzzling at his whereabouts until remembrance returned and the fog of sleep cleared from his eyes. He struggled into a sitting position.

'Breakfast in bed, OK?' Helen pushed back the door with a bare foot and carried in a large tray generously loaded with delicious smelling food. There was sufficient for two. Rashers of crisp lean bacon, a dish of scrambled eggs, fried tomatoes. Grilled pork sausages and a rack of golden brown toast. Butter, a dish of thick-cut marmalade and a pot of hot coffee completed the tray-load.

'I'm sorry.' he apologised.

'What about?'

'Last night. There was so much I planned to tell you. So much to explain, and all I did was fall asleep. It's awful. I really am sorry.' He sounded like a contrite schoolboy who had neglected his homework.

'Don't worry,' said Helen with a wry little smile, 'I'm getting used to it.'

'Getting used to it?'

'Yes! Having my love life ruined by the long arm of the law.'

They sat comfortably, side by side in Helen's bed, happy and relaxed in one another's company, enjoying their meal like a long married couple.

'Is it over now?' Helen asked, 'the murder enquiry. Will life in the village return to normal?'

'Mmm! Well! Perhaps not quite, there's one final problem to be sorted. But I'll need to talk to the Chief Constable about it first.'

'Oh!' Helen gave a little gasp, 'I almost forgot, there was a phone call for you from your friend, Nigel Rowthorne. He wants to meet you, suggested eleven o'clock in the Snug at the Cock Inn. He said, "Tell him it's unofficial." He just wants to have an informal chat.'

'Nigel Rowthorne! My friend? He's the Chief Constable for Heavens sake. I can hardly regard him as a personal friend can I?

'You could give him a chance.' Helen suggested.

'Give *him* a chance? My God! He's like... he's like... like... *my* God!' Decker finished his protest lamely, unable to think of a suitable comparison for a man he held in awe.

He loaded the breakfast tray with empty plates and set it aside on the floor away from his half of the bed. Helen remained silent for a few minutes, thinking of a reply.

'You know, you're wrong. Just because he's reached the top of his profession doesn't mean he has lots of friends, people he can trust. Quite the opposite in fact. I'm willing to bet that a man in his position has very few *genuine* people around him who he trusts one hundred percent. It stands to reason. They all want his job. They're all fighting to get to the top of the tree. Stabbing one another in the back, using one another like stepping stones, all trying to curry favour and hoist themselves one more rung towards the top of the ladder.

'Now you! Well, you're completely the opposite. The nicest part about you Ted Decker is your complete *lack* of ambition. There isn't a mean streak in your entire body and I doubt whether you've ratted on a colleague in your life... and certainly not for gain. Now have you?'

'No but...'

'There you are then,' she swept on effusively, 'it's like I'm saying, Nigel Rowthorne values a man like you. A man who is completely loyal. One who will give him an honest and straightforward opinion, one without fear or favour. You see if I'm not right?'

'Mmm!' Ted meditated on Helen's words. She could be right. With her uncanny perception of human nature, who was to say her assessment of the Chief Constable was anything but true? A sudden question sprang into his mind.

'By the way, how come I failed to hear the phone ring?'

'A-ah! That's because I unplugged the extension in my bedroom. The wonders of science you know, also I turned down the volume on the beep. Sunday mornings should be sacrosanct.'

'Sacrosanct?'

'Mmm-mmm! Sacrosanct. Especially for what I have in mind.' She slid out of her dressing gown and snuggled down the bed, moving eagerly towards him.

'I never knew you were so religious.' Decker murmured, pulling the bedclothes over their heads.

*

'Two pints of bitter if you please landlord.' Nigel Rowthorne paid for the drinks with a crisp five-pound note. 'Oh! And have one yourself.'

'Yes sir! Thank you sir.' The landlord was so polite that an amused Decker half expected him to tip his forelock. Even out of uniform the impressive presence of the Chief Constable commanded respect.

The Snug was a popular place for courting couples. It had four little alcoves formed by high-backed seats made of polished pine and was an ideal place to hold a private conversation. Rowthorne carried the foaming glasses over to the corner alcove where Decker was already seated.

'You look very relaxed Ted,' remarked the Chief Constable, 'And you're fully recovered?'

'Yes sir.' Decker replied. Rowthorne had insisted that the policeman address him by his first name when they were off duty but the ingrained habit of respect for his authority was hard to break. 'Yes sir, I had a good night's sleep and thanks to Helen I'm feeling fully relaxed.'

'Are you now?' the Chief gave him an amused, knowing look, 'Here's to you then Ted. Cheers!' They raised their glasses together and swallowed hard. Rowthorne stretched back in his seat and heaved a contented sigh.

'This is wonderful, just what I need. Sunday morning over a pint of bitter, you can't beat it. I should do it more often, escape to my roots. Did you know that Ted? I was born here in Briseley T'ill and all I ever wanted to do as a young man was leave, to escape out into the big wide world and claw my way to the top. Well! I did that... I succeeded. But sometimes I wonder...' He looked pensive for a few seconds before adding, 'was I wise? You're a lucky man Ted, a lucky man.'

The lucky man allowed himself a smug little smirk of satisfaction. He nodded happily. This was one morning he felt inclined to agree.

'Yes sir, I think I am.'

'I'm sorry to intrude on your Sunday morning but there was a hint, just a suggestion in your report that needed explaining. Am I right?' Rowthorne's massive head cocked quizzically to one side inviting a reply, 'and of course it's provided me with a perfect excuse to re-visit one of my old haunts.'

He looked around the public bar with its relaxed informal atmosphere, at the regulars leaning against the counter or perched casually on stools caressing their Sunday morning pints. Yes, it was definitely an aspect of his life he'd sorely missed.

'How is that young lady friend of yours? Ms Argosy isn't it? I must say that she was very protective of you when I phoned. She was most reluctant to disturb you. She's a lovely young lady. I do hope you're not going to let her slip through your fingers... Eh!'

'No sir... Nigel... sir.'

Decker had a sudden mental picture of Helen politely but firmly putting the Chief Constable in his place. Her motherly instincts now included him. What was more surprising, her judgement of Rowthorne was proving to be astonishingly accurate.

'I... er... I asked her to marry me,' confessed the Constable, 'about an hour ago.'

'Have you now? Well good for you Ted Decker,' enthused the senior officer, 'Did she accept?'

'I think she's adopting police tactics,' replied Ted with a rueful little smile, 'She's leaving me to sweat on it.'

'A-ha! Good for her. You know what they say, "Half the fun lies in the chase." I wish you both every happiness, every happiness.' The big man's head bobbed up and down in genuine pleasure. Then his eyes became serious as he returned to the fundamental reason for their meeting.

'I read your report,' he continued, 'It was first rate, a satisfactory conclusion to the investigation and in the circumstances, one that may well prove to be for the best. It will save that poor man, John Mole, from a lot of unpleasantness which he would have suffered had his son been brought to trial. There is the other son, Norman; the one who's gone missing. He *was* an accessory to the murder, however unwillingly. I expect we will soon track him down.'

'I fear not.' Decker replied with a sorrowful shake of the head, 'I hope to God I'm wrong but I doubt we will find him alive. My fear is that the sense of guilt was too much for him to handle. He doesn't have the strength of character of his father, and that some way or other he has taken his own life.'

'Oh Jesus! Surely not. That poor man, hasn't he suffered enough? If what you say is true then John Mole has lost three members of his family in a matter of days. How on earth will he cope?

'And then there is Elizabeth Mole, where in the world will he find the money to support her... to keep her in the security of Marston Grange? Without the financial assistance of his sons it will be impossible.'

'On the contrary,' said Decker, 'Lenny Mole being killed in the way that he was may be the only beneficial part of the whole sorry mess.'

'Benefit! What benefit?' Rowthorne's massive brow creased as a puzzled expression spread across his face.

'Fortunately, if being killed accidentally can be considered as fortunate, Lenny was playing cricket at the time of his death. He's covered by the club's insurance policy. His next of kin is his father. That means the money will go to John Mole, and it's considerable, something like five hundred thousand pounds if I'm not mistaken. Properly used, say put into a trust fund of some kind, it will provide John with financial security for the rest of his life. It's enough to allow him to devote his time to caring for Elizabeth. That could give him the will to live on... just about the only reason he has left.'

Nigel Rowthorne listened to the constable's calm and logical explanation with approval. He knew he'd been right to trust in Decker's pragmatic approach, and yet, from the report he had read there was still one final unexplained mystery to be solved.

What had Decker uncovered that he still had to learn about?

'I'm beginning to think you missed your vocation,' Rowthorne informed his subordinate, 'you seem to think of everything. Now, perhaps you would like to tell me what it is that's still on your mind? Take your time... there's no hurry.'

Decker had no intention of hurrying. What he was about to reveal could well have a significant effect on the life of a man he had known and respected for over twenty years. A man upon whose head he wished no harm... and yet!

*

'In all,' began the policeman in a quiet voice, 'there have been six deaths connected to this case. Each one had a different reason. And each death led on to the next, which in turn led on to the one after that. It was a tragic chain of events that had their origin in the actions of one man. The event took place over twenty-three years ago when Seb Mole attacked and assaulted his daughter, Rowena and the man she loved. We both know about the consequences of that attack. What I did not know, until now, was the depth of feeling and hatred that sprang from Seb Mole's violence.

'In John Mole it created an overwhelming desire to protect his handicapped daughter. A desire, so powerful, that it led him to hide her from the world for more than twenty years. He became obsessive in his secrecy. Indirectly that secrecy led to and caused the death of Daisy Kutter. She was the right person in the wrong place at the wrong time.

'If Lenny Mole had known about his sister, if he had known that she existed, then he would have understood why Daisy Kutter and his father went to Marston Grange together every week. It's tragic that he was never told and a greater tragedy that his immature mind completely misconstrued the relationship between Daisy Kutter and his father. His mother, Rowena died a natural death. It could have happened at any time but the suddenness of it tipped Lenny over the edge. I'm convinced that the balance of his mind was disturbed. What John Mole had feared for years happened… but not in the manner he'd anticipated.

'Lenny killed his victim coolly and professionally. Exactly the same way he slaughtered animals every day of his life. Inspector Moxon's death was a terrible accident brought about by his desire to bring the murderer of Daisy Kutter to account. He was over zealous to the point of being foolhardy, an aberration that had a disastrous result. I believe that when he heard about the Inspector's death the burden of guilt became too much for Norman Mole. He disappeared on the following day and there hasn't been a trace of him since.'

'What makes you so certain that he's dead?' asked Rowthorne, 'He could simply have taken off.'

There was firm conviction in the slow shake of Decker's head.

'If it were anyone else then I'd agree with you,' he said, 'but Norman for all his strength and size is weak. Lenny was always the leader, the one who made the decisions, Norman followed. How do they describe such people in the forces? As having no moral fibre – it fits him to a tee. It shows up in his sport. He's a big strong lad, with talent, but there's no fighting instinct. He hasn't got an ounce of aggression in his whole body. Otherwise he'd be a much better player.

'No, I'm convinced we'd have found him by now if he were still alive. Finally there's Lenny, he died trying to prove himself. His arrogance killed him. He just *had* to be the one who won the match.'

'That only adds up to *five* deaths,' the Chief Constable pointed out, 'You said there were six connected to the case. Who else died?'

'Seb Mole.'

'Seb Mole! Are you mad Decker? He died years ago... accidentally. It's all in the Coroner's report. Death by drowning, brought about by an excess of alcohol. In short, he was found to be pissed out of his tiny skull, fell into the stinking canal and didn't have the wit to pull himself out. I remember it well.'

'Yes sir, I know. I looked up the records, but they are wrong.' Edward Decker permitted himself a smile of satisfaction. He had heard the selfsame story from the Doctor. Until yesterday, he, like everyone else, had believed it to be the truth, until he had talked to John Mole. Until, like a priest in the dark privacy of the confessional, he had listened to a man unburden his soul.

'Are you saying that Seb Mole didn't die accidentally? That he was murdered?' Nigel Rowthorne leaned forward, his face alive with interest, pressing for an answer.

'Murder? That's what I can't decide sir. Murder, manslaughter, or was it just an accident?'

'Go on man. Good God! You can't stop now.' The Chief Constable's attention was aroused. His eyes glowed with the intensity of his curiosity.

'When his daughter was first born John Mole was a very relieved man. He'd been in a state of anxiety for Rowena's welfare following the vicious attack on her by her father. She appeared to recover well even thought the birth of her baby had been a difficult one. He knew there were problems with the little girl but the significance of how serious those problems were had failed to sink in.

'For the first two or three months Rowena was kept in hospital until she was considered well enough to return home. So John Mole didn't have to face the reality of Elizabeth's condition. Only slowly did the full meaning dawn upon him. As his realisation grew, so did the rage and anger against his father in law, Seb Mole.

'Well, in reality Seb wasn't really his father in law because they were never able to marry, but to all intents and purposes he was. Over the months a burning resentment grew and grew in young John Mole, fired by his terrible feeling of helplessness. There was absolutely nothing he could do to help his daughter. His inadequacy added fuel to the burning rage enveloping his soul, a bush fire sweeping to engulf him.

'On the day the hospital consultants informed him that his beautiful little baby, Elizabeth, would never lead a normal life he resolved to exact retribution. He decided to kill Seb Mole.'

'Go on man.' Rowthorne urged as Decker paused for effect, 'Then what?'

'His plan was simple. He knew, without fail, that Mole could be found at the Navigator Inn. He knew, as everyone in Briseley T'ill knew, that Seb Mole was there every night of the week and that he would drink himself into a stupor and that at some stage during the evening he would need to relieve himself, he'd stagger out, blind drunk, to urinate in the old canal under the bridge. All he had to do was seize his opportunity, make certain no one else was around, push Mole into the water and hold his head under until he drowned. It wouldn't take much force and there wouldn't be any signs of violence. A firm grip on Seb Mole's head would be unlikely to show bruise marks. It would be assumed that he had slipped into the canal and been incapable of getting out again.'

'My God!' gasped Rowthorne, 'And that's what happened.'

'Not quite sir,' answered Edward Decker, 'When it came to the crunch everything didn't go to plan. John Mole followed him to the pub alright. On a dark November night and with very little lighting about neither Seb Mole nor anyone else saw him follow his quarry. He watched his uncle go into the Navigator Inn and then he settled down to wait.

'He stood around the corner of the bridge. Pressed back into the hedgerow that ran alongside the towpath. It was dark and though other drinkers came out of the pub and used the canal it appears that no one saw him or realised he was there. For two hours he waited for Seb Mole to appear.

'The man was very drunk, he must have consumed several pints, for he stood for minutes on the edge of the canal relieving himself. It was the easiest thing in the world for John Mole to slip up behind his uncle and tip him into the canal.

'Despite all the hatred and rage bottled up inside him, John just could *not* do it. He couldn't move. His heart and soul cried out for revenge but the ingrained decency of the man held him back. The anguish became too much. He clenched his fist and beat the air at the futility of his indecision. A cry of despair burst from his lips. He shook his fist in an empty protest.

'Seb Mole was startled by the cry. He turned to be confronted by a tall dark figure apparently about to bear down upon him with the intention of a violent assault. He staggered back. His foot slipped on the slimy moss-covered stone coping of the canal bank. For brief seconds he swayed precariously and then plunged backwards into the murky waters.

'The water was only chest deep and a sober man might well have struggled to safety except that the bed of the derelict canal was littered in junk. An old iron-framed bedstead with coil springs trapped one of Seb Mole's feet. He was unable to balance upright on his one free leg.

'Despite himself John Mole rushed to Seb's assistance. It was a natural reaction, to help a fellow human being in distress. He stretched out and managed to grab one arm by the wrist. Seb Mole thrust out his free leg and gained a toehold on the bank. It was a precarious position for John, trying to lever a man up against his own body weight. The coiled springs of the rusting frame held Seb's leg like the tentacles of an octopus.

'Slowly, very slowly John Mole began to win the struggle. His arms felt as though they were being pulled from their sockets as he heaved against the resistance of the water, the drag of the submerged frame and the floundering bulk of the trapped man.

'Up... up... up came the body of Seb Mole, the heavy frame still attached to his leg. The muscles of John's arm screamed in protest as the terrible strain threatened to tear them apart. Slowly the faces of the two men drew close. The one contorted in an effort of will and determination, the other soft from the effects of alcohol and distorted by fear of drowning.

There was sufficient light for recognition. Seb Mole saw the face of his rescuer. Gradually, as realisation grew, his expression changed from one of gratitude to a look of pure scorn. His words uttered forth, slurred by drink, oozing with contempt and preceded by a short barking laugh of derision.

"Hah! You! You gutless wonder... came to kill me, and lost yer nerve!'

'It was all there in his face, the supercilious air of contempt, the hard black eyes, lacking all compassion, which glowed with sadistic pleasure when inflicting pain.

"I'm immortal," said the look, "And *you* are less than dirt. Dirt! Dirt! Dirt! Fit only to be swept aside as and when the fancy takes me. Dirt!"

*

Decker lapsed into silence. Eyes closed. The events projected like a film onto an imaginary screen in his brain. He could have been there, watching. So strongly were the images portrayed. He could see the two men, clasped together at the waters edge, the old humpbacked bridge and the dark scummy surface of the derelict canal. The evil acrid smell of its stagnant waters invaded his nostrils.

'Go on!' urged Nigel Rowthorne, 'What happened next?'

'He let go.' replied Decker, 'He just let go and watched the arrogance and contempt flee from Seb Mole's face. Saw disbelief... and fear in a last fleeting moment before he vanished under the surface. There was a ghastly gurgling sound as a stream of bubbles rose to the top. Then there was... nothing!

'The ripples ebbed away. The water became still. Seb Mole was gone.'
'Just like that.'
'Exactly like that. He walked away and left him to his fate. To this day no one has been any the wiser of what really happened. My problem is, what happens now?' He lifted questioning eyes towards the Chief Constable.

'Was it murder, manslaughter... or do we leave it on record as an accident?'

*

Long minutes dragged by as Rowthorne stayed silent. He sipped at his beer reflectively, leaving a thin foam moustache across his upper lip. An old biblical saying he'd been taught at Sunday school drifted, unbidden, into his mind.

'Judge not, that ye be not judged'

Until this moment it had been a meaningless religious phrase. A text to learn and to repeat to prove the efforts of his religious teacher had not been entirely in vain. Now it took on new meaning. *He* was in the seat of judgement. The last thing he needed was another murder enquiry. The County force was already stretched beyond its limits.

'Let's look at it logically,' he said to Decker, 'Did you caution John Mole at any time before talking to him?'
'No sir.'
'No. Did you take a statement or record what was said between you?'
Decker gave an emphatic shake of his head. John Mole's confession had been unforeseen and unexpected. The Chief Constable continued.
'So what have we got? We have one man's word against that of another, an unsubstantiated story of an event that happened over twenty-two years ago. There's no evidence, no proof of any kind. If John Mole were to change his story, say on the advice of a good lawyer, where do we stand?'
'Nowhere sir.' Decker replied with a helpless shrug.
'Precisely! Nowhere.' Nigel Rowthorne lowered his voice to a deep bass whisper. He leaned towards his companion, placed a large strong hand on Decker's forearm and squeezed it confidentially. It was a signal of trust stronger than any words.
'As far as I'm concerned we have never had this conversation... you get my drift?'
'But sir...?' came the half-hearted protest.

'Let me ask *you* one question Ted Decker. Knowing all you do about Sebastian Mole and what he did, if you had been in John Mole's shoes what would you have done? Hauled him out... or let go?'

Dear God, prayed Decker. In his heart he knew the answer.

Acknowledgements

My grateful thanks go to all the people who have helped me with the publication of this book. To Ruth E Glover, a friend and fellow author who gave me valuable advice about self-publishing. To Sue Barlow who taught me what precious little I know about computers and helped set up the cover designs. To my artistic brother, Robert, who designed and painted the original picture on which the cover is based. To Neil Turner for his advise on book binding. To Geoff Clark who supplied my computer and continues to give support and to all those friends and colleagues who have encouraged and supported my efforts and finally to my wife, June without whose help, patience and encouragement none of this would be possible goes my undying gratitude.

A well-known author once wrote to me that a novel does not really exist until it has readers. So to everyone who picks up my book, turns the pages and reads the story may it give you as much pleasure to read as it gave me to write. Thank you.